THE OUTSIDER

ALSO BY PATRICIA GERCIK

On Track with the Japanese:
A Case-by-Case Approach to Building Successful Relationships

Book design by Ricardo Bloch

THE OUTSIDER

PATRICIA GERCIK

To Lou, Abe, Larry
in loving memory

It is my pleasure to acknowledge all those friends, colleagues and family who have offered support, editorial comments, and encouragement during the writing of The Outsider. *Martha Sweezy tirelessly read many drafts of the novel and gave wholehearted support and thoughtful editorial comments. John Low-Beer's comments were critical in the final stages of the book. My good friend Ricardo Bloch, renowned photographer and book artist, designed the book. I want to thank my agent Anne Hawkins for her belief in* The Outsider. *– PG*

CONTENTS

PART ONE

Tokyo: Winter 1946

THE HOUSE

The Nishiguchi house, like old houses everywhere, held secrets, stories whispered in the dark, tales etched in dark wood, confidences that if exposed would diminish the teller and scar the listener. Sarah opened the door to Scalia's room, high above the treetops, a place forbidden and filled with treasure. O'ba's urgent voice commanded from below, "Sarah-chan. Where are you? Come to the kitchen right away. Scalia-san has a surprise for you."

Sarah crossed the threshold, stepping cautiously between the trays of pearls—pink, white, gold, black, round, and irregular—and headed to the eight-hundred-year-old Kannon perched high on a lacquer stand. It was long, half as long as she was, and most forbidden. She pressed her lips against its round mouth, and embracing its graceful curves, fell to the floor.

She could not stay long. O'ba's footsteps were just below. Surrounded by the scent of Scalia's talcum powder, dried flowers, musty-smelling oils, and trays of multicolored South Sea pearls, she hugged the Kannon close. Her mother called Scalia the "collector." His walls were lined with *samurai* swords, African masks, small tables crammed with jade, ivory, and coral statues and *netsuke* carvings, and a zebra skin on the floor. All of them wondrous. Scalia grabbed, he bargained, he left dealers breathless. "It's essential to have the right eyes at the right time," he liked to say.

Sarah was only six but knew she had the right eyes. O'ba knew it too and smiled when Sarah neatly lined up her collection of Japanese, hand-painted dolls. But now O'ba was on the steps, wheezing and cursing, and Sarah swiftly replaced the Kannon, took one last look at Scalia's treasure, and slipped out the door.

"Naughty Sarah-chan," O'ba hissed, her rough hands seizing Sarah's shoulders as she spelled out Scalia's rules: only O'ba allowed in Scalia's room, quiet during Scalia's afternoon nap, Scalia's hot bath at four.

"Let me go," Sarah cried, struggling. But the landing was too narrow. The world moved backward, O'ba's breath hot against Sarah's neck until they reached the bottom.

"There," O'ba said, tucking a stray hair into her bun, "no more snooping. Scalia-san puts disobedient little girls in the granary, fattens them with sweet rice, and roasts them. But for good girls, he has presents and big surprises. You want to be a good girl, don't you? Today he has a present for you. Something wonderful."

"What?"

"He wouldn't tell me. Be good."

Sarah pressed close, longing for that loved feeling, that tenderness that made her think of herself as Atsuko-chan, O'ba's daughter, the small girl with wide eyes and giant hair bow, the child who had died in the war. Atsuko-chan, forever solemn and earnest, framed in dark wood on O'ba's bureau, was O'ba's most precious possession. Sarah touched O'ba's lips and stroked her cheek, but O'ba's voice remained severe. "Be Japanese, Sarah-chan. Be sincere. Accept your obligations."

"I'm not Japanese," Sarah declared, furious at O'ba's harsh tone. "You can't make me be!" She raised her leg to kick O'ba, but O'ba gently seized it. They dared each other, waiting for the other to surrender, conscious of their strong characters, temperaments that had bound them from the start.

"You will be Japanese, Sarah-chan," O'ba said, her voice at once rich with tenderness as she brought Sarah close. "You're a child of the maid, *jochuuko*. You belong to me. You're not the same little girl who got off the boat from Shanghai. That girl lived among filthy Chinese and barbaric foreigners. But now I check you at night. You lie in bed just the way I taught you with your legs straight. You don't move a muscle."

"I want my mama," Sarah said in a solemn tone she reserved to make ordinary requests that adults would take as seriously as she did. She pressed her head against O'ba's soft breasts, knowing that more than her mama, she wanted assurance that O'ba's welcoming flesh would always protect her, a shield she had come to depend on.

"Your mama's not here," O'ba answered gently. Changing the subject, her voice dropped to a whisper. "Your mama and papa live in this house because Scalia-san wishes it. You will never leave this house."

"Why?" Sarah whispered, forgetting her need for her mother and Scalia's surprise, forgetting everything but the secret embedded in O'ba's low voice, one of O'ba's trove of secrets that emerged suddenly in a hushed tone.

You will always live here," O'ba repeated. "You're mine. Look at you," O'ba said, turning her so she could see her reflection in the glass door. "You hold yourself like a Japanese." But Sarah knew this last statement was false. She did not look obedient or dutiful. Dark curls outlined her small face, with its iridescent skin, red mouth, and sparkling, blue eyes, eager and alert. She glowed with an appreciation of possibilities that Scalia referred to as mischief. This immediacy drew people to her, Japanese and foreign alike. It was a look that did not belong to any nationality, one that was full of life, curiosity, and magic. Scalia called her a forest nymph, a fairy child, light and airy, who danced in the full moon. Her parents claimed she was golden. "You are beautiful," O'ba now whispered, and Sarah knew O'ba was thinking of little Atsuko-chan.

"Let's go to the kitchen," Ob'a said with feigned excitement, sensing Sarah's distress. "Scalia's surprise will be wonderful, something that only Scalia-san could dream up. Maybe it will be a beautiful doll with skin of crushed eggshells and real hair. He wouldn't tell me except to say that this is the best present of all, a present you will remember always and will make you thank him forever. He said that the present was worth more than a treasure chest, more than anything you could imagine. He said the present would change your life. He wouldn't tell me more."

Sarah clung to O'ba's thick flesh as they moved down the long corridor, past her parents' bedroom, the dining room, and living room to the kitchen, O'ba muttering all the while about the impossibility of working for *gaijin*, "foreigners," the lack of *tatami* mats, bare wood, and the *shizen*, "natural feeling." But Sarah didn't care about all that. She loved the house just as it was, so different from the crowded apartment in Shanghai—the smell of pine and cedar, the bare spaces, the clay walls, and the dark wood along the corridor that linked the servants' quarters to the rest. *Shoji*, "paper doors," let shadows of bamboo play on clay walls, flickering shapes from the vast forest behind the house, also forbidden. This grand house felt safe, a place where nothing could hurt her. Mama said so.

"At last," Scalia said, greeting them, dressed in his customary white, silk suit and silk ascot. His dark hair was combed straight and curled around his neck, giving him the appearance of a storybook prince, slender and tall, with high cheekbones and full, red lips. His grace and knowing smile caused a ripple of excitement when he entered a room, making woman turn and whisper. He bent his head over their small hands, his lips hovering, never quite touching the skin. The women laughed and slanted their eyes towards him. Even so, Sarah remained unconvinced.

Small things triggered Scalia's rage. At once his mouth would tighten, his voice would fill the house with shrill demand, and his hazel eyes would sharpen to a bright green. At those moments his face jutted forward and his mouth narrowed to a half moon. At those moments Sarah was truly frightened. Last week, upset the pasta was overcooked, Scalia fell to the floor, gnarling the table leg until Mama shook him out of it. When Sarah protested, Mama explained that Scalia was from Naples, and she mustn't worry because his behavior was Italian.

"Where did you find her?" Scalia asked softly in his perfect Japanese, straightening his silk ascot.

"I found Sarah-chan in the back hall," O'ba lied, giving Sarah's arm a squeeze, "looking at the garden."

"Garden? What garden? Even a dreamer like Sarah-chan wouldn't sit in a cold hall staring at a pile of dust."

"Sarah-chan imagines the garden as it was before the war, before the American bombs," O'ba answered, glaring at Scalia. "I've told her about the fish pond, the weeping willow, and how my uncle and I washed the rocks and hand-fed the one-hundred-year-old *koi* at sundown. I've told her that of all the summer villas outside Tokyo, it had the most beautiful garden. It needs repair."

"Nonsense;" Scalia answered, "we don't need a garden. We live in a summer villa surrounded by an ancient bamboo forest, one with a lake even."

"You said that you had a surprise," O'ba said, walking over to Emiko, the young maid who'd recently come from O'ba's village in the north. She placed her hand protectively on Emiko's shoulder. "You said it was a special surprise, something that Sarah would remember always. Where is it?"

"Sarah-chan," Scalia commanded softly in English. "Come. O'ba is right. The surprise can't wait. It's the most extraordinary gift. I looked all over Tokyo and found it at last. It's just for you. Did O'ba tell you? It will change your life forever. That is my wish. Do you want to see?"

"What?" She walked cautiously toward him. Scalia's finger beckoned. His body swaying in excitement, he reminded her of the Russian puppeteer at the Shanghai French Club pulling strings—his fierce expression intense, commanding, lights glinting off the chandelier, the puppets moving right, left, and back again. The room felt off kilter. Scalia smiled, and as if tugged by invisible cords, Sarah tiptoed, moving forward, her arms extended for balance. They were playing a game, a sport of chance, one in which Scalia alone knew the ending. She felt a bolt of excitement, yet she moved with care, her face flushed, her body in tentative equilibrium, conscious of Scalia's absolute control and his delight in that.

"Sarah-chan," Scalia's voice chanted, "I've got a surprise for you." His smile broadened as she came closer. And closer.

THE SURPRISE

Scalia jerked open the door and dragged in a small boy. "Saburo-chan," Scalia announced loudly. "He's your surprise, Sarah-chan. You like him? He's cute, no?"

The boy had a large head and closely shorn hair and wore a loose-patched jacket and baggy, black pants. In his right hand, he held the end of a short, braided rope that dangled to his feet. His large eyes absorbed Sarah in a single glance and then moved to Scalia, Emiko, and O'ba. Despite his frozen, starved look, he seemed indifferent to the food that lined the counters and the warmth of the room. His eyes widened. A smile played on his lips.

Sarah studied him. He looked like the child priest she'd seen in a Kamakura monastery, a boy with the same large, shorn head and thin neck, a boy whose straight back made her notice. Like the monk, his confidence created an aura. O'ba stared, Emiko covered her mouth, and Scalia smiled. Bluish ears, raw from the cold, stuck out at right angles, and there were sores on his cheeks. He stood with his feet apart and his small chest thrust forward as if he owned the room. He snapped the rope against his thigh. Scalia put his hand on the boy's shoulder. "He's just a beggar child," O'ba snorted. "Where's his mother?"

Scalia again reached behind the door and pulled a small woman into the kitchen. Except for the red, sequined scarf around her neck, she was dressed like Saburo in a loose quilted jacket and baggy pants. "Fumiko-san," he announced. "Fumiko-san worked for me in Shanghai."

Ragged bangs covered her forehead and framed high cheekbones lacerated by the cold. Her chapped lips puffed red over slightly protruding front teeth. Dark eyes fringed with thick lashes lingered on a plate of rice balls, a basket of tangerines, and a row of large, green pickle jars as she scanned the room, taking in the stove, the counters loaded with food, the polished floor, and beamed ceiling, as if the house and everything in it belonged to her. She arched her slender neck, laughed, stretched her arms wide, and moved swiftly toward the warmth of the stove.

O'ba grunted in disgust. "What thing have you brought to this house? Sarah's mama and papa are not here now. You know that. I don't have to tell you how they will feel about this. You said you had a surprise for Sarah-chan."

Saburo's green-gray eyes widened with an energy that made Sarah want to play. He smiled, and she smiled. He insisted that she notice him, and she did. The adults disappeared as she thought of her Shanghai friends, Cousin Irina, and the hours of make-believe, stories that tumbled into each other, scraps of information pieced together from adult conversation, their bodies trembling with the telling. Saburo laughed, and she laughed. Scalia and Fumiko nodded at each other. O'ba frowned.

Saburo walked deliberately toward Sarah, his rope dangling beside him like a loose vine. He smelled of Tokyo, a city of ashes where people moved slowly between piles of ruin, a city of grime, of rancid oil, of mold that clung to stone. Saburo ignored O'ba's protest and Fumiko's laughter. His eyes didn't leave Sarah's face, a look that commanded her attention. They were the only ones in the room who mattered.

He moved closer, and the rope swung next to his leg. His eyes narrowed and she stepped back, but he quickly grabbed her wrists and tied them in a "knot." "*Yoshi*. Well done, Saburo-chan," Scalia exclaimed enthusiastically in Japanese. "You got her." Sarah flushed. The smell of dirt and the bound-in feeling made her furious. She had expected a bow, a smile, a friendly salute, but not this. She had believed in his bright-eyed look that invited her to join him in a world apart. Where was her friend? Who would she make up stories with? To whom would she tell her secrets? Adult laughter filled the room. Even O'ba laughed.

Blood rushed to her cheeks, and the skin on her forehead stretched. The pressure hurt her eyes. He had tricked her. Shame. "*Baka*, 'idiot,'" she cried and pushed Saburo. Saburo stood stiff and expressionless. She pushed again. "Baka." The adult laughter grew. Saburo did not move. Sarah bit the knot, freed her hands, and with a wide stroke whipped the rope across his face. His right eye closed, but his left eye, still bright with mischief, made her sad. She covered her own eye with the palm of her hand.

"Saburo-chan," Scalia called. Saburo turned slowly and, disregarding Fumiko's outstretched hand, walked toward Scalia. "Listen!" Scalia commanded briskly in Japanese. "Sarah-chan, Saburo-chan. You'll be friends. You'll play with each other. You'll be like this rope," he said, taking the rope from Saburo and stretching it between his hands. "Sometimes the rope will be shorter and sometimes longer, but it will always bind you. That is my wish."

No one moved until suddenly, in a quick gesture, Fumiko tossed her head, loosening the bun at the nape of her neck, and her thick hair cascaded around her small face. She laughed, revealing her protruding teeth and tiny pointed tongue, and wetting her lips, placed her hands on her hips. O'ba hissed, and Scalia held up his hand, but Fumiko did not stop. She turned slowly, her mouth open, her eyes scanning the room.

"Stop!" O'ba screamed. "The master and missus. I hear the car coming. You waited until her parents were out. Don't you have any respect? You shouldn't have brought them here. They belong in Shanghai. They are the past." Her parents' low voices came from the entryway. Sarah longed to run to Mama and press her face against her swollen belly. Papa would lift her high and, spreading her hands, she'd soar like a plane. Her parents would laugh. Soon the baby would be born, and they'd take care of it together. Mama promised. Yet, the room held her in place.

"What do we have here, Beppe?" Her mother addressed Scalia from the doorway. Despite the swell of pregnancy, her slim figure was graceful. Her small head faced Scalia with a questioning look. The rose-colored skirt, matching sweater set, and pearl necklace looked out of place in the crude kitchen. Sarah loved Mama's creamy skin, her grace, and the knowing expression that made the corners of her eyes crinkle. After lunch Sarah curled in her lap, touched her full lips. Now she wanted Mama's embrace, but the stillness of the room and Mama's cold stare stopped her.

Papa's lips tightened at the sight of Fumiko and

Saburo. He lit his pipe as the room waited. Papa's dark hair, set against white skin, curled down his neck. His high cheek bones gave him an elegant, thoughtful and mysterious look. Mama claimed that Sarah looked like Papa, that like her Papa she liked books, ideas and learning. Now Papa puffed slowly on his pipe, and the smoke slowly curled toward the ceiling. Sarah knew from the flush that crept up his cheeks that he was angry. He was waiting for an explanation. Sarah edged toward her parents. Her father pulled her against him.

"Beppe," her mother demanded as she put her arm around Sarah. "What is the meaning of this? Who are these people?"

Scalia gazed at her, bewildered. "Tamara, dear Tamara." Scalia made a brief bow and spoke in his finest English, "Meet Fumiko and Saburo, old friends from Shanghai days. I found them living under a bridge right in the center of Tokyo next to the Imperial Palace. I'd been searching for them. Good, they were found. They'll live in the granary in back of the house."

"The granary?" Sarah's mother was incredulous. "That shack on stilts next to the fence? Are you mad? It's filthy. It has no insulation or heat and is full of rats."

"Tokyo, 1946, my dear. Not exactly New York." His Italian voice growled, low and menacing, as he spoke of the hell of Tokyo: the flattened city; the smell of cinder, charcoal, and rot; the mass starvation; the old and young weak from hunger, orphaned and desperate, clogging train stations and living in tin huts and tents under bridges. His voice rose as he described tiny, frozen babies wrapped in newspapers stuffed in trash cans, and men's waists the size of a dinner plate. He ended in a high whisper, and when he finished, Sarah felt the horror. She wanted to wrap the people in blankets, give them food, and save the babies, small and defenseless, from the jungle of ruin. Mama closed her eyes. Papa looked at the floor.

"We are fortunate to have all this." Scalia waved his hand around the kitchen. "A villa, a Japanese noble-man's estate an hour's ride from the city, an hour from beggars, rubble, and madness. Quite a find. We even have a forest and a lake nearby to cool the summer's heat. Imagine."

"The granary will not do," Mama said softly.

"Will not do?" Scalia snorted in a dismissive voice. "Fumiko and Saburo have been living, wet, cold, and starving in a tent. Before that they begged at a train sta-tion. The granary will suit them just fine."

Then Scalia's voice sweetened as if he were telling a bedtime story, a promise that Japanese values of sim-plicity and frugality would save the day. Fumiko would cover the floor with straw mats and insulate the win-dows with oilpaper. Each morning she would light just three pieces of charcoal, and at night they would bathe in the neighborhood public bath. Life would be reduced and meaningful, as it was for the ancient heroes of Ja-pan. Sarah believed him.

Scalia's voice became more intimate. "It is high time Sarah had a playmate. She needs a friend, and Sa-buro will be that friend."

Her mother threw up her hands and turned to her father. Using his Russian name, she said, "Sasha, stop this. They'll freeze. The hut won't do. We do not agree. This boy can't be Sarah's friend. He is a beggar child. Look at him."

"Sasha," Scalia imitated her mother. "Remember, Tamara dear. Alexander-Sasha may be a thinker. He may have lofty ideals about democracy and America, but it's not his house."

Then Scalia explained patiently that the house, the

grounds, and the servants would return to his friend, after the occupation. Sarah knew from Scalia's tone, the same careful pitch O'ba used to describe her parents' entrapment, that he was letting everyone know the situation. Sarah wanted him to stop; she wanted Papa to make him stop.

Her father lowered his pipe. "Why, Beppe? Why do you want them in the granary?"

Scalia did not answer; the only sound was the flick of his rope. "I want them for my own reasons," Scalia finally said.

Her father looked at Fumiko, who tossed her head, folded her hands across small breasts covered by her sequined scarf, and smiled.

"Yes, of course," her father admitted slowly. "But Saburo will not be Sarah's playmate. Tamara's right. A dirty Japanese boy. You can't be serious. You weren't in that Japanese jail in Shanghai, Beppe. You didn't hear the screams, cries of terror, sobs that tore your heart out, night after night. I screamed till I spat blood. You don't know."

The room was thick with anger. Scalia and her parents, large and red-faced, filled it with dread. The rage made Sarah's ears buzz and her eyes dim. She wanted Scalia to disappear. She wanted the kitchen quiet, the way it was when O'ba told stories, and she helped Emiko chop vegetables. She pressed her forehead against Mama's stomach, and feeling the baby move, blurted, "Do you eat children?"

Scalia threw back his head and laughed. "I do eat children, Sarah-chan. But only if the children disobey the rules. So listen."

"Rule number one…" Scalia spoke each rule in Japanese and repeated it in English, cracking his rope. "Fumiko and Saburo must never ask for food." Crack.

"Two: Fumiko and Saburo must never enter the house." Crack. "Three: Saburo and Sarah must never play in the forest." Crack.

As the rules kept coming, Scalia's voice never paused, leaving no room for doubt. Why didn't Papa grab the rope? He was as tall as Scalia. She wanted it to stop. The adults seemed paralyzed except for Fumiko, who tossing her head impatiently, stared at Scalia with a raised chin and insolent eyes.

"Ten: Saburo and Fumiko must not bathe in the house." Crack.

"Rule one hundred," Saburo yelled and grabbed the rope from Scalia. He raised it high and turned slowly so everyone could see. With one eye nearly closed, the skin puffed red around his eyelid, he walked triumphantly to Sarah, his good eye shining.

Yes, Saburo would be her new best friend. They would make up stories, tales of samurai bravery, and learn about each other to create more games until nothing mattered but play. They would be chums, the kind who called to each other every morning and spent every minute together digging for treasure under the hut, under the boulder by the well, and under the fence. He would tell her his secrets, and she would share her own. They would have adventures.

Papa said Japan was full of buried treasure, gold and valuable jewels from China and its colonies, and precious metals from wartime factories. It was beneath tree stumps, in deep wells, and in dark caves. Every inch must be explored. They would find enough gold, silver, and goods, enough to buy Fumiko and Saburo a proper house, enough to feed small babies and beggars in railroad stations and families under bridges, enough to leave for America. In America she'd have her very own puppy to replace her spaniel, Natasha.

Fumiko walked to Saburo and put her hand on his shoulder. They stood together in their matching jackets, baggy and torn with great patches. Fumiko wrapped her red-sequined scarf around his head. He did not look like a young monk now but like a small girl with red lips, wide eyes, and a soft smile. Then Fumiko took the rope from Saburo's tiny fingers and threw it at Scalia's feet. Scalia laughed. Fumiko's full lips curled as she picked up Saburo and slid the door open, sending a blast of cold into the room.

"Wait," O'ba called. She moved swiftly to the counter and wrapped the rice balls, tangerines, and pickles in newspaper. The package was between them. Fumiko stared at it and then at O'ba. O'ba's face was impassive. The room was still. Everyone understood that with this act, the rule broken, all bets were off. Scalia stood by the door with a quizzical expressioin, his lips turned at the corners, a smile suggesting he knew the outcome.

Saburo laughed and reached for the parcel. Fumiko pushed his fingers aside. The room waited. Fumiko lifted her chin. Theb O'ba stepped forward. Fumiko backed away. Her eyes narrowed. O'ba moved close as if to reassure her. O'ba smiled and handed her the package. Fumiko tucked the parcel next to Saburo. She did not bow, but held her head high. The room was still. Fumiko walked swiftly out the door.

FRIENDSHIP

The next morning Sarah woke to the scrape of bamboo and remembering Saburo, she ran to the window. Fumiko, dressed in baggy pants and a white headkerchief, swept the stairs with a stiff broom. Saburo dumped armfuls of empty jute bags from the balcony.

Sarah watched. The family watched. O'ba and Emiko whispered. Fumiko and Saburo worked in synchrony, their arms and legs bending and lifting with speed and efficiency. They did not speak and, ignoring the watchers, plied the task at hand. The yard, littered with straw and debris, looked like the aftermath of a storm.

That afternoon two workers arrived in a small truck. They carried a large straw box, a table, two urns, a *hibachi*, and cushions and quilts up the rickety steps. Fumiko tacked oilpaper over the window frames while Saburo wedged newspaper into cracks in the walls.

When O'ba called Sarah for supper, Saburo and Fumiko were still working. The rich smell of clams wafted down the hall, and she hurried to the dining room. *Spaghetti alle vongole* was Scalia's favorite dish, and Sarah had learned to love the garlicky sauce. In the candelabra's flickering light, the Chinese tablecloth, gold goblets, hand-painted *Imari* pottery, and walls decorated with intricately carved wooden trays, created a warm glow.

Her mother leaned close and whispered, "I missed you. I wanted to show you the picture that Uncle Max sent from Australia of Cousin Irina looking quite grown up and feeding a kangaroo. Where was my Sarah?"

"Watching," Sarah replied, looking hungrily at the plate of pasta piled high with clams.

Scalia said, "Sarah-chan is always watching."

The table was silent, and Sarah knew from her parents' sidelong glances that there was trouble.

"Sarah-chan is brave," Scalia continued. "She wants adventure and assumes that her smile will subdue the world. But the smile is just a mask. She can't be controlled." His voice lowered as he described her brazen bargaining in the antique markets, her defiance of authority, and her need to explore every forbidden place.

Her parents smiled and shrugged. They called Sarah "treasure." They taught her Russian songs and clapped to the music while she danced. At night she joined her mother in the handkerchief dance while her father scissor-kicked the Kazatsky. During arguments she distracted them with funny faces. Sensitive to Scalia's dark mood, she sang Neapolitan folk songs. When O'ba was sad, she made *origami* birds and turtles.

"Sarah is like her mother: willful but brave. Tamara, do you recall that time in Shanghai when you took on the Japanese navy?"

"Flattery won't help, Beppe," her mother replied. "Stories from the past won't help either. We don't want Fumiko and Saburo in the granary. We will find them another place. Beppe, listen to me. We live here too. Our wishes must be considered."

"Tamara, remember the young Japanese naval officer," Scalia continued softly with a wave of his hand as though she had not spoken. "It was August, and you'd just returned from Karuizawa, the last time you vacationed in the Japanese Alps. The summer of '39."

"Yes, our last vacation in Japan before the war," her mother said, her voice soft with memory. "Such fun. Remember the bar on the boat from Shanghai to Japan, Sasha? Remember, we bet drinks on rats that scampered across the glass roof."

Sarah listened, wishing she had been on that boat full of laughter, wishing too that she had sat next to Mama on the long train ride from Yokohama into the Japanese Alps. They would've waded in Karuizawa's clear streams, picked mushrooms, and had afternoon tea on the veranda of the Mampei Hotel.

Scalia's matter-of-fact voice echoed her thoughts. "The Mampei Hotel, full of Nazi officers, German sympathizers, and spies from everywhere—a gruesome bunch, an unsafe place. You couldn't trust anyone or anything at the Mampei Hotel. But that's another story.

"It was the day after a terrible typhoon. The air was fresh," Scalia continued, his voice reverting to a soft storytelling mode. "You wore a blue and white silk dress with ruffles in the front and a broad-brimmed hat, your hair tied loosely at your neck. You looked so young, so very young, and so very beautiful"

"We all remember, Beppe," Sarah's father muttered.

"A young, grim-faced, Japanese officer with a neat mustache pushed his way up the gangplank, shoving passengers aside with his stick. He stood in front of you, but instead of stepping away, you faced him square on. It was a stupid challenge. He pointed a pistol at your belly. You put your hands on your hips."

"Then what?" Sarah asked.

"For a moment, Sarah-chan, everyone in the line froze: an old woman in a flowered hat, a young boy in a sailor suit, twins with large hair bows. Everybody stood still. Your papa moved to protect your mama, but she stopped him with one hand and with the other brushed away the officer's gun. He stood for a moment as if uncertain as to how to proceed—his gun dangling, his expression puzzled, and the passengers staring. Japanese soldiers held their holsters. We all waited. What would he do? Would he shoot her in broad daylight? It was Shanghai. Anything was possible. I imagined the worst. But the Japanese officer retreated, and as your mama passed, nearly everyone gave her a salute."

"He looked sixteen," Sarah's mother said and laughed.

Scalia twirled the pasta around his fork and swallowed a mouthful. Sarah followed his example. The pasta slid down her throat, pepper blending with parsley. The room smelled of spice. Emiko served toasted garlic bread and there was more wine. Sarah sat up straight, proud that Scalia recognized that she was as brave as Mama and immensely grateful that the story ended well.

"Remember the night we learned the war was over?" Scalia said.

"I'll never forget," her father said and drained his wine.

"What?" Sarah pulled on her father's sleeve, glad of Mama's laughter and Papa's open expression. Papa put his arm around her, and she was glad about that, too.

"It was our wedding anniversary," her father said. "We were celebrating with Beppe and some friends."

Her mother picked up the story. "The restaurant had a screened-in patio with flowers everywhere. We had the center table, but all around us Japanese officers with guns were eating and drinking. We tried to ignore them, but there were many more guns than usual. Then the news came. From table to table, chair-to-chair, everyone whispered, hands over their mouths, eyes lowered. The buzz filled the room."

Her father cupped his mouth to her mother's ear and whispered, "The war is over."

Scalia whispered, "The war is over." Her parents and Scalia all leaned toward Sarah and whispered, "The war is over."

Sarah covered her ears and giggled. They whispered again and again until she howled with laughter.

There was a long pause. She knew from Scalia's frown, Papa's quick glance at Mama, and Emiko's retreat, that there was trouble.

"Tamara, Sasha, a lot has happened since then." Scalia's face became serious, and he gestured to Emiko, wide-eyed in the doorway, to proceed with serving the veal with tuna sauce.

"Today Japanese and Americans are friends," he said softly and smiled a false smile. "And there's money in that friendship."

"Not for us, Beppe," Mama said, the warmth gone from her voice. "We will not be drawn into your black market schemes that take money from America, a country we admire. As soon as we've made enough from the pearls, we're leaving Japan."

"Of course you will leave Japan," Scalia spoke even more slowly, as if his words were coming through the finest silk, rippling through the room, leaving no doubt about the seriousness of the conversation. "But for right now, just as you say, Tamara, let's focus on pearls, jewels from the sea, their luster created by living creatures, the ones Cleopatra treasured above all else. She wore them in her hair and sewed them into her dresses. American wives love pearls and American men will pay anything to keep those wives happy. This is our chance."

"Americans will eventually leave," Sarah's father snapped. "We need more than pearls; we need a steady business that will provide a legitimate income. We need land."

"No one can resist Tamara's neck," Scalia interrupted. "Silk and pearls. Tamara prances into a party, and the women gather round, asking, 'Where did you get that, honey?' We made six big sales at the last party. You want money? Forget your downtown office, forget the forest, and forget buying parcels of land."

The room was silent.

Scalia cleared his throat and gazed at the tops of the bamboos, bushy with silver-tipped leaves against the setting sun. His Italian voice rose and fell like a song, the rhythms lifting her spirits, catching her in its ebb and flow, letting her dream. He had done this before, describing the girth of the trees, the clear lake, and the grassy clearings. In those moments her parents forgot the scramble for passports and money, imagining only the thick forest, blue hills, and the sandy beach in the first morning light.

The forest had the magic of *Shinto*, touched by *kami* spirits that inhabited its groves, boulders, and streams. Ancient bamboo, straight and tall, needed honor. It was home to the samurai, warriors disciplined through practice, whose every act realized perfection. Samurai recited *haiku* under the bamboos, did *kendo*, *judo*, *karate*, and *Zen* meditation on the shores of the lake. At O'bon, festival for the dead, hundreds of tiny candle-like lanterns dotted the water. Her parents held hands and did not interrupt.

"Tamara," Scalia said in the same tone. "Tell Alexander about the ladies swarming over you. Remind him how we were able to purchase lots of South Sea pearls, pearls the Mitsubishi Corporation and the Japanese navy had stolen — pearls destined for Italy to produce cash that would support the war." Scalia paused and wiped his brow.

"Remind him, your dear Sasha, how he danced a jig when he learned the war was on, and submarines full of pearls would never make it to Italy. Remind him that we bought the pearls for next to nothing. We are obligated."

"Obligated," her father snapped, "to your comrade Nishiguchi. He may be owner of this house and owner of you, but not me, not Tamara."

At the mention of Nishiguchi, the one O'ba called *Sensei*, the room was quiet. It was a hush that no one dared interrupt, a quiet that spread fear. Sarah felt his presence, an enormous man, tall with a long beard and a great sword. He stood over them, his muscles thick and his eyes black with hatred. He owned the house, the forest, and an island in the Inland Sea. He would ruin the family, storm into their lives, and take all. O'ba spoke of him with awe. They were trapped. Sarah put her hand on her mother's arm.

Her father broke the silence: "Nishiguchi gets a cut on each pearl, and he expects us to sell every one. When there are no more pearls, Nishiguchi will disappear. We need land."

"Sasha is right," her mother said, tossing her napkin on the table. "We must be independent, beholden to no one. Nishiguchi is a listed war criminal. You hold on to the dream of a powerful Japan. You and Nishiguchi."

"You're correct, but it's not a dream," Scalia said. "In time, Nishiguchi will live in this house again. He loves the house and roamed the forest as a child. Nishiguchi's soul is in every bamboo and rock, and every tree and rock is in him. The forest gave him the 'Japanese way.' Yes, Nishiguchi will be back. He will be powerful again and so will Japan."

Scalia paused. There was more. The room waited.

"We have a perfect setup, Sasha," Scalia said in a low certain tone, pulling his chair close to her father, as if they were on the same team.

"Perfect?"

"Saburo's mother, Fumiko-san," Scalia said.

"Beppe, stop this."

"Fumiko knows pearls," Scalia insisted. "She knows how to separate them by size, color, and shape, and how to string them." Scalia turned his wine glass against the light. "She's been trained in dyeing, too. I couldn't find better in my uncle's shop in Naples or anywhere."

"Beppe, stop," her father repeated, moving his chair away.

"I first saw Fumiko in '38," Scalia continued. It was an old story, and he wanted them to know it. Once again his voice flowed. He lifted his head as if he were gazing at a bright star. Her parents exchanged a worried glance, but Scalia didn't seem to notice. "I met Nishiguchi before the war at a club in Tokyo, the kind with oriental carpets and dark wood, the kind where diplomats and agents gather to make connections. I had just arrived from Naples to buy pearls for my uncle's store. The Italian vice-consul invited me to the club. We had a few drinks. I was interested in pearls and Nishiguchi, a naval intelligence officer, was interested in Italy. I understood he wanted to use me in some way. He told me that his family owned an island in the Inland Sea surrounded by pearl beds. He invited me to his island.

"And there on the island was Fumiko, high on a rock, hair streaming down her back, her *Ama-san* diver's costume wet from the sea, sculpting her body, perfection. Only seventeen then—a bundle of talent. I knew it right away. She dove longer than the others and could sort pearls quicker than anyone. Late one afternoon I was walking on the beach. Suddenly Fumiko, wet-faced and laughing, rose from the sea, a giant octopus clinging to her arm. I dove into the waves and pulled her to shore. It took the villagers hours to get the suckers off. Throughout, Fumiko tossed her head as if the incident was of no consequence. She has the scars to this day.

"The next time I saw Fumiko was in Shanghai. She'd been married off to an official who managed a string of Japanese-operated, Manchurian opium dens. Eventually he was killed in a fight with a local drug runner. Hardly a hero's death."

"Beppe, enough," her mother interrupted. "Not in front of Sarah." Mama's arm crept around Sarah and pulled her close, her breath tickling the back of Sarah's neck, her face buried in Sarah's curls. Sarah wanted to go to the Inland Sea, to dive into the waves and search for pearl oysters. She wanted to know about the drug business in Manchuria, too. But Sarah had Mama's attention now. "It's Sarah-chan's bedtime," her mother cooed. "Sarah-chan has heard enough stories for tonight."

***

Late that night she was awakened by Papa's low voice followed by Mama's muffled crying. Rain pelted the roof, and still Mama wept. She covered her ears and flattened her body against the bed. After a long while, when the house was quiet, Sarah crept to the window and pulled back the curtain. The rain had stopped, and a mist covered the stairs. The hut appeared floating, its dark, curved roof etched against the night sky. Behind, the forest, dark and forbidding, rose like a wall. With each gust of wind, the bamboos bent in a sweeping caress. Above the swaying branches, a round moon, light blue and shrouded in clouds, hung low.

Sarah pressed against the cold glass, flattening her cheek until it was numb. A dog barked in the distance. A crow shrieked. Then silence. She watched for a long time. The single light against the black filled her with longing. Then a dog sounded low and long, a wolf's howl. Other dogs joined. The cry, short barks punctuated by longer wails, made her skin pucker. Soon the dark was filled with sound. She trembled, left the window, and folded the quilt over her head. Scalia was determined. Mama and Papa were angry. For the first time, the house felt unsafe.

OBLIGATION

The next day Scalia rose early and left for town. At lunch her parents gazed at the granary as if they expected Fumiko and Saburo, but the hut remained quiet. Her father gently rubbed Mama's hand, and Sarah picked the other hand and held her index finger. But soon Sarah became restless, went to the kitchen, and sat between O'ba and Emiko, who were snapping green beans into a large bowl. They too stared across the yard at the granary.

"Tell me more about the garden," Sarah said.

O'ba stared at the bare soil outside. "I first saw the garden when I was twelve. It was all shades of green, a world of moss, grass, and trees. I had never seen anything so lovely. I knew then that the beauty would ease my pain and make separation from my family bearable."

"Did you want to come here?"

"We were poor. Niigata is cold. We couldn't afford leaves for our tea. All winter we sat next to the *kotatsu futon* drinking hot water. With my swollen hands and face, I looked worse than Saburo. One day my father served real tea and talked about the poor potato harvest. There was a long silence while he contemplated the tea leaves in the bottom of his cup. I waited. I knew something terrible was coming. Still I waited. Then he told me that I would go to the Nishiguchi house to pay off a family debt. I would work in the garden with my uncle."

"What did you say?"

"I cried," O'ba said, her mouth tightening. "I lowered my head and the tears dribbled down my cheeks. After that I cried every day. They could have watered rice fields with my tears," O'ba murmured.

Sarah's eyes moistened, and she immediately thought of O'ba's little girl, Atsuko-chan. Emiko said O'ba cried when Atsuko-chan was sent away. Sarah blinked so O'ba would not notice and placed her hand in O'ba's large palm. O'ba squeezed her fingers. She must not ask questions. She must not mention anything that would remind O'ba of her baby.

O'ba said, "Life isn't simple, Sarah-chan. When a person accepts gifts, they take on responsibilities. Obligation, gives life meaning. In Japan all life depends on relationships, and all relationships are based on obligation and loyalty." O'ba's voice lowered. "Never forget loyalty."

"What's loyalty?" Sarah whispered back, her voice low with anticipation.

"Loyalty is death," O'ba answered with certainty. "Loyalty means you are ready to die. That is loyalty. Without loyalty life is meaningless, pointless, nothing."

Sarah nodded as if she understood. Her throat tightened. "I understand obligation," Sarah said in a solemn tone.

"Take this," O'ba instructed, handing her an apple from the fruit bowl. "Now you have obligation. Repay me."

Sarah handed her an orange. "There."

O'ba shook her head. "You don't understand anything."

Sarah blinked. Pain stretched her cheeks, her forehead tightened. She bit her lip to keep from crying and quickly whispered, "Fumiko-san was married to a drug dealer in Manchukuo, Manchuria. He died in an opium den."

"Married?" O'ba asked in the same serious tone. "A good story. Don't talk to me about that one."

"Scalia-san told me."

Emiko's eyes were eager for more. O'ba waited, too. She had them now, news they craved from a foreign place, the world of her parents and Scalia. After each family meal, they questioned her. Sarah knew her stories would be discussed over afternoon tea and rice crackers.

But just then Saburo climbed down the granary steps and stood in his oversized jacket, his chest puffed and his small feet pointed toward the kitchen window. His lip, swollen and cracked from the cold, exposed a thin line of blood at its center. His cheeks were also chapped and raw. He took a stout bamboo flute from his sleeve and began to play. The high, eerie sound stilled them. Saburo closed his eyes and the skin around his temples darkened. A vein pulsed in his neck. The sound grew. No one spoke. O'ba put her arm around Sarah.

"What's he doing?" Sarah asked in a soft voice.

"He is being Japanese," O'ba replied in the same tone. "He has the discipline of a samurai, enduring cold and physical discomfort. Nothing matters but his will— loyal, strong, and true. People are cautious around a man playing a flute. With one stroke the flute can and will kill for truth."

"I have discipline," Sarah said, mimicking his posture. "I have endurance. When I sleep, I lie on my back and never move, not one muscle. I am strong. I know about obligation, duty, and loyalty. I would die for truth.

I could beat Saburo-chan."

"You're foreign," O'ba said.

Sarah flushed, but instead of a retort, she moved closer to the glass. Her legs itched to run to Saburo. The cold and wind didn't matter. Saburo demanded her presence; the discordant notes made her pay attention. If he could, Saburo would march into the kitchen, take her hand, and lead her outside. He wanted them together. Sarah knew it because she felt the same way.

O'ba drew her back. "No. Your Papa said no."

* * *

The next day Saburo returned with the same remote expression. He removed the flute from his sleeve. Its high sound filled the air.

"He looks like a *bodhisattva* statue," Sarah's mother exclaimed. "It's freezing cold. How can he stand so still?"

Saburo appeared again the next day and the day after. "He must come from a samurai family," her mother finally admitted on the fifth day. "Samurai are trained from a young age to endure hardship. *Bushido*, they follow the samurai code to serve Japan. Look at his chapped hands, swollen joints. Even his earlobes are raw and bleeding. If this keeps up, he will be ill. No one can stand this cold. Why doesn't Fumiko make him stop? We don't have authority. Is she putting him up to it?"

Her father shook his head. "Nonsense. The boy simply has nothing to do. This is intolerable. I told Beppe that Sarah would never be his playmate. Never. He needs a decent place to live. He needs boys his own age."

"Saburo is a samurai," Sarah said and repeated O'ba's story about the *ronin*'s flute doubling as a sword.

"He does come from a samurai family. He is strong."

As Sarah said this, she stood squarely in front of the window, her arms folded across her chest. Saburo approached the window. They grinned at each other, and seeing that Saburo's front tooth was missing, Sarah pointed to her own before her mother dragged her away.

On the sixth day, the household watched as Saburo climbed down the steps, crossed the yard, and stood in front of the glass. He spread his legs, taking possession of the space, and began to play.

"Did you speak to Beppe?" her mother asked sharply. "He has to understand this won't do."

"Saburo is just a small boy," her father muttered. "Let's move to the living room."

"It's not just Saburo," her mother said. "Fumiko encourages him. The other day she stood on the veranda for over an hour, glaring at the house while he played. I fear she might do something terrible. There was a bitter wind, but she didn't seem to care. I don't know how she bore the cold."

Sarah settled between her parents on the living room couch. The flute and gold peacock screen seemed as if they were in a temple. Sarah rubbed her feet on the Shiraz rug absorbing the texture and color of the ivory, coral, and carved wood.

"Why was Papa in jail?" Sarah asked as the flute gained volume. Her father closed the door. "Radio was the only way to keep informed about the war. It was against the law. I had a radio."

"What happened?" Sarah whispered. The flute stopped. She felt Papa relax.

"A downstairs neighbor reported him," her mother answered, "and the Japanese put Papa in jail."

"Then what happened?"

"I froze," Papa replied in a low voice. "The jail had

no heat, and the guards were terrible. I became ill, and Beppe talked to Nishiguchi, who talked to the right officers and persuaded them to let me out."

"Did a doctor come?"

"Beppe nursed me," Papa said in a voice rounded with memory that made Sarah glad. The flute started again. Her father's face reddened, but her mother steadied him with her slim hand. "Beppe saved me," her father continued in the same low voice, determined not to allow the flute to interfere with his story. "He took care of me night and day, sponged my body, and never left my side. I've never had such a gentle nurse. Every day he came with a new package of medicine. I would have died without Beppe."

"Beppe is not a doctor," Sarah said.

"Beppe was all we had," her mother explained. "Papa's body was covered with sores. Beppe got medicine from his friend Nishiguchi. The medicine and Beppe made Papa well. When Papa felt better, he and Beppe played chess every afternoon. Beppe brought flowers and hired Italian sailors to help us with chores."

"O'ba says you're obligated to Beppe," Sarah said, knowing she was on dangerous ground. "She says you will live here always because Beppe wishes it. She says there are obligations that can never be repaid. Never."

"Why, Sarah, that's rubbish!" her mother exclaimed. "Japanese nonsense. I will speak to O'ba about putting such ideas in your head. We are not obligated. We are good friends. We love each other. We may have our differences, but Beppe is steadfast. He helped us. We appreciate it, that's all. It's not obligation; its friendship based on giving, on true concern and love."

Her parents moved close, mumbling, their bodies bundled together, foreheads touching and hands on each other's waists. Sarah wanted her father to continue in his full warm voice with words that were comforting. But the flute filled the room, and her parents remained huddled, absorbed in their own conversation, closing her out with a garbled mixture of German, Russian, and English—words she could not understand, names and places she'd never heard of.

Sarah rose and slammed the door. "I want to play with Saburo," she demanded, swinging the door back and forth. "I want to play. Saburo has done nothing wrong. I want to play. You're stupid. Let me play."

Her father, his face red with anger, reached for her, and for a moment Sarah thought he would shake her. But instead he pushed her aside, and hand-in-hand with her mother, left the room.

COMPULSION

Fumiko stood straight backed, glaring at the house with her head held high, her arms folded, and her feet apart. A strong wind pressed her short tunic and black pants, outlining her lean torso. She looked wild and beautiful. Her hair billowed around her small face, and her red fingernails pressed against the banister.

Fumiko's eyes narrowed to slits. She faced the forest, spread her arms wide, and lifted her head skyward. The bamboos bent, the sky darkened, and the clouds swiftly blocked the sun. At once the yard was in shadows. Sarah felt the magic of Fumiko, a force that made things happen, a power that awed her parents and O'ba. She wanted to stand next to her.

O'ba knocked on the window and shook her head, but Fumiko paid no attention. O'ba banged harder. Fumiko raised her chin. Sarah looked at the dark hut. Where was Saburo? She wanted him next to Fumiko. Lately when she asked about Saburo, O'ba ignored her, muttered, and dragged Sarah from the window.

※ ※ ※

The next day O'ba yelled, "Look!" Sarah scrambled to the window. Crumpled balls of newspaper like small stones littered the yard. Dressed in a thin cotton blouse and trousers, oblivious to the freezing wind, Fumiko hurled papers. "I want a bath!" she screamed and threw a ball toward the house. "I want to eat in the kitchen!" she demanded. More paper descended. "I want glass windows!" The balls kept coming. More and more balls landed on the bare ground.

"O'ba!" her mother hurried down the hall. "What's happening? Come, Sarah, I need you to translate. How dare Fumiko make such a scene!"

Before Sarah could ask anything, O'ba proclaimed, "Fumiko, Saburo must leave."

Sarah translated that O'ba was angry.

"I can see that she's angry."

"It's a fire hazard," O'ba continued, glancing uneasily at the hut as if responsible for the current state of affairs. "Yesterday I told Fumiko-san she couldn't stack newspaper near the hut. She refused to answer. Now this. She's an animal. She shouldn't live next to decent people."

"What is she saying?" her mother asked.

Sarah took a deep breath. Mama must never know. O'ba and Mama would breathe adult anger into the yard, a rage that would force Saburo and Fumiko to leave. She had seen it happen, grownups all thinking the same thing, their energy focused and absolute. She wanted to avoid that at all costs. Now the air thickened with that determination, a unified force that brooked no conversation.

Her mother mumbled that Fumiko and Saburo wanted to control the house. Life had become impossible. She would find a respectable place for them to live. Tokyo had some apartments. No one asked Sarah to translate.

But Sarah imagined Fumiko and Saburo, their belongings tied to their backs, walking down the road. Tokyo was full of homeless beggars. Scalia described their lives. Her mother covered Sarah's eyes when the sight was too awful. Yesterday four small children, their swollen hands extended, begged for food. Mama ushered them inside and gave them hot chocolate. Sarah bathed the smallest in a warm tub. Before they left, Mama dressed them in thick sweaters and pressed money, rice balls, ham, and chocolate into their pockets. Mama cried as they marched out the gate to the main road.

She imagined Saburo's little hands waving while Fumiko stared ahead. They would disappear into Scalia's Tokyo—people who lived under bridges and in tin huts, hordes of beggars, war veterans, ragged children, and refugees at train stations. Their faces would swell, and sores would cover their bodies. At night they would huddle against the station wall and wrap their arms around each other for warmth.

She would never let this happen. Never. Sarah folded her hands like the female samurai she'd seen in a movie, a ronin disguised as a man, who traveled alone armed with a stout flute, stopping only to protect the defenseless. She felt deliberate and strong, able to make the world right. Sarah lowered her voice in an effort to sound unconcerned, as if Fumiko's requests were normal desires that anyone would agree to. "Fumiko-san wants to bathe in the house and eat in the kitchen."

Her mother turned to O'ba. "Of course she can't bathe in the house. There are public baths. She can't eat in the kitchen either. She has a hibachi. That was the agreement."

Just then Saburo emerged from the hut and put his thin arm around Fumiko's waist. Fumiko dropped the rest of the newspaper. They stood proud and stiff high above the yard, their clothes billowing in the wind.

They turned to the forest. The wind tangled their clothes, wrapping them closely, making them a noble unit indifferent to O'ba and the household. Fumiko moved, and Saburo followed. His head turned to the right and then to the left. He lifted his foot and then his hand. Their movements were slow, methodical, a dance that mesmerized.

O'ba and her mother's silence acknowledged Fumiko's determination to be part of Scalia's Japan, a Japan that had defeated Russia and China, bombed America, and planted its flag in Asia. Scalia said Japan would rise again. O'ba whispered that Fumiko had gone to Manchukuo and had returned alive. Fumiko laughed when Saburo played the flute, used impolite Japanese, dismissed her mother. Sarah had never heard Fumiko say thank you or bow. Her sequined scarf, sparkling against the bare yard, signaled her revolt. It was obvious to everyone. Fumiko would win.

Saburo looked tall against the hut. He stood with his back to them. Fumiko lifted her head to the treetops, her hands spread as if she was ready to fly over the fence. Sarah pressed her face against the glass. Mama said Japanese killed themselves on railroad tracks or in apartments or hotels. Would Fumiko dive to her death?

Her mother covered her mouth.

They waited.

Then with one swift turn, Saburo ushered Fumiko into the hut.

＊＊＊

The next day the hut was quiet. Sarah waited for Saburo to appear. That night she peered out the window, but the hut was dark. The second day was the same. On the third night, O'ba left rice and vegetables in a ceramic bowl at the bottom of the hut's stairs. In the morning the bowl was gone. O'ba placed a bowl of noodles at the foot of the stairs. Sarah's parents chatted as if Saburo and Fumiko did not exist.

Scalia was silent.

That afternoon during tea, the yells began. At first they sounded like a dog in pain. Then the cry became high pitched. Her parents rushed to the window. Scalia cursed, slammed his teacup on the table, and strode across the yard to the hut. Sarah expected Fumiko to emerge with more demands, but instead Scalia descended the stairs cradling Saburo.

Saburo's small hands covered his ears and his head moved from side to side. His cries pierced the air, making it impossible to think. Scalia rushed to the back door and placed Saburo on a futon in the spare room behind the kitchen.

Sarah's mother rolled up her sleeves and ordered O'ba to boil water and bring towels. Sarah sat on her father's knee next to the kitchen stove. Her mother emerged from the spare room with a handful of bloody cloths. There were more screams.

A shout sounded at the back door.

"Fumiko," her father muttered. Fumiko burst into the room, her face covered with soot, hair knotted with dirt, *hanten kimono* stained and pants torn at the knee. She did not look proud now. Scalia pointed to a chair next to Sarah. Fumiko sat sullen and dark. Her father handed her a glass of water and covered her shoulders with a blanket.

They waited.

The screams continued.

"Will Saburo die?" Sarah asked that night as her father tucked her into bed.

Her father was silent. "No," he finally said softly. "Will you let us play?"

"No," he answered in the same soft voice.

***

The screams continued for two days. Sarah sat in the kitchen with O'ba, Emiko, and Fumiko, listening to Saburo, his cry soft like a puppy's whimper. Scalia remained on the second floor and her father went to his office.

On the third day, Emiko tried to distract Sarah with a shopping trip, but Sarah would not move. Fumiko sat near the back room and covered her face with a cloth. O'ba gently ushered her down the hall to the bath. She returned an hour later, her wet hair tied in a ponytail, wearing O'ba's *hanten* and pants. O'ba made her eat a bowl of beef and noodles. Saburo was quiet. Fumiko ate another bowl.

Sarah's mother emerged from the back room, held Sarah, and whispered that she mustn't worry. Her mother seemed happy, and that made Sarah glad. Saburo would be all right. His eardrum burst, but his fever had broken. He would stay in the house until he was well. In a few days, he'd have a bath. She took Sarah's hand and opened the door to the back room.

Saburo, his mouth open, looked like a small frog. His large head balanced on his thin neck pressed against the pillow. Fumiko lay down beside him. Sarah's mother shut the door. Sarah wanted to ask if she and Saburo could play, but the words would not come. Mama was too happy.

For the next three days, Sarah stayed by the kitchen stove. Fumiko ate bowls of noodles with sliced beef. She told stories about her childhood on the island and her time in Manchuria and in Shanghai. They were funny stories about the giant octopus fastened to her arm, about her house full of servants in Manchuria, about tricking Japanese authorities, about smuggling pearls and semiprecious gems. Sarah translated, and Mama laughed and encouraged Fumiko to say more.

Sarah had never seen her mother so relaxed. She didn't care if dinner was on time or what they ate or Sarah's table manners. She looked young and purposeful as if all that mattered was the kitchen, Saburo and telling stories. Her mother talked about Russia, about the cold, about sleigh rides and her revolutionary brother who studied biology and joined the Menshevik party. She spoke of hiding from the Cossacks in a neighbor's basement, about picking wild strawberries in the woods, and about family picnics and summers in Riga at the beach. The words poured out in her high Russia voice. Sarah translated. Fumiko listened. O'ba smiled and made more noodles.

Except for Saburo, too little and too sick to count, there were only women in the kitchen. Everyone wanted Saburo to get well. O'ba claimed Saburo was a great flutist; Mama agreed, and Fumiko nodded. They hummed the song that Saburo had played to help the healing. The room had a cozy feeling focused on good. They were part of the same team and wanted the same things—nice things, like making noodles and telling stories about tricking police, smuggling, and happy rides in the snow. Emiko taught Sarah a song about the apple festival and how to make paper cranes for good luck. Sarah hummed the song, made a string of cranes, wished for Saburo to stay in the backroom always and O'ba to keep making noodles. Scalia did not appear and her father only came for a short visit at the end of the day.

That night Sarah woke to a full moon. The house was silent, the blue-black sky streaked with white clouds. She slipped out of bed, walked down the corridor to the kitchen, and opened the door to the back room. Fumiko lay on her side with her arm around Saburo. Sarah lifted the corner of the quilt and slipped in. Saburo's large head, a balloon perched on a thin stem, made him frail. His soft breaths filled the room. A white bandage covered his right ear, his hair felt crusty, and a streak of dirt smeared his neck. He wore her father's sweater. Sarah curled against it.

Her breathing matched Saburo's. The darkness and weight of quilts made her drowsy. The clay walls pressed in. The room warmed, closing in on Fumiko, herself, and Saburo. It felt right, so natural, that she didn't mind the mildew smell, the sharp edge of Saburo's bony body, or the heavy sound of sleep. Lying next to Saburo and Fumiko was where she belonged. Soon she was sound asleep.

A streak of morning light filled the room. "Good morning, Sarah-chan," Fumiko whispered in her ear. "Saburo-chan's friend, Saburo's always best friend." And with that Fumiko smiled a broad, satisfied smile, and welcomed the day with her arms stretched wide. Sarah crept out of the room.

***

The next night Sarah snuck down the hall to the room. A glass of water with a flower stood next to the futon. Saburo was clean and smelled of soap. She touched his thin neck, her fingers trailing to the bandage. His skin felt smooth and silky. She slipped in beside him. He smiled and put his hand on her head. The pressure warmed her, and she moved close. Saburo rubbed her skull. She felt his breath on her lips. She put her hand on his head and touched his thick hair.

Night after night Sarah woke, ran down the hall, and slipped in beside Saburo. Each time she felt his hand on her head. His fingers massaged her scalp, his hand roaming over her head as if exploring her one minute and pressing down the next. The pressure sent currents down her neck and back, warming her body till she closed her eyes. In some deep way, Saburo was taking care of her. In turn she rubbed his head and traced his soft smile with her finger, curled against the small of his back, and fell into a deep sleep. The days in the kitchen with her mother, O'ba, Emiko, and Fumiko and nights with Saburo gave the world a rounded feeling.

On the tenth night, Sarah ran to the room. The door was open, and she went inside. The room was dark, and as her eyes adjusted, her heart froze. The futon sat folded in the corner of the room; otherwise the room was bare, devoid of the memory of Saburo or Fumiko. The clay walls, gray and stark, were cold and demanding. She stepped back, hoping that there was some mistake. In moments all would be restored, and Saburo would lift the quilt, and she would slide in beside him and feel his hand once more. But nothing happened. She stared at the empty space and felt chilled, aware something precious, something she had counted on, had vanished.

She walked to the kitchen window. The hut's remoteness made her sad. There was no hint of life. Had Saburo gone away? Would the drama continue? Would they be allowed to play? Would Scalia win? The forest, the treasure, and Saburo were off-limits. Would that ever change? She should have been told. She had a right to know. They were a team. Why hadn't Fumiko said anything? Why hadn't O'ba or her mother told her? She felt of no consequence. She did not exist. No one cared that she wanted a friend, that she wanted to play, that she and Saburo were chums. As she walked back to her room, a deep loneliness took hold, dark and troubling, a loss that made her move quickly.

THE FLIGHT

The next day the hut was silent. O'ba left food for Fumiko at the foot of the stairs. In the morning the food was gone. Sarah's mother ordered clean clothes and blankets for Saburo and Fumiko. Mama looked worried. O'ba made chicken soup. O'ba grumbled. The household waited.Nearly a week passed before Saburo appeared in the yard with his arms folded. His stony face did not blink in the glare of the winter sun. His puffed lower lip, split down the center, was encrusted with blood. A big toe, peeking from his torn sneaker, was swollen, too. Mama's eyes widened with horror. Saburo began to play his flute.

"Fumiko and Saburo have to go," her father said. It was after breakfast, and they were still seated at the dining room table. "Tamara has nursed Saburo back to health, bathed him, fed him, and gave him new clothes. We are willing to pay for a place for them to live. Look at Saburo. He looks demented. He is dressed in rags and filthy. He needs proper care. We spend all our time waiting for Fumiko to make a scene or for Saburo to appear at the window playing the flute like some ancient samurai ghost."

"They are harmless."

"They have to leave. Today."

Scalia stood. It had been building to this all week, short remarks about the hut as living quarters, other quips about Fumiko's temper tantrums, land deals, pearl business, and the like. Now Sarah held her breath. All that Papa hated about Saburo and Fumiko, Sarah admired. Since Fumiko's tantrum and Saburo's illness, they were as haughty as before, rude and unyielding when they should have been humble. They were above the law.

"Sasha, never order me," Scalia said. He stood and clenched his fists.

Papa rose.

Scalia's fingers pointed at Papa's eyes. He zoomed in. Again. Scalia's hand darted, his fingers hovering centimeters from Papa. Again.

"No," Sarah cried.

"Beppe," Mama snapped.

Scalia jabbed. This time he touched Papa's eyelid. Papa remained still except for a slight trembling of his right leg. Scalia's fingers kept moving, in and out, back and forth, a blur of motion, darting nearer and nearer. He danced on the balls of his feet, his hands and legs moving in rythem. Papa's eyes widened. Mama clutched her arm. The room was silent. The dance continued. Scalia's pointed nails and fixed expression terrified her. Sarah imagined Papa's bloodied eyeball on Scalia's nail, in Scalia's hand, on the floor. She pressed against Mama. "Stop." Scalia whistled a warning. The whistle continued. Scalia's lips pursed, and his fingers moved. His eyes blazed. Scalia's fingers, quick and sure, centimeters away from Papa's eyeball, loomed large.

"Beppe," Mama's voice cracked the air. "Beppe!" As if waking from a dream, Scalia dropped his hand. His whistle softened. He stepped close, letting his hand fall to Papa's cheek. His fingers lingered on the rounded curve of Papa's jaw. He cupped Papa's chin. The room was still. They faced each other. The clock ticked. Emiko entered the room and left just as quickly. Beads of perspiration covered Scalia's forehead and dribbled down his chin. He turned to Sarah and pointed to the door. Sarah ran. She didn't stop when O'ba called. She pulled at the back door. It wouldn't move, and she pulled again. It opened.

Saburo appeared tiny in his oversized, frayed jacket and pants. His skin reeked of dirt, and his hair, coated with dust, made her think of child beggars. Sarah stepped back, but he grabbed her and pressed his small forehead against hers until she saw his eyes, green in the center, glowing with a force that drew her to him. Saburo put his hand on the top of her head, and rubbed. The pressure, reminiscent of their close nights in the back room, made her giggle and she placed her hand on his head.

"I knew you would come," he said.

"We are friends."

"We are friends," Saburo repeated in a solemn voice as if taking an oath.

They remained silent for a moment, absorbing this information.

"They are fighting," she whispered.

"I know, Mother told me."

"How does Fumiko know?"

"They talk all the time. Even now Scalia is with Mother. You ran out the back door, and he left by the front."

Sarah had just left Scalia, but she knew that what Saburo said was true. She imagined him storming out of the room and crossing the yard to the hut. Scalia visited the hut when her parents were out, bringing Fumiko soap and sweet treats for Saburo. Scalia held Fumiko when Saburo was sick and brought her warm clothes. Emiko did their laundry and O'ba left them noodles at night.

"Let's run," Saburo said. "Let's find treasure. Mother took me. There was a big mound of earth. I know where to go."

The forest's soft light beckoned, and the bamboos swayed. Birds circled overhead. The winter sun lit the earth with specks of light that turned the woven fence silver. The watery glow, thin and airy, made her feel anything was possible. A crow swooped and then flew skyward, soaring above, a dark spot against the gray sky.

Saburo squeezed her hand and pulled her across the yard. She went with him, certain that they would find a box of gold or jewels or coins. Treasure is what she thought about each time she looked at the forest; treasure made her think of obligation, about the ones that could be repaid and the ones that couldn't. The hunt would provide escape from the anger and confusion of the house. They would flee into the trees and run down the path to the lake.

Her excitement grew as she reached the fence. Sarah looked back. The house was quiet. There was a split in the bamboo weave. Sarah yanked, and they squeezed through. On the other side, they ran into a bamboo grove.

BLOOD OATH

They were in the forest. Sarah smiled into Saburo's tea-scented breath and said, "We will find treasure." They jumped, feet pounding the frozen soil, and the forest rang with their laughter. The sound made her glad, as if they owned the stone, trees, and all of it. Sarah pulled Saburo down the path that wound through the grove of bamboo. She had dreamed of the forest and its magic, and now it flowed through her.

The massive trees and moss made her feel tiny and large at the same time. Greens were everywhere— gray green, dark green, yellow green, blue green. Moss spread over boulders, shades of olive flowing to lime. The trees broke the wind, and the dark earth between bamboos held the quiet. It was very cold. The trunks of the oldest bamboos rose like the giant pillars in the Kamakura temple, letting sunlight flood through their branches. Even when she stepped into the warmth of that pale sun, Sarah was cold.

The trees thinned, revealing a bare lot filled with rubble and a bombed-out house. A low mist swirled around the charred *tatami* mats and doorframes, seeping between the slabs of concrete that pointed like giant pillars skyward. Sarah's cheeks stung, and her fingers hurt, but Saburo kept going. "The treasure is not here. It's much deeper in the forest. You must have strength. Endure," Saburo said and pulled her forward.

"I am strong," Sarah yelled back and covered her ears against the cold. She knew this was a test. Physical hardship was nothing. She would find treasure so her family could leave Nishiguchi's house and Scalia. But aside from the test and the hunt for treasure, she delighted in the trees, moss, and filtered light. It was just as Scalia had said, just as she imagined. His soft voice embedded in the forest had prepared her for the shadows, dark recesses, wide clearings, and winding streams.

They passed another destroyed house and then another. These bombed lots were not like the flat ruin of Tokyo, where every inch, inhabited by squatters, smelled of rotted wood and fire. The remains of houses, outlined on fields, were part of the mystery. Treasure could be anywhere—plunder hidden behind the thin row of trees, jewels stuffed under rocks, gold bars buried in caves. They should stop.

The path turned, and they were completely surrounded by trees. Except for the beating wings of crows swooping against the sky, the forest was silent. It was even colder than before. Saburo dropped her hand, folded his arms, and walked on with lips pressed tight. Sarah assumed the same posture. The path dipped, and the bamboos bent inward. The mist grew dense, and the cold nipped her earlobes. Dim light turning to dusk made her uneasy, but Saburo kept moving. Sarah hurried to keep up. The path split. "That path goes to the squatter village where Sensei lives," he said with dogged insistence, "but we must go deeper into the forest, to the deserted part, to the ruins of the big house near the lake."

Sarah didn't agree. Enough! The cold burned her

cheeks and lips and made her head hurt. Saburo forged ahead, his face pinched, his arms crossed. Mama would miss her. It was almost time for a story. She wanted Mama's soft lap, her low voice, her smile, and her smooth cheek. She closed her eyes, held her ears against the sting, and pressed on.

Saburo stopped. He pointed to a large field with a mound that rose above a deep hole. The crows swooped low, their cry claiming all. She and Saburo marched across the frozen ground, knelt, and peered into the cavern. It was dank and smelled of rot. The mound with broken glass, bits of metal, and charred wood looked like a large pyramid. Saburo pointed to the top, secured his footing, hoisted up, and kept moving. Sarah found one foothold, then another, and forgot about the cold, climbing step by step, up and up, with only the crows' dark bodies and bright eyes for company. Saburo sat cross-legged above her and pulled her up beside him.

A field opened up before them. Beyond the crater, beyond the faint footprint of the house, beyond the dark trees and empty lots, a lake's rippled reflection glittered through a wall of mist. The fog covered the lots and cloaked tree trunks. Soft light filtered through bamboos, and the forest beckoned. She spread her arms and gazed at the purple, pink, and orange bands that arched to a rainbow. She felt grateful for being perched high and for the rays of light.

Voices. Faint sounds. Laughter. The air moved, the crows flew higher, and Saburo's grip tightened. Fumiko's laugh was followed by a low voice. Scalia. But who was with them? Sarah's heart pounded, and she was cold again, too cold to move. The sun vanished behind a watery cloud. The forest, ominous and forbidding, surrounded her with danger. Saburo, his eyes wide with horror, his hands shaking, inched his way down. Sarah followed, her hands slipping on the icy dirt. A glass shard pierced her knee; blood spurted. She picked out the glass. There was more blood.

"Please, don't let Scalia see me," she said to herself. "I will never come into the forest again. I will listen to O'ba, sleep with my legs straight, speak polite Japanese, and never eavesdrop on Mama and Papa's conversations. A few more steps." Her foot skidded down a slide of dirt. She crouched against the mound and brought her bloody knee to her mouth.

"Nishiguchi Sensei," Saburo whispered and placed his trembling arm on her shoulder. She trembled, too. Nishiguchi: the officer her parents and Scalia were indebted to, the owner of the house, the man who lived in the squatter village and about whom O'ba told stories. This was the man who filled the room with fear and made Emiko cover her face and her mother close her eyes. Dressed in white, Nishiguchi stood straight backed, a ponytail halfway down his back. His flowing robes made Sarah think of the white-garbed veterans at train stations playing harmonicas and accompanied by small dogs. But Sensei had a different energy, moving swiftly, his quick eyes taking in everything. The deep lines around his mouth gave him authority. Only a head taller than Fumiko, Sensei dominated the circle. Fumiko and Scalia bowed low.

Sensei leaned on his silver-handled cane as Fumiko, composed and neatly dressed, took a large, wood *soroban* abacus from her jacket and placed it on the ground. Then she knelt and began calculating while the two men watched. The clicking stopped. Fumiko bowed, and with her forefinger inscribed her calculations on the palm of her hand. Sensei nodded. Using the tip of his cane, he wrote in the earth. The three huddled over the figures. Scalia and Fumiko bowed, then bowed again and disappeared into the forest. Sensei stood alone.

The forest was quiet.

"We must run now," Saburo whispered and tugged at Sarah's sleeve. "Run."

Sensei's feet stirred the low mist as he walked to the edge of the crater. He untied his ponytail, letting his hair flow, laid his cane beside him, and slid off his tunic. He folded it carefully with the sleeves down — a perfect rectangle — and placed it to one side. Lithe and muscular, he removed his *getta*, bowed, and clapped. Then he faced the mound, assumed a *Za-zen* position, his legs tucked under, his thumbs touching, and his rib cage lifting and falling. His body whitened from the cold, and his nipples darkened like pebbles at the bottom of a stream.

Saburo scrambled across the bare ground to the forest. He beckoned. She wanted to follow, but Sensei's steady, in-out breaths puffed white against the dark of the forest, and his ashen skin held her. His eyes stared ahead, his mouth curved in a deep-creased smile. Mist covered the field, blanketing the crater. He floated on the cloud. Saburo waved frantically from the edge of the forest. She froze. He called her name. She could not move. Saburo impatiently jumped up and down. Still Sarah remained, huddled next to the mound, her muscles frozen. Sensei clapped. The sound broke the silence. Sarah crouched and ran. Cold rattled in her throat. She looked back. Sensei stared, eyes focused, piercing her core. Sarah went as fast as she could through the underbrush, past large boulders and into the thick bamboo grove. The memory of Sensei's pale figure, his rigid posture, hair flowing down his back, stuck with her. She closed her eyes, felt his hands on her, and her legs moved faster.

Suddenly the granary, with its dark roof and shuttered windows, loomed ahead. Within seconds she'd be inside her house shouting the news of treasure. The cold and fear would fade as she described Fumiko on the soroban. Tomorrow she'd take Mama and Papa to the mound. They'd return with their arms loaded with gold. But Saburo was there first, his body squarely in front of the opening. "Not yet," he said, his voice guttural, determined. His eyes bored into her. She tried to duck, but he blocked her. "Don't even think of telling," he said in an even deeper tone. "Treasure. Sensei. Any of this."

A crow cried and flapped its wings. Night closed in, turning the trees to purple, its deadly dark making her shiver. Saburo's voice lowered to a hoarse whisper. "Sensei wears white because he is still a soldier. He'll hire Ninja trained to climb walls and walk on ceilings to drip poison into our mouths as we sleep. They'll murder your mother and father first, then O'ba and Emiko, and finally you, Mother, and me."

"You can't scare me," Sarah said, even though in the dark she imagined her house filled with black-hooded figures with poison vials creeping along the ceiling. She wanted Mama and Papa's praise, to be heroic, and to save the family. But Sensei had seen her.

"*Yubikiri.* You must promise, and you must keep your promise," Saburo said softly and pressed his forehead against her temple. She tried to move away. His forehead followed. "Yubikiri," he said. "Always." She no longer felt the scrape on her knee, the cold, or the hurt from her bruised arm. She wasn't a messenger of good fortune but a destroyer of all she loved. She tried to push past Saburo. He held his ground, reiterating: "Yubikiri."

Broken glass, its tip pointed, sparkled. Saburo edged it close to her hand. Her heart pounded. She twisted left, but Saburo caught her. When she stepped back, he followed. Her knees buckled. He pulled her up, grabbed her middle finger, and held it tight. It swelled. He did the same. The glass cut. Their blood flowed, a thick stream of red, mingling, dripping down their fingers onto the dark ground. Saburo pressed his finger to hers. The sharp pain went deep. Then nothing. The release was immediate. Her fear dissolved. She had survived the cut. She felt strong, purposeful, and certain. She leaned into him. Yes, this was right. They would be buddies, chums to the end. Saburo stroked her cheek, and she let him, a tie that nothing could destroy.

"Yubikiri," Saburo whispered in a tender voice, a tone that acknowledged the change in her.

"Yubikiri," she repeated.

TREASURE

Before Sarah put her hand on the back door, it slid open, revealing O'ba's worried face.

"Sarah!" Her mother reached past O'ba, and her father lifted her into the kitchen. "Where have you been?"

"Lost," she admitted, knowing she had misbehaved and that she would be punished. She was ready to be punished. "Your finger's cut," O'ba said sternly.

"You could have been hurt," Mama said.

"You're here," Papa said. "That's all that matters."

For a minute, she didn't understand, waiting for the anger she deserved. Papa held her, the cold receded, and Mama's soft hands replaced Sensei's long stare. The click, click of Fumiko's soroban faded, and she could almost forget Saburo's *yubikiri*, too. She closed her eyes and burrowed into Papa's warmth.

Mama carried her down the hall, undressed her, and Papa slid open the bath door and brought her inside. The steamy room smelled of wood. He sat her on a wooden stool and cleaned the cuts on her knee and elbow. "You're hurt," Papa said in a gentle tone that made her cry. "Beautiful Sarah," he continued in the same voice, "so little with shining eyes. So very little, our little wood fairy who makes us laugh. Did you run into the forest because you were afraid? Because of my fight with Beppe? Did you? Sometimes grownups fight. Beppe and I don't agree on a lot of things, but he is close, a brother." Buckets of steaming water cascaded over her. She closed her eyes and felt nothing but the downpour. Papa was still saying nice things about Beppe when he placed her in the cedar tub. She was nearly asleep as he wrapped her in a waiting towel.

❊ ❊ ❊

In the days that followed, she ran to her parents' room each morning and leapt on their bed as if she had just discovered them. She laughed, and they laughed and showered her with kisses as though they had just found her, too. She snuggled, and they sang soft Russian songs and buried their faces in her hair and the small of her back.

The hut was silent, and Sarah didn't ask questions about Saburo or Fumiko. Her parents kept her close, and her Japanese world disappeared and with it her Japanese self. She no longer aped Japanese behavior or tried to speak Japanese. O'ba served the family silently, her eyes narrowed as if holding a great secret. At times Sarah tried to engage her with reports of conversations between Scalia and her parents, but O'ba turned away.

But after nearly two weeks of this, Sarah wanted O'ba and Emiko back. She missed the smell of tatami in the maid's room and chopping vegetables with O'ba in the kitchen. Most of all she missed the stories. She tried to slip away, but each time her parents intercepted her. One afternoon when she was about to run, her mother held her close.

"I was almost lost once," her mother said, gazing at the plate of *blini* and jam. Sarah leaned closer.

"When were you almost lost?" Sarah asked.

"It was the First World War, and I was your age. We lived in the Ukraine, where my grandfather owned a textile factory. That was before my father went to Hong Kong to work for his older brother—before the family split up, before Communism, and before the Germans. We were a big family then."

Sarah's mother smoothed her hair. She nestled close. "The Czar ordered Jews from the Ukraine sent back to their place of birth. They were afraid Jews would befriend the Germans. They sent us to Riga, where my father was born. We had only days to pack. Grandfather panicked because he couldn't bring his beloved books, piled in the center of the room. He climbed a ladder and spread himself across the books, books that were his life, books he'd collected over the years and that he couldn't be parted from. Finally father relented and hired a *muzhik* to load the books on a cart. The boxcars were crowded. It was hot, and the smell was terrible. Babies were sick, and everyone was hungry. The train went so slowly," her mother's voice lowered with the memory, "and I needed to pee."

Her father put his hand on her mother's arm. "Tamara, do you want to tell this one? Sarah's too little. Please don't, Tamara."

"And I needed to pee," her mother repeated, her eyes still with a glazed look of memory as if her father hadn't spoken. Sarah leaned close. "Finally the train stopped near a large field covered with tiny white and yellow wild flowers. My brother Michael lowered me down, and I ran into the tallest grass. I smelled the warm earth, and as I pulled down my pants, the grass tickled my bottom. Suddenly a bee buzzed, and I stood quickly.

"'Tamara! Tamara!' my mother's voice cried in a high-pitched voice mixed with the train's hoot. Mother called again, and my brothers joined in. I ran! I never ran so fast! My head buzzed with stories of lost children—children left in fields, children lost in crowds, children forgotten during a hurried escape. The wheels of the train turned. The train was moving. Michael was on the rear platform. I stretched my hands to him, screaming, 'Michael! Mama! Michael!' My legs went faster and faster. Michael's fingers were just in front of me. Others leaned from the train, waving, shouting 'Come on! Come on!' The wheels spun fast. I reached up, and Michael seized my blouse, caught me, and lifted me onto the train."

"Mama," Sarah wrapped her arms around her mother's neck.

That afternoon she wanted Saburo. They had taken an oath of friendship. Where was Saburo? Why didn't he play the flute? Why wasn't he in the yard? Had Scalia sent him away? Had Scalia sliced him open and eaten him? At night she pressed her face against the window and watched for Saburo's shadow. But the hut was dark.

The next morning, Fumiko, neatly dressed, met O'ba at the back door. O'ba gave her noodles, and Fumiko did errands. This went on for a week. There was still no sign of Saburo. Sarah stood next to O'ba as Fumiko discussed chores. When Fumiko walked away, O'ba pulled Sarah close and whispered, "Saburo shouldn't be cooped up in the hut with Fumiko. He's too big. He should be playing with boys his own age. It is not good. Something has to be done."

"Does Saburo-chan still live there?" Sarah asked in a tiny voice. It was the first time she'd spoken to O'ba since coming back from the forest. Her Japanese voice, high and hesitant, made her realize how much she missed O'ba and Emiko.

"Of course he still lives there," O'ba answered

with a gentle look and pulled her close. "Something is wrong in the hut," she whispered.

Three days later Saburo appeared. He did not play his flute but stood as before with his arms folded, maintaining his straight, samurai-like posture. Sarah's father drew the curtain and informed O'ba that Saburo must not stand in the yard, but Sarah understood from O'ba's absent look that O'ba would do nothing. He repeated his request. O'ba turned away. At lunch Sarah's mother turned to Scalia and said, "He has to stop."

"Forget him," Scalia declared in a satisfied tone. "We can talk even with little Saburo staring. He may look like a half-wit, but Saburo has brains. He'll get bored." Scalia spoke slowly, as if content with his world and accomplishments. His eyes roamed, then settled on Mama, with her perfectly manicured nails resting on the napkin in a dancer's pose. It was the smug look of a man who has everything and feels powerful. The look scared Sarah. Had Mama seen it? Had Papa?

After lunch Sarah ran to the veranda and waved at Saburo. He extended the little finger that sealed their oath. Sarah lifted hers in return. Yubikiri. When Scalia saw her signaling to Saburo, he looked at her in the same way as he'd looked at her mother. "What games are you playing?" he asked gently. He repeated the question. She remained silent.

That night, Scalia's footsteps paced the floor above. Her ceiling creaked with each turn, back and forth, guarding his realm, and making the house alive with his march. Her stomach tightened. Were Mama and Papa also listening?

Several weeks after the flight to the forest, Saburo appeared wearing new, dark pants and a white shirt. He stood in front of the dining room glass doors and smiled. She smiled back. Saburo jumped with little hops, smiling the whole time. She hopped. Then he did a cartwheel, and she copied. He strutted, and so did she. This game went on for quite some time. No one interfered. That afternoon, Saburo returned with a ball. Sarah ran to her room and got one, too. He bounced the ball, threw it in the air and she followed suit. The ball hit the window. The adults watched. O'ba muttered. Her mother sipped her coffee. Her father left the room.

The next day at lunch as Saburo descended the stairs, Sarah asked if she could play. "Saburo is a good boy," she pleaded in a whisper. "He hasn't done anything wrong."

"You're right," Papa repeated. "Saburo has not done anything wrong. He is just a small boy."

"They are children after all," Mama said.

"You can play," her father conceded, "but only for a short time. You're not to leave the yard. You're not to play in Saburo's house. And the forest is forbidden. Do you understand?"

Even before her father had finished, Sarah ran from the room, down the hall, past the kitchen, and out to the yard. Saburo stood at attention. He jumped up and down. As his feet pounded the earth, Sarah shouted, "Let's play!"

"Let's play," Saburo returned and extended his small, chapped hand to her.

❊ ❊ ❊

Every day after lunch from that day on, Sarah sat beside her mother on the long couch in the living room listening to her read. Her high voice filled the room. They read *The Jungle Book*, *The Secret Garden*, and the *The Little Prince*. Sarah asked questions about the story as if Saburo didn't matter. The clock ticked. Sarah fidgeted. Finally her mother nodded. Sarah rose and walked slowly toward the door.

For the rest of the winter and into the summer, Sarah and Saburo became a unit. Victorious against the adult world, they played with confidence, their bodies churning with excitement. They dug for treasure — string, old coins, marbles, and bits of pottery from the soft sand around the house. Treasure would change their lives, make them heros and allow them untold freedom. It would make their parents glad. It gave their games purpose. They placed the treasure in a large, tin box under the hut, where they enacted stories of samurai: of triumph, courage, and loyalty, of Bushido, and of ronin, who protected the weak and served the emperor until their last breath.

Sarah spoke Japanese and spent more time in the servants' quarters. After her brief banishment, she eagerly returned to her Japanese world. She mimicked low, respectful bows, mincing steps, and a high voice, and created harmony through humor and small favors. O'ba and Emiko smiled when she entered the kitchen, calling her *jochuuko*, 'child of the maids,' the one they could trust, the one who understood. She in turn related her parents' conversations, stories for discussion and analysis.

And with that Sarah slipped from her parents' world into that of Japan — a world of empathy and relationships, of obligation and history. It was a place where she felt most comfortable, a place where she could anticipate each person's reaction, and a place that gave voice to a generous heart.

SENSEI

Sensei was the focus of their games. Sarah pressed O'ba for stories, and O'ba responded with tales of Sensei as a young boy wandering the forest path and as a young man carousing in the Yoshiwara teahouses and dining with fawning *geisha*. Late one afternoon as they sat in the kitchen peeling potatoes, O'ba began to speak in a trance-like voice. Sarah sat close. "Masako was Sensei's favorite. She was young, still a *Maiko*, a 'young geisha in training,' but beautiful, headstrong, and witty. The mistress expected a great deal from Masako. She was given French lessons, riding lessons, classical piano lessons. Rumor had it that she rode bareback in tight pants with her hair free on the beach at Kamakura. The mistress of the geisha house didn't mind all this. In fact she enjoyed Masako's rebellious nature. But when she discovered that Masako had been seen watching fireworks on the Sumida River with Sensei and meeting him in a Ginza coffee shop, she was furious."

Sarah wanted the story to end well but knew from O'ba's sad voice that a happy ending was impossible. "Old man Nishiguchi was angered by demands of the geisha house. The house had already sold the right of Masako's first night. Sensei was threatening their investment, you see." Sarah didn't see but nodded as if she understood. O'ba took a deep breath and said, "The situation was impossible. After that nothing was the same. Old man Nishiguchi arranged for Sensei to be accepted on government scholarship to Harvard University. I'll never forget Sensei, pale and desperate, sitting day after day on the veranda, just as you do now. He did not eat and refused invitations from his friends. He was ill. The house was swollen with worry.

"We hoped America would be good for him," O'ba continued, "that he would forget Masako and learn another way of life, another way of thinking, but none of that happened. Sensei returned to Japan bitter, enraged at Harvard and the West. He became convinced that he must follow the true path, *Shinto*, the only path for Japanese. He argued with his father, claiming Harvard professors belittled Japanese, were greedy and stupid, and had ignored him.

"Old man Nishiguchi, who also had studied engineering in America during Meiji, disagreed, claiming that America had much to teach Japan. Sensei became enraged, screaming, yelling about his belief in Japanese values, frugality, loyalty, obligation, empathy, and more. He called westerners barbaric, people with no understanding or descency. Old man Nishiguchi threw a *sake* cup at Sensei and stormed out. The next month, the military took over Manchukuo."

If she remained still, O'ba would continue talking.

"Sensei never saw Masako again. I know he missed her, but her name was never mentioned. Instead he spent time at the family temple and read books on Japanese history, Bushido and Shinto, and great Buddhist leaders like Nichiren. Six months later he became a Shinto priest.

"At first old man Nishiguchi was pleased because

the Nishiguchi family supported several Shinto shrines and worshipped kami spirits and paid homage to the Imperial House. You know, Sarah-chan, Japanese are a *hoshi gari,* 'wanting,' nation. We pray at Shinto shrines for good luck and things we desire. That is normal. We also believe that kami, 'gods,' live in streams, mountains, sea, lakes, and the forest. With the help of kami, nature enters our souls; *shizen* allows for empathy. That is the Japanese way.

"But Sensei's Shinto had nothing to do with the hoshi gari, or shizen, 'nature,' small shrines overlooking the sea, or planting rice and the rituals around building. No, Sensei's Shinto was about Japan first: the superiority of the Japanese, special people descended from the Sun Goddess Amaterasu Oomikami, the Japanese way, and the emperor. It was about Japan's mission to create a 'Greater East Asia Co-Prosperity Sphere.' It was about the conquest of Manchukuo and the rest of Asia. His father called Sensei's Shinto *'baka,'* and they had more fights."

O'ba paused, waiting to see if Sarah understood. Sarah nodded.

"One day Sensei's old schoolmate Ito, a captain in the navy, came to see him," O'ba continued in a low voice. "They sat in the garden for many hours. I never liked Ito. He had a narrow mean face and thin lips. Terrible man. I pretended to weed but listened. Only when it got dark did I go inside. They spoke softly, heads together—their conversation went on for half the night. Ito came the next day and the next and many days after that. In the end Sensei never returned to the family shrine. He joined the Japanese navy, became an intelligence officer, and achieved the rank of admiral."

Although Sarah didn't understand what an intelligence officer or an admiral was, she knew from O'ba's pained expression that she must not ask about Sensei. "Did you serve the Emperor, too?" she asked instead.

"I was with Sensei in China," O'ba snapped, put down the bag of beans, and left the table. Suddenly O'ba was back. She handed Sarah a photo of a young woman with short, curly hair in a short-sleeved, flowered dress, smiling at the camera. "I was in Shanghai for ten years," she whispered. Sarah picked up the picture, trying to imagine her plump O'ba, in a wide apron with her hair in a tight bun, as the open-faced, laughing girl in a short, puffed-sleeved dress. What had happened to O'ba? Then she realized it was something terrible, something that involved Sensei and Atsuko-chan, a deep secret, and she must not ask.

"Relationships you make when young will haunt you, influence your whole life, make you do things, sometimes terrible things, things you try to make right," O'ba said softly and took the picture from Sarah. "Those cuts, buried deep, are part of you, always there, even though you might not realize it. Sensei is obsessed with the past. That's why he lives in the squatter village, why he walks in the forest, why he takes care of Ryuzu-chan, the son of Masaru-kun, his best friend. The past haunts Sensei, and if you're not careful, it will haunt you, too." Sarah thought of Saburo and the vow to be best friends always. She wanted to tell O'ba about that but instead put her arms around O'ba's broad shoulders. She stroked O'ba's cheeks and murmured her name. O'ba rocked her gently and whispered in turn. "Beautiful child, my child. You must be careful."

During family lunches Sarah heard about foreign life in Shanghai, a world she barely remembered. Her parents spoke of Shanghai's Victorian homes surrounded by beautiful lawns, about the parks with signs that read "no Chinese or dogs allowed," about Shanghai's badlands, where machine-gun nests controlled the streets, about the carts that collected frozen bodies, and about the children sold for less than a dollar. They spoke of private opium rooms furnished with velvet couches and long nights starting with drinks at the Grande Hotel and ending with gypsies and dancing outside the city. With each account Sarah made up new games. Saburo matched her stories.

"White is for sorrow," Saburo whispered one very hot day. "Passengers on ship dressed in white. My friend Hisashi-kun carried his parents' ashes in a box around his neck," Saburo continued. "My baby brother, Kyoshi-kun, died the day before we reached Japan. His ashes are in an urn next to my father," he said, pointing to the hut. "I pray in front of Kyoshi and my father's urn every day."

"Saburo-chan," Fumiko's high, cool voice called from above.

Sarah looked up, wanting to hear the rest of the story and knew from Saburo's flushed face that he wanted to tell it. Since Fumiko's tantrum and Sarah and Saburo's adventure in the forest, Fumiko rarely spoke to Sarah. Now she stood on the hut's balcony with her hands on her hips and smiled as if she didn't feel the heat. "Come inside where it's cooler."

"I can't. I'm not allowed," Sarah said, annoyed by Fumiko's presence.

"Don't worry. We can do something else," Fumiko said, tossing her head and starting down the stairs. "We can go swimming in the lake. You would like that. It's cool by the lake."

"I'm not allowed to swim in the lake," Sarah said. "The lake has germs that make you get sick and paralyzed."

Fumiko smiled, ran her fingers through her hair,

and placed her hand on Saburo's head as he yelled, "Let's go."

"You are a good girl, Sarah-chan. Saburo-chan is a bad boy," she added with a laugh. "We won't swim. We'll sit on the shore and feel the breeze from the lake. On the island the sea breeze cooled us. O'ba and your mama won't mind that. They are sleeping now. We'll be back soon."

Sarah hesitated. Saburo laughed. Then Sarah laughed. Fumiko led the way across the yard to the main road. Fumiko swung her arms and sang a children's song about a meditating Indian monk. Sarah and Saburo joined in. They passed several burned-out homes and crossed an empty lot to the woods. Fumiko paused each time they passed a ruin. Her eyes gauged Sarah's reaction. With each stop, with each look, Sarah remembered the large mound, the cold, and Sensei's white skin. Though summer had transformed the forest to a vibrant green, and crickets filled the air, she remembered. Fumiko sang of *O-Bon*, the festival for the dead, when lanterns of dead souls floated out to sea. The slow walk and Fumiko's throaty voice let Sarah's thoughts turn to treasure.

The path narrowed, and trees bent close. The power of the forest—the tall bamboos, the sound of crickets, and boulders covered with moss—made her glad. Saburo grabbed her hand, and they broke free of Fumiko and ran from tree to tree, slamming their hands against the crickets. Fumiko laughed, and they laughed.

Before she realized it, they came to the spot where the crater and the mound had been. Burnt wood and other refuse had filled the crater. The mound was flattened. Fumiko stood with her hands on her hips, her face severe, and pointed at the field. Her voice was harsh. "You saw nothing," she said. "The hill is gone, the hole is filled, a dream. There was nothing." Frightened by Fumiko's tone, her glare, all of it, Sarah ran ahead. She rounded a bend.

Water glistened between the bamboos. The lake, its small waves rippling, was before them. A strip of white sand stretched like a pale ribbon around the deserted shore, and clumps of water grass stood in the shallows. Birds swooped to the water's edge, coasting above the waves until caught by a draft and soaring skyward. More forest loomed beyond. Fumiko spread her arms and ran to the shore, her cruel smile replaced by the gentle look of a young girl, wide-eyed, cheeks rounded, lips soft and expectant. Her laughter rang across the lake as she took off her blouse and pantaloons. Then she shook her hair free so that it covered her shoulders, swollen breasts, and large nipples. A welt and several bruises discolored her lower back, but the rest of her skin had the same smoothness as Scalia's Kannon. She held out her arms.

Sarah forgot her anger and her mother's warning of dirty water, sea snails, and polio and took off her clothes. Saburo undressed too. Fumiko wrapped her hair around their necks. Sarah held the thick, charcoal-smelling strands as Fumiko walked into the lake. Saburo rubbed noses with Fumiko and giggled. Her nipples pressed against their skin. Saburo squeezed her breast and laughed. Sarah nuzzled Fumiko's neck. They were in deep water now, and Fumiko released them to float side by side on their backs. Sarah stared at the tops of the bamboos moving against the sky. She was glad Fumiko was happy, the mound was flattened, the sun was bright, and the sky blue. The lake reflected the green forest and the clouds overhead. She felt the water, clean and fresh, wash over her.

The kami sparkled in the bright sky, in forest

caves, on boulders, and under trees, just as O'ba and Scalia had said. Her body stretched with happiness, a joy that encompassed the lake and hills and the sky beyond. This world, harmonious, flowing with good will and feelings that expressed her innermost being, had to last.

BEPPE'S PLAN

Sarah, you're daydreaming," her mother said the next morning at breakfast. She smiled an encouraging smile that made Sarah want to tell everything. "What are you dreaming about?"

Scalia interrupted. "Tamara, there is a big party at the American embassy this week. Will you wear your choker?"

Her mother's hand rested on her large belly, and she shook her head. "Beppe, I don't think I'm up to it."

"So we will take Sarah-chan," Scalia said quickly. "Good American ladies love children just as much as they love pearls. I know just the assortment that would intrigue them."

"That's not possible," her father said. "We don't want the ladies pawing at Sarah."

"Not possible?" Scalia asked and leaned back in his chair. "Let me remind you, we're in business. Americans like families. They feel good when they buy for their wives. And if they can't buy for wives, they buy for children. You know what they buy? They buy what they see, pearls they see on Tamara or Sarah."

"Impossible," her father repeated.

"Alexander, we need cash." Scalia tapped his fork against the table as a reminder. "Nishiguchi wants a nightclub, classy, with top US acts, where Americans can relax and do business with Japanese. His navy buddies will provide land. We have to come up with cash."

"I don't want to be involved."

Scalia, his eyes narrow with tension, considered this. His voice would soften now and would remain barely audible until the explosion that was sure to come. Since the fight between Scalia and her father, there had been a truce of sorts. Scalia would tell stories, and her parents would listen, but unlike before the atmosphere was cold, and by the end of each meal, Scalia's shrill voice dominated. "

But Mr. Berman," Scalia said in a sarcastic voice. "You love America and believe in American democracy and American law, but we have to earn a living. We have to take care of the family. Remember your brother executed in '36 by Stalin for nothing except being a student and a Jew? Remember your uncle taken in the middle of the night for being a rich Jew? Never to be heard from again. Remember your cousins, the twins, sent to a work camp in Siberia? I don't even know about the nameless others, marched into the forest by the SS, stripped and shot, each with a bullet so they fell neatly into the pit. Very German."

Be quiet, Beppe," her father ordered, glancing at Sarah, who sat like a stone listening to the list of dead — names that were whispered, names that made her father sad and her mother cry, names that were mentioned suddenly and then disappeared just as quickly. She knew there were more: cousins, friends, aunts, and uncles, whom her mother had played with on the sandy beaches of Riga, all killed in turn by Germans, Latvians, and Russians. Her mother called them "holes in her heart," and her father remained silent.

Scalia's expression became animated. He ticked

off the dead. He knew the family history better than her parents, keeping track of who was related to whom, when they were born, where they went to school, and exactly how they died. He knew the name of the street in Riga where her mother had lived and the details of the watch business that brought the family to Hong Kong and to Shanghai. He knew her father's favorite operas, his apartment number in Harbin, and the personal histories of his parents and grandparents.

He loved them so. When she felt that love, she called him uncle and sat on his lap, and he explained the history behind a netsuke carving. He would smooth her hair and speak first in English, continuing in Italian and then Japanese as he described each Tokugawa carver. She touched the fine details, the witch's turning head, the romping puppies' rounded limbs, and the octopus's tentacles. She giggled and nestled against his shoulder. When they saw Scalia's arms around her, her parents smiled as if he were cradling them, too. Now her parents glanced at each other as if they didn't know how to proceed.

"The Flamingo will promote everything you stand for, and you'll be helping America too, Mr. Berman," Scalia continued in an even softer tone. "Americans need a relaxing place, a place where they can drink whiskey, be entertained by singers like Sinatra, a place where they can even bring their wives. Conquerors like to feel at home in countries they control. They want to recreate themselves. Otherwise what is the point? The Flamingo is important. America needs Japan and Japan needs America. It will work."

"Beppe," her father said, "I was at the US military headquarters. Nishiguchi was there."

"Why were you there?" Scalia asked.

"Americans wanted facts about the Chinese left

wing in Hong Kong and Shanghai, about my student days. God knows what they were asking Nishiguchi, but I'm sure he gave them plenty and asked for plenty. The US officer covered a brick of gold bullion with a cloth just as I entered the room. He had a foolish smile, but I saw the gold, bright and large. Leave it alone. Don't get mixed up with Nishiguchi's club, his friends, his gold, and his drugs. You'll be dead in the end. You'll be one of the people who disappear."

"We're already involved in the pearl business and renting his house, this house. Nishiguchi is Japan. Japan will never change. Nishiguchi is yesterday, today, and tomorrow."

"Beppe," her mother said in a reproving tone with a glance toward Sarah.

Scalia took a deep breath. The room was silent except for the distant screech of crickets. Her mother gazed out the window and ignored Scalia's stare. Sarah waited for Scalia to leap to his feet in a rage and attack her father.

"The world's turning, Tamara, Alexander," Scalia said in a reasonable tone. "Americans may be liberal, but America hates Communists, especially Russia. There is a Cold War, Alexander. Our job is to stay on America's good side. If they imagined you were left wing, you'd be finished in Japan. No more invitations to parties. No more selling pearls. No more hope. Americans don't buy from black-listed people."

"Are you threatening us, Beppe?" her mother hissed. "Don't think we are so weak. Don't think you can threaten and bully, bring up those who weren't lucky to make your point. We are not that indebted. Alexander was never a member of the Party. He was left but never a member."

Scalia lowered his eyes. He looked desperate,

aware that he'd gone too far. He gave her mother a soft smile. "Of course, Tamara; I know that, and you know that, but he's a Jew," Scalia murmured in his gentlest voice. "That means nothing to me. I love my pale Jews, but imagine how it sounds to an American diplomat educated at Yale or Princeton. A left-wing Jew, born in Harbin, war years in Shanghai, mother tongue Russian. All that makes no difference to me," he repeated, "but it doesn't sound good today. Today Russia is the enemy."

The table was still, and Sarah asked in a timid voice, telling her lie cautiously, her voice hesitant, worried that she would be discovered. "Can I go shopping with Saburo-chan? Fumiko-san said she would take us."

"You like playing with Saburo, don't you?" Scalia asked abruptly.

Sarah thought of the lake. She wanted nothing more than to leave the tension of the room and the frozen adults. She could not dispel their rage with a joke or a small story. She was a small child without power. With Fumiko and Saburo, she would run to the forest and down the path to the lake. She had not died from germs, snails, or snakebites. This time she would leap into the water and dunk her head so that she was cool all over. Saburo would follow, and they'd splash each other, and let the little fish nibble their toes. After that they'd collect things on the shore while Fumiko slept.

FUMIKO

Saburo," Sarah called from the top of the stairs to the hut. "Asobimasho."

Whispers and Fumiko's soft laughter sounded through the door.

"Saburo-chan, asobimasho, 'let's play.' Let's go to the lake again. It's hot. We can swim." Sarah kicked the sill. The door slid open, and Saburo pulled her into the entryway, into smells of burnt food and mildew that filled the narrow space, into the place against all rules. She had never been in the hut before. It was hot, and Sarah kicked off her sandals.

Saburo pushed open the *shoji* door to the main room and bowed solemnly to the brass urns on the opposite wall, the urn of his father, and of his little brother, Kyoshi. Fumiko, dressed in a blue and white summer kimono, sat on a large, orange cushion. "Come," Fumiko beckoned, smiling and flicking her tongue over red lips.

"Can we go swimming?" Sarah asked.

"Perhaps," Fumiko teased in the same baby voice she had used in the past. "Perhaps not." She pulled Sarah onto her lap. "Feel how deep," Fumiko said and ran Sarah's fingers under her bangs, through her hair, and over her pocked skin. "When I was six, I almost died. They called it the great sickness. I lay in bed for months."

"Did you get sick from the water?" Sarah asked.

"No, I grew up on Sensei's island. The island of pine trees, rock, and sand. The sea was full of sea bass, halibut, oysters, scallops, sea urchin, shrimp, octopus, squid, and many good things to eat. Our water came from a river so clean the pebbles on the bottom glowed like jewels. The sickness was the air. I got sick from the air." She brushed back her bangs. "Look." A dozen deep, whitish scars, tiny blinking eyes, dotted her forehead. Fumiko moved Sarah's palm back and forth across the pitted surface. "My mother said that because of the scars, I would never marry, and I would have to be sold, but Sensei arranged a good marriage. In Manchuria I had three servants."

"I got sick, too." Saburo ran to the cushion, pushed Sarah off Fumiko's lap, and pointed to the scar on his forehead.

"You weren't sick. You fell, silly." Fumiko laughed at Saburo's belligerent expression. "I am talking to Sarah-chan now. Go and pray to your ototo-san and oto-san."

"I've already prayed." Saburo's face reddened. He hugged Fumiko around the waist. Fumiko pressed his head close.

"You didn't pray enough," Fumiko said, switching once again to baby talk. "You are my naughty baby."

Sarah stood. Saburo and Fumiko rubbed noses, nostrils touching, skin blending. As their bodies meshed, Sarah remembered O'ba saying that Fumiko and Saburo were too close. Sarah thought O'ba was right.

Plump larvae the color of her pale-pink arm undulated up the wall to a crack in the ceiling. She folded her arms so her skin was less visible. She looked at Fumiko and Saburo's black hair and brown skin, tears welled behind her eyelids, and she kicked the corner of the table.

"*Gaijin*!" Saburo shouted as if he read her thoughts. He nuzzled Fumiko's neck.

"Those aren't my parents," Sarah shouted back. "They found me in Shanghai in a shoebox wrapped in newspaper. I was blue and small. They thought I wouldn't live. O'ba took care of me. O'ba knows. I'm really Japanese, pale Japanese from the north."

"You are not Japanese!" Saburo shouted. "Gaijin."

Fumiko's eyes narrowed and she pushed Saburo off her lap. "Do you think you are true Japanese, Saburo-chan?" Fumiko teased. "Then why are you bad? Your little brother, Kyoshi-kun, listened; he was not bad like you. Your papa is angry. He was a good Japanese. There was nothing your papa wouldn't do for Japan. Even in death, he knows everything. His ashes darken when he's mad. You're a bad son. You're not Japanese, real Japanese. Your papa knows."

Saburo stood with his feet apart and arms folded. His eyes searched for approval, and his body trembled. Sarah felt his desperation, a need so powerful that it filled the room.

The neighborhood laughs at you," Fumiko continued. "They think you are the foreigner. You make the family lose face. You should be ashamed."

"I am Japanese," Saburo shouted. "I have the Japanese spirit. I have endurance, strength. No one laughs! Sensei gives me presents. She's the gaijin." With that he crawled on Fumiko's lap and began prying open her yukata.

Fumiko laughed again and at once reached inside, cupped her right breast, shrugged off the top of her yukata, and with a teasing gesture pushed away Saburo.

"Mama wants to play," Saburo shouted and leapt to his feet. Seizing Sarah's hand, he yelled, "Mama." He pointed to Fumiko's loose yukata and screamed again. Fumiko shook her head and slowly drew the flaps of her yukata together.

"Mama, mama." Saburo jumped up and down. Sarah flushed and jumped, too. Their feet pounded the floor. "Let's play!". Sweat dripped from her forehead, the floorboards creaked, and the urns wobbled on the dais.

Fumiko undid her hair. Her small hands smoothed and flattened it until it framed her large eyes and her small chin. Then she opened her yukata again, revealing a breast; a blue vein encircled the nipple puffed dark at the center. Fumiko raised her breast and pointed the nipple at Saburo. "You won't get me," Saburo shouted and ran.

Fumiko slid her index finger toward the nipple and squeezed. A stream of milk shot out, landing on the floor near Saburo's feet. Fumiko angled her breast and squeezed again. The spray dotted Saburo's skin. She squeezed again. This time the milk hit him directly in his face. He screamed and ran across the room toward the urns. Fumiko laughed, and her small tongue flicked. She moved her breast once more and aimed at Sarah. Milk landed on Sarah's arm. Milk hit her face. Sarah didn't know where to run. More milk hit her neck and cheek. The walls were close. The heavy, sweet, sticky odor made her stomach turn. Saburo pulled her against him. "You're wet," he laughed.

She laughed too, and they jumped up and down. The milk dotted their skin and sprayed the urns and walls white. They screamed, racing from one side of the room to the other. Saburo's rough tongue licked the milk from his skin and from hers. She licked, too. They stomped, yelled, bumping against the walls and each other. The cabin shook; maggots dropped.

"Come," Fumiko said, spreading her yukata to reveal both her breasts. "I have enough for both of you. Saburo knows how much I have."

Saburo ran to her lap and reached for her breast, but Fumiko grabbed his hands and squirted milk on his nose. Again he grabbed, and she lifted the breast away. He howled with a desperate rage. At once Fumiko drew him close and closed her eyes.

The sound of Saburo's sucking filled the room. Fumiko pressed his head closer, and the sound grew louder. Sarah stepped nearer. A drop of milk grew on Fumiko's other nipple, round and white. Sarah knelt and reached, but just as her fingers grazed the nipple, Saburo pushed her back.

The sucking grew loud. Maggots dropped. Her hands were wet with perspiration. Fumiko rocked. Saburo sucked. The room felt close. She backed onto the scorching-hot porch. "I'll find treasure alone," Sarah thought, descending the steps to the space where the earth was soft, to their best imagining and digging place.

The high walls comforted her. Above, the hut was quiet. She banished Saburo and Fumiko and focused on mixing water and dirt, shaping them into mud patties. The pile grew. She molded the mud into a castle wall.

The big house back door slammed. Leather shoes scraped the flagstone path. The steps creaked, and a shadow blocked the light. Sarah held her breath. A man's shoes were visible. The sliding door opened. Fumiko's low laughter filled the space. The man laughed.

Scalia.

Sarah sat very still. There was a giggle. Then more giggles. Had Saburo left? Was he waiting for her by the back door of the house? She would make him beg to play with her. She would force him to his knees and demand an apology for the word gaijin. He would promise on their yubikiri oath never to insult her again. Then they would escape to the forest and run to the lake. They would splash each other and collect shells. No one would know. Yubikiri. She put three stones in her pocket for luck and hoisted herself out of the hole.

The outer door of the hut was open, but shoji separating the entry from the main room was closed. She peeked through a tear into the room. Fumiko's bare shoulders glistened. Scalia and Fumiko undulated like an enormous wave, their shadows making the room alive, oblivious of anything except each other. Sarah wet her finger and extended the tear. Saburo lay on a quilt next to the shrine, asleep with his head facing the door. A shaft of sunlight outlined his full mouth and square chin. Her heart pounded. She'd wake him with a lucky stone. She wobbled the door open, aimed, and threw. The stone clanged against Ichiro's urn.

Saburo's eyelids fluttered. Scalia murmured. Scalia and Fumiko were suspended in space. Then their motion resumed, their pace quickened, and the dark crack of Fumiko's bottom widened. "More," Scalia called in his hoarse voice. "More." Fumiko straightened, picked up a thick, silk sash and held it high over her head. "Yes," Scalia whispered as she hovered. "Yes," he repeated as she tied the cord around his neck. "Yes. Yes." Fumiko pulled. "Ahh." Scalia's moan filled the hut. "Ahh." His head thrashed violently. "No," he gasped. His voice was hoarse. He wanted her to stop. Fumiko pulled the sash. He protested. Again. Scalia raised his fist and smashed Fumiko's skull. Fumiko's buttocks rose. She stared wide-eyed toward the door before slumping sideways. Scalia's shiny penis rested against his leg. He pulled at the cord as if untying a necktie. Sarah closed the door and extended the tear in the shoji. "Mama," Saburo's voice was sleepy. "Mama," his voice was louder. "Please Mama! Are you sleeping?"

Scalia pulled on his pants and faced Saburo. "She is sleeping," he muttered. "Now you must sleep, too."

Scalia's shadow towered against the shoji. His acid-sweet sweat filled her with terror.

"Is Mama sleeping?" Saburo asked.

"Go to sleep," Scalia commanded.

Saburo whimpered and reached toward Fumiko.

"Rest." Scalia pointed to the quilt. His hairless, bruised chest and the welts around his neck made him look diseased. His skin shone with perspiration.

"You hurt Mama," Saburo said. He rose and lunged at Scalia. Scalia caught him and threw him down. A tray of pearls cascaded across the floor. Saburo scrambled to his feet and lunged again.

"You want to play?" Scalia taunted. Saburo attacked. Scalia hit. Saburo rose and dove. Scalia tossed him back. More pearls scattered. The lids of the urns toppled, sending up a fine ash. It hung like a cloud and then descended slowly.

"Papa! Kyoshi!" Saburo screamed.

The ash clung to Saburo's skin. It mixed with perspiration, dark bands smeared across his cheeks. He rolled on the tatami, but it stuck to his back and legs. Saburo rose and charged again. Scalia pushed him back. Saburo fell. This time he squatted on his haunches like a runner, uttered a wild cry, and ran at Scalia. This time Scalia caught him in midair and flung him hard. Saburo's small body held the wall for a moment and then slowly, ever so slowly, like a leaf caught in the wind, hovering and unsteady, flopped to the ground. Except for pale maggots that fell like small pellets from the ceiling, the room was still.

Sarah waited. Saburo did not move.

Her fault—she had seen, heard, and smelled what was forbidden. She had broken her promise not to enter the hut. She had thrown a stone. Fumiko was dead. Saburo was dead. Bodies strewn across the thin mat, heads pitched at odd angles, legs akimbo, mouths open. She must vanish. It was the only thing to do. She descended the steps and ran toward the hole in the fence.

She was well into the forest. The crickets' high-pitched siren screamed. Her head throbbed as her feet hit the earth. She ran into the dark world outside the inner circle, the family, where anything could happen. It was a place full of strangers, a place where shame, obligation, and all the things that mattered did not count. Human relations counted for nothing in that world. It was savage. She'd been warned about it, yet she ran.

The lake glistened and the sandy beach stretched before her. Her pace slowed, and she spread her arms. A dragonfly hovered over the tall reeds, its wings inches above the ripples, before disappearing into the glare of the sun. Spongy sand squeezed between her toes, and the breeze stroked her skin. Water lapped at her feet and covered her knees. She opened her arms to the chill and plunged face down, her dress billowing like a parachute.

FLIGHT

She floated on gentle currents between clumps of lake grass. Dancing water beetles zigzagged across her path. Water smelling of mud and grass lapped against her skin, and stretching her arms wide, she drifted.

Then Saburo.

His terrified cry, his scramble toward Fumiko, and his small neck turned awkwardly filled her with horror. Saburo was dead. She must tell Mama. They would go to the hut together. She would show Mama just how it happened—the stone, Fumiko, Scalia. Mama would fix everything. She planted her feet in the mud and started toward shore.

Dark silhouettes appeared against the sun. "Look," the men called from the narrow beach and waded into the lake. Fear pricked the back of her neck, and she backed away. Their shaved heads glistened, and they came crab-like through the murky water. She moved to the right. They followed. She turned to the left. They were right behind her. She swallowed water and coughed. They laughed. She backed into deeper water, lost her footing, and gasped for air. The water stung her eyes. They were on either side of her, closing in; the younger one laughed again and opened his arms.

She gulped water and went under. Strong hands seized her elbows and pulled. She kicked the younger man in the face, but the older one tucked her under his arm and hauled her to a clump of young bamboos on the narrow beach. In coarse Japanese he said, "Stop struggling, foreign fish." He flashed a gold-toothed smile and touched her hair, then her cheek and neck. "Look, white skin, Hiro-kun," the older one said.

"Freckles, Jiro-san," Hiro responded.

"Light blue veins," Jiro replied, his weathered hand moving to her shoulder. "Brown, soft hair, curled eyelashes, blue eyes right to the brain." Jiro's eyes dulled as he touched and stroked, lifted her skirt, and felt her leg. Their fingers sickened her. "Stop," she yelled, but it continued, Jiro patting her thigh and Hiro the back of her neck.

"Japan lost the war," she shouted the insult with all her strength.

The men inhaled. "She speaks Japanese," Hiro finally said. "We will take her to the village."

Hiro pushed Sarah against Jiro's back. She kicked, but Jiro grabbed her hands and twisted the rope around. She could not move. They stuffed a cloth in her mouth. Sarah bent to avoid lice that scuttled onto her cheek. More lice jumped, disappearing under the collar of her dress and down her back.

She sobbed quietly.

Blackness.

❀ ❀ ❀

She woke to the hut's metallic scent. Tiny, red ants marched across her cheeks. She brushed them off and stood unsteadily. How long had she been here? Where was she? She remembered the lake, the chase, and that was all. Sarah pushed open the door. The village was separated from the forest by a dirt road. Tin huts formed a half circle by a collapsed bridge, and the metal roofs glinted in the bright sun. Fishing poles rested against each hut. Muddy ground dotted with potted plants sloped to the lake.

Jiro spoke to a crowd. Hiro smiled proudly. Children pressed close, women bobbed their kerchief heads, and men patted their wide, wool waistbands.

"Gaijin." It rang through the small clearing like a chant, and with each utterance the villagers looked expectantly at the hut and became more animated. The chant built. They pounded their feet. Children raised their hands and ran toward the hut. The adults laughed. More children came. They stuck their tongue out and pulled their faces in odd grimaces. She retreated but Jiro went to the door and pulled her outside.

A hush fell. A stocky boy, broad faced with tiny eyes, pushed his way through the crowd. He jabbed his rod at her, shouting, "*America kaere*, 'America go home!'" His face reddened, and he continued to shout, "America kaere." Other children shouted while the adults laughed. Sarah backed against the hut's ribbed wall and covered her ears. The shouts grew. The stocky boy dangled the hook close to her face. He brought it close again. He stepped back, took aim, and swung. The hook sailed through the air and landed next to her head. The children urged him on with more screams. The adults laughed and pointed. The hook kept coming, striking to the right and to the left. She turned. The hook pinned her hair. A cheer rose.

"You're a bully, Michio," a tall boy shouted.

Michio raised his rod, but before he could swing, the tall boy charged.

"She is gaijin, Ryuzu-chan," Michio yelled and

swung at him. He swung again. Ryuzu jumped to one side. The hook kept coming. Ryuzu bent low, charged, and mounted him. The two boys rolled in the dirt.

The crowd closed in. Michio punched. Ryuzu dodged. Michio rammed his head into Ryuzu's stomach. "Ahh," Ryuzu cried and grabbed Michio's ankle. Ryuzu leapt on Michio's chest and flattened Michio's arms on the dirt. Michio bit Ryuzu's hand and Michio was on top. Ryuzu sprayed Michio's face with dirt. The crowd chanted, "Go, go."

"Stop."

A figure strode across the road, white robes flapping, and entered the village. He carried a silver-handled cane. He moved swiftly. The children regrouped behind the adults and peered cautiously. "What's going on here?" the man shouted. "Have you forgotten everything? Is this the Japanese way? Get away from her."

The villagers retreated.

It was Sensei. His robe swayed as he approached Sarah. He knelt so that he was at eye level and held that position for several seconds. A hush descended. "We know each other, don't we, Sarah-chan?" he said gently. "You have nothing to fear."

"I'm not afraid," she answered, even though she was.

"Good. Saburo-chan has told me that you are becoming a brave samurai. You live in my house, the house where my family and I lived before the war. Back then it had a lovely garden and a pond with one-hundred-dred-year-old *koi*."

Sarah froze at the mention of Saburo. She wanted Sensei to know about Saburo but didn't know how to begin. Sensei put out his hand, and Sarah extended hers. His palm felt cool. She squared her shoulders and answered softly, "O'ba told me about the garden and the koi. She told me that you played the flute and walked in the forest with your friend Masaru." Sarah stepped close. The villagers pressed in.

"Yes, a long time ago," Sensei said. "Masaru-kun was my best friend. Is O'ba still noisy?" Sarah nodded, and for a moment she forgot about Saburo and smiled because she wanted Sensei to like her. Sensei laughed, she laughed, and behind them the villagers laughed.

"How did you get here?" Sensei asked.

"I ran into the forest and swam in the lake. Jiro caught me and brought me here," she replied. Sensei nodded as if her explanation was all he needed.

"Everything is going to be all right," Sensei reassured her. "The children got carried away."

"They are dirty and mean," she said, looking past him at the children who had gathered around them.

"I'll introduce you, and you'll all be friends." Sensei beckoned to the stocky boy and said, "Michio-kun, apologize to Sarah-chan." Then he called to a round-faced girl with a mucus-filled nose, "Noriko-chan." One by one the children stepped toward her, bowed briefly, muttered words of apology, and retreated to the end of the line.

Finally Sensei called, "Ryuzu-kun." The tall boy stood in front of her. As he bowed, his face broke into a smile, and his clear eyes shone with humor. His long forehead and full lips reminded her of Scalia's Kannon. His height and good will set him apart. Sarah immediately wanted to be his friend, to whisper and share secrets. Her eyes went to his cut knee. She bowed. She could tell from Sensei's smile that he loved Ryuzu best, too. That made her glad. Everything would be fine now.

But Saburo. His ash-streaked chest, his desperate eyes, and his still body made her tremble. The crowd faded. Even Sensei didn't matter. Her body shook as though she were cold. She couldn't stop shaking. The children watched, and an old woman closed in and murmured, "There, there," to her while several others dabbed their eyes.

"Saburo-chan," she whispered to Sensei. "He is in the hut."

"What about Saburo-chan?" Sensei asked and drew her near until their faces almost touched.

She was about to tell. She wanted to tell. He must know. Her breath came in short gasps. Sensei would help. He was the Sensei, who rode a white horse, who saved the children in Chinese villages, who served the Emperor. He meditated on the coldest ground. His voice was soft, his eyes gentle. Saburo was wrong about the Ninja warriors. Sensei would never hurt her. Now he would bring Saburo back to life.

Beep! A sharp horn interrupted.

"Americans!" the villagers yelled, "Americans!" Sensei swiftly thrust her behind him.

A jeep rounded the bend and pulled to a stop. A narrow-faced officer with thinning blond hair combed flat scanned the crowd. He walked toward Sensei. The driver, his black face shining, followed. The crowd stirred.

"Black!" Michio yelled, and others took up the cry. "A monkey," one yelled. And then, "A black monkey. Pale palms. A beast from the forest." Sensei held up a hand. The children became quiet. Sarah pressed against Sensei's back.

"Nishiguchi-san, we've come to visit you again," the officer said.

"I'm happy to have you visit, Major Anderson," Sensei said quietly in English. He bowed to Anderson and the black driver while the crowd watched. Sarah peered out. Sensei pushed her back.

"This time we have come for answers," Anderson said. "We will stay until we get them. No double-talk. Just answers. You understand? This is my third visit, and I want it to be my last. I know you understand because you speak English well. I studied at Harvard, too. Yes, we know all about you."

Sensei's hand remained, large and warm, on her head. Sarah pressed against his back. Sensei's hand fell to her shoulder, cradling and protecting her. She closed her eyes and imagined it was Mama's hand and that she was safe. It would be all right—O'ba praised Sensei. His voice was kind.

Just then Sensei stepped aside and commanded gently in Japanese, "Sarah-chan, please say hello to the Americans."

"My God, she's white! A white child!" Anderson stared. "But she's not American. I know an American when I see one. She's not even wearing shoes or socks. What is this?"

"It's good you're here," Sensei informed Anderson quietly. "Her name is Sarah. She speaks English. She lives in the big house on the other side of the lake. My house. She got lost, and my men found her. Her parents must be worried. You must take her home."

"How in God's name did she get lost? Look at her. She is covered with mud. Her dress is wet. What happened to you, Sarah?" Anderson asked. Sarah was not sure of her English. She felt tired, very tired.

The black driver knelt and took her hand. She pulled away, but he held tight and picked her up. He smiled and stroked her cheek. "It's OK," he said gently. She touched his curly hair and ran her finger down his brown-black face. He let her touch him, cradling her, speaking softly, and she put her arms around his neck.

The crowd murmured, "Black." Their voices grew

loud. "Black monkey." And again, "black—black." The slurs, guttural and indecent, made her ashamed of Sensei and the villagers. They were nasty. She didn't want the driver to hear. He mustn't know. He would be sad. Sarah covered his ears and brought her face close so she had his full attention. The driver let her hands stay as he carried her through the crowd.

"Nishiguchi," Anderson said in a louder voice than necessary. "Obviously we have to get Sarah home. It's very convenient that she is here. Too convenient. We know you're hiding war materials. Gold, too. We have solid information about you and this village."

"No war materials," Sensei answered quietly. "No gold."

"We know there is stuff hidden all over this village. Wire, iron, precious metals. It comes up for sale on the black market and then disappears." Anderson's voice lowered. "Where are those materials?"

"Search the village," Sensei said calmly. "You will find nothing. Japan is poor. Japan is defeated. We are a poor island nation dependent on others for raw materials. We only have our people, the Japanese people. People are our only resource. And of course what America gives us. America has been very generous. Our children eat American cornmeal."

"Now what's wrong with cornmeal? There is nothing like a good cornbread straight from the oven. Your children are lucky to have cornmeal."

"America is a great country," Sensei stated gravely.

"Sir," the driver interrupted. "The girl feels hot." He pulled a Hershey bar from his breast pocket and handed it to Sarah. She shook her head. He tossed it at the children. Michio caught it, tore off the remaining wrapper, and broke it in small pieces. He split it among all of them except the tall boy, Ryuzu, who smiled at her shyly.

"We'll be back," Anderson said in a voice as soft as Sensei's. "You still have a great deal to learn about America. We are a determined people. We don't take 'maybe' for an answer. We'll be back, and there won't be any more diversions."

Anderson walked to the jeep, climbed into the rear seat, and nodded to the driver, who handed over Sarah. "Let's get out of here," Anderson muttered, glaring at Nishiguchi and the children, their mouths coated with chocolate, surrounding the jeep. The driver revved the motor and backed into the lane. Anderson continued in an angry voice, "The more I learn about Japan, the more irrelevant I feel. Nishiguchi, Japanese Naval Intelligence, Manchurian opium dens, slave labor, plundering Manchuria's natural resources. Nishiguchi was in jail. Nishiguchi should be in jail. Crazy. The occupation let him out."

The children yelled, "America!" The driver smiled but Anderson continued, "Many of these poor bastards served in the Japanese army in Manchuria and were clubbed by their own officers. Officers like Nishiguchi."

"I understand, sir."

"Well, I don't," Anderson muttered. "There is stuff in these woods and maybe even in the village, but they won't squeal. Never. Loyalty to the end."

"I understand, sir," the driver said again and gave a final honk to the villagers, shouting, "America! America!"

Perched next to Anderson high on the seat of the jeep, Sarah felt tall. She was part of the occupation, and Sensei knew it, the children knew it, and she knew it, too. Now she didn't care that they had tormented her because, in the end, she was the one who sat next to Anderson, who smelled clean and whose eyes were as blue as her own.

"Sarah-chan!"

She turned to Ryuzu's smile and warm eyes. He lifted his hand in friendship, a gesture that made her forget that America had won the war, a sign that they were pals. She raised her hand. Their palms flattened in midair, and with that, the occupation disappeared. Her pulse quickened. The children waved, wrists flapping, fingers extending, making the air alive with motion.

She called Ryuzu's name.

"Sarah-chan," Ryuzu returned, running close to the car and repeating it so others took up a chant, "Sarah-chan, Sarah-chan."

She imitated their round motion with both hands. The chants increased. She moved back and forth, swaying in rhythm, her hands revolving. Anderson pulled her close, but the children jumped, and she jumped. They yelled, hooted, and called. Anderson put his arm around her and whispered jolly words. She made faces. Ryuzu laughed. She laughed. The jeep honked and went faster. The children's cries grew faint, and soon the village, Sensei, and the children vanished in a swirl of dust.

ILLNESS

Sarah didn't think she had fallen asleep, but she must have because before she knew it, they were already at her house. Sensei's house. The jeep pulled to a stop, and the gate opened. Papa clutched her to him. Mama's worried face floated above a belly that appeared much bigger. Mama hugged them both. "Sarah."

"Where in God's name did you find her?" her father snapped.

"We found her in a village of squatters," Anderson said. "You see, she's wet. She must have gone to swim and gotten lost."

"The lake. How would Sarah know about the lake? Is that village near the bridge? That's a long way."

"Yes, sir," Anderson said. "We went there to talk to their leader, Nishiguchi, the one they call Sensei. He had taken charge of her. He would have brought her back to you. It's not a pretty place—mud, tin huts, and hungry children."

"We are grateful," her mother said. "Very grateful. We were frantic."

"I'm sure you were," Anderson said, eyeing the string of large, gray pearls around her mother's neck. "I believe we've met before at an embassy function. Anderson is my name. Pearls, very good ones. You suggested the gray."

There was an awkward silence. Anderson smiled as if he expected to be invited in, but her parents stood with their arms around Sarah.

"She's burning up, Sasha," her mother said. They touched her cheeks, looked into her eyes, and headed toward the house. The driver waved from the jeep. Sarah tried to raise her hand in turn, but the gate had closed, and her head went down on her father's shoulder.

She was sick. She was in her bed. She had a fever. She was cold, hot, and cold again. Day and night merged in a continuous blur. Her throat was dry. It hurt. Her body burned. O'ba placed an electric fan next to her bed. Her skin felt raw. She cried. Papa pressed pills between her lips. She slept fitfully. O'ba was next to her bed. She made Sarah sip water and gave her more pills.

"Mama," she called. Where was her Mama? She searched for a comfortable position while O'ba sang a lullaby: "Sleep, sleep." Sarah placed her finger against O'ba's lips. Blackness. She dreamt she was in a forest clearing. Saburo and Sensei moved with slow hand movements. The air stilled, and Scalia, wearing his silk dressing gown, crossed the clearing and put his hands around Saburo's throat. Sensei's white robes flapped, and he hurried forward, yelling, "Stop!"

Her father took O'ba's place. He wiped perspiration from Sarah's face and neck. He turned her over, inserted a hose in her bottom until her stomach tightened and water gushed. "Mama!" Her father cleaned her and pressed more pills into her mouth. Sarah wanted her Mama.

Seven days later, Sarah opened her eyes and whispered to O'ba, "Where's Saburo? Is he dead?"

O'ba pressed more pills between her lips and whispered, "You've been sick for nearly a week."

"We must help Saburo," Sarah said. "He died, and I promised."

When Sarah woke again, the house was silent. She stood unsteadily and called, "Mama."

O'ba entered the room and scooped her up. "Your mama is in the hospital. You're still sick."

"Is my baby sister born?"

"Your papa will explain. He is at the hospital. He will be home soon. You are getting well." O'ba's heavy breathing filled Sarah's ears. Sarah stared at O'ba's worn fingers, crisscrossed and swollen with old scars and new kitchen cuts.

"I want Mama."

A few hours later, her father lifted her gently and hugged her so that his beard scratched her face. "Sarah, you're better!"

"Where is Mama?"

"Mama will be OK," Papa reassured and glanced at O'ba. "They put her in a big machine that helped her breathe. We were lucky that the American army hospital took her. Today she moved her toes."

Sarah was glad, but there was something else. O'ba coughed and wiped her eyes. Her father said softly, "It was polio."

Her father's tight lips forbade more questions. "I gave Mama polio," she whispered in a solemn voice, "and I killed Saburo."

"No, Sarah," her father said, rubbing his dark stubble chin with his fingers as if washing, up and down, his hands moving quickly. "You did not give Mama polio. You were sick but not with polio. Polio is everywhere. Anyone can get it. We are so lucky that you are well. Mama will be well soon," he said and paused. Sarah waited. "It was too much for the baby," he continued in a whisper. "The baby died, but Saburo is not dead. Saburo and Fumiko have left the hut. Someday they'll come back for a visit. You mustn't worry. They are well. Very well."

"I loved my baby sister, and I promised Saburo."

"You mustn't worry about Saburo or the baby," her father said. "You are a brave little girl, my brave, little Sarah, our golden girl, the one who makes us happy, the one we love so much. Our beautiful little one — white, white skin, dark hair, and blue, blue, eyes. Our forest fairy. You are everything. Mama asks about you every day. You are our life. Mama will be home soon. The past is over. You will go to the American army school. No more samurai games, no more Bushido. We were wrong to let you play with Saburo. You'll play with American children and learn about Donald Duck and Mickey Mouse. You'll make friends, and one day you'll be an American."

***

For the next week, O'ba brought her thick soups, puddings, and white bread on a tray. At night she heard Scalia pacing, back and forth, his tread shaking the floorboards above her bedroom. No one spoke about Saburo or Fumiko.

Ten days later after her father left for work, Sarah ran to the window. Except for a loose board that flapped against the hut, the granary was still. Sarah slipped out of her room, crept down the hall, and out the back door. She walked across the yard.

"Rap. Rap." It came from above and behind, from the big house. "Rap, rap." Scalia glared, knocking his ring against his bedroom window. "Rap, rap." He shook his head. She must not enter the hut. She challenged him with a hard look, scaled the steps, and opened the door. The room was bare except for beams dotted with maggots. Sarah took in the clay walls, the pine floorboards, and the pile of ash along the wall. Her footstep sent a thin spray of silt into the air. It stuck to her arm. Sarah remembered Saburo's streaked skin. She knelt and gathered. The ash was light, lighter than she imagined, and mixed with tiny bones. She knelt and gathered, holding the ash carefully. Then head high with great ceremony, she crossed the room to where the urns had stood. The pile grew. She patted it to a cone. Finally the floor was clean.

Saburo. Sarah took a deep breath, lowered her head, and waited. Now he would come. He would walk through the door, smile, and fold his arms across his chest. He'd tell more stories about Sensei and his adventures in China. They would make up more games. She'd apologize for the stone, and he would hold up his small finger, a reminder of their promise. She kept her head bowed and clapped her hands. Nothing. She clapped again. Except for the occasional maggot that fell from the ceiling, the room was silent.

Only then did she finally understand. Saburo and Fumiko were gone. O'ba, Emiko, and her father had tried to tell her, their voices tender, then abrupt, and finally determined, but she hadn't listened. They had disappeared while she was sick, while she slept with fever, while she was too weak to walk. They were dead. She had killed them. She could have run to her parents, or even told Sensei, but she hadn't. She had gone into the forbidden lake and brought back germs, bugs that sickened Mama and killed her sister. Tears pricked her eyelids, and her chin trembled.

"Sarah-chan." O'ba entered the hut and knelt on the floor next to her. "No more crying about Saburo-chan. Saburo-chan is safe. You must believe me. Saburo-chan is well and happy.

"I lost a friend once," O'ba whispered, holding her close. "I was seven, and Makiko-chan and I were best friends. She had short hair and big ears. We walked to school hand in hand and played every day. One morning she was gone," O'ba paused. "No one would tell me where she went."

"Why?" Sarah whispered.

O'ba was silent.

Sarah smelled the dust and the rot. The maggots dropped.

"Sarah-chan," O'ba said softly. "You must have strength. You must endure and never show pain. Don't you want to be Japanese?"

Sarah was silent. She didn't care about being Japanese. O'ba frowned. Sarah pressed against her wide bosom. O'ba's voice tightened: "Scalia-san wants you for tea. You must change your clothes and be good. I'll be with you the whole time. Scalia-san ordered your favorite apricot tarts with cream sauce."

"No!" she screamed. Sarah wanted to tell O'ba that Scalia killed. "Rap. Rap." His knuckles pounded the glass. He'd thrown Saburo against the wall and strangled Fumiko. "Rap. Rap." His rage seeped through the walls, pounded the floor at night, an anger that filled the house with fear. "I'll tell you a secret," Sarah pleaded. "Saburo-chan and I are going to make everyone rich. We found a mountain of treasure. I'll take you there. I'll give you some."

"You must stop talking nonsense," O'ba said. "There is no treasure. All that digging was a game. Saburo won't be back. He is being taken care of in the Japanese way. You're a big girl now. You have to accept life. Come, the tea will be short."

"I won't!" Sarah screamed and kicked O'ba. O'ba reached for her, but she bit O'ba's hand and kicked again. O'ba toppled on the ash. It smeared across O'ba's face and hands. Black streaked her white apron.

Now O'ba was angry.

"*Okyu*," O'ba said. She grabbed Sarah, carried her down the steps and across the yard. "With okyu you won't have tantrums like this. Okyu will cure you. It will teach you to endure. After okyu, tea with Scalia-san will be nothing," O'ba said, putting Sarah next to the hibachi. "School will be nothing. Missing Saburo will be nothing."

Tears rolled down Sarah's cheeks. "Does oky- hurt?"

O'ba didn't answer. She unbuttoned Sarah's dress, removed a small packet from a drawer under the hiba-chi, and sprinkled white powder on Sarah's shoulder blades. O'ba lit incense and pressed the burning tip on the powder. It hurt. Sarah squeezed her eyes shut. She covered her nose against the smell of burnt skin. She didn't scream.

❀❀❀

"Sarah-chan," Scalia said, tapping the place next to him. The low table set with flowered English china and heavy silver dominated the room. Sarah had only been in this room twice, but she remembered every de-tail—the leopard skin, ancient swords, ivory statues, Japanese prints and gold screens, Kannon, and trays of pearls. She gazed at the Kannon's serene face. Her shoulders burned.

She felt Scalia's smile as she folded her hands on her lap. A platter piled high with fried apricot tarts sat next to the Bunsen burner. O'ba poured liqueur into a pot of cream, set it on the burner, and stirred the sauce carefully while Emiko loaded tarts onto Sarah's plate. The pungent aroma made her cough. Scalia snapped his fingers. Emiko pressed a towel against Sarah's mouth.

"I learned to make those apricot tarts near Harbin," Scalia said in a low voice, "after I escaped."

Sarah still did not look at him, but she listened.

"It's a long story," Scalia said as his thin hand fondled the ascot around his neck. "Do you want hear such a long story, Sarah-chan?"

Sarah nodded.

"O'ba, you and Emiko may go. I'll take care of the tarts."

O'ba hesitated, then backed out of the room with Emiko.

"It was a long time ago, when I was captured by the Russians along with my Japanese friend," Scalia said. "We had crossed the border from China into Russia. The Russians suspected we were spies. They put us on a train and took us deep into the forest with other prisoners to be shot."

"Were you scared?"

"Yes," Scalia said. "The train stopped in a town at the edge of the forest. All the prisoners were chained. We had barely enough room to move, and the wood floor was covered with straw and piss. The smell was terrible."

"What did you do?" Sarah asked. She still didn't look at him or move, instead imagining the snowy railroad tracks, the acid smell, and the sound of moaning prisoners.

"I had a file," Scalia said.

"Did you kill the guard?"

"I sawed through the chain and chipped a hole in the floor boards. It took two days."

"Then what?"

"That night my Japanese friend and I made the hole larger. We squeezed through, lowered ourselves onto the tracks, and crawled toward the back of the train. When the dogs slept, we ran into the dark. We were lost. It was cold, so cold that my toes froze and my eyes stung. I covered my face with a cloth, but it was no use. We were doomed. We scrambled toward a distant light and collapsed at the door of a wooden house. Two black-eyed sisters pulled us in. They were kind—fed us, made us well." He paused. "They taught me to make the apricot tarts, and I taught O'ba."

That was all? It would have been better if Scalia had stabbed a guard or if his Japanese friend had been caught by dogs, or if Scalia had found a bear's cave and lived on honey until spring.

"Do you know who my Japanese friend was?" Scalia asked in a voice so soft that Sarah knew the question was the point of the story.

"Sensei," Sarah whispered.

"Yes, Sarah-chan," Scalia continued in a low mumble. "It was 1940, and the Japanese were frantic. The Russians were frantic, too. They didn't know if Germany would attack Russia, or whether the Japanese would attack Russia, or if the Japanese would go south to Asia. Everyone spied. You met spies in Karuisawa at the Mampei Hotel, at the international clubs in Tokyo and Kobe, and in bookstores, bars, and restaurants in Shanghai. They were diplomats, businessmen, and newspaper reporters, all on the take for money, for glory, for ideas, or for country. Sensei was a spy. I was Italian. Italy and Japan were friends. I helped him, and we got caught."

His voice sounded far away. He put his arm around her and stroked her cheek. His ascot was loose, and his bony, freckled shoulder jutted under his collar.

She turned away, but he cupped her chin and brought her back. His sweet talcum smell turned her stomach. "Sensei said he saw you and Saburo in the forest. You spied on us. You met Sensei in the village, and he introduced you to the village children. Is that true?"

Sarah said nothing. Scalia repeated the question. Still Sarah was silent.

"You look so much like your mother," he whispered. His large hand rested against her hip. "The same blue eyes, the same chin. Even more beautiful. Red lips. So red. Like cherries. Your white skin: translucent and glowing against dark hair. High cheekbones—the Mongols. One day when you enter a room, men will stare. They will want to know you."

Sarah pulled away, but Scalia held fast. The sun glanced off the gold-threaded tapestries. Sunspots moved across the wall. Scalia came close. He had the slightly sweet, woody smell of sandalwood mixed with brandy and powder. His touch, lingering and insistent, was different from the American ladies and made her wince. She thought of okyu. She thought of how she had been bad. So bad. Her shame meant she had to endure this.

"Sensei wants you to be friends with the Japanese children, especially Ryuzu-chan. You will like them. They will help you be even more Japanese. Your future must be Japan. All of you—Tamara, Alexander, and Sarah. You are my family, and families must be together always. Don't you agree?" Scalia paused. "Your mama and papa don't have passports, but Sensei knows people and will help with that, too. You want to help your mama and papa, don't you?"

The weight of Scalia's hand against her hip held. Again when she tried to twist away, it pressed her down, an immobilizing mass. She stood. Scalia towered above, his hand held solid. Her hipbone ached, the pain lodged deep. His hand burned through her dress. She would never stand straight again.

"Sarah-chan." O'ba stood in front of the tea and the tarts. She had emerged suddenly. Her voice was loud and full of business as if Scalia's room was her kitchen. "Have you finished? Come with me, Sarah-chan. It's time for a rest."

Scalia's hand dropped.

O'ba led her down the stairs. "I'm sorry I left you, Sarah-chan," O'ba said, her voice low with regret.

Sarah did not reply. She remembered Scalia's woody sweet scent, his freckled shoulder, and his thin fingers as he cut the apricot tart. She remembered the same fingers squeezing the flesh on her back. She remembered the weight of his hand on her hip. She remembered his whisper against her ear and the brandy on his breath.

SCHOOL

Her father bent close. "I have two very important things to tell you, Sarah." The stubble on his chin was gone. He smiled and continued, "A wonderful thing happened. Your mama walked the length of the hall without any help. She will be home soon."

"When?" Sarah asked, glad that he was smiling.

"Soon," her father whispered. "The second important news is that your school called. Your first day is Monday. Happy?"

Sarah nodded because she wanted to please him, her young father, with a clean, white shirt and broad smile. She imitated his smile.

He ruffled her hair. "It's over. Everything is going to be fine," he said softly.

* * *

On Monday O'ba woke Sarah early and dressed her in a plaid skirt and white blouse. Fuji-san, the driver Scalia hired, drove while she sat next to her father in the back seat. Her father explained that her new school, Jefferson Heights, was on a large American base and located in the middle of Tokyo. Sarah gazed out the window. The car turned down a narrow street. "We're almost there," her father said, pointing at the guard box surrounded by barbed wire at the end of the street.

The street narrowed. Posters of short-skirted, young girls plastered the lampposts. Red, paper lanterns flickered, their light casting rose shadows on shoddy buildings. Girls with permed hair and spiked heels slouched against the signposts, and more girls stared from windows. A tall girl with narrow hips waved, and the others laughed.

Fuji-san slowed. The tall girl and two others sauntered to the middle of the street. Their bottoms twitched. They puffed cigarettes and tossed their heads. Smoke curled, and they swayed back and forth and laughed, a sound of mischief, rich and low, that reminded her of Fumiko. The passersby laughed, too. Sarah pressed her face against the window.

Fuji-san honked, but the girls paid no attention. Instead they linked arms. Fuji-san leaned on the horn. "*Pan-pan*," Fuji-san yelled. "You sell yourself to Americans. Pan-pan."

The girls threw back their heads. The growing crowd roared. A thin boy in short pants stuck out his tongue and yelled, "America, *akachokobe!*" His small finger pulled at his lower eyelid. The crowd raised their fists and shouted, "America, akachokobe." A policeman's sharp whistle sounded, but the girls continued to block traffic, hips twitching and smoke blowing. The whistle blew again. The girls paid no attention. Other girls joined and locked arms, their bottoms gyrating. Her father ordered Fuji-san to honk, but he did nothing.

A child's nose flattened against the glass. More faces grinned and pulled the skin under their eyes, exposing red. "Akachokobe!" The tall pan-pan hit the hood, and her red lips smiled as she hit it again. She led others, pressing their red fingers against the wind-shield, taking turns, slowly, methodically, as if they had all the time in the world. The red hurt Sarah's eyes. Her father brought her close, and she burrowed into him.

A policeman's blue uniform flashed. A whistle blew, sharp, piercing the jeering crowd, the grate of nails, and yells. Another policeman appeared. There were more police and more whistles. The girls kept moving, their eyes smiling, their nails scratching, as if the police were of no consequence. A policeman pushed the tall girl. She stood her ground. He pushed again. She threw down her cigarette and mashed it with her heel. The police came close. She faced him head on. The policeman raised his club. The girl waved, the crowd roared and she walked with her head high across the road.

Fuji-san drove quickly down the lane and through the marine checkpoint. At once, the narrow streets were replaced by an expanse of sky and low houses with large windows and grassy lawns. Her father touched her cheek, wanting her to be pleased, but the open space and the sun reflecting off the bay windows felt foreign. By the time Sarah reached the school, she was sure that she didn't belong.

"Don't leave," she whimpered to her father. "I'll be good," she whispered. "Please."

"Don't worry, Sarah," Miss Woodlock said and led her away. "The first day is always the hardest."

The day began with explanations of homework and class procedures. Sarah was between two blond boys, one freckled and the other with light green eyes. She tried to pay attention, but Miss Woodlock spoke quickly. At recess she sat on the bleachers while the boys played kickball. A cluster of girls stared at her and whispered.

After recess Miss Woodlock had the class draw,

"something that impressed you. Something you can explain to the class." Sarah sketched three, red-lipped women in tight skirts holding hands.

"Sarah, explain your drawing."

Sarah knew from Miss Woodlock's smile that she was trying to be nice. She also knew this was her chance to make friends — friends for secrets, friends for stories, friends for giggles and fun games. Her father was right. Her classmates looked like her, tall with long legs and freckles. The boy with the green eyes smiled. She wanted them to like her, to run to greet her in the morning, to choose her for their teams, and to laugh at her jokes.

Her classmates waited.

Sarah held up her drawing. Her thoughts went to Mama's nod of approval. Mama liked it when "her best girl" knew the answers. Miss Woodlock waited, and the children stared. The room seemed small and then large. Sarah floated, time receded, sounds magnified — the hum of a bee trapped by the window, the cry of a crow, the children's giggles. Red, blond, and brown heads turned, with round eyes and bright smiles, curious and aware of her dilemma. Sarah took a deep breath. The words would not come. The silence lengthened.

Miss Woodlock stepped forward. "Sarah?"

Still she could not speak. The green-eyed boy nodded encouragement. She took a deep breath. Her legs shook. It was the first time she'd been asked to speak in public. She wanted to do well. She wanted Mama to be proud.

"Pan-pan," she said in a loud voice like Fuji-san's. She was treading on thin ice but wanted to astonish them with her knowledge, facts that would reveal her understanding of Japan, the Japan beyond the lawns and neat houses, the Japan of manners and custom. They would love her. She would be the guide to that crowded place with moss-covered gutters, small lanes, tin shacks, and wooden houses.

"These women sell themselves to Americans. They're called pan-pan."

The class was absolutely silent. Miss Woodlock's eyes widened as if she expected an explanation. The green-eyed boy Tommy hiccupped, snickered, and hooted. His freckled friend followed. The others did the same. They banged their desks with their fists and roared. "Pan-pan!" Tommy yelled, followed by another round of laughter. "Pan-pan." The laughter reached a pitch. Miss Woodlock's face reddened, and there were more gales of laughter.

"Silence!" Miss Woodlock shouted.

Sarah blinked back her tears. A trickle of pee crept down her leg and then her ankle before sliding into her shoe. More followed, streams of pee pelting down, rivers of shame that made her shrink. Her honor violated, and her socks sodden, an ammonia smell, pungent with an acid finish, filled the space. The pee burned her toes. Her stomach tightened, but she couldn't stop. Holding her body straight, Sarah walked in small steps, jerky and abrupt, dripping and wet, across the room to the door.

After school Fuji-san drove her home, and Sarah slowly entered the house. The smell of pee clung to her sock. Her shame folded around her like a dirty blanket. It made her shrink from herself. She was nothing, a person without a place, a home, or a mother. They were right to laugh, to ridicule, to scorn.

"Sarah," her father called, "I have a surprise for you." He stood next to Scalia at the end of the hall, held out his hand, smiled, and then stepped to one side.

Her mother, deep creases around her mouth and more around her eyes, stood at the end of the hallway fingering the yellowed lace on the collar of her blue and white dress. Her lined face and still expression made the hurt apparent. No one moved. Mama lifted her hand. Sarah ran toward her, yearning for her light laughter and lilac smell.

Mama's arms went around her. She could not breathe. This gaunt woman, bone and skin, wasn't her real mother. Where was the Mama of her dreams? Where was the beautiful Mama who would take care of her? Listen to her? Protect her? Who was this woman? This wasn't the Mama who cuddled her, who pinched her cheek, and who she could depend on.

Her father steered them into the dining room. Scalia followed.

"I love you," her mother said and blew her a kiss. Sarah blew it back. Her mother smiled. She looked younger now, and Sarah recognized the delicate eyebrows, soft mouth, and tender gaze. Yes, this was her mother, the one she needed. She'd waited so long to feel Mama's hand against her head and lips on her cheek. Mama would come to school, sit next to her in class, and answer all Miss Woodlock's questions. During recess they'd share O'ba's *onigiri*.

Sarah came close. Her mother brushed back Sarah's hair and kissed her eyelids until they closed. Sarah pressed closer. Yes. Yes. This is what she wanted. The children's taunts and laughter faded. Scalia seemed unimportant, too. All that mattered was Mama's touch, her gentle voice, making the world safe, a round, rosy place. Sarah turned so that her mother could braid her hair. Her mother sectioned Sarah's hair, creating order first on her head and then in the room. Her father smiled, Scalia looked content, and even Emiko nodded as she placed a tray of tea and sandwiches on the table. "It's going to be all right," Sarah thought. Mama was home now.

Mama's hand stopped. "Oh, God. Look."

"Tamara, what the devil?"

"Worms."

"Ringworm," Papa said and peered at Sarah's ears and scalp.

"Worms," Mama declared. "Her hair is crawling with lice. You were in charge."

"Pus. Just a little pus." Her father turned Sarah's head.

"She's filled with every rotten worm in this rotten country," her mother said bitterly. "I never wanted to come to Japan. We should have applied for visas to Australia. Max got in. Japanese are the worst hypocrites, with their emperor worship and carrying on about the Japanese spirit. Animals!"

Sarah knew about worms. Her parents had told her of worms that curled in little round circles under her skin and laid eggs that made more worms, worms that had made her skin grainy and her ears pusy. Each month her father gave her worm medicine, and that next day she'd count thin white lines in her stool.

"I left her in O'ba's care," her mother continued, unbuttoning Sarah's dress. "If she'd been Japanese, this would not have happened. I'm sure of that. We will shave her head clean. We'll wash her inside and out. Scissors," her mother commanded.

Seconds later her mother's pointed scissors cut, and hair dropped in large pieces. With each snap of the scissors, more hair fell, landing in clumps on the white tablecloth and on the hardwood floor. The curls, dark and streaked with gold, twisted in large loops. She remembered O'ba's story of a greatly admired, ancient, Japanese princess whose long hair reached from her palace to the street. She wanted Mama to stop. Except for the clicking sound of the scissors, the room was silent.

"Powder," Mama said in a firm voice. Emiko ran, and soon Mama rubbed the powder on her bristly scalp. It settled on her arms, her chest, and dusted the clumps of fallen hair. The sweet smell made Sarah's nose itch, but she did not move or make a sound.

"Tamara, stop this," her father said.

Her mother pulled Sarah's dress over her head. Sarah tried to shield her bare chest with her hands, but the dress was already gone. She stood in just her panties and smelly socks with only her raised hands against Scalia's stare.

Her mother pointed and said, "Alexander, look."

"My God!" her father exclaimed. "What is this?"

"It's okyu," Scalia said softly in his highest, whispery voice. "O'ba meant no harm. She did what she thought best," he added and went on to describe okyu as traditional Japanese healing, performed on old people to help rheumatism, sleeplessness, and aches, and on children to cure tantrums. "Sarah has been tense and having tantrums. Okyu was undoubtedly done to O'ba as a child, too. Sarah will survive, Tamara, just as you will get well."

"I'll tell you what will make me well," her mother snapped. "My own home, my own land."

With that the room fell silent, so quiet that Sarah could hear the adults breathing, a wheezing sound, thick and terrifying that made her want to run. Scalia stared at his jade collection as if seeking reassurance in the beauty of each object, his lips moving silently as if in prayer, words that he could not utter aloud. He hung his head while her parents sat stiffly. With an abrupt bow, Scalia left the room.

Her father cleared his throat. "Mama needs rest," he said gently, a definitive request she must not refuse. He pulled her dress back over her head. "We will all take a nap now. We will see you at dinner."

Sarah wanted them to stay. Mama had just come home. She wanted to be held. She wanted Mama to read her a story, tickle her, and kiss her forehead. She wanted to lie between them and repeat Scalia's story of his escape with Sensei from the train in Russia. She wanted to tell them how Sensei wanted her to play with Ryuzu and the village children. She wanted to tell Mama about Miss Woodlock and the picture, to explain why she was ashamed to return to the army school and why she wanted Mama to teach her at home. She wanted to talk about Saburo. She wanted Mama to say that despite her shame, the worms, the shaven head, and the okyu, she was "Mama's best girl." She started to ask, but her father gave her a warning look, wrapped his arm around her mother's waist, and left the room.

Tears pricked her eyelids. She walked woodenly down the long corridor. No one will know, she thought, as she went out the back door and through the yard to the hole in the fence. She knew she mustn't. The forest was forbidden. Mama and Papa would be angry, and she wanted to be their best girl, she thought, as she squeezed through the hole to the forest on the other side.

THE CHILDREN

She ran, arms flying, legs moving, her feet hitting the dirt. Faster and faster she bolted between trees, the late afternoon sun slanting through branches, lighting the dark earth, bushes, and rocks. The path turned. A boulder, flat on the top, dominated a clearing. She walked to the boulder and lay on the rock. At last. The sun warmed her face, and her body relaxed, her arms and legs melting into the contours of the stone. Except for the scream of crickets, the forest was silent.

A hand touched her ankle. A tall boy in ragged clothes stood at the edge of the rock. Ryuzu. Sarah recognized his long forehead and full lips. He smiled. Noriko appeared wiping her runny nose and then Michio, the squat boy who'd attacked her. Other little ones followed. They stood in a tight circle.

They came close, so close that she smelled the dust on their skin, clothes, and shoes. Noriko's swollen eyes were yellow at the corner. Ryuzu's arm was bruised. Blank-faced and intrusive, they moved in. There was no Sensei here. She was utterly alone. Her heart pounded, her muscles refused to move. They would kill her, she thought, scanning the circle for knives and fishhooks. She measured the distance between the boulder and the path.

Again Ryuzu touched her ankle. He was the one who had helped her, but that did not matter. It had all been terrible: school, pee, Mama, worms, her hair. Enough. She needed to strike back, defend herself, and make them understand that she was a person not to be trifled with, ridiculed, or hooked with fishhooks.

Her leg shot out and hit Ryuzu's chest. She jumped from the boulder and before Ryuzu could move kicked his legs and slammed his head with her fists. He fell to the ground. She was on him, pinning his shoulders to the ground with her knees. The children moved close and screamed, "More, gaijin, more!"

Ryuzu shouted for her to stop, but she couldn't. The boulder was hers. The squatters belonged by the polio lake, not here, not in the forest, her forest. Her mother was sick, her baby sister had died, and Saburo had disappeared forever. The children at school had laughed at her, and she had disgraced herself.

Ryuzu tried to rise, but she forced his head back against the ground. Ryuzu pulled himself up. Dirt blinded her. She dropped to one knee. More spray. Ryuzu grasped her shirt. The children shouted, "*Sumo! Sumo!*" Ryuzu's thumbs dug into her waist, his hips swayed, and she turned with him, gripping the earth with her toes. She leaned low, head against his chest. They fell to the ground.

Their pants filled the air. Ryuzu stood. She jumped to her feet also, wiped the dirt from her eyes, and stared them all down. Ryuzu came close. They were the same height. His long forehead and wide eyes reminded her once again of Scalia's Kannon. He had the same straight posture and quiet gaze, confident and assured. His eyes, warm with forgiveness, lit up his face. Her anger vanished. They stared at each other for a long moment punctuated by the shriek of crickets. Sarah wanted to turn away, but Ryuzu held her, forcing her to accept his good will, waiting to make amends.

The children crowded close. It hit her that she had no other friends. Saburo was dead, and the children at school detested her. Ryuzu was kind. She felt equal to him and the others, content in her own skin with no apologies for its whiteness. Her anger disappeared, gone suddenly as if it had never happened. She reached in her pocket, handed him a handkerchief, and said softly, "here."

Ryuzu took the handkerchief and wiped his cheeks. The others stood together in a tight circle, so close she saw their cuts and bruises, the thinness of their bodies, the dark rings under their eyes, and the dirt encrusted in their necks and wrists. Ryuzu took a *sumo menko*, "wrestler card," from his pocket and motioned to the others. Noriko placed a jump rope in Sarah's hands, Kohe offered a slingshot, and Michio gave a fistful of marbles. The gifts piled up. It didn't matter that the frayed jump rope had rough, splintered handles, that the slingshot was made from a tree branch, that the bent menko cards were black with dirt, or that the marbles were broken. The children turned out their pockets and, grinning, pushed their treasures into her outstretched hands. Noriko took her hand, pointing to Sarah's powdered head, her own, and to the heads of the others. The children laughed, she laughed, and they touched each other's bristles.

"It's beetle season; tomorrow we have a hunt," Ryuzu said. "The beetles live under dead wood and drink the sap. You have to have good eyes to find one. Meet us by the fence. We will teach you to play beetle sumo. Beetles are better at sumo than humans. Will you come?"

Sarah nodded.

"Tomorrow, Ryuzu repeated softly."

❈ ❈ ❈

After school the next day, she waited. Finally she heard, "Sarah-chan, lets play." The call echoed across the yard and down the corridor to her room. The voices swelled, then dropped and grew loud again. The crickets shrieked, the children shouted, and she pressed her hand against the window. O'ba was shopping, and Mama and Emiko were napping. She tiptoed down the corridor, across the yard, and out through the hole in the fence.

She was in the forest.

Ryuzu and the others met her. Each held a small bamboo cage with a tiny door. They were eager to start. Michio bragged that he would find the biggest beetle and win the match.

"You've never won before," Noriko said.

"I will today," Michio said. "A foreigner won't. Sarah-chan doesn't know anything about finding beetles or sumo."

"Michio's always in a bad mood," Ryuzu said as they started down the path. "Don't pay attention to him. Here, take this," he offered, handing her an empty cage. He was dressed in a clean shirt, his cropped hair glistened, and he smelled like soap. There was a bandage on his cheek where she had kicked him.

"Are the beetles hard to find?" Sarah asked.

"Beetles live on sap," Ryuzu said, and pulled a thin nature book from his pocket and flipped to a picture of a large, black beetle with two curved, claw-like pinchers.

"You think you're smart, Ryuzu the scientist," Michio taunted as he pushed Ryuzu from behind. "You read science books because you're older and know more *kanji.* Who gave you that book?"

"Sensei." Ryuzu said and turned to face Michio. He was not smiling now. "Sensei gives me lots of things to read. Sensei and my father were best friends."

"The military killed your father because he was pink," Michio said. "Sensei hates Communists, too."

Ryuzu wrapped his fingers around Michio's throat and pushed. The children waited. Ryuzu tightened his grip, and Sarah was certain he would strangle Michio, but instead he dropped his hands and said in a deadly tone, "Sensei was in China and didn't know about my father's arrest. Sensei would have helped. He was my father's friend. They played in this forest together, always together. He didn't know."

"Sensei knows everything," Michio spat. "Sensei hates pinks."

Michio spat again, the children mumbled, and Sarah waited for Ryuzu to stick up for the pinks. Last night Scalia called Mama and Papa pink and, even though Mama had denied it, Sarah knew from her shrill voice that it was true. Sarah wanted pinks to stick together. She stepped close and put her hand on Ryuzu's shoulder.

Before Ryuzu could respond, Michio stormed angrily ahead. No one spoke. But as they went deeper into the forest, harmony took hold. Bamboo leaves shimmering silver, beams of sunlight highlighting moss and earth made her feel like a forest fairy. Crickets shrieked, subsided into silence, and shrieked again. Noriko took her hand. Sarah squeezed Noriko's fingers and swung her cage.

The path narrowed. They took the right fork at the boulder and soon reached the field near the lake. Michio and the others ran to a pile of bricks. Sarah and Ryuzu headed for the remains of the mound, which was filled with logs, glass bottles, and tin cans. Ryuzu picked up a board. Centipedes and small beetles swarmed for cover, their legs racing from the light, burrowing into the dark earth, boards, and moss.

"Some stag beetles are as big as my hand," Ryuzu said. "They're powerful. We will find a champion." Ryuzu split a beam.

"I found one," Michio yelled with great excitement.

Sarah touched a dark spot. The stag beetle's iridescent green-black reflected the sun, and its mantle, like the finest lacquer, made her think of a dark pond. Its squat body, powerful and low to the ground, sat on hinged legs beneath its sculpted back. The beetle raised its pincers, legs churning, and burrowed into the sludge. Ryuzu's hand darted toward it, but Sarah intercepted and seizing its rear placed it in her cage.

Michio drew a circle. "Let's fight. Tojo against MacArthur. Japan against America. These are Japanese beetles, and only Japanese can make them fight. The beetle that gets flipped or leaves the ring loses."

"I can make MacArthur fight," Sarah protested, stroking MacArthur's back as it lifted his horn. "MacArthur will win."

Michio and Sarah picked up sticks. MacArthur spread its claws. Tojo opened its orange-brown mouth. MacArthur raised its pincers and stood on its hind legs, its squat body moving forward. Sarah pushed MacArthur. Michio poked Tojo. The children screamed. Clack. Clack. The beetle's pincers clipped at each other. Clack. MacArthur reared. Its shiny back gleamed bright; its legs moved across the narrow space, banging Tojo's antlers. Tojo staggered. MacArthur pushed again. This time Tojo held its ground, and its pincer grabbed MacArthur's left claw. Tojo turned, and MacArthur wobbled.

"*Nippon, Nippon,* 'Japan,' 'Japan,'" the children yelled. MacArthur shook loose and seized Tojo's fore-leg. Tojo twisted, but MacArthur held fast, raising his horn like a trumpet. Tojo flailed and flipped belly up, his legs churning.

The children stood, mumbled, and looked uncertainly at Sarah.

"*Banzai.* Sarah-chan," Ryuzu yelled.

"That was unfair," Michio said, his face flushed with rage. "MacArthur was bigger." He held up Tojo. "Look how tough Tojo is. Look at his wide back and strong legs. He would have won against a normal-sized beetle." He pushed Ryuzu's chest. "You like Sarah-chan because you're Communist, pan-pan sister Sachiko-chan taught you foreign ways. You smell foreign."

Michio's eyes went dead. Sarah had seen that look, a flat look, disconnected, and removed, the look of Japanese soldiers in Shanghai when they checked her parents' papers. It was a look she would always re-member. Sarah reached for MacArthur. Michio's shoe slammed. She tried to lift Michio's heel. Michio pressed hard, turning his shoe back and forth, again and again, the mud spattering, was blackening the toe of his sneaker.

MacArthur. His shell cracked, a dry pop resonat-ed. Pop, pop, a broken sound, busted and wrecked. The unmistakable crunch of MacArthur shattered made her cringe. Yellow liquid oozed, thick and mixed with white mucus and chips of mantle. MacArthur's horn, shiny and pointed, lay on the ground.Michio lifted his shoe and scraped off MacArthur. Sarah stared at MacAr-thur's tiny leg nearby, twitching with sporadic bursts. She covered it with a stone, placed a leaf over his horn, and buried the ooze. Her hands moved quickly as she piled leaves over the rest. Her friends watched. No one moved. Only when she patted the grave flat did Noriko hand her a twig. The children were silent as she pushed it in the ground.

Sarah took a deep breath, rose, and faced them. The children, with their ragged clothes, dirty faces, and thin bodies, reminded her of Saburo. They watched as if waiting for a play to begin. Their expression begged for words they could hold onto, words that would erase Michio's violence and allow them to be children again. She had them. Now they wanted to believe.

"I don't smell foreign, Michio-chan," Sarah said slowly in an imitation of a deadly Scalia voice. "I am not foreign. I am Japanese, pale Japanese from the north. O'ba found me wrapped in newspaper in Shanghai and gave me to my parents. O'ba is from the north, too. I was blue, and O'ba thought I wouldn't live, but I had strong, Japanese blood."

Noriko looked puzzled, and Michio seemed uncertain. Taro held hands with Ichiro and his small friends. The others looked at Ryuzu. Ryuzu smiled, his eyes full of admiration, brimmed with pleasure, and urged her to say more.

"See, I have proof," Sarah said in the same tone. She unbuttoned her dress and slipped it over her head. There must never be any question, she thought. For the first time since Saburo, she realized her terrible loneliness, a feeling of desperation, hollow and estranged, that made her alien. She must imagine, disappear into stories, and feel the children's skin next to hers. Like Sensei and his friend Masuru, she would play in the forest, smell its dank smell, listen to the swell of crickets, and splash in its streams.

If she could convince them that she was worthy, they would join her. Their voices would call for her by the back fence, demanding her presence. She wanted that more than anything. It wasn't enough that her hair was powdered and cropped, that MacArthur had beaten Tojo, and that Ryuzu, Noriko, and Taro liked her. There must be no question of their loyalty. She must win. She had no alternative.

Ryuzu frowned, unsure of her sudden nudity. Michio jeered. Sarah turned and pointed to the wounds inflicted from an adult world, scars that meant she had disobeyed and had been branded.

She said, "Okyu. Only Japanese endure that."

The children nodded solemnly at her battle wounds. Taro pulled up his pants and pointed to a shiny, round scar on his ankle. Michio did the same. Noriko showed a scar on her shoulder. The round dots gleamed bright on their dusty skin, badges of honor, hurts endured with pride.

Ryuzu yelled, "Banzai!" He looked relieved, his face flushed with knowledge that he had made the correct choice and had been right about her all along. He joined hands with the others, and they made a ring around her. Michio shouted too. "Banzai!" The cry resounded through the forest. "Banzai!" It echoed across the empty fields and ruined houses. They yelled it again.

She turned slowly, letting them touch her hands, shoulders, face, and hair. The feel of their skin made her strong. She stood tall, even taller than Ryuzu. Her eyes traveled up the bamboo trunks to the blue sky. The children's voices faded, and sheltered by the trees, the boulders, and the fields, she felt nothing could hurt her. The forest banished the hatred in the house and the strangeness at school. These were her wild friends. They depended on her, and she them. In the forest they made up rules that had no connection to the outside. Forest creatures, moss, earth, stone, and multi-colored greens would feed their imagination. They would wander under the ancient bamboos and through groves of trees, leading the group as true samurai, as one.

She spread her arms wide. Noriko took her hand, her small fingers curled, tight and hard, around her own. Everyone formed a circle. The little ones pressed against her and raised their arms. Ryuzu put his hand on her shoulder. Together they screamed, "Banzai!" again and again until her throat hurt, and the forest rang with joy.

PART TWO

Tokyo: Spring 1952

BLOODY MAY DAY

It was a bright spring day, the air fresh with the first hint of summer. On May Day—a day for workers, Maypole dances, and Communist demos—Sarah noted Fuji-san's frown in the rearview mirror. The roads were congested, and Fuji-san was in a bad mood. That did not matter, for Ryuzu would be waiting by the boulder. Sarah thought and flushed.

For six years Ryuzu and her Japanese friends had provided a buffer from the tense meals with Scalia and her parents and long days at the army school. Sarah endured school and home, waiting until she could slip out the back door, bolt across the yard, and squeeze through the hole in the fence.

The forest had its own rules, and with Sensei's blessing she and Ryuzu led the pack. Each year the world made new demands, but among her friends an unspoken agreement remained—the forest must never change. They refrained from mentioning the pressure of juku and junior high entrance exams, and in turn she did not speak of the army school. In the forest she wore baggy clothes, tied her hair in a loose ponytail, and played childish games.Surrounded by bamboo groves, they worshiped ancient gods and acted out Sensei's stories. When Sensei interrupted their play, they ran to him, eager to hear about ancient heroes and his China exploits. Sensei described Bushido, the "Way of the Sword and Horse," and famous samurai who protected the weak and understood obligation and honorable death.

They met by the boulder, clapped, and prayed to the kami of trees, moss, and streams. They were a powerful, nakama group, bound by loyalty and Bushido principles. Nothing must interfere with their solidarity. Nakama made life possible and gave meaning to the impossible. Quarrels were settled easily for it was understood that there must be no permanent rift, nothing that would create lasting hurt. Every game had rules, and the rules were obeyed without question. This insider group was everything.

Her parents slowly acknowledged her double life. In the late afternoon, her mother invited Ryuzu and the others for cookies and milk in the kitchen. Those were awkward moments. Her friends gobbled sweets and looked with wide eyes at the mounds of food—the rows of pickle jars, piles of vegetables, and plates of fruit and pastries that lined the kitchen counters—while her mother asked questions in primitive Japanese about school and plans for the future.

Last week Ryuzu spoke of his interest in biology, handing her mother a book on worms. Her mother opened the book slowly, peering at the pictures and turning the pages with care. "My brother Osyka was interested in biology," her mother said in the tender voice usually reserved for Sarah. "He was a student in Moscow. Osyka died young. Just a boy, really. Stalin's police came for him at night."

The room was still. Her friends shuffled uncomfortably in their chairs. Then Ryuzu spoke. His voice lowered as if sharing a great secret worthy of attention. He talked softly of his father's conversion to Communism, his arrest by the Japanese secret police, and his death in prison. He spoke of his father's journey to Beijing and his friendship with young, Chinese Communists. "My father believed that what Japan was doing in China was wrong," he said. "He wanted to stop it. He was against the Greater East Asia Co-Prosperity Sphere dominated by Japan." Her mother's eyes softened, and dabbing her eyes, handed Ryuzu a large bag of cookies.

"Fuji-san," Sarah asked from the back seat. "Why are you taking this route? It's a lot slower. Look at the traffic."

"It's May Day, there are demos, you look American," Fuji-san answered. "They wouldn't dare have a May Day demonstration in front of the Imperial Palace. There will be too many police."

Sarah hated Fuji-san's superior tone, his spotless white gloves, and the way he opened the car door in front of her American classmates. She hated his deference to her parents and his rages against foreigners. Now Fuji-san, his skin creased with worry, spoke quickly of the end of the occupation. "There will be trouble today," he finished quickly. "We must get home before anyone sees you."

Sarah glanced at herself in the rearview mirror. She did look American in her red shirtwaist dress and ponytail. Dark curls framed her pale face, her luminous blue eyes sparkled with energy, and arched eyebrows over high cheekbones gave her an exotic look. Her impish smile was immediate and provocative. She was tall and growing taller. Her nose grew, then her cheeks, and today her neck seemed too long. Gangly and uncertain, she looked in transition. Her father called it 'a time between' and her mother just smiled. She had friends at the army school now, friends who listened to her stories and told secrets. She was invited to their homes for barbeques and sleepovers. But despite this her Japanese world dominated.

"Ryuzu-chan and his sister Sachiko-san went to the demonstration," Sarah informed Fuji-san in a haughty tone. "The demonstrators are peaceful. They will just hold signs and sing songs. They are meeting at the Meiji shrine; that's blocks from here. You don't know anything."

Fuji-san's voice dropped. "Listen," he whispered. "Sachiko-chan had better quit her union. America is still boss, and America supports the right, always the right. Owari. 'Finished.'" He made a gesture across his throat.

Sarah blocked out Fuji-san's nasty tone. Ryuzu knew politics, more than Fuji-san or O'ba or even her parents. He lectured on Sachiko's union fight for worker rights, on America's trade concessions in exchange for bases on Japanese soil, on America's support for the Japanese right. Even Michio was impressed.

Last week Ryuzu locked pinkies. He was learning Russian to win a union scholarship to Russia. "No one must know," he said. "Sensei hates Russia. Russia still has Japanese soldiers in Siberian camps." She squeezed his finger in a promise to the death, yubikiri. His trust made her feel adult, part of history and a larger world. Yet as their fingers locked, she remembered Saburo, the cut, drips of blood, and the yubikiri pact of eternal friendship. The remorse that haunted her dreams and quiet hours took hold.

The street widened as they neared the palace moat, a grassy embankment dotted with stunted pine trees that ended in a high stone wall. The Emperor's Palace was unchanged, squat in the center of Tokyo, surrounded by green water and occupied by the imperial family. Rituals uninterrupted for a thousand years dominated. The palace, which was ringed by samurai estates, had always been protected. Sarah imagined the imperial family: the grim mustached botanist, the stout wife, and the puffy-faced children going about their day, oblivious to the realities of Japan.

The traffic slowed. Cars, police vans, and army jeeps made it impossible to move. Honks and police whistles filled the air. "Get down," Fuji-san hissed. But before she could move, police ran from their vans, crossed the boulevard, and took up battle stations, blocking off the Palace Plaza. Hundreds more, helmets gleaming, raised clubs and formed a line. Sarah's heart raced. She yanked the bright, red ribbon from her head, wiped her lipstick, and pulled her bangs over her forehead. More whistles blew. Demonstrators ran between the cars, moving left and right. A small woman pointed. Protesters started toward them.

Bang. A fist hit the car. Bang. And another. Bang. The sounds echoed. Bang. Bang. Sarah screamed. Men kicked the tires. A man with a mop of black hair raised his stick. Fuji-san shouted. The hit was direct. Crack. The windshield shattered. The man struck the side of the car, the hood, and the bumper. Others pounded. More protesters appeared, like pop-up dolls, leaping through the maze of cars and trucks and screaming, "America! America! America, kaire, America, kaire; America, 'go home!'"

"We'll be killed," Fuji-san blubbered.

The police advanced. The demonstrators ran, their wild eyes focused, intent on taking the plaza. They shouted for unions and against America, hoarse voices rising above the din. Rocks flew. A policeman fell. A demonstrator held a union flag high and charged. Others raised their banners and followed. Another policeman fell, then another. Demonstrators raised flags, stretching their arms, leaping in triumph. Shouts of victory filled the air.

Demonstrations rocked an American jeep. "America, kaire," the shouts grew. "America, kaire." A soldier attempted to jump but was forced back. His companion raised his hands. The demonstrators dragged both soldiers to the edge of the moat. They swung the Americans, once, twice, and then with an extra wide swing hurled them into the water.

Police closed in. A squat policeman ran toward the crowd, lifted his club, and hit a young man across the back of the head. He jerked and stood straight for a moment and fell face-first onto the ground. Blood dripped from his mouth. The crowd backed away. A thin boy with a high forehead rushed forward. He lifted the wounded man's head onto his lap.

Ryuzu.

He cradled the man against his chest and spoke to him, but the man remained still. Ryuzu stroked the man's face and Sachiko wiped the blood from the man's mouth. Their foreheads touched, and their lean bodies hovered like large birds while the demonstration raged. A policeman swung his club. Ryuzu crumpled. Blood dripped from his right temple.

"Ryuzu!" she shouted and turned the car door handle. She was on the sidewalk. The crowd swirled, moving aimlessly. Sarah wanted everything to stop, but the people kept coming. Police canisters of tear gas exploded. Demonstrators doubled over, coughed, and spat. Her eyes burned, and she felt her throat swell. Tears flowed down her cheeks. She could not see. Her face felt on fire. She moved with the crowd, pushing and shoving and gasping for breath. When they went forward, so did she; when they angled to the left, she veered there.

A loose stone caught her heel. She was on her hands and knees. People pressed in. The crowd was dense. She covered her face. Dreams of glory, of charging the police were replaced with images of her murdered family, of cousins dragged from their beds, of children lined up to be shot. What if the crowd recognized her as a foreigner? What if people kicked her, beat her, or threw her into the moat? Sarah clutched her burning throat, and rising unsteadily to her feet, charged in Ryuzu's direction. Her feet moved quickly. The crowd cleared. Yes, just a few more feet. She was almost there. Half blinded and in pain, she yelled his name.

A hand grasped her waist. She pulled away, but the grip tightened. Her body twisted; she could not move. "Don't even try," Fuji-san threatened. She kicked, moved her head violently, and clawed at Fuji-san's arm. It was no use. Her legs dangled helplessly. There was a roar from the crowd. Fuji-san ran, the car door opened, and she was back inside.

Ryuzu lifted his head. His blood-matted hair stood on end, and blood dribbled down his cheek. His eyes were wide with horror. Then he saw her. His lips tightened. He shook his head as if bewildered and pointed. Sachiko turned and moved close, speaking earnestly and gesturing toward the car. Ryuzu shook his head, but she kept talking, cradling his head, her mouth pressed against his ear. Ryuzu's expression changed slowly from disbelief to confusion to rage. He pushed Sachiko away, but she was back, talking and pointing.

Ryuzu raised his hand. He shook his fist. "Baka, 'idiot,' baka!" Tears streamed down his cheeks. He shouted, "Baka, baka!" The words were heavy with hatred, anger she did not deserve, rage that broke her heart.

A policeman blew his whistle. Police quickly formed a line in the center of the road. Fuji-san threw the car into first gear. Sarah spread her hands against the back window. Again their eyes met. She raised her hand, and Ryuzu's hand went up, too. His eyes burned with intensity.

She reached toward him, but the car sped into traffic, and he grew smaller and smaller.

BETRAYAL

When they arrived home, Fuji-san, pale and trembling, hurried to the servants' quarters and described the demonstration to O'ba, who in turn told Sarah's parents. That night her parents lectured about safety. Her mother's eyes were moist with worry. Her father shook his head. But in the end they laughed. She was part of a great family tradition that knew the good from the bad. "I'm sure Ryuzu is fine," her mother added. "He is lucky to have you as a friend."

The next day Sarah, dressed in baggy pants and a loose shirt, ran to the empty lot where her friends gathered. A US Army jeep parked next to the wall blocked her way. Two blond soldiers wearing dark glasses with their caps cocked sideways sat in the front seat puffing cigarettes. Smoke rings drifted above their heads.

American soldiers often stopped her, making comments and joking as if on the same team. She put them at ease, answering questions quickly with a smile. But knowing Ryuzu would be furious if he saw her speaking to Americans, she tiptoed past the jeep and began the climb to the lot above. She glanced back. The soldiers had not moved, eyes closed, cigarettes perched on slack lips.

Sarah ran toward Ryuzu and the others at the far end of the lot. She was eager to hear about the wounded man. She had risked her life. Her friends knelt in a closed circle. She ran faster. "Ryuzu-chan!" she yelled. "Ryuzu-chan!" Still their heads remained bent. At last! She pushed into the circle.

Ryuzu held a pair of long, bamboo chopsticks over a wasp nest. The wasps swarmed. Ryuzu's hand darted, lifted a larva, and dropped it into a tin can. The chopsticks snapped. He lifted another. The plump bodies wriggled. Ryuzu's grip was steady, his face creased in concentration, a look of absolute focus. The chopsticks snapped again.

Ryuzu walked slowly to another nest swarming with bees. Her friends followed, whispering as if witness to religious ritual. Ryuzu lifted a larva and placed it carefully on the nest. Then he dropped another and then another. Several wasps walked around the larvae. Then one attacked, his feelers moving rapidly, signaling the others. The wasps swarmed. Their mouths darted at the plump bodies. The hum grew. More wasps arrived. Bits of white splattered. Sarah reached for the chopsticks, but Ryuzu pushed her away.

"Even wasps know a stranger," Ryuzu muttered. "They kill gaijin."

Sarah stared at the knot of wasps swarming around the pale larvae and then at her own pale skin. For the last six years, for all that time, Ryuzu had stood by her, forcing Michio and the others to accept her as their own. He had spoken earnestly about the importance of nakama. Nothing must disturb the harmony of the group. That was the Japanese way. Sarah was nakama. Ryuzu loved her: her strangeness, her make-believe games, her humor, her sense of adventure.

"Ryuzu-chan," she whispered her mind numb and

her body cold. The words came in a rush, tentative and then sputtering, as she described the tear gas, her attempt at rescue, and Fuji-san's interference. But Ryuzu turned away, his face closed, an expression she had never seen. She kept talking, speaking quickly as if the words had been stored just for this telling.

Then she knew with certainty that this public shame might never be lived down. Ryuzu blamed her. She was gaijin, and her friends knew it. Real nakama would have helped Ryuzu, Sachiko, and the wounded man to the car, real nakama would have forced Fuji-san to drive to hospital, and real nakama would have stayed while they were cared for. From the start her friends had labeled her as unworthy and as a foreigner who could not be counted on. They were right. She was no better than the army brats with their plastic lunch boxes, football scores, and grade averages.

Ryuzu put his arm around Noriko. Other arms followed. They pressed their foreheads together, dark heads blending. Taro and Noriko's small hands grasped Ryuzu's shirttails, completing the closeout. "I'm sorry," she whispered, at once willing to tell any lie, make any promise to feel the familiar weight of Ryuzu's hand on her shoulder. She trembled, and the sound of her own teeth rattling made her shake even more, but Ryuzu remained unreachable—his gray skin and tight lips, the gash on his forehead pressed together with tiny stitches, a person she did not know.

"Hiro died," Ryuzu said. "He died in my arms. Just eighteen."

"Gaijin," they chanted. "Gaijin."

"I'm not gaijin," Sarah cried in desperation. "I'll prove it," she said and stood back. They waited, their eyes expectant. Even Ryuzu watched. She had their attention now. In a low voice, she described the American soldiers parked next to the wall. "We can fight America," she said. "Unless you are scared. Unless you are afraid of guns."

Taro, Ichiro, Michio, Noriko, and the others looked at Ryuzu, their spokesperson for peace, Gandhi, and the will of the people. He showed them again and again that true samurai protected the weak. Ryuzu was against war, bombs, and the military. He said Japan did terrible things in Asia, things that no one wanted to hear. He defended Sarah and the little ones from Michio. It was Ryuzu whom they turned to for justice. He was their leader.

But this was a different Ryuzu. He had murdered larvae to make a point, he had betrayed his best friend, and now he stood with his fists balled and his face contorted, thinking only of revenge. Where was his gentle smile? Where was his humor? Where was his empathy? Where was his friendship? They did not know this Ryuzu. Taro whimpered, and the others mumbled.

It was up to Ryuzu; he knew it and they knew it. He folded his hands and looked back toward the forest. For a moment Sarah thought he would put his hand on her shoulder and lead them into the woods. But Ryuzu did not move. He faced the crowd with a grave expression, raising the can above his head for several seconds before turning it upside down. Larvae dotted the ground like small pellets. "Let's get them."

Ryuzu led, gathering stones, moving low across the field. Others gathered rocks, too. They climbed over the ruins, boulders, broken glass, and burnt planks, a long column on hands and knees heading to the wall. Ryuzu raised his hand for quiet. Sarah peered down. So did the others. The sun glinted off the windshield of the jeep. The driver smoked with his eyes closed. The other lay on his side, the sun highlighting his hair, strands streaked white, pale against dark freckles. A small boy stretched long.

Sarah hesitated.

"For Japan," Ryuzu whispered.

"For Japan," the others whispered back.

A cloud passed overhead. The soldiers, with pistols black and ominous in bulging holsters, now appeared enormous. She raised her hand. Others followed. She chanted: "America, kaire, America, 'go home!'" The others joined. The air vibrated with their cries and their stomping feet. "America, kaire."

The soldiers looked up. Sarah's stone hit the side of the jeep. Ryuzu's rock cracked the windshield. Michio hit the driver's forehead. Sarah grabbed a bottle. Taro heaved a large board, his small body panting with the effort, while others threw anything they could find, their arms moving quickly. The soldiers, pistols in hand, jumped out of the jeep and pointed high.

Taro began to cry. Noriko also wailed. Others started, "Scared." Their limbs trembled, and paralyzed in place, they looked to Ryuzu.

"Run!" Ryuzu shouted. "Run," they echoed his command, scrambling across the lot, skirting metal planks and the bags of garbage, hopping over the rotting logs like startled birds. Sarah scooped up Taro, his small body smelling of old eggs. He was so light that she held him fast like a small pillow. He clung to her, pressed his nose against her cheek, and jabbed her stomach with his scabby knees. The soldiers mounted the wall.

Taro clutched her harder. "Scared,'" he whispered in a terrified wheeze. The others were at the forest. The others were at the forest. She moved quickly, skipping between wooden planks, broken glass, and worn bricks. Taro's nails bit into her neck. She tried to loosen his grip, but he only grabbed harder. Ahead was a large log.

She leapt, her feet almost clearing the wood, but then tripped, landing hard on an old quilt. Taro scampered away. She rolled, grabbed the edge of the quilt, and covered her body. Grubs tickled her legs and stomach. She stiffened. The soldiers' boots moved close, the air thick with the dense smell of oiled leather.

"Japs," one soldier said in a deep voice.

"Kids," the other said. "Those brats think we don't want to go home? I'd go today. Leave the dump to commies and North Koreans."

"We have to report this," the other retorted. "The commander wants to know everything. One was white."

"White?"

"Yeah, white," the soldier said.

"Couldn't be," the other said. "No American kid would play with Japs. I know an American when I see one. No sir."

The soldiers went back and forth until their voices quieted. They pointed their guns at the forest. Panic set in. Now they would shoot. It had been her idea to stone Americans. She must explain. It was only a game— childish, cowboys and Indians.

Taro's small legs were visible behind a large tree. He was only eight and loved candy and lived alone with his mother. Ichiro, his best friend, was even thinner. Noriko's red hair bow was just to the right. Sensei had arranged for her adoption by an uncle. Michio had just passed his junior high exam. A gun clicked.

There was a long silence. A bird chirped. More silence. Another chirp, clear and bright, gave her courage. Sarah stood, faced the forest, and slowly turned. Her heart pounded. The field was empty. Gone! Where were they? The jeep's engine sounded in the lane. It was over. Like the Japanese soldier emerging from the Guam jungle with wild hair and glazed eyes, the one who hadn't surrendered, she had taken on the American army. The others had fled, but she had remained and faced the enemy.

One by one her friends came, Taro dancing across the field clapping his small hands, the others following more slowly. They buzzed around her, touching her hair and clothes. They knew she was brave, a hero. They called her name softly, "Sarah-chan." Sarah closed her eyes.

But Ryuzu turned away and refused to look at her.

"Let's play war," Michio said at last. "Sarah-chan will be the Japanese captain, and Ryuzu will be the American captain."

"Yes," everyone shouted and laughed.

It was time to leave. Except for Ryuzu, her friends liked her again. If she left now, they would plead for her to stay; if she left now, Ryuzu would miss her, too; if she left now, they would come for her at the back gate tomorrow, their voices rising over the scream of crickets, demanding her presence. But she wanted Ryuzu. She knew it was a mistake to want him so much. O'ba said they were too close, a closeness that would lead to misunderstanding, too much dependence, *amae*. "You are not Ryuzu, and Ryuzu is not you," she had scolded. "You must be yourself. You must be Sarah-chan." But O'ba had said the same about Saburo.

She followed Ryuzu and the others into the forest. Immediately they were surrounded by tall bamboos. Beyond the bamboos were more thickets, fields, empty lots, and small brooks. The light streaming through the leaves created shadows on the stones, boulders, and dark earth between the bamboos. The patterns transformed as the wind blew. Wild flowers carpeted the fields, and thick moss disguised the ruined houses. All of it banished the outside world.

Noriko took her hand, Taro pressed against her leg, and Ryuzu pasted leaves on his face and arms. Sarah pasted too. Michio cut young bamboos into spears and laid them one by one on the boulder. Through all this Ryuzu glared. Her friends glanced furtively in her direction. Now the game was not so much fun. Being the Japanese captain made her not want to play at all.

Noriko, Taro, and Ichiro walked along the patch of blue wild flowers to the bushes. Except for the rising screech of crickets and the distant sound of tractors on the other side of the lake, the forest was still. Noriko held Sarah's hand. Each shadow reminded Sarah that Ryuzu's team lay in wait.

"Look," Sarah whispered and pointed to a tiny, bright red spot in a far thicket.

"Michio's jacket," Noriko whispered. "Sensei gave it to him last week."

"We'll ambush from both sides," Sarah ordered, splitting the group.

They crept through thick underbrush and sharp grass, and stones cut their knees. She crept for the glory of Japan, to be the best Japanese general, to be accepted by Ryuzu, to end the war. She would win. The demonstration would be forgotten.

"Banzai!" she shouted and ran at Michio's jacket with her spear. "Banzai." Noriko, Taro, and the others did the same.

Even before she speared the jacket, she knew, as the others did, that it was a trick. The forest was too silent and the attack had been too easy. The jacket hung limply from a branch. She pierced it again, knocking it to the ground.

"Kneel," Ryuzu commanded from behind. "Kneel." His voice was cold, and his bamboo hurt her back. Other spears poked at her legs and arms. The rule—the loser kneeled—must be obeyed. Noriko and her team were on their knees. But Sarah would not kneel. Ryuzu had been too mean. He was cold and distant. He had betrayed her publically. There was no nakama with Ryuzu. It was a question of face, of humiliation. Nothing would make her obey.

"Gaijin!" Ryuzu and Michio shouted. "Kneel, gaijin. Gaijin, gaijin." Even her teammates wanted her to obey. The rules had been agreed to. She must comply. Taro hit her thighs, and Ichiro poked her legs. Her body shook.

"Kneel," Ryuzu commanded again. "Kneel." With each cut her body stiffened. Spears ripped her clothes and sliced her skin. Still she stood, her arms stiff, her neck unbending. Ryuzu thrust his spear, this time slowly with his weight behind it. Blood dripped. More drops fell. Her apologizing babble had been a mistake. It was one she wouldn't repeat. She would never kneel. Never.

"Surrender!" they shouted. "Rules!" She backed against a bamboo trunk and shielded her face with her hands. The spears came fast. She screamed. The sound caught in her throat, a high explosion, stuttering and shrill.

Then it stopped.

THE FAR SHORE

Sensei walked toward them, his movements grace-ful, supple as the day she and Saburo had first seen him, robed in white, hair flowing, assuming the za zen position. Now despite his gray business suit, with hair trimmed below his ears, she was impressed.

"Ryuzu-kun," Sensei said, "what is happening here? Why are you fighting? Sarah-chan, what is going on?"

"We were angry, Sensei-sama," Ryuzu said, bow-ing deeply. "Sarah-chan broke the rules."

"What rules?"

"Stupid rules," Sarah said, wiping a tear.

Sensei glanced at the others, but they were silent.

Sensei lifted Ryuzu's chin and stared at him. "This is not the Japanese way." He lowered his head and spoke in a tone so soft they leaned forward. "We Japanese do not behave like animals." Sensei's thick lashes gave his eyes an exaggerated slant, straight and dark. She wanted to touch them.

"Sarah-chan is one of you. You were brought up to protect everyone in your group. A true samurai pro-tects the weak. He understands that we are all one, and what happens to one happens to everyone. That is the meaning of obligation. That is what I have taught you.

Has it meant nothing?"

Ryuzu lowered his head. His stitches were dark against his pale skin.

"Ryuzu-kun," Sensei continued in a lilting tone that reminded Sarah of a bubbling spring, a voice that she could respond to and could believe in. "You of all people should know this. I depend on you to carry on the Japanese way, to create harmony. I am disappointed."

Ryuzu was silent.

"I heard you were in the demonstration at the palace. Sachiko-san should not have taken you there. You are hurt."

Ryuzu lowered his eyes and Sarah saw from his pursed lips that he was trying not to cry.

"Don't you have *juku*, 'after school lessons,' today? I saw your teacher, and he said you have not been at juku for several days. I came to the forest to find you. This is not like you, Ryuzu-kun."

Ryuzu froze.

"Sarah-chan, do you know why Ryuzu-kun is not in juku?" he asked, drawing her close and repeating his question in children's Japanese. He wiped the blood off her arm, lifted her blouse, and examined her back. "These are bad cuts," he said. In a quiet voice, he repeated his question about Ryuzu's juku.

Sarah felt Sensei's breath on her face. His hands gripped her shoulders. He trusted her and her alone to give him the answer. It was a heady feeling. She wanted to touch his thick lashes and stroke his broad cheeks. His tea-colored skin, wide forehead, and curved nose gave him a lofty, aristocratic look, like a *Kabuki* actor, unafraid, disciplined, and forceful. Sensei smiled. And Sarah knew the answer, the information that would allow Sensei to nail Ryuzu. Ryuzu had skipped juku for his Russian lesson taught by a Japanese veteran who'd been interned in Siberia. Ryuzu said his teacher's nose was white from frostbite. Russian language was a union scholarship requirement for study in Russia.

Sensei waited. The children waited. The crickets screamed. Sensei's eyes had the flat expression of a man confident of his facts, who'd come to the forest with purpose. Sensei was toying with her. He already knew about the Russian lessons and the scholarship. Now Sensei wanted a public admission. Ryuzu, her very best friend, had blamed her for Hiro's death, excluded her from the group, and attacked her. Sensei's demand gave her power. Her friends fidgeted, trying to distract her, but she was mad, so mad that nothing mattered but providing Sensei with ammunition.

Sensei repeated his question, his voice soft and cajoling as if he understood her dilemma.

Her mouth opened then closed. Then she realized nothing could make her tattle on Ryuzu. It was the same stubbornness, determined and forbidding, that made her refuse to kneel, the same resolve that had forced her parents to accept Saburo and now her life in the forest. It was a large part of her, a will she depended on with right on her side. The murmur of her friends, like buzzing bees, grew louder.

Sensei waited.

"Ryuzu-chan is sick," she said. "He has a fever. He should be in bed."

Friends sucked in their breath. It was over. She had kept her bargain to the group. She knew it and so did her friends and Ryuzu. Her cuts did not hurt anymore. She felt whole and strong. She stepped away and straightened her shoulders.

Sensei sighed. "I didn't know you were sick," Sensei said to Ryuzu softly.

"I study Russian," Ryuzu blurted. "Russian is the reason I was not at juku."

Sensei nodded and moved closer.

"Is Russian Sachiko-san's idea? I got her a job in the factory to better herself, not to become a Communist, not to study Russian, and not to go to demonstrations that expose you to danger."

Ryuzu's face reddened.

"Masaru-kun, your father, died because he was a Communist," Sensei continued. His voice softened with memory as he spoke of Masaru. Each morning they walked to school, and in the afternoon they would roam forest paths. Then step by step, Sensei described the liberal influence of Masaru's father, who knew Sun Yet Sen as a student in Tokyo and with other Japanese liberals even attended his funeral in China. He taught Masaru about the left and Japan's domination of Asia. But Masaru went even beyond his father. He converted to Communism and withdrew from school, from seeing Sensei and his friends. In Beijing he worked as a reporter, made friends with young Communists, and spread poison about Japan's intentions. Masaru's mother refused to leave home. "She died of grief," Sensei whispered. In Shanghai Sensei learned that Masaru-kun had been jailed. Then Sensei learned he was dead.

"Japan hates Communists," Sensei continued, his voice so compelling that Sarah put her hand on Sensei's arm. She and her friends had heard the story in bits and pieces, but this time they pressed close. "Even now, the Russians are at war with Japan," Sensei said. "They haven't returned our soldiers. They have killed their past. Communists want to control Japanese unions. You must have nothing to do with Russia." His hooded eyes glowed with intensity. His skin tightened, outlining his skull and cheeks. At once everything about him stretched taut as if about to break and rip apart. Sarah backed away.

"You know all this was once my estate," Sensei addressed them in a louder voice. "Part of this forest and your village belonged to my family. That's why I feel responsible for you and take care of you. That's why I buy you clothes and help you with your lessons. I am teaching you the Japanese way. You are Japan, the future, all I care about."

Sensei put his hands on Ryuzu's shoulders. "Ryuzu-kun, I see Masaru-kun, your father, in you, the man I knew before university before he was seized by the left." Sensei's voice was so tender that Sarah forgot her fear. Her eyes filled with tears. Sensei's beautiful face, sincere in its mission and resolute in his memory, absorbed her. "Many friends in Nagatacho knew Masaru. Those friends want you to take his place and study for the University of Tokyo exam and serve Japan. They know that you are one of us, the real Japanese who put Japan first."

"Forgive me, Sensei-sama," Ryuzu said and hung his head. His misery was so infectious that Taro and Ichiro began to cry.

Sensei's tone gained strength. "We must rebuild Japan and make it strong, strong enough to rise from the ashes of defeat. We must catch up and surpass the West. You must study for Japan's sake and win this war, the economic war. Japan's resource is its people. You are the future."

Sarah wanted more. She wanted Sensei to say something amazing, words that would resonate and guide her. She wanted the truth about life, its dangers, limitations and opportunities. Her friends wanted it too. They were waiting. She shook his arm. He turned away. The children whispered and called his name, but

Sensei went silent. Then without a backward glance, he strode down the path.

One minute the forest was full of Sensei, his words, his energy, his dictates, and then he was gone. Emptiness. Her friends stared at each other. He must be replaced. Ryuzu must fill the void. They wanted direction, something that would bind them, create a sense of purpose. Even Michio turned to Ryuzu. Ryuzu nodded toward the path that led up the hill and said gently, "Let's go the forbidden side of the lake."

They protested. "But Sensei said we shouldn't," Taro said.

"Sensei will be mad," Noriko said.

"Sensei said we would be eaten by bad people who live there," Michio said.

They repeated all they knew about the forbidden part of the lake, speaking at once as if talking would make the fear disappear. But with Taro's high chant, "the other side of the lake," the mood switched. Noriko joined, then Ryuzu, and then Michio. The chant gained strength, and they jumped up and down until Ryuzu broke into a smile. Noriko laughed, Taro pounded Ryuzu's back, and the others cheered.

"Let's go," Ryuzu called, pointing up the narrow path. The little ones cheered again.

She should leave. Her uneasiness increased as she thought of Sensei and Ryuzu, their tangled history occupying each other's minds. They reminded her of Scalia. His feelings seeped into the walls of the house, permeating each room with ownership.

Ryuzu put his hand on Sarah's shoulder and nodded toward the path. "Come with us, Sarah-chan," he invited in a voice meant for her alone. "You have never been to this part of the lake. Sensei took me long ago. We can swim. It's beautiful."

Still Sarah did not move. Her friends waited, their faces so close she smelled talcum rice on their lips.

"Come," Ryuzu coaxed, and the others murmured the same.

Sarah hesitated. She shrugged Ryuzu off, but his hand went to her cheek. Her friends pleaded. Noriko bent close.

She went with him. What else could she do? They were her whole world, and she was theirs. They climbed quickly, the bamboos giving way to shrubs and rocks and the sky opening up wide and blue before them. Even Taro was silent by the time they neared the summit. The lake reflected the forest and shone like an emerald pool edged by a ribbon of sand. A tiny bird flew low across the water, fluttering in midair waiting for an updraft, and circling higher, disappeared into the blue. The hills surrounding the lake were backed by more forest, and the slate blue sky stretched as far as the eye could see.

They stood for a moment taking in the contrast of green and white and blue and turning to the breeze let the wind caress their cheeks. Sarah's friends pointed, but she still felt distant. Ryuzu set Taro down and lifted his arms high. The others did the same. "Yoy!" he yelled down the mountain. "Yoy!" In this mood she followed the others to the water and stripped to her underwear.

Polio lake. Since her illness Sarah had avoided the lake and refused invitations to swim. Her mother had nearly died, the baby had died, and she had been deathly ill. All that seemed in the distant past, too. Today she needed the purity of the sand and the inlet. She wanted something that would banish her hurt.

The water stretched before her. The lake was clean, so clean that she saw swarms of minnows clustered around the reeds. The wind created white-crested waves dotted by sunspots, dancing silver beams of light, on the water. She felt the mud between her toes as she went through the reeds past the minnows and water beetles into deeper water.

Ryuzu dog-paddled along the shore, but Sarah, who had her own strong stroke swam straight across. She cut through the small waves, stretching her arms to a powerful crawl. With each stroke the water ran through her. She hit a cold current and felt her stomach tighten as she gained speed—one arm over the other, her body driving through the water. The cold numbed the cuts on her back. Her head turned and plunged, her power increasing with each lift of her arm. The sun glinted off the lake as she headed toward the far shore. For the first time since the demonstration, Sarah felt confident; she could do anything or be anything.

She'd entered the shallows on the opposite side, and as her feet touched the soft muddy bottom, she was sorry to have reached the shore. She walked up the beach, sat on the sand, and watched the sun sink to purple. The breeze puckered her skin, but she was not cold. She lay on her back, at one with herself and the world. It was a delicious feeling, this harmony of not wanting, of unity with the trees, sand, and water. Her eyes filled with colors. She spread her arms and legs wide so that the sand slipped between her fingers, cushioning her shoulders and pillowing her head.

Ryuzu ran up the beach holding her clothes like an offering. "It's getting late. We must hurry." She laughed, pushed him back, and took her time getting dressed. "Hurry. Bad people live here." She threw off his hand. He grabbed hers again. "Come."

"*Konnichiwa*, Sarah-chan, 'good day.'"

The voice came from behind her, a voice Sarah knew. She turned slowly. A short woman in *mompe*, "baggy pants," and a *hanten*, "jacket," stood before her. The woman's hair was tied in a bun at the nape of her neck, and long bangs covered her forehead. Her face was darker than her neck, and the contrast set her features apart. The tanned skin, heart-shaped face, and slightly protruding teeth made her old and young at the same time. Her face tilted toward Sarah, and with a knowing smile, she seized Sarah's fingers and gave a short nod.

Fumiko. It was Fumiko.

Behind her was a pale boy about Sarah's age wearing a Mickey Mouse T-shirt and new Mickey Mouse sneakers. Dark hair framed his face and curled around his neck. She saw the scar on his forehead. His straight nose gave his features a regular look. She took in his square chin and full lips. He was tall, lean, and carried himself easily. As he stepped forward, she remembered his squared shoulders, his blunt movements, and his white teeth. Most of all she remembered his eager eyes and energetic smile, welcoming and playful.

Saburo.

"We must leave now," Ryuzu said firmly, tugging on her arm. The wind came off the lake in strong gusts. Sarah shivered. Ryuzu's arm went around her, his body pressed against her wet skin. He held her tight, propelling her along the beach. Her feet sunk into the wet sand.

She dug in. They stood still. Ryuzu looked worn—black circles creased his eyes and his skin, gray with fatigue, made him seem desperate. He appeared soulful, his rage gone, aware of his betrayal, conscious that their friendship might never be mended. He pleaded with her to leave, to come with him away from this place and the people in it. His speech faltered as if he'd lost authority. She wanted to reassure him, but the anger was too recent.

She turned.

Fumiko and Saburo stood side by side, silhouetted against the fading light, their arms around each other. Sarah remembered them standing tall and defiant, challenging O'ba, her parents, and Scalia, on the hut's balcony for all to see. She remembered them wild, beyond rules, flaunting principles that others accepted. It all came rushing back.

Enormous dark clouds billowed above, and at once a strong wind came off the lake. Fumiko's hair came loose and swirled around her face. Her face tilted forward as if she were talking to Sarah along the long shoreline. Their eyes met. Fumiko held her with a long look. Then Fumiko lifted her arm and waved in a round motion, slowly, deliberately, as though washing a pane of glass.

Sarah waved back.

THE WEB

Sarah-chan, hand me another plant," O'ba said. Dark earth, loose and crawling with worms, piled to the right of a shallow trench. O'ba repeated her demand. Sarah did not move. She was after answers.

Saburo and Fumiko were alive, lived on the other side of the lake, and Saburo had grown tall with dark hair that framed his face and curled on his neck. Just last week she had asked O'ba if she had any news of them. O'ba had remained silent. Why? Did her parents know that they lived so close? Did O'ba? Did Fumiko still work with Sensei and Scalia?

"Where were you yesterday, Sarah-chan?" O'ba asked. Sarah remained silent and prepared for the worst. O'ba dug another hole, lining it with fertilizer. "Emiko-san said when you came home your dress was filthy, covered with old cotton, and your hair was wet," O'ba continued in a flat voice. "Your dress was cut. There was blood. Someone hurt you. You were so tired that you went right to bed."

Emiko nudged Sarah to reply. When Sarah complained about O'ba's bad temper, Emiko reminded Sarah that O'ba loved Sarah more than anything, like her own daughter, Atsuko-chan. Sarah moved close and

laid her head on O'ba's shoulder. O'ba let it rest there,
wrapped her arms around Sarah, and rocked, singing the lullaby nen, nen, "sleep," "sleep," while Sarah
hummed. The gentle sway of O'ba's body made her feel
nothing bad could happen. They stayed that way, hum-
ming the lullaby, with the dank earthy smell all around.

"Excuse me. Wada here." A middle-aged policeman with cropped hair stood by the gate. He looked
intently at O'ba and shuffled his feet. A younger policeman entered. O'ba remained with her back to them, let
go of Sarah, and thrust her spade into the soil. Sarah
recognized Wada and Ito, policemen who visited the
house every New Year. They drank tea, their hands
turning their cups slowly as they asked O'ba questions
about the house, the number of visitors, Sarah's father's
work, and her mother's friends. O'ba answered each
question with studied indifference while Ito and Wada
took notes.

Wada came forward, his severe expression focused on O'ba as he took out a pen and notepad. "We
have come to have a chat," Wada said. "I hope that we
are not disturbing you." O'ba's spade moved swiftly, digging and dumping dirt on Wada's leather shoes, cover-
ing the shine with smatterings of mud. Wada shook off
the dirt and retreated. "I have come on a serious matter.
Yesterday we had word that a foreign child with dark
hair and about Sarah-chan's age stoned American soldiers with a group of local children. The complaint was
from American occupying forces. We are investigating."

O'ba kept digging, and more dirt splattered. O'ba
wiped her forehead, bent over a hose, and sent a spray
of water onto Wada's trousers. Wada stepped back.
Sarah wanted to run into the house, but O'ba's determined look stopped her.

O'ba said in a rude tone, "What do you want to know?"

"Where was Sarah-chan yesterday at 4:30?" Ito spoke for the first time.

Sarah's heart thumped, a wild hammering so loud that she put her hand on her heart. Wada and Ito knew, O'ba knew, and even Emiko knew. If O'ba nodded in her direction, the police would haul her away. With that nod her parents would never get American visas, and the family would be trapped in Japan forever.

Ito walked toward her, his large lips curled in an insinuating smile. She felt ashamed. He knelt in front of her and spoke in a gentle whisper. "You must tell the truth, Sarah-chan. If you tell the truth, nothing bad will happen. But it could be terrible if you were to lie. Really terrible."

Sarah hung her head. She felt tired. Ito's low voice, the syllables broken, sounded like he spoke from under water. It felt like a dream, Ito, Wada, and O'ba, all glaring and determined. Ito put his hand on her shoulder. "Everyone knew it was not her fault," he whispered. Village children were to blame. They were wild and uncontrolled. Their parents had been informed. Sarah backed away, but Ito's hand followed, its weight like a large stone holding her down. A pain shot through her stomach. Her temples pounded. She felt dizzy. Ito's hand moved to her temple, pressing in until she lowered her head.

At once O'ba was between them. "How dare you touch Sarah-chan," she said in her most guttural voice. "Do you want me to report you?" she yelled. "You walk into this garden uninvited and touch this child. There are laws against this. You cannot slap people for not answering your questions and then slap them even harder for answering those same questions. This is not prewar

Japan. The power of the police is gone. We are through with you. Over. No more bullying. You say Americans asked for an investigation. Americans will not like you touching a foreign child."

"Be reasonable," Wada said.

"Reasonable," O'ba continued in a thunderous voice. "This child was napping at 4:30. She always naps in the afternoon. I gave her cookies and put her to bed myself. She is tired after school. She has to speak English all day. It's exhausting. It was some other child. It was an illusion. How dare you! Get out! Out!"

The policemen stared at each other, looking bewildered.

"Are you insane?" Wada asked.

O'ba put her hands on her hips, fierce and unrelenting, and pointed toward the gate. Wada kicked the diggings, sending loose dirt flying, and turned on his heel and left the garden. Ito followed.

Emiko whispered for Sarah to apologize and beg forgiveness. She wanted to. She wanted to be O'ba's little girl, Atsuko-chan, again, the lost child, the cherished daughter. O'ba picked up her spade, and Emiko gently mopped her brow. O'ba grunted and kept digging, her spade moving quickly through the hard surface to the soft, dark earth underneath.

When she finally spoke, her voice was steady. "*Ware, ware Nihonjin*, we Japanese do things very carefully, Sarah-chan. We think before we act, and we never act alone. We are never rash. We plan. We are *shima guni*, an 'island nation,' nothing but stones, mountains, and the sea. We prepare to get the best results. We know otherwise all will be lost. That is the Japanese way."

O'ba took a flat stone, placed it carefully next to a strawberry plant, and kept right on talking. "You see what I am doing, Sarah-chan? I place this stone here.

All day the stone will absorb the heat of the sun. At night I tie a bag over the plant and the stone. This way the heated stone will warm the plant. Nothing is lost. The berries will be twice as big. That's how we Japanese prepare, that's how we leave nothing to chance, that's how we help each other survive."

O'ba hesitated. Her face creased to a frown, and she put her hand on Sarah's head. "Sarah-chan," O'ba said softly. "You cannot play like a child any more. You saw what just happened. Wada and Ito have threatened our household. You have responsibilities." Her voice lowered, and she spoke passionately of Sarah's obligation to study, to help her once-again pregnant mother. "Your mother needs you. You must be her best girl."

Sarah nodded, thinking of her father's happiness at holding her mother's hand at dinner, stroking her wrist as if she might disappear. Her mother seemed glad, too. Yet their joy excluded Sarah. She willed the dinner to end. Beppe felt rejected as well. When her parents stroked and whispered, he stormed out of the room.

A cloud shrouded the sun, and at once the garden was in shadows. O'ba's eyes were round and clear. She looked steadily at Sarah as if gauging her response. Sarah returned her gaze. They faced each other, the plant between them. Sarah felt small next to O'ba's massive certainty.

"It's time you stopped playing in the forest, Sarah-chan," O'ba said. "Those children are not suitable friends. They will get you into trouble. Look what just happened."

"They are my friends," Sarah asserted, remembering that Fuji-san had said the same.

"You are gaijin," O'ba's voice dropped, and Sarah knew the important part was coming. "The occupation is over."

"So what?" Sarah said, feeling brave again.

"Watching is our way," Oba said. "That is why neighborhoods are close and why police like Wada and Ito want to hear about anything that might threaten the wa, 'harmony,' of Japanese life. Police come in pairs. Why? Because we Japanese check on our neighbors, and we check on each other. Nothing is left to chance. Wada was right to come here today. He was right to bring Ito. A warning. Warnings mean we prepare. Warnings are serious. We understand consequences. That is the Japanese way."

"I didn't do anything wrong," Sarah protested.

"Wrong?" O'ba continued. "Wrong?"

"Wada and Ito are stupid," Sarah said.

"Stupid?" O'ba asked.

Sarah was silent. She kept on digging, aware that O'ba still sat on her haunches, squat and alert like a large frog watching for prey.

"Did you think that you, Sarah-chan, Ryuzu-chan, and the others could take on America?" O'ba asked. "Are you listening to Ryuzu-chan? He is brilliant but a dreamer. His father, Masaru-kun, was a dreamer, too. Fuji-san said that at the demonstration you went into the crowd looking for Ryuzu-chan. You could have been killed! When he got home, Fuji-san was so upset he ran to the bathroom and threw up."

"Did Sensei kill Masaru, Ryuzu's father?" Sarah asked. "Did he turn in Masaru to the military police?"

"Who told you that?" O'ba snapped and sucked in her breath. Dirt flew, Oba's lips narrowed, names tumbled out: Masaru, Ryuzu, Sensei, familiar names uttered with ferocious energy, an intensity that silenced her. It was clear from O'ba's tone that she thought about Sensei every day. Sarah was frightened. She wanted to take back her question. She wanted to hear more.

"Myoshin-ji."

"Myoshin-ji?" Sarah asked.

Emiko stepped away, shaking her head to warn Sarah into silence. But Sarah said it again.

Now O'ba's voice rippled as she spoke about the Myoshin-ji, a Zen cult that was part of the Japanese army, a nationalistic, racist sect that believed Japan was superior and hated Jews. Myoshin-ji trained and disciplined Japanese soldiers. Sensei belonged. Did Sensei hate Jews? She had never heard of Japanese who hated Jews. Sarah waited for O'ba to continue, but O'ba closed her eyes in exhaustion. Wada's questions about stoning American soldiers seemed trivial compared to this large world of nationalism and hate, a world that her parents referred to over dinner, one that made her mother whisper about passports and visas and made her father incredibly sad.

The silence grew, and Sarah knew that it must not be broken. O'ba's story about Sensei, about the Myoshin-ji sect, was a warning. Sensei—a member of Myoshin-ji, a right-wing machine that would crush anyone or anything that stood in its way—had power. He had sent Atsuko-chan away; he had killed Masaru, he had warned Ryuzu. O'ba wanted to terrify her and she had.

"You will know Ryuzu-chan for the rest of your life, Sarah-chan," O'ba gently changed the subject, "just as Sensei still knows Masaru-kun. He remembers those golden days with Masaru-kun, his boyhood friend, the chum he walked to school with, the one he could not live without. He thinks of him every day. That friendship is in his body, in his bones, and in his blood, imprinted on his soul. It controls him, and he can do nothing about it."

O'ba then spoke quickly about Masaru-kun's distress when Sensei was sent to Harvard. They wrote each other every week, and when Sensei returned, Masaru-kun was at the dock to greet him. "Sensei pretends Ryuzu is Masaru-kun," she said. "Sensei is reliving his youth. Ryuzu has Masaru's high forehead, dreamy manner, and kind heart. I warned him against being too involved with the past, living in the village, and mentoring Ryuzu. Nothing good can come of this. I warned him, but he would not change his mind."

"Ryuzu-chan is my friend, that's all."

"That's not all," O'ba said. "In time you will remember your carefree days, days that you will dream about, days you will want to relive. You have the heart of Japan, a brave and loyal heart. You know truth and beauty, and you understand people. But you don't know your own power. People want what you have. That will be a problem — their need and their anger because of it."

"You're stupid," Sarah said, annoyed with her own uncertainty.

"Truthful," O'ba answered. "This must stop. You and Ryuzu are too tight. You finish each other's sentences. You speak with one voice, but you come from different worlds. All is an illusion, a dream that will be terrible for you. It may be already too late. It was the same with Saburo, always together, reliving a past that never happened, making up stories in each other's minds and hearts. Too much amae, 'enmeshed dependency.'"

Saburo. Sarah was still. It was the first time O'ba had mentioned Saburo. Now she understood. O'ba knew they had met by the lake. News traveled fast from Fumiko to Sensei and then to Scalia and O'ba. She waited for more, but O'ba turned away, her face bent and her spade deep in the soft soil. "Ryuzu-chan is my friend," Sarah repeated in a soft tone, hoping O'ba would talk about Saburo.

"You must behave like a Japanese," O'ba warned.

"Treat life the way I treat the strawberry plant—carefully and with respect for danger. You must look in front of you, then to your right and left. Most important, know what lurks behind you. Wada and Ito gave us a warning, a Japanese warning. Next time they will act."

Sarah remembered the Myoshin-ji Zen look in Sensei's eyes as he had waited for her to tell on Ryuzu. Was O'ba right? Was Sensei replaying his past with her and Ryuzu? Is that why he told them stories about loyalty and the Japanese way? Is that why he wanted her to betray Ryuzu as he had betrayed Masaru? She was certain that was true. Sensei's rage, a pool of anger that lay just beneath his calm, was the issue. Her friends backed away when Sensei drew Ryuzu close, his hand on Ryuzu's shoulder, speaking tenderly of Ryuzu's family and the past. They held hands, uneasy with Sensei, his energy and need, waiting patiently till Sensei left.

The setting sun sent shafts of red light across the yard. A sudden breeze made the cuts on her back hurt. She felt tired. Myoshin-ji, Sensei, Scalia, Masaru, and the house—more secrets than Sarah could or wanted to absorb. The once exciting stories now meshed in a powerful knot with no beginning or end. She wished Atsuko-chan were alive, and O'ba was happy. She and Atsuko-chan would play with dolls, make origami cranes, and be best friends. With Atsuko-chan, there would be no Saburo or Ryuzu.

Sarah wanted to say that but instead put her hand in O'ba's large palm.

"You are mine," O'ba said in a low voice meant for Sarah alone. "Always remember. Mine alone. No one will meddle with you, no one. Leave the forest. Those friends must disappear. They will only bring harm. You will learn to be careful, Sarah-chan. You will remember

Wada and Ito. You will behave like a Japanese."

Sarah lowered her head. At once the world was a serious place.

RYUZU

The next day Sarah slipped through the hole in the fence. It was a cloudless day, and ordinarily she would have walked the path slowly, savoring the warm air, dappled light, and sprinkling of wild flowers next to the path. But O'ba's words of caution and her own unease at meeting Saburo made her hurry. What if her friends, furious at her bold swim across the lake and aware that the occupation was over, never came to the forest again?

"Look," Noriko yelled as Sarah rounded the bend. "Sarah-chan, look at this!" She pulled a pair of jeans and a T-shirt over her clothes. The ground was littered with stuff, and her friends, who were absorbed with pulling on the new things, hardly looked in her direction. Michio's hands trembled as he patted a shirt embossed with Superman. Noriko handed her a T-shirt.

The smell of newness, sharp and acid, made them bury their heads in the cloth. Even Ryuzu smiled a slow grin of pride and pulled on a pair of new American jeans. "America," Noriko pointed to her Mickey Mouse shirt and strutted.

The sound of a Japanese flute, the same reedy, temple note — high, atonal — that Saburo had played as a small boy floated down the path. The sound rose and fell. It did not have the harsh sound of a call for attention that Saburo had played in the yard but rather a coaxing, teasing, seductive tone of invitation. Her friends joined hands. They had heard the flute in temples, its discordant tone breaking apart and coming together. Taro squatted. Michio, Ryuzu, and the rest did the same.

"Saburo," Michio whispered and pointed. Saburo's pale face peered from a thicket. Sarah's friends shouted his name. The face disappeared.

Moments passed. The music started again, hovering like an invisible cloud. Michio hummed, and the others joined him, their voices rising with the flute and filling the small circle. Ryuzu took her hand.

Again Saburo's face appeared a pale flash against the green. Ryuzu's grip tightened.

"Banzai," Michio yelled. "We'll come and find you, Saburo."

"Banzai," Sarah joined them. They ran down the path between tall bamboos. The flute moved ahead, its weedy sound mingling with the crickets and birds, echoing across the open lots. Then it stopped. They ran to the right and to the left, yelling first in anticipation and then disappointment. Nothing. They circled back to their boulder.

"Look!" Noriko screamed.

More belts with cowboy buckles hung from the branches. A flashlight dangled above a Superman lunch box. The sun danced off the plastic and tin, the forest sparkling with lights and colors as if its trees had grown iridescent fruit. Her friends ran from one shining object to another, grabbing and screaming with joy. "I love America," Noriko shouted.

The next day Sarah and her friends sat by the boulder waiting. There was nothing. They grew restless. Still nothing. The new T-shirts, now smeared with dirt, made them look like beggars. They walked slowly down the path to the lake. Still nothing. They went to the empty lot. Nothing was there either.

"This is stupid," Ryuzu said, putting his hand on Sarah's shoulder as if she would agree. "We must stop running after Saburo's American things. Saburo is having a good laugh."

Sarah's friends nodded, but even so their eyes flicked back and forth, scanning the path for bright plastic, goods from another world. Sarah wondered where it would end.

"Let's go to the cove where we met him," Sarah suggested. Ryuzu dropped his hand from her shoulder.

"Yes, take us, Ryuzu-chan," Taro and the other younger children cried. "Let's find Saburo!" The yell became a chant: "Let's find Saburo. Saburo. Saburo."

Ryuzu cautioned, "We should not go there. Saburo is with America, with the black market. Even if Sensei supports it, the black market is dirty money. It's American money. We hate America. Yesterday Sensei came to our house. He made Sachiko-chan cry." His friends listened in silence as Ryuzu explained that Sensei was against Ryuzu going to Russia on a union scholarship. "If you want to find Saburo, go alone."

But after much pleading, Ryuzu relented. Once again, his hand on her shoulder, he led them up the hill and down to the shore and the cove. They stood on the beach stamping their feet and calling, "Saburo."

Sarah left the group and walked to edge of the forest, whispering Saburo's name, willing him to her. "Come. Come. Come." Her mind reached out, commanding his presence. He must. Nothing. Again she called. Nothing.

Suddenly a man wearing a green work uniform and a hard hat ran toward them. "Stop! Stop! This is off limits," he yelled. "We're building here. Go away."

The rumbling grew loud, mingling with the smell of exhaust, a sooty, acid smell that made them cough. A horn sounded. Three huge bulldozers breaking trees, pushing trunks onto the beach, descended. Noriko and the little ones screamed. A man in green blew a whistle. Bulldozers, their exhausts belching clouds of black smoke, dropped their loads and turned toward the children.

Her friends fled. But Sarah turned and ran up the beach. The tractors blasted. The children called. Ryuzu grabbed her by the wrist, his grip hard and unyielding. He pulled her along the shore, running back to the hill and familiar territory. A strong wind off the water pressed them together; her hair whipped across his face, and his arm tightened. They climbed the hill hand in hand. By the time they reached the boulder, Sarah clasped him close. They collapsed in a heap, laughing and calling Saburo's name.

❀ ❀ ❀

Look," Taro said the next day, pointing to a Hershey bar next to the path. "Saburo."

Along the path, half hidden by stones, leaves, and branches dribbled sweet treasures: bubble gum, jelly beans, licorice, and more sweets under rocks, behind trees, and under moss. Just when they thought there was no more, screams of joy revealed another stash.

Michio bit into an M&M bag, chocolate smeared across his face. Colored pieces dripped on the front of his shirt. Taro and Noriko shoved gumdrops down their throats. The candy had a dense, sweet taste, sweeter than *unko* cakes or hot sweet bean soup at New Year's. They couldn't get enough. The sugar made them scream, run, and laugh at bad jokes. They forgot their play. All that mattered was candy. They found more in the empty lot and more by the stream and more hidden under leaves.

They gobbled all the way to the lake.

Michio lay on the sand and dumped a bag of M&M's into his mouth. Ryuzu lay next to Sarah with his arm around her shoulder pouring chocolate bits down her throat, laughing into her cheek. "Sarah-chan," he whispered. She let him stay, and feeling him close, something intimate and heady stirred inside her. It was a new feeling. She touched his cheek. Taro burrowed his head in her shoulder. Ryuzu pushed him off. Taro laughed and climbed back on. Ryuzu held her hand. His long fingers grazed her palm. He whispered her name.

They guzzled, rested, and guzzled more, their new clothes covered with chocolate, thick and mixed with sand. "We love you, Saburo," Michio screamed. "America!" Taro yelled and grinned. "We love America."

Ryuzu was next to Sarah with his arm around her shoulder pouring chocolate bites down her throat, laughing into her cheek. "Sarah-chan, he whispered. She let him stay, and feeling him close, something intimate and heady stirred inside her. It was a new feeling. She touched his cheek. Taro buried his head in her shoulder. Ryuzu pushed him off. Taro laughed and climbed back on. Ryuzu's long fingers grazed her palm and he whispered, "Sarah-chan."

SECRETS

The next day Sarah's mother caught her by the back door. Without makeup her mother's thin cheeks, luminous eyes, and high forehead gave her an ethereal look. She was dressed in tan cashmere with a coral necklace and earrings. Her beauty made Sarah move close, as if by association her mother's elegance would pass to her.

"Tell me what's going on," her mother said softly and led her to the living room. From her decided grip, Sarah understood that her mother knew everything about soldiers, police, and cuts on her back.

"I want to see my friends," Sarah said. "I'll do my homework."

"You are too big for all this play," her mother said, explaining in a hurried voice that her father was worried, and O'ba was concerned. They all agreed Sarah must focus on school, be in the top sections, and get top scores. The family intended to buy property in America and follow her.

Sarah's throat tightened. She wanted to still her mother's fluttering hands. "Your friends have exams, too," her mother continued in her high, Russian voice. "They go to their juku after school. The Japanese system is full of exams. You want Ryuzu-chan to do well, don't you? He is trying to win a scholarship."

Sarah didn't answer. She watched her mother watching her. She wanted to tell the truth, the whole truth, that the hunt for Saburo, the chase, made them forget tests and juku. Since Saburo appeared their games had disappeared. Sarah knew Saburo played for her and her alone. The excitement was infectious. Saburo might be anywhere. She had not killed Saburo. She no longer felt guilty. It was just as O'ba had said. Saburo was fine.

She really wanted to know about Sensei. The occupation was over. Would Sensei reoccupy the house? Would he force her father into the black market business? Now she would ask all of it.

Her mother moved close. Surrounded by her lilac scent, Sarah felt little again.

"Are you happy about the baby?" her mother asked.

"Very happy," Sarah answered. Her mother smoothed back her hair with her soft hand and whispered, "*Ya tebya lyublyu*, 'I love you.'" The baby moved.

"Sarah," her mother said. "O'ba is worried. I am worried. You heard too many stories about the family, about Russia," her mother said. "I'm to blame. Stories that burst out of me, stories I needed to tell. I couldn't stop myself. But don't confuse those stories with your life in Japan. That was then; this is now. You are not fighting oppression. Until last week Japan was occupied. If American soldiers are threatened, they must shoot. They have orders to shoot. They are trained to kill. You could have been hurt. Your friends, too."

Her mother spoke in a gentler tone. "Sarah-chan, Japan has a different law. Bribes don't work here as they did in China," she continued to herself. "In Japan it's who you know, how you know them, and how they are obligated. No one is obligated to us, and we aren't obligated to anyone. That is how your father and I want it. Beppe thinks he is connected to Japan through Nishiguchi, but he is wrong."

"What about Nishiguchi, I mean, Sensei?" Sarah asked, glad the conversation had moved away from her and glad to know more. "Aren't we obligated to Sensei?"

"Sensei didn't do us any favors," her mother replied in a flat voice. "There is a lot of blood on Sensei's hands, Sarah," she said in a strained tone. "He was with Japanese intelligence in China. Sensei had tremendous power and killed many. He was accused of war crimes. He is a criminal." Her mother sighed. "He should be in jail, but Americans wanted information and let him out. Now that the occupation is over, Sensei will reclaim his property. We are not part of Sensei's world. We don't want to be part of that world. Beppe does not understand that. Like all foreigners Beppe will be tolerated while useful and then thrown out."

Should she tell her mother that she was the exception, that Sensei loved her, insisting she was Japanese, a person to be trusted, loyal with a true heart? That Sensei would never hurt her? Should she say it?

Her mother continued talking, this time about her father. He had been called to the Japanese tax office for questioning about their Swiss bank account. A well-known foreign lawyer advised them on how to handle the case: which bureaucrats to visit, what papers to sign, how to bow, when to apologize, and whom to pay. "I don't know who turned us in to the tax office, but we are under scrutiny. We could be kicked out of the country," her mother continued in a terrified whisper. "Where would we go? We have Red Cross passports. Uncle Michael can't get us papers for Australia.

I'm about to have a baby."

Her mother's arm felt cold. Her lips pursed with worry.

"Did Sensei report you?"

"Why would he?" her mother answered. "He has nothing to gain from getting us in trouble. He knows we will leave when he wants the house. I don't know who would gain from telling. I asked Beppe, and he didn't know. Who knows about our affairs, about the account?"

They sat quietly for a few moments sifting through the possibilities. Her mother was asking for reassurance. This was an important conversation. Sarah felt grown up. Her parents' circle of friends included reporters, diplomats, Jewish refugees, and Japanese artists. They wouldn't know about the Swiss account. Then Sarah understood. It was not Sensei or any of her parents' friends. It was Beppe. Beppe. Since her mother's pregnancy, he'd become bitter; he wanted to punish, his acid tone making the house miserable, filling each corner with hate.

Mama began speaking again, this time whispering in an excited voice. "I have a secret. Promise not to tell?" Sarah nodded, relieved the worry lines on Mama's face dissolved into flushed happiness. "Your father is involved in a very big deal," her mother said and nervously glancing at the door, drew her close. "It's the land deal," she said.

"Land?" Sarah asked.

"Yes," her mother answered. Her father had patiently purchased adjacent lots in the forest until he had amassed a parcel large enough to sell. "It will be a new town," her mother announced. "The town will help Japan grow. It will help us, too. We will use the money to make a new life in America."

Sarah felt blood drain from her face. She tried to smile, but her lips would not move. She blinked back the tears. Beppe had laughed at her father's land deals, and she had laughed with him. The woods would never change. Thick bamboos had survived American bombs, explosions that had demolished twenty-six Japanese cities. The forest, a reminder of the past, of the soul of Japan, would remain always.

She liked Scalia best when he spoke of the forest, winking at her as if he and she alone knew about the kami spirit that allowed them to fuse with nature. Kami of stones, moss, trees, lakes, and waterfalls entered their soul. Kami spirits created empathy in language, body gesture, and concern for others. No foreigner could understand that.

"Just a couple of days and it will be done," her mother whispered. "Don't mention it to your father. He wants to tell you himself. Don't tell O'ba. She doesn't like change. She is very fond of you. But I am so happy. It's great news."

Her mother spoke of how the secret Zurich bank account, loaded with gold, protected the family. Sarah mustn't talk about that either. Her mother moved closer, and they stayed clasped like dragonflies hovering over the lake, fastened together unto death. "It's all so complicated, Sarah-chan, this business of not having a country."

Sarah closed her eyes. She didn't want to hear about the forest. If she hadn't seen the green men in tractors, if they hadn't chased her down the beach, yelling as if they owned the lake and the trees, she wouldn't have believed it. They could never really demolish miles of fields, trees, and the broad lake. It was too big. Impossible.

She felt tired. The baby pushed, and her mother murmured about being stateless. As their bodies swayed, her mother's uncertainty became her own. Her mind churned with questions. Was O'ba right? Am I being used by Sensei to snare Ryuzu? Does Ryuzu not really love me? Am I just a stupid foreigner? Is all an illusion?

Things were changing fast, too fast.

FACE

The next day Noriko screamed, "Saburo," and pointed toward a grove of trees. There, amid green bamboos, Saburo stood, arms folded, looking disdainfully at her friends.

"Do you have candy?" Michio shouted. "We will let you play if you have candy."

"I don't need your silly games," Saburo said.

"Go away," Ryuzu shouted. "We don't need your American junk."

Saburo shouted back, "I'm samurai. While you play, I steal boxes and boxes of American stuff to sell on the black market. American people pay. They pay and pay. Americans are ridiculous, fat people who have too much of everything, and you are stupid, thin people who have lost their way."

"You're a fool," Ryuzu yelled. "We threw American soldiers into the Imperial Moat. American bases will leave Japan, and the black market will vanish. You will have nothing. We are changing history."

"Changing history!" Saburo shouted. "I am history!"

Ryuzu raised his fists. Saburo followed suit. They faced each other with crazed expressions, a look that meant a fight to the death. Saburo spat, and the wad glistened against the dark dirt. Ryuzu and her friends spat, slowly pursing their lips and collecting their saliva until it burst out, thick and white. They were quiet, the shining sputum between them.

Then Saburo spoke with care, imitating their screams of joy. "If I bring candy, you make me your leader. What kind of Japanese are you? No real Japanese would behave this way." His eyes blazed. He turned abruptly and stepped into the shadows. Her friends waited, mumbling that he was a coward. Ryuzu laughed. They had defeated him. It was over.

But just as she imagined Saburo gone, he was back, this time wearing black, American jeans and shirt. He hooked his thumbs in his belt. "Aren't you happy today?" Saburo asked. "Wasn't the candy enough?"

"What do you want?" Ryuzu demanded. He threw off his American shirt and kicked it toward Saburo. "Here are your American things. We don't need them. We were playing with you. The game is over." The others discarded the same. Soon the dirt was littered with tangled material, silver chocolate kisses, buckled belts, and plastic lunch boxes. They formed a circle, their arms spread, feet moving quickly, kicking the discarded clothes and shouting, "America, America."

Saburo's gaze never left Ryuzu. "You know what I want?" Saburo asked in a deadly tone. "You know why I bother with all of you?"

"Because you're crazy!" Ryuzu shouted.

Saburo dismissed Ryuzu's remark with a toss of his head. His face relaxed. He swayed as if singing a song. His body, hypnotic and mesmerizing, caught them off guard. It beckoned and dismissed—cobra-like—putting them under his spell. All eyes were on him. "I want Sarah-chan," he said finally with a smile. "I want her to come to me."

The dance stopped.

Saburo stood still and repeated his request, his low tone explaining that Sarah took an oath that she would always be his friend. "She promised to be one with me forever," he said. "Forever. You remember that yubikiri, Sarah-chan?" He held up his small finger.

Sarah remained still.

"Sarah-chan is with us," Ryuzu said. "She is part of us."

Sarah knew from Ryuzu's tone, confident and full of emotion, that he had finally forgiven her. It had happened yesterday as they lay stuffed with chocolate, giggling on the grass with Ryuzu's arm around her and Taro on top. She had rested her head against his shoulder, and he'd whispered her name again and again until the gentleness in his voice made her weep.

Still Saburo's words resonated. The savagery of Ryuzu's attack, her wounded pride, and the painful cuts remained. Ryuzu had led the assault and even the little ones had put weight behind their thrusts. The inside group, always just out of reach, was tiring. She wanted to assert herself, to tell them that she was a person, one with self-respect who knew right from wrong. Reason told her Ryuzu would now stand by her; she was his true friend, and he loved her, but reason was not enough. She hated her need of them, a want that made her bend to their will, while they could turn on her, even Ryuzu.

Saburo was different. Saburo didn't care that she was gaijin. He understood they were both outsiders, not Japanese and not really foreign and had to make their own way, living by their wits, creating strategies for survival. They had taken an oath in blood, ubikiri, a bond, a sacred trust that would last forever. Now they would honor their promise. In time Ryuzu would know that he had made a grave error, a mistake that no promise could fix. He would understand she mustn't be tampered with.

Memories of recent insults, layered like multicolored limestone, piled one on another. Saburo's presence gave her courage. His raised hand offered the freedom of childhood, a rebirth, and a way to create something different. His demand was simple. She only had to walk across the bare ground to the edge of the grove. Hand in hand they would disappear into the forest. Her face flushed with anticipation. Excitement centered in the pit of her stomach, an urgency that she had never known. She felt herself spin out of control. She no longer thought of consequence. Her friends' whispers sounded loud, calling her, reminding her that she was part of them, but she paid no attention.

She pushed Ryuzu's hand away.

Ryuzu pleaded. His voice filled with longing, pulling her against him, his forehead touching her own. He spoke of Hiro's death, apologizing and saying it had not been her fault. He explained that the crowd, smoke, and police bully clubs made him crazy. He had never been so afraid. She mustn't join Saburo, evil, corrupted by the black market, and America, Japan's worst enemy. "Saburo is not like you; he is not one of us. He has no place in Japan."

Ryuzu tried to grab her, but she went ahead. Ryuzu called, "Sarah-chan!" She kept going. Her friends took up the chorus, their voices shrieking across the space, echoing through the trees. It was the same tone when they called for her by the back gate, voices rising like the crickets' shriek: "Sarah-chan."

It was not far, yet it felt she was traveling a great distance. With each step she broke the rules of the group, shaming them, a breach of trust so public that there was no going back. Most of all, with each step she humiliated Ryuzu. He had claimed her as part of his small band, and this time it wasn't Sensei who made him do it; this time it was because he loved her, feelings he'd admitted publicly.

At last she stood in front of Saburo. The scar on his forehead shone in the sunlight. His skin, like pale ivory, glowed in the sun, and his black hair curled. His leg muscles tightened, and his shirt, open to the waist, revealed his broad chest. He wore a thin, gold necklace around his neck. She wanted to touch it. She returned his bold look. He stepped back. She advanced. He looked straight at her, long and hard.

His eyes narrowed, icy and distant and his lips pursed. He raised his hand as if to push her away. It must be a mistake, she thought. She had broken with Ryuzu and come all the way across the clearing, a long crossing, and one that would change her life. He must know that there was no going back. She stepped closer.

"Why?" she asked as she reached to touch him. "Saburo-chan," she said as he turned away. Sarah repeated his name again as if it would bring him back. Saburo stepped aside. He was no longer handsome but looked foxlike, light on his feet, crafty and wild. She came toward him, reminding him of their promise, their ubikiri oath to be forever true. Saburo hesitated. He closed his eyes. She repeated their history. She spoke quickly with urgency. She babbled, the words a torrent of pleas. Saburo moved close. His face softened. He touched her shoulder. Then with one turn, he disappeared into the forest.

The ground was bare. Gone. Her skin was cold. She stepped unsteadily to the edge of the clearing. There was no sign of Saburo. The trees surrounded the forest like a dark wall. He'd slipped between the tall bamboos, merging with the trees and the moss, leaving only a faint shadow, a footprint of his passing. She could follow, but it would end in nothing. Her friends knew it, too. The forest was silent with understanding.

Ryuzu's public declaration of love was her disgrace. A true friend would have never let this happen, a true friend would have protected his face, and his pride. She should have left. There were alternatives. Michio's suspicions were correct. They could never trust her. A person who didn't understand honor. A self-loathing took hold. O'ba was right. Nothing good could come of this. Saburo had broken the group, destroyed what she loved, and she had helped him. She was always an outsider. She should have listened.

Sarah turned back, but her friends were already walking stiff-backed down the path toward their village. Don't leave, her mind said. Don't. Her throat choked. She closed her eyes and willed their return. They must not go. She had been wrong. She called to them, her voice cracking, but they kept going. Ryuzu led. No one looked back, not Ryuzu, Noriko, Michio, Ichiro, or even Taro. Sarah watched until the bamboos closed around them and the last of them had vanished.

They will come for me, she thought, because they have no one else. They will return because they want to be different, special, with something to talk about. They are noticed because of me, and they are proud of it. I am everything to them. In a couple of days when we meet again by the boulder. I will bow, and they will bow. I will tease Ryuzu, he will smile, put his hand on my shoulder, and the games will resume.

But even with these thoughts, deep down, where the pain had lodged, Sarah knew all was an illusion.

SHAME

The next morning Scalia's determined footsteps paced above the dining room. Her parents ignored the noise, eating eggs, smoked salmon, black bread, and strong coffee. The steps grew louder.

"We have wonderful news, Sarah," her father said quickly. "The land deal is finished." He smiled brightly as he told her what she already knew. The parcels of forest he'd bought one by one had been sold. "Sarah, things are going to be fine now, really fine. We have already started clearing for apartments and factories."

Scalia's footsteps stopped. Her father kept talking. "Now we have enough money to buy a house, send you to the American International School, and to an American college. We will buy property in America and follow."

The footsteps started again. Sarah's mother reached across the table and squeezed her hand. "We have found a house, American-style, with a rose garden next to your bedroom. You'll like that, won't you, Sarah?"

Then banging, loud and demanding, filled the room. Her father's arms went around her, and he said, "You'll be happy in the new house. Oh, Sarah! You're going to love it. We know you hate the army school and the base."

"Our friends from Shanghai, the Cohens and Shapiros, send their children there," her mother added, looking nervously at her father, who kept talking, this time about the Jewish Club in Azabu, with a swimming pool, lovely garden, and large hall for events. Her father's voice grew stronger as he described the dark wood in the synagogue, like the one in Shanghai. "We will go there for high holidays," he finished.

"Beppe is mad," Sarah whispered and glanced at the ceiling

Her parents ignored her remark. They wanted her to share their excitement, a new life with money, friends, and a real business.

"When?"

"In three days," her father said loudly, looking at the ceiling as if he wanted Beppe to hear. Then he added, "The movers will pack this afternoon and again tomorrow. We'll leave the day after that."

Emiko entered with a tray of burned toast. "Emiko-san," Sarah's mother admonished. Hands on her hips, Emiko turned and slammed the dining room door.

"We can't leave Emiko-san and O'ba," Sarah whispered. "Emiko-san is scared of Beppe. He yells at her. She cries. O'ba loves us. She talks about you, about the baby."

"Beppe yells at everyone," her mother said. "Now that the occupation is over, this house and everything in it, even O'ba and Emiko, will be returned to Nishiguchi. Beppe will still rent the second floor, but we must leave. This is a chance to have our own home."

The room felt frozen. Sarah couldn't imagine a life without Emiko and O'ba. Who would scold her when she was late? Who would worry about her table manners? Who would care what her mother and father said at the dinner table? Who would tell her stories of Sensei's family, the war, Scalia, and Shanghai? Whom would she drink tea with after school? Then she thought of Ryuzu and her friends. She must apologize, ask for forgiveness, and beg for mercy.

"Sarah," her father said. "Don't look so pale. Please understand. These are Japanese matters. Emiko-san and O'ba must pay off family debts to the Nishiguchi family. It's their obligation. In Japan, obligation comes first."

"I don't want this," Sarah whispered. "I don't want any of it."

* * *

That afternoon workmen arrived with large, woven baskets, straw, and rope. Sarah followed them through the house. She picked up a coral octopus carving. "Can we take this?"

"That belongs to Beppe," her mother said.

Sarah nodded and slipped the octopus into a packing crate. Sarah hid ivory carvings: a bird, a woman clipping her toenails, an old witch, a netsuke of three romping puppies, a badger, a fox, and more. She would steal his collection, things he cherished, netsuke carvings he admired. By the time he realized his treasures were missing, everything would be in her new home. After a glass of wine, lonely and confused, he would look for a particular netsuke, one he knew well and liked to hold.

The second floor was silent.

This was her chance. She tiptoed up the stairs and opened the door. For a moment Sarah took in the wonder of Scalia: pearls, zebra skin, African swords, netsuke, okimon, wood, ivory, jade carvings, and the gold screen. Scalia's sanctuary, the colors, shapes, and lines, each piece collected with care, bought from refugees, at auctions, or received as gifts for favors, on shelves, on walls and tables, the space wild with beauty. The room, a temple to art with its ability to influence, made her humble.

In the center stood the Kannon, its slender body, with a soulful expression and hip thrust forward, reflected the afternoon light. She went directly to the statue and gathered it close. Her finger traced its downcast eyes, the full mouth, and long cheeks. Compassion etched in its features made her hold the statue close. The Kannon, more precious than everything combined, would be missed most.

"Sarah-chan, welcome."

Scalia stood naked but for a towel around his waist. Water dripped down his chest, arms, and legs. A purple bruise swelled above his nipple.

"I didn't mean to," Sarah whispered and set the Kannon back on the table.

"Don't you know I always have a bath at four? It's my favorite time—not quite day and not yet evening. A Japanese bath, that deep soak in my wood tub, calms me. It's Japan's contribution to civilization, don't you agree?"

Scalia blocked her exit.

"The Kannon is my favorite piece," Scalia said in a calm voice. "But you know that, don't you, Sarah-chan?" He smiled easily as if they were at the dining room table.

Thick hairs on his arms and belly, dense, ape-like, made her afraid. She darted toward the door, but he caught her elbow. "It was given to me by a Japanese officer. I never knew where he got it. You didn't ask questions like that in Shanghai. Not in those days."

"Why not?" Sarah asked, trying to sound as normal as Scalia, even though she had been caught redhanded and was standing next to his naked chest.

"Why not?" Scalia laughed. "Curious Sarah. Because Shanghai was a dangerous city in the middle of a war, full of soldiers, refugees, and spies. Everyone did what everyone had to do to survive. No one wanted anyone to know. People met at clubs and hotels. You kept it simple. You kept it direct: little talk about the war, little philosophy, and a few drinks. You might make a trade, one thing for another, done quickly. You never saw each other again."

Scalia stepped nearer. His fleshy body smelled of sandalwood, a raw smell of cut logs. His look, possessive and commanding, made her step back. He followed. He took another step. She moved to the right. He was there. His towel slipped, revealing a protruding navel. Water trickled across the floor. He was almost against her. There were dark hairs around his nipple. Sarah stared at the bruise.

"I had done a favor for the Japanese officer who gave me the Kannon. Japan is a country of favors, even when there is no war. Isn't that right, Sarah-chan? Just one little favor can create ties that grow thick, ropes that cripple. A little favor got that beautiful statue, but the statue, more valuable than the favor, created an imbalance. It meant there were more favors. That's Japan. One good turn leads to five. Then you are part of a team, doing things that you wouldn't have dreamed of. In the end you come to feel differently about yourself and everything. Another person, one you don't recognize. Of course your friends don't notice. You fool yourself into thinking that you haven't changed. You make excuses. But inside where it matters, you are less shocked by life, more flexible but often in an unpleasant way. But you already know that, don't you, Sarah? Clever, curious, beautiful Sarah; what do you dream about?"

Scalia's breath was on her cheek. "I have to go," she whispered at Scalia's naked chest.

"Why, Sarah-chan? Because you got caught?" Scalia pointed to a table crowded with the carvings: octopus, woman clipping her toenails, romping puppies, witch, dharma, fisherman, jade mouse, and others, things Sarah had taken.

"You've been naughty, Sarah-chan. Did you think I wouldn't notice? I'm a collector, and collectors notice everything. You're a collector, too. I have seen your Japanese doll collection—the emperor and empress, the sets of dolls for Girls' Day and more dolls that advertise plays. Many are Edo period. Did you know that? Of course you did. You have quite an eye. Your mother says that you bargain like a native. Dealers give you a good price because you are young and earnest and foreign. I had to look through all the baskets to find everything. What a bother, Sarah-chan."

"I didn't mean to," Sarah whispered, stiffening against his touch.

"But you did mean to, Sarah-chan. You wanted those things, and you took them. You are like me. That's how I knew it was you. Tamara or Alexander would never have dared. They would feel guilty. Yet they feel no remorse when they destroy the forest. They have no shame about replacing ancient bamboos, moss, and streams with concrete. It doesn't occur to them that the forest has a right to live, that it is full of kami spirits that link our souls to the forest. Its history of samurai is part of Japan. They simply chop down trees, think its progress, and feel good about it. You and I would never do that. You and I are different, aren't we?

"Never the trees. We love the forest and want it to stay lush and green. We love the bamboos, tall and straight, silver and bushy next to a blue sky. We love the noise and the silence. We want the scream of crickets by day and the croak of frogs at night. Our hearts stop when we see a boulder covered by moss, the wild flowers growing by a stream, and the dark earth between the bamboo groves. Isn't that right, Sarah-chan?"

She was silent. Scalia put his hand on her shoulder, warm and heavy, a deadening weight. He waited for her to answer.

"Yes," she whispered and knew it was true.

"You see, Sarah-chan, I know everything about you. I know you keep your makeup in your top drawer under your purple scarf. I know that you eat a rice ball after school. On Monday you wear a green skirt and on Tuesday a plaid one. On Wednesday a red shirtwaist dress. I sit in that chair and listen to the floorboards creak and follow you around the house. I know what you do every moment, Sarah-chan. And I know that you want Saburo. Do you know why he turned away?"

Sarah shook her head.

"Because of me," Scalia said. "I told him to back off. That's why. Do you believe me?" Sarah shook her head. "I have questions, and I expect you to tell me the truth, Sarah-chan. Do you hear me?"

She was silent.

"How did you meet Saburo-chan?" Scalia's voice asked in a calm, matter-of-fact voice.

"We are best friends from when he lived in the hut," Sarah whispered.

"That was a long time ago."

"I met him by the lake."

"Do your parents know that you went to the lake? That you met Saburo?" Sarah shook her head. "Do they know that he brings you and your friends clothes, toys, and candy?"

Sarah was silent. Scalia put his hand under her chin and turned her face up. She held her breath. His waxy fingers stroked her arm. She'd been bad. She had betrayed Ryuzu and her friends, stolen, spied, and stoned Americans. She didn't care about her baby sister, her swim in the polio lake, or her mother's feelings. O'ba told her that she was wicked, and O'ba was right. Now she was paying for all of it.

"I'm surprised you recognized each other at the lake. It's been a long time since you and Saburo played."

"Fumiko-san remembered."

"Of course. Good old Fumiko. She must have liked you and Saburo meeting again. That would have made Fumiko-san happy. Don't you agree?"

She must not answer. Her eyes fixed again on the bruise above Scalia's bare nipple, flat and red. At close range it looked like a shiriveled dried cherry. No one would save her. She was alone, isolated, and at Scalia's mercy. O'ba was busy in the kitchen, her parents were out, and the movers had left. She wanted to scream. Her throat felt paralyzed.

"My God, I'll miss you," Scalia said, his voice soft, his eyes hooded. "Beautiful Tamara. Serious Alexander. Curious Sarah. You're so much like your mama, your papa. Graceful. Dark hair. White skin. Snow White. Wood fairy. Princess. I dream of your mother in a sleigh on the Russian steppes, blanketed in fur with bells tinkering. I imagine her porcelain skin, smooth to touch, her long neck and tiny earlobes. I hear her laugher."

Scalia stroked her back. His face flushed, eyes glazed, a non-seeing look, one that made her realize he could do anything. Sarah wanted to tell him to stop, but her throat clogged. He pulled her gently against him.

His finger moved across her arm. Again and again like a feather, his cold touch numbed her skin. Except for his fingers stroking her arm and his hand sliding up her back, Sarah felt nothing. When his hand reached the nape of her neck, her lips tightened, and her tongue flattened against the roof of her mouth. She wanted to push him away. Her body would not move. Nothing worked. She did not exist.

A fly landed on Scalia's bruise, flexed its legs, advanced slowly across his chest. It stopped at his nipple, moving cautiously between hairs, its antennae scouting the skin and beads of perspiration. The fly searched, nose against Scalia's torso, his iridescent body made its way around the nipple, edging up his chest. The wings whirled. At once Scalia slapped. The fly dropped to the floor. With that hard smack, Scalia's eyes opened, and now alert, pushed her away.

Scalia gazed out the window as if he'd forgotten her presence. The afternoon sun cast a long shadow across the room, muting colors. She stood at a distance waiting for a chance to run. Scalia blocked the door. He turned toward the window and folded his arms. No one moved.

Etched against the shadows, Scalia's features, a black-and-white drawing, took her by surprise. It was Saburo. Scalia, imprinted in Saburo's high cheekbones, aquiline nose, broad forehead, and full lips, stopped her. His eyes, green at the center, were Scalia's eyes, his skin dusty with a light undertone was from Scalia, too. He had Scalia's sudden smile, roar of laughter, possessiveness, and immediacy with life. She had seen shades of likeness before, but this was irrefutable. Why had she not known? Scalia and Saburo, father and son, twined from the beginning. She tried to look away, but her eyes returned. Scalia. Saburo.

O'ba and her parents knew. That was why they let Fumiko and Saburo live in the hut. Now she understood why Scalia tolerated Saburo's presence, why he excused Fumiko's tantrums, gave them food, defended Saburo, and wanted them to play, to be best friends, and to love each other always. O'ba shook her head at the situation but gave Fumiko extra food and put up with her insults. O'ba was against Saburo and her becoming fast friends. Yes, now she understood. She was the only one who hadn't seen the obvious.

Scalia stepped aside, bowed, and waved her out. His smile was knowing and confident, the smile of a man who had made his point. Mission accomplished. This was her chance. At any moment Scalia might resume his dreamlike state, think of new insults, and bar her from leaving. His mood switched abruptly, moving swiftly from wise, worthy, and honorable to a place where anything was possible. The door was partially open, and taking a deep breath, she ran for it. On the landing she heard Scalia's laughter, loud and certain, a laugh of victory. She descended the stairs, Scalia's laughter following her to the bottom.

LOVE

Sarah sat on the veranda. Her heart thumped against her chest. She felt ill. Saburo and Scalia — father and son. Hopelessness took hold, a feeling that life was beyond her control. She looked across the bare earth to the hut's broken windows, crushed door, and broken floorboards. One side of the building sagged, and the wood siding lay scattered in large sheets on the ground. Wood, moldy green with white streaks, encased the veranda and roof. The change had happened gradually: one winter a broken window, the next summer the door caved in, and so on. Soon nothing would be left.

Suddenly she needed her routine, the comfort of the servants' quarters, and her cushion next to the *kotat-su*. She needed O'ba's stories about Sensei and Shanghai. She needed O'ba to massage her back. She needed O'ba to scold her for not combing her hair. She needed to hear Emiko's tales of snow and mountains and hot springs, tales that made her yearn for the North Country. Most of all she needed the comfort of being O'ba's special child, the one she protected.

Emiko's smile and the fresh smell of tatami greeted her. O'ba's gaze remained fixed on the table. Sarah took her usual seat by the kotatsu and poked the charcoal with long metal chopsticks.

"Your new house sounds pretty," O'ba said, snatching the metal chopsticks. "I hear that all the walls are painted white. That's how Americans like it. All white. No wood. You'll forget about this Japanese house, so shabby and difficult to repair, so many paper doors that need fixing. Japan should learn from America. Japan is poor and ignorant. We should change."

"I love this house," Sarah said cautiously. She hunched over the hibachi and parroted O'ba's description of the smell of tatami, the wooden beams, and the deep bath.

"This house is old," O'ba interrupted. "It's cold in the winter, and the bath is shabby. Your new house will have a heated bathroom with a white bathtub and a flush toilet. So convenient."

"I don't like hot bathrooms," Sarah said. "I like the smell of the wooden tub."

"Japan is poor," O'ba said. "Small and poor with cold bathrooms. You'll live in a warm, American-style house. The house will be painted white and carpeted, so your feet will never be cold. You will have a shower in your bathroom. Baths will no longer be necessary. You will go to America and and forget all about small, impoverished Japan." O'ba continued to speak rapidly about rich America and impoverished Japan, comparing America, strong and certain, to poor Japan.

Sarah interrupted: "I'll never leave Japan."

"But you will," O'ba said in a bright voice. "You are foreign, and foreigners are not wanted here. Foreigners have no place in Japan. They are here for a time and then move on. Your parents know that. They want to live in America."

"O'ba is in a bad mood, Sarah-chan," Emiko said.

"You should come back later."

Sarah took a deep breath. O'ba stabbed at the charcoal. Sparks flew. Hatred filled the room, a dark irritation with everything Sarah said, the way she moved, the clothes she wore. Sarah wondered if O'ba had ever loved her.

"I'll play with Ryuzu and my friends," Sarah said. "They'll be glad to see me."

"Your friends are gone," O'ba said solemnly. "You have no more friends, but never mind, you'll make new and better friends at your new, American school. Forget your poor Japanese playmates. They are cold and hungry. Not suitable for a rich foreign girl like you."

"My friends are not gone," Sarah answered carefully, wondering how much O'ba knew about the last few days. "I have to apologize. We had a fight, that's all. They would never really leave me. You don't understand anything. You're old and stupid."

"They are gone," O'ba said. "They have been sent away. You will never see them again. They were taken away in trucks."

"O'ba, yamete, stop," Emiko said.

"They're in the forest right now waiting for me. I'll go visit them and Saburo-chan, too."

"Saburo-chan is gone," O'ba continued in a rush. "He left with Fumiko-san for an apartment in the city. You will never see Saburo-chan or Fumiko-san or Ryuzu-kun again. All gone."

"I don't believe you!"

"Come with me," O'ba demanded. "It is you who doesn't know anything." O'ba, her face set rigid, a mask, mouth downturned and eyes narrow, rose and walked to the door. Sarah followed.

The sun was low in the sky. O'ba hurried down the street and across the vacant lot to the forest. Her friends weren't there, but Sarah knew where to find them. So did O'ba. They took the right fork at the boulder. The path narrowed. O'ba moved so fast that the green whizzed by, a blur of plants and trees. They crossed a small stream and then a meadow surrounded by the remains of a wall. O'ba slowed. The path widened. They had reached the village.

But the village was not there.

"Look," O'ba ordered. "Look what your father has done. He sold the village to a development company. It was demolished in two days. Look at what has made him so happy. This will pay for your new, American-style house, your new school, and your America."

The air smelled of raw dirt. Machines like the ones by the lake, like the ones in the city, loaded debris onto trucks. Shovels, forks, and lifts were creating Japan's new subways, bridges, offices, aqueducts, and factories. They worked day and night on boarded streets lit with great overhanging lamps. Under the boards was a subway system that would link Tokyo. The banging never stopped. It was Tokyo's way, of progress, of the future. Now trucks dumped great loads of earth into the lake. Whistles blew, and lights spotlighted the water. The beach, loaded with moving machines and men with whistles, looked like a highway.

She wanted them to stop. It was her lake! It was her forest! They had no right. It was where she imagined, played, loved her friends. It was a place where nothing could change, would change. How had this happened? Everything in ruin, piles of sand, dirt, and tress dumped on the sand. The muddy water, choked with silt, stones, and debris, looked like a vast dump. O'ba was still talking, but she paid no attention, instead gazing at the shoreline—metal and stone heaped on flattened earth, the mud dark and unyielding, everything destroyed and broken.

"Where are your friends, Sarah-chan?" O'ba asked. "Scalia-san would never have done this. Your father planned this—years of going through records, locating survivors of each family, knowing they had nothing and offering them nothing. That's what he was doing at the office, buying and buying until there was nothing left." Her voice thickened as she spoke of little Masaru and Sensei running through the forest, playing flutes, swimming in the lake, about fireflies dancing among the water reeds and the laughter of families gathered at sunset on a summer evening.

Sarah covered her ears, blocking the sound of the tractors and O'ba. Where were Ryuzu and all the rest? Had Ryuzu taken his books? Had Taro and Ichiro and the little ones cried? Did Noriko have her doll? Was Michio scared? Did he have his beetle cage? Had they been loaded on trucks in the middle of the night, sleepy and bewildered? How would they live? Did Sensei know? Why hadn't he stopped this? Didn't his family own the forest and the village? Hadn't he told them that again and again?

Then Sarah understood. The realization came slowly. It was a truth that tied the story together with an invisible thread, a tie that connected and made sense. Her father could not have done this alone. He didn't read Japanese. He didn't know the laws. He didn't know how to find people. Sensei. Sensei had contacted his old neighbors now living in small flats or under bridges. Sensei arranged to have the land sold to her father, even as he lectured about the kami spirits and the Japanese way. Sensei destroyed the past to make way for a new Japan—Sensei's Japan with Sensei's friends in power. Nagatacho and politics had sanctioned this as they had all construction in Japan. Sensei often said impermanence was the Japanese way. She hadn't understood till now what that meant. Sensei's Japan had been a façade, an illusion. Sachiko knew. Ryuzu knew. Even Saburo knew. Only she believed, never imagining such a betrayal possible.

"O'ba," Sarah pleaded. "O'ba."

O'ba started walking back along the path to their house, back to Nishiguchi's house.

"O'ba," Sarah called again. Her eyes hurt, and tears ran down her cheeks. She stuttered in fits and starts.

O'ba hesitated, turned, and slowly walked back. Sarah stepped toward her, wanting O'ba's arms around her, needing that familiar hug and low laugh. But O'ba's face was creased with fury. Her anger was so apparent that Sarah stopped in her tracks.

"O'ba, please," Sarah pleaded. But it was over. She no longer had O'ba or Ryuzu, friends, or Saburo. All she cherished had disappeared. She could not think or be. Shame entered her soul. It diminished her. Her being was at stake. Gone was illusion and with it all hope.

O'ba raised her hand, and Sarah closed her eyes, preparing for the blow, the crack hard across her cheek, a hit that she deserved. She would endure that for all her father had done, for all the deception. It didn't matter that Scalia had touched her. She deserved that. Her dream had ended. Scalia was right. She should have scolded her father and she should have set things right. She was responsible for this. She stepped forward.

But O'ba's fingers ran gently down the side of her face, brushing away her tears, stroking her cheeks, and smoothing her forehead. O'ba lifted her hair, touched the back of her neck, and massaged her shoulder blades. She murmured soothing sounds. O'ba's rough skin roamed over her, memorizing the outlines of her face, neck, and back, as if she could never let her go. Her fingers lingered on her cheekbone, the shape of her lips, and the dimple in her cheek. She caressed her, kneading her flesh with the palm of her hand. "Sarah-chan," she murmured, and again, "Sarah-chan."

Sarah closed her eyes. "Gomen," she returned. "Gomen, 'sorry,' gomen."

The noise of machines and the smell of raw earth disappeared. Sarah leaned into O'ba, their foreheads touching. Surrounded by O'ba's thick flesh, all disappointment faded, evaporating like a morning mist and filling her once more with hope.

"Sarah-chan, please don't forget us," O'ba said softly. "Sarah-chan, my girl, my only girl."

PART THREE

Tokyo: Spring 1958

AMERICAN INTERNATIONAL SCHOOL

Alan Buttericks, the teacher at the American International School she had grown to cherish, had grown up in Japan. In their first meeting, Buttericks spoke in Japanese, choosing his words carefully, asking about her family and previous school. Her voice choked when she mentioned Ryuzu, the deserted village, broken trees, and piles of mud. After a long while, Buttericks pulled out a picture of him in a summer ukata, small and freckled with a wide smile, surrounded by Japanese boys dressed the same. Since the seventh grade, she had often checked in with Buttericks. Today was no different.

"College," Buttericks said as she stood in front of his desk. "As one of our best graduates, you will have choices."

"Thanks for writing my Stanford recommendation," Sarah said softly. "Thanks for everything." Buttericks's sad, deep-set eyes stirred her. Her classmates sneered at his worn jacket and mismatched socks, at the way he strode back and forth in front of the class, threw back his head, laughed too hard at his own jokes. Sarah felt at home with his humor.

The American International School was a culture of transplants, with students from thirty-five countries, sons and daughters of diplomats, American businesspeople, Jewish and Chinese refugees, Korean gangsters. It was its own world and was determined to remain so. A stone wall separated the school from the tangle of small streets, the press of people, and all things Japanese. Unlike the army school, there were no guards, fences, or guns, yet it was a fortress.

At school Sarah's friends weren't American or Japanese, but were a "floating world," as she described them, uncommitted, coming from places—Shanghai, Harbin, Taiwan, Seoul—they barely remembered and immigrating to places they could not understand. They mocked the dominant American culture of cheerleaders, football, grade point averages, and SAT scores. All sought help with their studies. By the end of her senior year, Sarah was the center of a tight circle of misfits.

"Any school would be proud to have you," Buttericks continued in a low, intimate tone. "Talk to me when you're ready to decide. If you're not sure, I'll try to help. I favor colleges on the East Coast, but if you want Stanford, I'll help."

"Why the East Coast?" Sarah asked, trying to be conversational.

"Hard work and sound values," Buttericks returned.

It didn't sound like much fun, but Sarah nodded as if they were on the same team. Buttericks must never know that tonight she, his prize student, would ride on Eddie Wei's cycle, let Eddie fondle her breasts, stroke her bottom, and plunge his thick tongue down her throat.

"I'll think about the East Coast," she said, rising.

"You will do prelaw?" Buttericks asked. She sat back down. "You'll do well in law. You think like a lawyer. Take a look at my thesis on Yukichi Fukuzawa, the Thomas Jefferson of Japan. A great man, an honest man, one who believed in Western law. Read it." He handed her his thesis.

"I read Fukuzawa's diary," Sarah replied, remembering Ryuzu hated Fukuzawa for supporting the Sino-Japanese War and wanting Japan to dominate Asia.

"Then you know," Buttericks said. "With your knowledge of Japan and Japanese, you should come back and be part of fixing things."

Buttericks was a missionary after all. Did he really think that Japan wanted to be fixed? Did he think Japan wanted Western courts? "Japanese are emotional, not logical," Sensei had insisted. "Disputes are settled outside courts through relationships. That is the Japanese way."

"Your midterm will be on Monday," Buttericks continued in a comforting voice. "Soon you'll be off to America. Every time I've returned to the States, it's been a shock."

Sarah was immediately curious about what kind of shock it was, but Eddie was parked at the corner, impatiently revving his Honda. "I have to meet someone."

"That's OK," Buttericks said, reaching for a stack of exams, signaling that it was safe for her to go.

Moments later Sarah peered at the bathroom mirror, dabbed her lips, highlighted her cheekbones, and outlined her eyes. Her pale skin, deep, blue-black eyes, full lips, and glossy, dark hair resembled her father's. But her bearing, graceful, head high, her liquid movement at ease with her surroundings, was from her mother. Young men whistled, and older men gave her long looks. Friends wanted to share her grace, her excitement, and her imagination—all of it. She told stories, tales from her childhood—Shanghai opium dens, spies on trains in Siberia, Chinese warlords, ancient Samurai, and a submarine laden with pearls—that made them yearn for more.

Yet still haunted by the past, she often slipped away from her chattering friends to the library, where hidden by rows of books, invisible to the world, she sat for long periods. The solitude, the still surroundings, the musty paper, kept her whole. This pensive part of her, reflected in her eyes and still expression excited interest. But Sarah was largely oblivious to the impression she made on others. Here amongst racks of books, she dreamed of another Sarah, another time, a freedom that had disappeared. Tears rolled down her cheeks. She skipped class, encased in a mothy cocoon, until the last bell rang.

During these moments her friends tried to engage her with gossip fell silent. Her friends engaged her with gossip, but she remained aloof, the conversation diffusing to a blur. Eddie jokingly called her "the black hole," sucking in light but giving nothing in return. She smiled, but the memory of Saburo and Ryuzu made her shy away from real friendship. She no longer longed to be part of a group or have a best friend. That was over. She depended on no one.

Eddie was no exception. He didn't understand obligation or shame. In short, Eddie didn't know Japan and barely knew himself. His Japanese mother lived in seclusion, and his Taiwanese father was busy. Eddie bragged that his father's fortune was from operating a prewar billiards parlor for Japanese naval officers. In lieu of debt, the officers allowed Eddie's father to smuggle amphetamines in naval ships from Taiwan. Now Eddie's father, rich and powerful, owned an island near Tokyo stuffed with a collection of Buddhist statues. Sarah raised her collar, unbuttoned the top three buttons on her blouse, and left the building.

"You're late," Eddie said impatiently. Sarah slid close, shoved Buttericks's thesis between them, and pressed her legs against Eddie's thighs.

"Let's go," she said and grabbed onto Eddie's leather jacket. The cycle roared, and spreading her arms wide, she felt a rush between her legs. Soon they were on the outskirts of the city, racing along paths between flooded rice fields, the air rich with Dogwood and mud.

Ahead, eight bikes belonging to her classmates and *Keiobotchan* were lined up beneath an abandoned bridge. The boys wore hachimaki bandannas across their foreheads, and the girls, dressed in short skirts and tight sweaters, rode behind.

No one spoke.

The boys revved their engines, the girls wound their arms around the boys, and Eddie pointed across boulders to a tall pine a few kilometers away. "Banzai!" Eddie yelled. The bike took off, skidding between boulders, stones glancing off the exhaust. Eddie bent low, shifted into third, and screamed, "Banzai!" at Mohamed, the Turk, who pulled ahead.

"Banzai!" the cry was taken up by others.

Eddie sped, grass whipped Sarah's leg, and Rita, riding behind Mohamed, spread her arms wide, so wide that she blocked the lane. Eddie braked, the bike skidding sideways at a dangerous right angle. The riverbank and boulder circled beneath an almost night sky. Sarah's world rotated, Eddie on the left and then the right, fast then slow. Eddie shouted. Sarah screamed. Air rushed under her skirt, pebbles sprayed her leg, the world tipped, and the Honda moved from under her. Everything went black.

Eddie was above her. A sharp pain shot from her knee to her chest.

"Can you talk?" he asked.

Sarah nodded.

"You've been out," Eddie said, smoothed back her hair and wrapped her in his jacket. Sarah shook, saw double, and threw up. Eddie held her gently until she stopped shaking, righted the cycle, and drove slowly back to Tokyo.

Hours later Sarah approached her house. The accident was a close call. Eddie could not afford police involvement, questions that would make his gangster father furious. The others felt the same. No one must know. Even the *Keiobotchan* worried.

Her parents stood in the hall. "What happened to your knee?" her mother asked.

"I'm tired," Sarah responded.

Her parents didn't want to know about her friends, motorbike rides, her hot trysts with Eddie, cheating, or smokes in the soba shop. They wanted assurance of acceptance into a good school. If she brought up the past, the house, O'ba, Scalia, they changed the subject; if she asked questions about business, they excused themselves. They wanted things to be pleasant.

"Emily Chan's mother called," her father said. "She was concerned, thought Emily might be here."

Sarah was silent. Her mother's face, always beautiful, was thin with worry. "Were you on a motorcycle? Did you have an accident?"

"No, I fell at school."

They stared, faces tight with disapproval, their tone full of condemnation. Her head pounded. The pressure was on. She was their passport to America, a ticket they counted on. She must get good grades, play with her little sister, Vera, and be polite at supper. Her father's face reddened with anger. "I was worried," he said and pulled her into a hug.

"What's this?" her mother asked.

"It's Buttericks's thesis on Fukuzawa. He wants me to read it."

"Mr. Buttericks believes in you," her mother said in a voice that suggested Buttericks would solve any problem, "and we need his help to get you into a good college, one that is near San Francisco. Stanford." Her voice dropped to a whisper as if somebody was listening. "It's so important."

Sarah broke away. "I do what you want."

"Last week," her mother continued, "Beppe threatened to tell the American Embassy that your father was a Communist unless I agreed to a trip to the Inland Sea. He sounds insane. We will leave Japan soon, Sarah, sooner than we thought—right after graduation before Beppe can interfere."

"Were you a Communist?"

"Socialist," her father answered.

It was rare that her parents mentioned Scalia. She wanted more, but they turned away. Was Beppe's accusation true? Sarah wondered. The American school had just fired Miss Murray, a math teacher, for making anti-McCarthy remarks. It was possible that her parents had been members. More than possible, she thought, remembering late-night parties ending with "The Internationale," passionate voices ringing through the house.

Her parents brought Sarah close, rocking back and forth, the smell of lilac perfume and tobacco mingling, a scent that calmed her as a child, making her feel warm and protected. They assumed she wanted what they wanted. In their arms she would have told them about her life if they'd ask. It was a familiar wish, one in which she could be transparent, truthful, and still loved. But her parents did not ask. The gentle sway of their bodies, moving like a large wave, calmed her. Her mind cleared. She wanted to help. Vera clung to her, her small voice demanding a goodnight story. Her parents depended on her being top in the class. They hovered over her report card, smiled when she mentioned Buttericks, and bragged about her accomplishments.

In the warmth of their embrace, her terror was transformed into a promise, a vow to look after them, a shield that would get them to America and insure their happiness. Yet the shock of the accident remained. One minute she'd been on top of the world, with the wind in her face and the smell of Eddie's leather all around, and the next, nothing. She had been careless with herself. Eddie and the others were afraid too, touching her tentatively as if she did not exist. She felt adult. Naïve and trusting, her parents were sure America would fulfill their dreams. She could not fail them. That promise gave her direction, a pledge she would keep, one that put her in control. Yes, she was the master. It was up to her. O'ba was right. She was responsible for the family, for her small sister Vera, for her parent's dreams. She must make up for all the people who had died, relatives who had not made it to the safety of Japan.

They were not asking much. It was what she wanted as well. No more cheating, rides on motorcycles, or smokes in the soba shop. She would distance herself from Eddie, too. The library would be her sanctuary. She was safe there. In two short months, the family would leave for America. What was left of her Japanese life would disappear as if it had never been. The old house, the forest, and her friends had already faded. She must be the girl they wanted.

DILEMMA

Buttericks stacked a pile of blue midterm exam booklets on the corner of his desk. He smiled at Sarah. She smiled.

"Sit next to me," Emily Chen whispered and took Sarah's hand. "I worried about the accident. You look OK. My mother called your mother. I got into plenty of trouble, but I didn't squeal. What did they say about your knee?"

Sarah didn't answer. Her mother had taken her to the bathroom, soaked the wound, picked out the stones, rubbed iodine on the cut, and bandaged it. Her parents tucked her into bed. When the door closed, she heard worried mumbling.

"We need your help," Emily and Suzie whispered. "I don't understand any of it. We love you."

Rita and Eddie took seats behind her. Bill, a football star and the leader of an American, anti-cheating, vigilante group, scanned the class. Bill's father was an oil executive, sat on the school board, and was responsible for firing Miss Murray. Last month Bill caught Johnnie, a Chinese refugee, cheating. He bragged that the note in Johnnie's file would keep him from getting into an American university. Johnnie left the school.

Sarah glanced nervously at Buttericks as he distributed blue books. Eddie whispered her name, but she waved him away. The test began. Sarah focused, filling in the blanks on alliances between Austria, Hungary, Russia, Germany, France, and England, moving on to the "what if" essay. Rita and Eddie kicked from behind, but Sarah kept on, line by line, paragraph after paragraph, theory supported by particulars. The classroom faded; she wrote quickly, creating a Europe connected by competing treaties. Finished, she closed her eyes but kept her pencil upright as if still working. She ignored Eddie. Emily bent over her paper. Suzie was quiet. The period would end without event. Sarah felt calm, content–a new start.

Emily's hand grabbed quickly, so quickly that Sarah didn't have time to respond. Sarah moved to retrieve her blue book, but Buttericks looked up, his gaze roaming the classroom, and fixed on her. Sarah's heart pounded. She returned his stare, smiled, and Buttericks went back to his book.

The clock ticked.

Her paper passed from Emily to Rita to Suzie, all writing as fast as they could.

Five minutes.

Two minutes.

Eddie had it. His body hunched over his desk. She hissed his name, but he ignored her and kept working. Her foot slammed against his ankle. Still he did not respond. The clock was almost on the hour. She lunged, knocked Eddie's books on the floor and reached for her test, but Eddie's hand, flat and steady, remained on her book. The bell rang. Eddie leaned back, his chair toppled, and he lay sprawled on the floor behind her. Her blue book was on her desk. Sarah took a deep breath. It was over. She tried to steady her hands.

She was about to pass her blue book forward

when, Buttericks boomed, "I've seen cheating today!" in a thunderous voice. He stood straight and slammed his fist on his desk. "There is a cheater in this classroom!"

The class froze; the room was utterly silent.

"I'm not going to say who you are," Buttericks said. "You know who you are. Cheating is not just a crime against everyone in your class; it's a crime against yourself. Truth is critical to a civilized life. It's the basis for American justice. I expect you to admit your crime. You must. I'll be in my office waiting."

The Americans scanned the faces of her friends, their eyes narrow with fury. Bill whispered, and they marched out. The rest lowered their heads and followed.

By the end of the afternoon, eighteen of the thirty students had confessed, verbally or with a short note. They came alone, one by one, slipping in to see Buttericks between classes, before lunch, and after school. Buttericks did not lecture, but nodding, wrote each name on a card. The school buzzed with rumors: late-night meetings between administrators and parents, parents fighting with their children, parents bribing teachers, board meetings, and Bill and his vigilante group reporting suspicious acts. At dinner there was no mention of cheating, although her parents had attended a school meeting.

The next day Sarah received a hand-written note on yellow office paper. Buttericks wanted to see her in his classroom after lunch.

"Thanks for coming," Buttericks said, looking even more disheveled than usual. He gestured to the seat beside him. "I called you because I'm disappointed. Your class," he said, pausing and shaking his head. "I just don't know about your class. Miss Smith, Mr. Thomas, and I have been talking all morning. Smith thinks her math exams have been tampered with. Thomas says that someone has riffled through his desk and changed grades on the English exam. I thought communication was pretty good. I trusted the students; I thought they trusted me."

He was asking for approval, words that would restore confidence and support his role as a mentor. Buttericks was reaching out. She was his friend. He had the hangdog look of a small boy begging for understanding. They shared a background, foreigners who had come of age in Japan, strangers who spoke the same language and knew life in the same way. She wanted to help, remembering his gentleness and the long hours spent after school discussing politics, America, and childhood memories of Japan in a mixture of English and Japanese. The silence lengthened, and the clock ticked.

"They do trust you," Sarah finally said.

"Then why are they all cheating? They're stealing."

"They don't mean to," she answered cautiously in an adult voice, aware from his incredulous expression that she was on tentative footing. "Mostly they are scared. They help each other."

"Help each other? How is cheating going to help anyone?"

"To get to America, to attend an American college," she said simply, as if explaining the obvious to a small child. Buttericks took a deep breath. Sarah pressed on, describing the Chinese and Korean students who didn't speak enough English to pass their courses and who didn't know Japanese either. Even if they knew Japanese, Japanese law prohibited foreigners from attending Japanese national universities. "They can't get an education or work in Japan. American colleges are passports. Without that they'll be stuck here with nothing."

Buttericks listened but continued to appear lost, the look of a small, disappointed boy. With each sentence Sarah gathered courage, helping him understand about being stateless, about the fear of deportation, about her own family. Her great-aunt Amelia, marched to a forest outside Riga with her baby, husband, and mother, all stripped and shot, Uncle Alex murdered by Bolsheviks. The many cousins, some barely a year old, killed. Now she would make him know it, too. When Buttericks understood, she would invite him home to play chess with her father, discuss American liberty, taste her mother's stroganoff, and read stories to Vera. It was up to her.

Buttericks would be on her side. Her imagination soared. Her mother was right—with Buttericks anything was possible. There would be meetings between teachers, parents, and students. Conversation would create a community, a dialogue between the Americans and the others. Together they would abolish the secret student files—no more fear, no more incriminating letters sent to faraway schools. They would give students advice and build a new system, one that fostered trust. Yes, it was all so easy now that they had begun to talk.

"You don't cheat, do you, Sarah?"

The question hung in the air. The clock ticked. A bell rang. A student yelled. Buttericks tapped his pencil on the desk. Tap. Tap. The sound made it hard to think. Students were just outside the door. Tap. Tap. She wanted to speak of history, displacement, and survival. Tap. Tap. She wanted him to understand this chance to make things right. She wanted him to be on her side, on the side of the displaced, on the side of right. Now this. What could she say? What did cheating mean? Buttericks sat erect, prim, waiting, and expecting the right answer, the only answer, validation that they were on identical teams.

She must smile and nod. She needed to. She had to. It was critical. She knew it, and he knew it. Before any conversation could occur, she must convince him they were on the same side with the same values. He expected that. Yet her head stayed motionless. It would not move. She thought of her mother's thin, worried face, of being the girl her parents wanted, of becoming an American lawyer, and of Scalia's threats. Her mind went to the stories of survival, outwitting naïve people like Buttericks to make good. She admired the tellers. They were right. It was crucial.

A bell rang. Students yelled. Footsteps. They would stream into the classroom. She must answer quickly. Her eyes widened. Her face felt paralyzed. The clock ticked. Buttericks nodded encouragement. He wanted her in his corner, and she wanted to be there. He was kind, spoke Japanese, and was funny. It would take just a nod, a quick signal of understanding, and an agreement that would cement their relationship. In moments the second bell would ring, the students would enter, and the room would fill. But the bell did not ring. Not yet. The clock ticked. Buttericks waited, his eyes wide.

"Oh, my God," Buttericks muttered. "Not you, Sarah. Tell me, not you."

The bell rang.

Nod, she thought, dismiss his worry with a wave of the hand. Bend and all would be saved. Bend and Buttericks would love her. It was easy, so easy. But she couldn't. Her stubborn streak, set and determined, emerged with terrifying energy. She would never agree. Never. The chair rattled, and she stood, holding on for balance, her hands shaking. The horror on Buttericks's face filled her with dread. It was devastating, a look of self-hate, anger at loving the wrong person and rage for believing the wrong story. He had written her recommendation, stuck up for her, advised her. She had betrayed him. He would never forgive.

She slowly backed out of the room, walked down the hall past Bill and the other Americans, conscious that one minute she was giving Buttericks advice and the next she was at his mercy. Where was the person who moved easily from one world to the next and left each smiling? Ryuzu, O'ba, Saburo, Scalia, Sensei, and her parents all wanted Sarah. She laughed at their jokes, bowed with Japanese, shook hands with foreigners, and left each wishing for more. She sensed what people wanted to hear and what they could hear. Had she forgotten?

She must convince Buttericks that cheating never entered her mind, that cheating was the same as stealing, that she agreed. Her vow to protect the family was important. Her stubborn, childish self must be buried. Explanations crowded her mind, making her dizzy. Why would she cheat when she knew the answers? He would agree. Why would she cheat when she prided herself on being the best? He would agree. Why would she cheat when her SAT scores were tops. Again he would agree.

She would enter his classroom, walk to his desk, and tell him that she had misunderstood, that she'd been too stunned by the question to respond. He would listen because he wanted to believe, because then he would be right. Within minutes life would return to normal, and they would speak softly in Japanese, smile, and laugh at the same things.

She stopped.

Next to Headmaster Williams's office stood a man in a white hat and suit with an ascot. Beside him stood a tall boy dressed in black. Headmaster Williams shook hands with each, as if they had concluded a conversation. The man fingered his ascot, laughed, and put his hand on Williams's shoulder.

Scalia.

And the boy was Saburo.

Saburo turned, smiled, and walked swiftly to her. His eyes, green and dark at the center, made her flush. He had grown since their last meeting and now was as tall as Scalia. High cheekbones made his angular face powerful. His skin was brown with pale undertones, a dusky look like earth under the first frost. Thick, black hair curled around the nape of his neck. His height and good looks dominated the front hall. Yet, despite his strong presence, Saburo seemed guileless, focusing on the moment as if the past and future did not exist. He was innocent, assuming people would and should like him.

"Sarah-chan," he said softly. His full lips broke into a smile. His hand seized her arm. She moved back. He followed. Several students, including Eddie, gaped, and sizing up the situation, their expressions puzzled, moved closer. Saburo's eyes glowed. He wanted her. His soft mouth made her remember. She wanted to tell him that lightly with a joke or a phrase, but the words would not come. Saburo playing the flute, Saburo asleep in the back room, Saburo making up stories, Saburo lying motionless in the hut, Saburo, tall and lean summoning her across the clearing. Saburo, despite his slanted eyes tea colored skin, was a young Scalia.

"Saburo," Scalia called in his high, Italian voice, as if this, like everything, were a joke.

But Saburo did not move. Scalia called again. Still Saburo remained. Scalia walked over, put his arm around Saburo, drawing him close, his hand on Saburo's cheek as if he owned him. Sarah froze. At once she felt a terror, different from any she had ever known. Buttericks's note in her file was nothing compared to this. Scalia had a plan. He had just spent a great deal of money. Williams looked happy. Scalia smiled. Enrolling Saburo at the American International School just before graduation was a plot.

Did Saburo know he was part of Scalia's revenge against her family? But what harm could Saburo inflict? He looked young, blameless, and oblivious to everything except her. His black shirt open at the neck, his thick gold chain, and his alligator shoes pointed at the toe made him alien. Even hoods like Eddie did not dress this way. Yet his outfit, a costume created by circumstance, had little to do with Saburo. There was nothing sophisticated or malicious in his expression. His eyes, youthful, open, and adoring, searched her face. He was in the moment, and that moment was hers.

She retreated. He smiled and came for her again, dismissing Scalia, Headmaster Williams, the students, and the fact that she stepped away. Since his rejection in the forest, Sarah had dreamt of this meeting. Now Saburo, with his blazing eyes, handsome and lithe, wanted her. His need was so apparent that the hurt faded as if it had never happened. He moved on the balls of his feet, quickly like a dancer, asking her to remember their childhood, their play, their promise, and she did. Memories that surfaced with lightning speed flashed before her. She felt dizzy. Her cheeks flushed.

She had been so alone, the center of a tight group, bound by a need to survive. Eddie liked her. The others wanted help. They rode cycles, smoked, and cheated, but there was no commitment or assurance that they were together. They laughed at themselves, their teachers, and Japan. Everything was ridiculed, loyalty never considered. Japan was temporary—a springboard, a stepping-stone to another world.

Saburo evoked old feelings, making her yearn for the warmth of his skin. He was her soul mate, bound together from childhood. She understood his smile and his determination to be with her. He was her wild part buried in dreams, a piece that caused her to toss at night. She felt that part surface, spreading through her, tossing caution to the winds. For the first time in many years, she felt free, unbound, and able to plot her own course. Scalia wanted revenge, but Saburo had come just for her.

SABURO'S WORLD

That night her parents mentioned the cheating, but Sarah said nothing. Her mother covered her face with thin fingers while her father's gentle voice probed for information. Things were worse than they could possibly imagine: Scalia's revenge, Scalia's deal with Headmaster Williams, Saburo in school, Buttericks's note in her file.

Rumors circulated: Saburo's father, a rich, Japanese nightclub owner, married a reclusive Manchu princess who smoked opium, wore thick silk, and was carried everywhere in a rattan box; Saburo made a fortune in the black market and lived alone in a small room near Shimbashi; Saburo came from Burmese royalty, was brilliant at chess, and rode a large Honda. Emily and Suzie reported that he had slept through one class and skipped another.

The next day, determined to set things right, Sarah headed toward Buttericks's classroom. Nothing would stop her, not Saburo or Scalia. She would clear any misunderstanding. It was not too late. Buttericks would be relieved. She had rehearsed her speech, explanations that would hit all Buttericks's vulnerabilities. It was certain to succeed. The Americans gathered by the drinking fountain called to her, but she ignored them and kept going. The last bell rang.

The front door opened. The doorway framed Saburo's lean body, dressed in black with thick gloves and hair that curled at the edges. He hooked his thumbs through his belt and scanned the Americans and the others clumped in small groups. Emily, Suzie, and Rita giggled. Emily sashayed toward him, her painted nails holding a small, red bag. Suzie and Rita followed.

Saburo ignored the girls and crossed the hall. She felt the warmth of his hand on her shoulder. She pulled away. Saburo followed. Her meeting with Buttericks would work. Timing was critical. Saburo's grip tightened. Her friends whispered. Bill whistled. Eddie glared. Saburo pulled her close, so close she smelled his pomade, dense and sweet. Saburo moved through things like the wind, doing what he wanted. He smelled of danger, of the outside, of things unknown. Everyone at school understood he wanted her. She tried to pull away but he whispered her name "Sarah-chan," over and over. The sound was so faint that she heard it as a breeze on a summer night. His lips were close. He led her across the entry hall and through the large doors to the outside.

"I have waited six years," he said softly in Japanese as they exited the iron-gate. "I thought of you every day. Did you think of me?" he asked, leading her down a small street of shabby houses. Saburo stopped at a black Honda with curved handlebars and a red, leather seat.

"School is nearly over," Sarah said in a flat tone, conscious that she should be in Buttericks's office making her plea. Saburo's voice, deep and slow with a touch of sadness, hypnotized her. It held a secret that would unlock mysteries and help her understand herself. She clung to all that was lost. She had lived another life. She'd been another person. She'd been so alone. No one else would validate her feelings. No one. "Why did you come?" she asked, her voice sharp, to create distance.

"Why does anyone come to the American school?" Saburo replied in the same mesmerizing tone. "I came to learn English, to learn about America," he said softly in her ear. "Our Shimbashi stall is big business." His breath tickled her neck as he whispered about Fumiko's black market deals. "If I work hard, if I learn English, Scalia-san promised I would manage the whole business. He gave me this cycle. I might become a lawyer."

"You hardly speak English, and you already skipped a class. I'm the lawyer."

Saburo's laugh was soft. "I came because of you. I want you, Sarah-chan."

Sarah flushed. Once again her thoughts went to Buttericks and the incriminating note in her file, the note that would keep her from becoming a lawyer. She was about to tell Saburo that, but he leaned close. His lips brushed her neck and her cheek.

"You're beautiful," he murmured. "More beautiful than you know. More beautiful than you realize. Beauty is a tyranny," he said in soft, female Japanese. "It makes magic, it destroys serenity. Men know that. You know it, too." His hand was on her breast. She pulled away. Saburo seized her palm. With his forefinger he traced a line. "Your love line is deep," he whispered. "It cracks through. A good sign. But look here," he pointed, "your lifeline is broken. See." He made her look. Sure enough the line scattered, fading into skin. "Soon you will have to make a choice. I'm here to help you make that choice."

"It's just a line," Sarah said, pulling her hand back. "How much did Scalia pay to let you in?"

Saburo laughed the same soft laugh. "Let's ride."

Soon they were in Shibuya. Her arms hugged his waist, and she closed her eyes.

"Japan will surpass the West," Saburo said. "Soon we will have more subway lines than New York or London. Tokyo Tower—higher than the Eiffel Tower. Buy low. Sell high. Everything comes together in the Shimbashi black market."

"Show me," Sarah whispered.

"I'll show you everything."

Twenty minutes later Saburo led her across a large plaza crowded with shoppers and tents to Shimbashi station, cavern-like, wood slated, and with a ceiling of wooden trellis. Inside, as far as the eye could see, tables were loaded with American jeans, T-shirts, belts, purses, sportswear, shoes, toiletries, and household items. There were no police. Hoods stood between tables eyeing customers as they filled bags with American goods. Saburo led her through the crowd.

"Mother," Saburo said. "Look who I brought."

"Sarah-chan, welcome," Fumiko said, standing behind a large table loaded with jeans and smiling her knowing smile. Her weathered face retained a rebellious look, and her nails were bright red. Like the other women, she dressed simply in baggy pants, a white shirt, and a white kerchief.

Sarah stood awkwardly. Fumiko's smile didn't reach her eyes. Sarah backed away, but Fumiko caught her hand. "It's been a long time, Sarah-chan," she said in a solemn voice, one that Sarah remembered from childhood. There was an awkward pause. Fumiko picked up a pair of Levi's jeans. "Here, I want you to have this. A present."

The presentation was so swift that Sarah didn't have time to respond. She folded her arms, glanced at Saburo, and he nodded as if the gift were normal. Fumiko and her helpers waited. A train rattled overhead, stirring sawdust and causing dirt to fall. The women brushed off the dust and glanced at Fumiko and Sarah, watching the story unfold. More dust fell. No one moved. All eyes were on her. Would Sarah accept the present, a public offering and a gift that would put her in debt?

Saburo cleared his throat. A child pointed. The women shuffled. Fumiko's dark bangs gleamed with oil. Sarah remembered the scars on Fumiko's forehead, her bare skin, the smell of tatami and the plump maggots that moved slowly on the beams. Her lips puffed over protruding teeth. Her thin cheeks gave her a worn look, one close to the bone, the look of a survivor. A train rattled. Dust fell. A child cried. The crowd was restless. Saburo coughed. Sarah hesitated. Saburo coughed again. Sarah took the jeans. Fumiko smiled. The women smiled. Saburo smiled.

Then Scalia, dressed in white and flanked by two goons, walked toward them. He did not resemble that man Sarah had seen at school. His pant cuffs were smudged with sawdust, and his shadow of a beard and large belly made him appear massive among the slight Japanese, who scattered out of his way.

The jeans felt heavy now.

"Who do we have here?" Scalia asked. "We do meet in strange places, Sarah. Shimbashi is out of bounds to young ladies. Saburo knows that."

"Saburo-chan and Sarah-chan are friends," Fumiko interjected. "I asked Saburo-chan to bring her to the market. I wanted to see her again."

"Of course, of course," Scalia said. "Saburo-chan and Sarah-chan are friends. Quite right. How is Saburo doing at school, Sarah? He promised he would study to prepare for law school because he heard you'd study law. Is Saburo keeping his promise?" Scalia continued without waiting for a reply. "Do you remember the first day you met? I knew that you and Saburo would be friends. You have a bond that must never be broken. Do you remember?"

Scalia repeated the question, bending close, so close she saw broken blood vessels on his sagging neck and smelled wine on his breath. His skin, paper thin, gray and mottled, looked as if it could tear. A vein pulsed in his cheek. Flecks of dandruff covered his shirt and shoulder blades. He had the unkempt look of a man who had stopped caring. She hated all of it.

"Why is that important to you?" Sarah asked, moving away.

"Always rude, Sarah-chan," Scalia said. "Rude because you think you can afford to be, rude because you're rich and can get away with it, rude because you're beautiful and because you think bad things won't happen to you. To others maybe, but never to you. But Saburo knows you're wrong. He knows that bad things can happen. He knows you have to be cautious. Saburo wears black and rides a big motorcycle with a red seat and acts daring, but actually he is careful, picking his way through life, looking to the right and left and behind, too. He will never cross a superior. Never. Isn't that right, Saburo?"

Saburo remained silent.

Scalia moved close. "How are Alexander and Tamara?" he asked softly, his voice pleading. "How are your dear parents? Do they talk about me? Do they say nice things? Do they remember Shanghai and the good times?"

"My parents are busy," Sarah said in a cold, deliberate tone. "Father manages the office of an American export company. Mother has her antique shop at the Imperial Hotel. At night they go to the Jewish Club or out with friends to concerts and dinners. They never mention Shanghai. We speak English at home—American English."

Scalia's eyes looked glazed, as if he couldn't quite absorb her words. What was she doing? She must return the jeans, walk through the market, past the crowded tables to the square. She would take a taxi away from the past; Scalia, Fumiko and Saburo. Antagonizing Scalia was stupid. He was in touch with Sensei and bureaucrats who ruled on taxes and visas. Scalia spoke loudly about Shanghai, her father's release from jail, her father's illness, and Scalia's connections that secured Red Cross passports. Fumiko shook her head as if she had heard it all. "Well, well," Scalia finally said, his tone hardened. "It sounds like Alexander and Tamara need some reminding." His voice rang louder now, a shout that reverberated across the market. "I have influence. I can make things happen, and I can stop things from happening. Don't believe that you and your parents will simply sail off to America."

"You don't scare me," Sarah retorted, conscious that Saburo, women workers, and customers moved close. She glared at Scalia, her arms folded with the jeans pressed against her. She wanted to bring him to his knees. Her voice came from a great distance. "And you don't scare anyone else either. You're a bully, and everyone knows it. Even Fumiko."

Fumiko's eyes widened, and Sarah was about to say more, but Saburo pulled her back. Scalia paled, and his mouth hung open, revealing yellowed teeth and spittle on the corners of his lips. He looked a mess, a ghost of the handsome man she had known, a shadow of the man, tall and commanding, who just days before had brought Saburo to school. Scalia raised both hands, at a loss for words, and turning toward Saburo smiled, a smile laced with sadness. He drew him close. Scalia and Saburo standing together made her furious. "Take care, Beppe," she said, even though she had already said too much. "You're too old and too fat for threats."

A train rattled. Dust filtered from the trellis above. Her arms were covered with sawdust that clogged her throat and dusted her hair. Tiny bits dotted Scalia's white jacket, streaking the silk with dark stains. Trains rumbled, and the dust fell in soft clouds making it hard to breathe. Women pulled bandanas over their mouths.

Sarah moved quickly away from the goons, the stalls, and the shoppers toward the open expanse of the plaza. "Go, go," her mind ordered. She quickened her pace, past the tables loaded with plastic to the light. "Go," she ordered. Her muscles knotted as she ran, dodging shoppers, sellers, and hoods. Now there were fewer tables and less noise.

At last! The sound of the trains faded. She inhaled fresh air and raising her head felt the full warmth of the sun.

Saburo was beside her. His hand was on her waist. His body shielded her from noise and chaos. He drew her close, his touch gentle, protecting her from the market, the goons, and the past. He stroked her face and smoothed her hair. She bent into him. He ran his hands down her back, bringing her closer still. She felt his rough cheek and soft lips. They swayed together, and he whispered, "Sarah-chan, Sarah-chan."

THE BEGINNING

Saburo parked the bike in a narrow lane, crowded with houses, dark and smelling of dirt. Shimbashi had been rebuilt after the bombing, but even the newest buildings looked old, swollen green with rot. Saburo's apartment, shingles loose, windows taped, and front door cracked, was no different. Saburo unlocked the door, led her to the second floor landing, and pushed back the shoji. The low ceiling, tatami floor, and mold reminded her of Fumiko's hut.

Saburo sat on worn zabuton with his arms folded. The clay walls matted with horsehair gave the room a cell-like look, bare except for a sink, folded quilt, and a low table. A beautiful bamboo flute lay across the table and Saburo immediately handed it to her. She smiled, felt its weight and carefully replaced it. Next to a Bunsen burner stood a framed picture of Saburo and Fumiko in matching hats standing on a beach. Fumiko wore a white Ama-san costume, and Saburo, his hat cocked and bare-chested, laughed into the camera. A straw basket filled with oysters stood squarely between them.

"That was taken after my first dive with mother," Saburo said.

"You look happy."

"Yes."

Saburo filled the kettle and turned on the Bunsen burner. "Don't fight with Scalia-san," Saburo said.

"I have to," Sarah answered slowly.

"When you and your family left," Saburo continued, "Scalia-san remained upstairs and wouldn't eat for weeks. O'ba stayed next to him day after day, coaxing him with chicken broth and tender bits of meat. He lost so much weight that O'ba took him to the hospital. When he returned much of the forest was gone. He took me down the path to the boulder, but that had been taken, too. Scalia kicked the dirt and said, 'Remember this, Saburo-chan; soon the moss and shade in Japan will disappear, and everything beautiful, riverbeds and the beaches, will be paved in concrete. All wonder will be lost.'"

Saburo continued in the same low voice talking, of the leveling of the forest, the draining of the lake, and the disappearance of lake breezes, and the sound of crickets. Sarah tried to imagine the concrete streets, apartment buildings, and train station. "Sensei's house is still there," Saburo interrupted her thoughts. "He keeps the house to honor the wooden beams his ancestors polished. Sensei replanted the garden, but car exhaust yellowed the moss. All you can hear is traffic."

Shamed by the tenderness, Sarah picked up the picture. "Sensei's island?"

"Yes, Seta Nan Kai, Inland Sea," Saburo said, moving his zabuton close. "We went to Sensei's island and fished."

Sarah studied the picture. A small shell rested against Fumiko's throat, her smiling eyes squinted against the sun, and her raised hand steadied the hat. She stood with her feet apart, toes buried in the sand, one hand dangling by her side, a comfortable stance, at peace, as if she had finally come home. Sarah felt the sun and the salty breeze against her skin. She imagined running into the ocean and the slap of waves against her face. Picking up a conch shell from the table, she rubbed its surface against her cheek.

Fumiko and Saburo had been fishing while she cried herself to sleep, filled with worry, feeling responsible for Saburo's death, a murder she dreamed about at night and remembered during the day. Why hadn't O'ba, Sensei, or Scalia told her they were safe and happy on the island? Why had everything been kept secret? Now she was sorry she had gone to the market and Saburo's room. Her parents were right. The past must be left alone. She'd been a fool.

Saburo whispered, "Scalia-san took us to the island when your mother was in the hospital. You were sick, too. Scalia-san was afraid you and your mother would die. Mother was ill."

"I thought Fumiko-san was dead," Sarah said. "I thought you were dead, too. I thought I had killed you."

Saburo nodded. O'ba had sent a letter describing Sarah's deep grief, her tears, her lack of appetite, and her restless nights. "O'ba should have let you write me. That would have been fair. I wrote many letters, but mother would not send them. We should have been in touch. It's what I wanted."

He wanted her to know everything. While Fumiko was ill, Scalia lived in the granary, cradling Fumiko, coaxing Fumiko to eat, to sit, to walk. Fumiko turned her head to the wall and wouldn't eat, but Scalia persisted until she ate a little and then a little more. When she was strong enough, Scalia wrapped her in a blanket and carried her to a waiting car. For the next three days, they traveled by car, train, and boat.

Saburo paused. When he started again, his voice

was dreamlike as he described the Inland Sea. Sarah saw the flat ocean dotted with islands like dark turtles, one rising behind the next. She imagined Scalia, Saburo, and Fumiko at dusk, watching the sea turn from blue to purple to black. "I first saw the island on a bright morning with the sun sparkling off the water and fishing boats bobbing." He spoke in a low voice about the thatched-roofed fishing village backed by a wooden hilltop shrine facing the sea. They lived with Fumiko's parents in the center of the village. The house had a sloped roof, thick tatami mats, and a large room that served as a bedroom by night and a sitting room by day. Saburo slept between his grandfather and grandmother and grew accustomed to their snores and the wash of waves. The room looked out on a walled-in moss garden with a single, stunted pine tree and a hollowed-out boulder that collected rainwater.

In the winter the kotatsu heated the room and the family gathered nibbled on sweet sembe, drank wheat tea, and gossiped. The talk was slow and repetitive, with long silences between stories. After school and on weekends, Saburo's grandfather taught him to mend nets and varnish boats. They worked together in silence, understanding what needed to be done. With spring they hauled nets, grabbed baby octopuses from under rocks, and caught small crabs in buckets at tidemark.

Sarah heard the ache in his voice as he and his grandfather climbed the hill to the Shinto shrine before his first fishing trip. They mounted the broad, stone steps, bowed and clapped, then marched to the harbor, boarded a stout, wooden boat, and traveled to a deserted island. For three days they fished for haddock, sole, and hake. On the last day, there was a terrible storm. Grandfather covered them in straw, and they lay on the bottom of the boat. The boat tossed and turned, but grandfather laughed and said he had been through much worse. When the winds died, they returned home.

That night Saburo's grandmother prepared broiled fish, salted fish eggs, and marinated baby octopus. Saburo ate three bowls of rice and for the first time in many months, Fumiko threw back her head and laughed. The sound echoed through the house, the village, and across the bay. Saburo and his grandparents joined her, rejoicing that they were still alive, their bellies were full, and they were together. Grandfather sang, and grandmother poured sake.

"Why did you come back?" Sarah asked.

"Four years later Scalia-san came for us," Saburo said. "He brought me a transistor radio, whiskey for Grandfather, and a woolen jacket for Grandmother. Then he took Mother for a long walk on the beach. When they returned, Mother told me to pack. I begged to stay with my grandparents, but Mother shook her head. Grandmother and Grandfather were upset yet said nothing. Scalia-san promised I could visit the island in the summer, the fishing season when the boats are out every day. I believed him.

"The next morning we left for Kobe and then took a train to Tokyo. Scalia built us a hut by the lake. He furnished it with a heater, a small veranda, and new mats. He came every day and brought me clothes and this gold chain," he said, pointing to his neck. "In the evenings, he taught me *Go*. He said again and again that we were family, and we would always help each other no matter what. He is gaijin but tries to be kind. It is difficult for gaijin." Saburo paused as if Sarah might take offense. Sarah was quiet, wondering whether Saburo understood that he was a gaijin, too.

Saburo began again. "Scalia and Mother went

into the black market business. I helped them. I have never been back to the island."

"You could go this summer," Sarah said, hoping for a good end.

"Grandfather died last year, and three months later Grandmother died," Saburo said. "Mother sold the house. There is nothing left."

Saburo's hand was on her knee. He flattened her to him and whispered, "You are my island, a bit of land floating in a vast sea, a world unto itself. You are where I rest, where I am myself. Together no one can touch us. I need only you. Always."

Sarah remained still.

Saburo's fingers touched her gently. She turned toward him. His face was cast in shadows, and his dark eyelids and set jaw made him look settled, trustworthy, and older than seventeen. "Why did you and Ryuzu make fun of me?" he asked. "You talked about me. I heard everything from my hiding place in the bushes."

"We were jealous," Sarah answered, mimicking his low tone. "You had American things and were teasing us, making fun of our ragged clothes and need for plastic things. The flute. The clothes. The candy. We were children."

"I came for you, Sarah-chan. I left all those things so that you would follow me into the woods."

"That's a lie," Sarah said in a rough voice, remembering her loss of face the moment Saburo disappeared into the forest. That feeling of disgrace had persisted, a humiliation that made her uneasy, anxious that she was not quite good enough.

Saburo was silent for a long time. Then he said in a pained voice, "If I had taken your hand, Sarah-chan, that hand I longed to hold, those fingers I wanted to caress, if I had pulled you to me, then there would have been no more Saburo. I can't explain it, but it was the most terrifying feeling I have ever had, a feeling that I would disappear, be nothing, and do nothing. You would take over, devour me, make me think as you do, behave as you do, and I would lose myself.

"For days after I was numb—couldn't eat or think. My chest hurt. The pains came in waves, traveling from my stomach to my heart. Mother took me to a doctor, but he could do nothing. It was terrible. Then I realized that I had done a great wrong, a mistake that would haunt me for the rest of my life. I need you; we are one, there is no difference between us, and it has always been so. There is no one else for me. There never will be. Understand that. No one. You are who I think about when I wake up and the last person I think about before sleep." Saburo paused. His fingers stroked the back of her hand, and he leaned into her.

"I went to find you that night, to tell you how I felt, to ask your forgiveness. I stood by your bedroom window, but it was dark. I tapped on the glass and called your name. The room was silent. The next night I went with a crowbar, but the window was bolted. The third night I brought a flashlight. Your room was empty. You were gone."

Sarah put her hand against his mouth.

"It took us just three days to pack."

The sun slanted red through the shoji. The fire-watcher's chops clapped in the distance, sharp and insistent, a rap that the wooden city depended on. Saburo picked up both hands and ran his tongue along her palm. His lips were soft. His arms wrapped around her. Sarah pressed against him.

"I dream of you every night," Saburo murmured. "I see you run through the forest. You find a chocolate, your lips part, and I see your pink tongue."

His hands touched her breasts and then moved to the insides of her thighs. His fingers were light, and she pressed close. He slowly unbuttoned her blouse, kissing her shoulders and her throat. She became dizzy as his lips slid down to her breast.

"I love you, Sarah-chan," he whispered in English. "I love you. I love you."

Sarah unsnapped her skirt and took off her panties. Saburo gathered her against him again. "Don't be afraid," he said and placed her hand on him. But Sarah wasn't afraid. She stroked him, and he closed his eyes, moaned, and moved over her.

The shoji shifted, inching open, a thin streak of light, a flash, and another. Fear rose in her throat. Someone was in the hall. The flash was a camera. They should stop. She struggled to sit up, but Saburo pressed her back and whispered, "Sarah-chan." His lips were on her neck and breast, encouraging her, moving with her, murmuring love. She held him, and although it hurt she rose to meet him.

They lay on the cushions. Saburo covered her with a quilt, and they smoked. The shoji was closed. Sarah wondered whether she'd imagined the light. Who would follow them to Saburo's room? Even Scalia would not be that bold. Her legs hurt. She wanted Saburo to say words that would make her confident, words she could trust and believe in. But he puffed his cigarette, his eyes uncomprehending, and said nothing. She nudged him and cleared her throat. He did not move. She touched his face. He remained still. It was hopeless. Shadows on the ceiling shifted. Sarah thought of the cheating, Buttericks, and the note in her file.

Saburo drew her close, murmuring her name, asking for her love. His low voice filled the room. It gave her confidence. In a soft, hesitant tone, she told him about the cheating, as if even she did not believe the sequence of events. The note in her file would ruin her American college education, the chance for her family to immigrate, and ultimately a legal career. Saburo was quiet. The cigarette smoke curled above their heads, and his arm tightened around her. "I'm going for it tonight," Sarah whispered. "I know the office, the file cabinet. The window is unlocked. I'll get Buttericks's note from my file and my friends', too."

Saburo took a long drag. "Not tonight, my love, but soon," he answered softly. "I'll help you. You can't go alone. Never alone. From this moment we will be together. We must prepare. You must know the office layout, so there are no mistakes. Learn every inch, where everything is kept. We will only have one chance." Saburo paused. She watched the smoke curl above their heads. The smoke rings enlarged and disappeared into the clay ceiling.

Then Saburo whispered in a low voice, "Tomorrow I'll take you to Sensei. Tomorrow. The Flamingo Club. Sensei wants to meet you."

Sarah went cold. She shivered. The chill hit every part of her. She wrapped her arms around herself. Still she froze. She could not move. Her arms felt leaden. She tried to rise, but it was impossible. She needed to run from the room, from Saburo and the past. She had been a fool. Meeting Sensei was deadly serious. Was this part of Scalia's plot? Was Scalia right about Saburo being most obedient? Would Saburo follow Sensei's orders above everything?

She remembered Sensei's stern expression, the feel of his hand on her head, his low voice making her friends listen. Sensei, the keeper of Japan, would smile when he saw them, understanding that she and Saburo were outsiders, people to be used for the good of Japan.

Saburo had no choice. He was in business with Sensei, a concern whose profits went to Sensei's cronies. She thought of Scalia's Kannon, its slim body and soft lips a reminder of obligations past and present. Had Sensei ordered Scalia to bring Saburo and Fumiko back to Tokyo? Yes. Had Sensei suggested that Saburo go to the American International School? Yes. Did Sensei know about tonight? Yes. Tomorrow Saburo would present her like a prize. Sensei would not ask to see her without wanting something. But what? Did Saburo know? She had nothing to give, Sensei must realize. Nothing.

Was loving Saburo—and she did love him—the price she had to pay for getting the note? Did lovemaking change everything? Why had she blurted out her problems, expecting Saburo to solve them? She could retrieve the note herself. Couldn't she? But now she was not sure. She was frightened. Saburo had caste a spell. The knot—Sensei, Scalia, Saburo—tightened. She tried to read Saburo's expression, stern and unapproachable, his eyes half-closed, his mouth pressed against his teeth as if there were words he could not say.

She hurt between her legs. She wanted to be alone, but Saburo turned to her, his breath on her cheek, drawing her close, and once again speaking softly about his need and their promise. They were the same, outsiders made from the same cloth. She had been in his dreams from the moment they met. He wanted to take her to the island, to a place where nothing could hurt them. He wanted to live with her, fish by day and hear the wash of sea at night. They would have babies and grow brown and wrinkled from the sun and wind. "You are my heart. You are my soul, Sarah-chan," he whispered. "Nothing can change that. Nothing."

And needing the reassurance of his touch, she turned to him, and his love burrowed into her.

THE DEAL

The Flamingo Club was at the end of a narrow street. She had expected more, but aside from the stream of black limousines dropping off a stream of well-dressed people, the club looked like any other low, innocuous post-war building. Saburo, in a white, silk jacket and black pants, stepped close as Sarah came up the steps. "My Shanghai beauty," he whispered in Japanese. "Sensei is waiting. Your Chinese dress is a good choice. Sensei ordered a fifteen-course meal from his favorite Chinese restaurant." ·

Sarah flushed at the memory of the lie she had told her mother about a graduation party at an American embassy. When her mother left, she opened up the slit to her thigh, combed her hair into a low bun, and matched the dress with turquoise earrings and bracelet. Her outfit, together with her rouged cheeks, colored lips, and highlighted eyes, was striking.

Saburo pushed past the men staring at Sarah's thigh and steered her through the dimly lit main room, rose-colored walls covered with paintings of black jazz musicians. A raised stage with a black jazz pianist dominated, his fingers rippling over the keys of a white grand piano. Men glanced in her direction, and noting their hungry looks, the rebellion that had brought her here vanished. Saburo gripped her elbow and ushered her past the tables, up to the balcony, and through thick curtains at the end of a hall. He knocked on a large, oak door.

"Sarah-chan, how good to see you."

Save his warm smile, Sarah would not have recognized the middle-aged man who stood in front of her. He looked like a Japanese businessman except for a small pin on his lapel—the Order of the Rising Sun with Paulownia Flowers, Grand Cordon—awarded by the emperor for his service to Japan. Yet his erect posture made him large. In seconds he dominated the room. His smile took in her outfit, makeup and her hesitation. He dropped his eyes, assumed a humble expression, and bowed once more.

"You're a beautiful woman, Sarah-chan," Sensei said. "Thank you for coming to see me. Thank you for humoring an old friend."

Sarah bowed.

"It was a long time ago," he said, his eyes soft with feeling. "It feels like another century. The forest. You. The children. I remember your bright laughter. You beat all the boys at the card game menko and sumo. They were afraid of you, and you were afraid of no one."

Sarah smiled. "The boys were weak."

"When I came to the forest, your faces would be flushed from play. You would run to me, and I would tell you stories of brave samurai. Your questions were clever, and I had to think carefully how to answer. I hope my answers were wise. Now here you are, and here I am."

The table, elaborately set with blue and white Chinese dishes, underscored the importance of the evening. Again she understood that Sensei wanted something very much. The dinner, carefully planned and ex-quisitely delivered, was a trap. Sensei smiled, Saburo smiled, and the waiters smiled. She sat in the seat of honor opposite the door.

"Try a little Chinese wine," Sensei suggested as the waiter appeared. "It's served hot with sugar and goes with the meal." The waiter poured the wine into thick glasses and stirred in large chunks of sugar. Sensei raised his glass, "*Kanpai.*"

"Kanpai," Sarah and Saburo responded in a chorus.

"Sarah-chan," Sensei said in a low voice. "Do you remember that when we met you were covered with silt from the lake? The children teased, but you were brave. You didn't cry. I thought to myself, this is a person to be taken seriously. This is a person I must watch."

"I remember," Sarah said, aware of his flattery.

"A long time ago," Sensei said in an intimate tone as if only they understood. "A different Japan." The food arrived, plates and plates of it. Sensei served one-thousand-year-old eggs, jellyfish, pickled vegetables, and fermented beans. The wine hit, and she felt dizzy.

"When the occupation ended, I returned to the house," Sensei said slowly. "I still sleep in my old room on the first floor. I think of you when I hear Scalia-san pacing upstairs like a restless cat. He must have kept you awake. Scalia, always a friend, my most obedient friend," he added, waiting for her to comment, but she remained silent.

Scalia and Sensei, living in the same house, eating O'ba's food, doing business in the black market and the Flamingo Club. But Scalia was not obedient. What was Sensei trying to tell her? Sensei, Saburo, Scalia, Fumiko: a world of thugs, greedy Americans, and Japanese nationalists—everything she detested. She should not have come. Sarah glanced at Saburo, but he looked removed, his eyes focused on the food as if that were all that mattered.

"My bedroom was your parents' dining room," Sensei said. "I have removed the carpet and put back tatami and shoji. The room overlooks the garden, and in the late afternoon, I take my tea there. Your parents were kind not to paint the woodwork. In many of my friends' homes, beams cured and polished for hundreds of years were whitewashed by the American occupiers."

"How are O'ba and Emiko-san?"

Sensei's voice became silky, as if the change of subject was expected, as if everything he said about O'ba being bossy and Emiko getting married to a sake maker in the north would meet with her approval. At the table they were all the same height. Sensei looked directly into her eyes. He nodded as if he appreciated her comments, but Sarah did not say much. Her nails dug into the palm of her hand. Again Sensei's eyes roamed over her, missing nothing with his military *Myo-oshin-ji Zen* focus.

"Do you want to know about your friends?" Sensei asked softly. "I am still in touch with them. They want to know about you."

"Yes, tell me," Sarah said.

The waiter poured more wine. He replaced the small plates with larger ones and served shrimp in garlic sauce, salted oysters, steamed ham with black beans, fried and steamed fish, and beef in oyster sauce. Sarah took small bites. The villagers live in small apartments near the highway. They had refrigerators and did their laundry in machines hooked to sinks. Sensei got them jobs as housemaids, waiters, and factory workers.

Sarah sat upright, absorbing Sensei's melodious tone, his smooth voice flattering, interested, seductive, making the evening feel like a dream. He made her yearn for her friends. She was lost in the past, its energy and innocence. She forgot her troubles and what Sensei might want. Again Sensei smiled, Saburo smiled, and the waiters smiled.

"I know you had trouble with Michio," Sensei said. "He is a traditional Japanese who dislikes strong women." Sensei laughed as he described her friends: Michio, a Hitachi factory worker, Ichiro's similar work at Toshiba, and Taro's ardent juku preparation for the University of Tokyo exam. Sarah drank wine, smiled, and commented. Saburo said nothing.

Sensei spread pictures on the table. "Your good friend Noriko works at a bakery. Look." A pretty, round-cheeked girl in a kerchief smiled at the camera. Sarah brought the snapshot close. She recognized Noriko's gentle eyes and, remembering the feel of Noriko's small fingers closing around her own, Sarah's eyes misted.

Where was Ryuzu? She was afraid to ask. He was not among the pictures. Sensei gathered the photos with a quick swoop of his hand. At once the room grew cold. Saburo's face looked frozen. The dream evaporated. She felt ill. She counted twelve dishes. The meal was almost over.

"I will tell your friends that you are doing well, too," Sensei said. "Saburo-chan tells me you are the best student in school. Stanford University will accept you. You will become a great lawyer. But you must not forget Japan, Sarah-chan, no matter what Stanford University teaches you. Japan will guide your life. You hold yourself like Japanese," Sensei continued, "but you speared your beef like a foreigner. Let me help you hold your chopsticks in the old way."

She had been holding her chopsticks in the old

way, exactly as O'ba had taught her, but Sensei's fingers closed over hers, touching her palm and her wrist as he positioned her fingers on the wood. His hand lingered, his small finger stroking her skin, a repeated caress, and a touch that made her cold. Saburo looked away. The room was silent except for the click of chopsticks. Sarah wanted Sensei to stop, but his hold was strong and steady. She knew he would not let go until he was ready. Finally he dropped his hand. She replaced her chopsticks on the holder. Saburo put down his chopsticks, too.

"Life is deceptive, Sarah-chan," Sensei said as the door opened and two waiters placed a mound of clay with great ceremony on the sideboard. "In that clay is Beggar's Chicken, a most impressive, magnificent dish disguised as a poor man's dinner. Japan is deceptive too, appearing to be a few little islands with nothing but simple people. What the Communists and the unions don't understand is *ware, ware Nihonjin*, we Japanese guard tradition. We don't show our wealth because real strength lies in appearing humble. We don't want disharmony and jealousy. We know how to act as one. That is all. We don't need Socialism or Communism."

With that, all confusion disappeared. Ryuzu. The dinner was about Ryuzu. Sensei had bided his time, seducing her with the past, pictures of her friends, flattering comments about her beauty and accomplishment, in preparation for his request. It was coming. The atmosphere was deadly serious. Sensei's lips tightened, and his shoulders straightened. It was always about Ryuzu, Sarah thought. O'ba had been right. Conversion of Ryuzu to mainstream Japan was Sensei's passion. Sensei's Japan—unions crushed, demonstrations smashed, and war criminals like Prime Minister Kishi let out of jail—had won.

The door opened, and a man wearing a chef's hat bowed with great ceremony and presented Sensei with a large, heavy knife. Sensei nodded, and the chef brought it down hard. The clay fell in large chunks, revealing a steaming chicken wrapped in gauze. The chef cut the gauze and carved the chicken in deft movements, placing thin slices on a platter. Sensei and Saburo clapped. Sarah joined in. The chef bowed.

"Did Ryuzu-chan go to Russia?" Sarah asked in a low voice.

"Ryuzu-kun is back from Russia," Sensei answered. "I was against his going. I fought with his sister Sachiko-chan. You know how much I helped her." Sensei sighed, looking momentarily satisfied as he described Sachiko's factory job and subsequent arranged marriage to a man from a good family. His voice lowered. "But Ryuzu-kun wouldn't listen. All that I had taught him about being Japanese, about obligation, about trust and loyalty, was of no consequence. Ryuzu went to Russia and came back a Communist. Even so, I tried to help Ryuzu. When I saw you playing samurai games or beetle sumo, I was reminded of the play in the forest with my friend Masaru." Sensei paused.

"Despite Russia I was sure Ryuzu-kun was true Japanese," Sensei continued. "Through my networks, I got him a job in a bank. At first I received good reports. But Ryuzu turned into his father, Masaru-kun, a Communist, an enemy of Japan, secretly attending a Marxist study group, writing articles on working conditions, encouraging his fellow workers' complaints about overtime. He didn't care about the welfare of his family, the bank. Revolution was all he thought about. He had forgotten who he was."

Sensei's voice imprisoned her, a cage she'd created with her own arrogance. She thought of Buttericks's note in her file, the note that would determine the future of the family, evidence she must destroy. Her vows meant nothing. She was a person of no consequence. A chunk of clay stuck to Sarah's chicken. The cook watched. She swallowed the clay. Her mind skipped to what Sensei wanted.

"Ryuzu-chan demanded bank workers be paid overtime," Sensei said. "The bank is family. It takes care of its workers like a father takes care of his children. Overtime is not something the bank could afford. Workers' demands are not part of the Japanese way. Demands create disharmony. Of course Ryuzu-kun was fired." Sensei took a deep breath. Sarah waited. Saburo grimaced. The waiters shuffled.

Sensei continued, his low voice, determined, purposeful, filling the room. "Ryuzu is in San'ya spending his days as a day laborer and his nights working for a union. We are rebuilding, Sarah-chan. American bombs—twenty-six cities flattened and mass starvation—devastated Japan. Remember that Japan? Do you want to see that Japan again? Does Ryuzu-kun? If the wages in San'ya rise, if the day laborers demand more, building will stop, Japan's recovery will stop. Even San'ya's outcasts must work for the good of Japan."

"San'ya?" Sarah said in a low whisper. Every winter her mother organized a clothing drive for San'ya's day laborers. San'ya—the end of the line, the most hopeless place in Japan, its streets filled with drunk, desperate men, Koreans, burakumin, "untouchables," and Japanese who had lost their way. Ryuzu was there?

"So you know how terrible it is," Sensei said. "Even in San'ya, Ryuzu-kun is a natural leader. He is causing trouble for construction companies and has caught the attention of the Nihon-Gijinto yakuza. You may not like yakuza—I don't either—but they have a tough job keeping order in a place like San'ya. Who else can we depend on? Yakuza must do their job, and we must help them for the good of Japan."

Sensei's love for Masaru and Ryuzu filled the room, a locked-down love, one of ownership. He spoke in an insistent voice, an obsession that defied time, justifying the Japanese right, war criminals like Kishi in cahoots with yakuza and in alliance with America. It was a deadly bargain to squash unions and protests in the name of recovery, surpassing the West, and celebrating the Japanese way. These were not her people. Her mother was right. They must leave Japan. Since Saburo's return she'd been living a dream. Danger lurked, a threat to her parents, to her, to small Vera. She must learn the office and remove Buttericks's note. Any flirtation with the past must end.

Sensei had received complaints about Ryuzu's refusal to comply with the traditions of San'ya. "Before the unions destroy San'ya, the yakuza will destroy Ryuzu. I will be powerless to stop them." Sensei finished in a slightly petulant tone as if he were the victim. His voice softened, his speech now feminine. "You are the only one he might listen to, Sarah-chan. You were his childhood friend, and he trusts you. When he came back to Japan, he asked about you many times. I think he might be in love with you."

"Ryuzu-chan is my friend," Sarah muttered.

Sensei's features tightened. The change was abrupt. She had seen it before, one minute kind and wise and the next Zen-like and focused. As a child this look frightened her, silenced her friends, and made Ryuzu bow.

"Yes, that is why I asked you here," Sensei continued. "You are Ryuzu's friend."

Sarah said, "You're Ryuzu's mentor. He will listen to you."

"You are wrong, Sarah-chan," Sensei replied sadly. "Ryuzu-kun stopped listening long ago. I told him not to go to Russia, and he went. When he returned I told him not to take part in Communist union demonstrations; again, he did not obey. I told him that if he kept this up, I would have to warn the bank. After all, I was responsible for introducing him to the bank. If we cannot get Ryuzu to change," Sensei continued, his head lowered as if in deep thought, "I will have to warn Sachiko's in-laws, too. They don't know about the years Sachiko spent as a bargirl."

Sensei's voice was clear, uncomplicated—blackmail offered as a simple fact of life that Sensei would do for Japan, just as he had done so many times, to keep everything in its rightful place. If he could ruin Ryuzu and Sachiko, then he could surely ruin her as well.

This was Sensei's warning, a threat that made no sense because Sensei must know, as Sarah did, that one meeting with Ryuzu would not change anything. Ryuzu was committed to following in the footsteps of his father. Sensei must have something on her, information that would scare her into convincing Ryuzu to leave San'ya. Ryuzu was stubborn and resilient and fearless. He had been her friend and finally her great enemy. Sensei's request was crazy. Fear knotted her stomach. But what did Sensei know? He couldn't know about Buttericks's note.

Sensei coaxed, "You must do this for Japan. You are his true friend." Sarah wanted him to stop, but he continued, explaining that his car would drive her to the union headquarters, wait while she met with Ryuzu, and take her home. "Ryuzu must quit the union. He must come back to the Japanese way."

The waiter served rice gruel with bits of green onion and chicken.

"Sarah-chan." Sensei spoke now in a light tone, his voice intimate, as if the Ryuzu question had been resolved. "Your stillness reminds me of a nunnery located on a hill just outside Kyoto. Every evening a long ring echoes down the mountain through the valley and into Kyoto. The bell is made from the purest iron. The pause between each ring allows the sound to penetrate the city. Once you have heard that deep gong on a foggy night, you know the essence of truth. Sarah-chan, you are like that bell."

Sensei's voice softened. "You read Haiku, Sarah-chan. Basho, Matsuo was the best. Like you, Basho was a traveler, coming from one place, stopping for a while, and then moving on. Haiku combines kokoro, 'heart,' and 'sincerity,' makoto. Haiku is Zen, a focus on the moment." He recited:

> A traveler's heart, .
> never settled long in one place
> like a portable fire.

"Is that not you?" Sensei's eyes bored into her, forcing her to consider the poem's meaning, words that did not really make sense yet made all the sense in the world. Was he urging her to leave Japan? She was not sure. She wanted to lighten the mood, but his voice held her with the tender rhythm of children's Japanese, a tone that gathered her to him, protective and loving. His face expectant, his eyes vulnerable, a look made her want to please. This was the Sensei she remembered, the powerful Sensei who loosened his hair before meditating on the cold ground like a beautiful god. This was the man she loved, who told stories that transformed the forest into a place of kami, spirits with human qualities so real they became part of her.

"There is an old inn at the foot of the hill," Sensei continued in the same low voice. "An immense weeping willow stands in a courtyard of white stones. You enter the inn under a curved beam that is more than six hundred years old. Each room smells of fresh tatami and each room overlooks a perfect moss and stone garden. It would be my greatest pleasure to take you there so that you and I, together, could sip sake at dusk and hear that ancient bell." His face came close:

> Will you turn toward me?
> I am lonely too
> this autumn evening.

Sarah picked up her rice bowl and drank the broth, letting the liquid soothe her, closing her eyes against Sensei's stare, a look that left nothing to chance. Sarah glanced at Saburo, who remained still, his face lowered as if in prayer. Yes, Scalia was right about Saburo. In the face of Sensei, he could and would do nothing. His finger touched her leg. She shifted so that her ankle pressed against his. Saburo squeezed her hand, and as his grip tightened, she felt his helplessness and her own as Sensei watched.

THE GIFT

The dinner put a wedge between her and Saburo. Their joy replaced by a careful silence; they smiled and touched, yet they were aware that they were part of a larger drama. They were watched. Sensei was Saburo's master. He had no choice but to obey. Saburo did not speak of the black market, or Fumiko, or Scalia. Sensei's politics, his cronies, and his proximity to the imperial house were likewise taboo. Both waited for something to change.

Yet late at night, after their cautious conversation, Saburo played the flute. She sat on the cushion — straight backed — listening to the familiar sounds coming together and breaking apart. They were sounds of her childhood, yet unlike previous times, the music was not demanding or seductive. Rather the notes were lonely, discordant, a yearning, a search for understanding that Saburo could not express, feelings that made her eyes mist. At those times, she felt humbled by what he could not say and what he did say. After, she would reach for him and they would make love slowly, holding each other gently, conscious of their fragility, of all of it.

Her parents, preoccupied with buying property in San Francisco that would entitle them to residency and eventual immigration, no longer interrogated her about friends or late nights. At school Buttericks called on her as if nothing had happened. Her friends, accepted to colleges in unknown places like Missouri and Oklahoma, places they could hardly pronounce, continued to copy her work. Hearing their soft voices pleading for help, Sarah weakened and slipped them answers on small scraps of paper.

Eddie never mentioned Saburo. "Are you all right?" he asked between classes. "Fine," Sarah retorted in a bright voice. "Let me know if you need something," he murmured.

Sarah focused on removing Buttericks's note from her file. She became friendly with Principal Wilson's secretary, Sato, making copies and running errands. Within a week Sarah knew Sato's cabinet key was in a lacquer box in her desk.

Saburo came and went as he pleased, reporting in at his first class then vanishing for the rest of the day, only to reappear for afternoon sign out. He waited for her by the back gate. His slicked-back hair, sunglasses, and black outfits continued to make him popular. Charmed by his vulnerable smile, his teachers allowed him great latitude. In return Saburo completed his homework, spoke English, and was polite. At school, he floated on the surface of things.

And Saburo had money, American partners, and a black market gasoline business. He met Jim ice skating. Jim's father, a quartermaster at Washington Heights Base, explained the system. Saburo would make local gasoline station connections, and Jim and his father would supply gasoline. "No one knows," Saburo whispered. "Not Scalia. Not Mother. Not Sensei. I have $50,000 in the bank. No more *senpai* and *kohai*. That's old Japan."

Two weeks after the dinner with Sensei, Saburo

waited by the back gate. Her friends knew, winking and nodding as she headed out. At his apartment she forgot Sensei, Ryuzu, and Buttericks's note, relieved just to feel his rough cheek against her own. They made love, and she stroked his bottom and back, wanting to touch more, but he grabbed her hands, and kissing her gently on the face and neck, ran his knuckles down the length of her spine. She twisted away, but he brought her back, his lips hard on her nipples. Saburo smiled, the love-making edgy.

In the soft shoji light, he looked Japanese, only a hint of Scalia in his smile. Sarah spread her arms and felt the weight of him, his teeth on hers, bone on bone, skin on skin. His tongue searched her mouth, and her body rose to meet him, biting his chest until he groaned and flattened his body to her. Afterward Saburo held her face between his hands and kissed her eyes shut. The rough chap of his lips brushed her skin. He kissed her again, murmuring her name like a mantra, rounding out each syllable as if he couldn't let go. She wanted to say his name in turn. Their voices would blend, push-ing away the world's ugliness until Scalia's threats and Sensei's tyranny were broken. Her throat felt dry. Time passed. Saburo's voice grew faint. Then silence. Saburo caught her hand and brought it to his mouth. "Here." His soft voice broke the mood. He placed a small, leath-er box in her hand.

She felt the gilded ostrich leather. It must contain an expensive jewel. "Italian," she whispered to please him, and slowly opened the box. A bracelet and match-ing necklace made of fine gold filigree, studded with small emeralds, pearls, and rubies lay on the velvet in-terior. "Beautiful," Sarah whispered. Saburo slipped on the bracelet and fastened the necklace.

"Ching—Manchu Dynasty made for a princess,"

Saburo said in a voice that caressed the jewels. "I got them through a Chinese dealer. I knew they were for you," he said with his possessive smile. He held a mirror, and she lifted her hair. The jewels sparkled against her bare skin. "My princess," Saburo said, his eyes wide with admiration.

Saburo filled a bucket with warm water, sat close, and wiped her arms and her legs with a wet oshibori cloth. He dipped the cloth again and squeezed warm water over her arms and legs. She lifted the necklace away from her skin, but Saburo pressed it back. The water kept coming, like silk, running over her bare skin and coursing down her sides onto the cushion and tatami mat. She raised her head, feeling its weight on her eyelids, cheeks, and mouth. Their knees touched. Saburo poured water on his own head. They laughed. He pulled her close. His lips felt soft. She smiled and pressed her forehead against him. He wiped her dry, slowly dressed her, and combed her hair. She wanted to ask about Sensei, all of it, but he silenced her with a long kiss.

It was ten thirty when they left the apartment. "Let's go to my club," he whispered. "I want everyone to see that you're my beauty. Your skin, your hair, your eyes, the jewels against your skin."

For a moment she hesitated. She wanted to be part of Saburo's world, to be that close, but Buttericks's note loomed large. "No," she whispered. "Buttericks's note. I need that note. I know where it is."

Saburo shook his head. "Together, always together."

The dark school building, high and ominous, rose before them. A dog barked, and they bent low. Another dog barked. A low mist covered the ground and the base of the building. She held Saburo's hand, and they ran across the grass to Wilson's office. She had left the window unlocked. They were inside. Sarah retrieved the key from Sato's lacquer box, unlocked the file door, and watched it roll back. Saburo lit a match.

Footsteps moved down the hall. Saburo blew out the match. Ito, the watchman and super, a veteran with a bad leg, made his way toward them. She had forgotten about Ito—bad-tempered, rule-abiding Ito. He was Sato's cousin. Sato and Ito were close. She felt sick to her stomach. The shaking would not stop. Her knees buckled. Saburo caught her.

Ito stopped in front of the door, the light flickered, and Sarah held her breath. The pain in her chest spread like a raging blaze. It was hard to breathe. She clutched Saburo. The light stayed, moving back and forth, searching. The doorknob turned. It turned again. Saburo covered her mouth, crushing her lips with the palm of his hand. She tried to think. Her mind went blank. There was nowhere to hide. She would be shamed in front of the school, in front of her parents, all possibilities lost.

Ito cursed, tried the door again, and struck it with his cane. The sound rang through the office. There was a long pause. Ito's light remained. Saburo kept his hand over her mouth. She twisted. He held on. Moments passed. The dogs barked, two, three. Howls filled the room. The doorknob turned. Ito swore. More howls. Ito limped away. His footsteps faded. The dogs were silent.

"Be quick," Saburo released her and whispered in a strained voice. "He forgot his key. He'll be back."

Her fingers trembled as she sifted through her file: her transcript, notes from teachers—all good—her SAT scores, the letter from Wilson. Nothing from Buttericks. She looked again. Nothing. He believed in her, she thought, remembering his look of approval when he returned her last test. "No note," she whispered. No notes in Eddie's, Suzie's, and Emily's files either.

Saburo blew out the match. "It's over then," he said softly, his voice caressing each word. "No worries. Now you must think only of me. We will celebrate. I'll take you to my club. With my jewels around your neck, everyone will know you're mine."

They were outside running across the lawn to the street and to a taxi, Saburo holding her, whispering that he loved her, that she was beautiful, that she was his princess. But she could only think of Buttericks. He had listened. He understood. He had saved her. He had saved her friends. She would fly to America, away from Scalia and Sensei, and become the woman she was meant to be.

The taxi turned down a side street of unmarked restaurants and stopped in front of a low, wooden building set back from the street. Unlike Sensei's club there was no line of cars or doormen. The building was unmarked except for a cone of salt placed next to a massive wooden door. Saburo pushed the bell, the door opened, and a slender man in a tuxedo holding a welcoming oshibori in each hand, knelt before them. His head remained bowed. They pressed hot cloths against their skin.

He led them across a Persian-carpeted room decorated with imitation Monet paintings, green-blue laced with pink, to a low, leather couch. Immediately two young women in short cocktail dresses approached with glasses of champagne. The taller girl introduced herself as Mitsuko and her partner as Hatsuko. Mitsuko wore a thin band of gold on her wrist and a delicate chain around her neck. Her classic features, powdered white, geisha-like, looked like a mask. Hatsuko's wide eyes and slightly protruding teeth reminded Sarah of Fumiko.

"Saburo-chan," Hatsuko teased in a nasal tone, "niichan, 'big brother,' you haven't come to see me lately. Are you too busy making money?"

Both girls laughed. Saburo smiled.

Did the girls know about Saburo's black market business? Sarah wondered. She shuttered, imagining Sensei's rage if he knew Saburo had a separate business.

A waiter placed a tray of small sushi on the table. The room was filling up with men in dark suits and curly-haired goons, yakuza, in white jackets, pants, and flowered shirts. She turned from the bold stare of a man at the next table. His yakuza-severed digit tapped against his whiskey glass. Mitsuko and Hatsuko moved close. Their knees touched her legs. They took her hands, telling her she was beautiful, that her skin was luminous and her eyes the color of the sea. They laughed at everything she said, admiring her Japanese, her ability to use chopsticks, and her plan to study at Stanford University.

The women's sweet perfume engulfed her. With knowing smiles, their painted fingers on her knee, they described their travels. Mitsuko came from a fishing village in Kyushu and Hatsuko from a tea-growing family in Shikoku. They bent toward her, blocking her view of the gray-suited men and their goons. Mitsuko poured champagne; the bubbles tickled Sarah's nose and made her sneeze. Mitsuko placed a special otoro, "tuna sushi," on Sarah's plate. The salty taste made her drink.

Mitsuko immediately refilled her glass and then took Sarah's hand, tracing her lifeline to the break. Sarah pulled back, but Mitsuko held tight. "Your lifeline is unusual," Mitsuko finally said in a low voice. "Few life lines have such a large break. You will have to make choices, important decisions, decisions that will force you to change." Then Mitsuko giggled as if she hadn't meant to say anything so serious. Hatsuko laughed as well. Sarah thought of Saburo's slow trace of the same line. The girls' perfume had a musky smell. She drank more champagne. The girls touched her neck and wrist, their fingers moving lightly over the gold, their eyes glittering with envy. "Expensive," Mitsuko said. "Someone loves you," Hatsuko teased and pointed.

Saburo sat near the bar speaking to a group of men in gray suits who laughed and raised whiskey glasses. How could he leave her with Hatsuko and Mitsuko and ogling men? Didn't he realize that she was unprotected, food for yakuza? A feeling of dismay, of being erased, took hold. It was a familiar feeling, one she had often as a child, her existence in jeopardy, tipped on the brink of an abyss. She tried to collect herself, but it was no use. She shook. Did he think of her as his mistress, little better than Mitsuko or Hatsuko? Was she to be adorned, used, and then discarded?

The women, with their white faces, knowing eyes, and painted lips, were women her mother pitied, their stories too sad to tell. "It could happen to anyone," her mother said softly. "Just a matter of luck." Sarah didn't know exactly what her mother meant by luck but knew the women—the half-Russian, half-Japanese beauty floating from one man to another, the American alcoholic whose cigarette lighter matched each outfit, the Japanese singer married to a foreigner who beat her, and a geisha bought by a foreigner who died and left her penniless. Where did she fit in the hierarchy? Not geisha. Not girlfriend. Not mistress. Not friend. Did Saburo sleep with Hatsuko? With Mitsuko? Would she ever know? His help tonight, his need for control, unsettled her. She could have gone alone. Or could she? Suddenly she was not sure, and that worried her, too.

The room blurred. If Saburo turned and smiled,

she could be certain of herself. If he would acknowledge her, respect her feelings, and care for her welfare, the club and the girls would mean nothing. If he loved her, he would send a signal. He must turn. If not, something would shatter, despite his jewels and his tender touch. It was a test. She waited. Saburo stood with his hand on the shoulder of a beefy man. The man peered at a piece of paper, nodded, and put the paper in his pocket. Saburo ordered another drink. His back was to her. She gulped her champagne. The man with the severed digit watched.

Her thoughts raced. She turned back to Hatsuko and Mitsuko, back to nothing. The large door opened. Four men entered, then another five. The waiter strode ahead of them, smiling and bowing. More men came through the door. Mitsuko refilled her glass. She felt their breath on her face. They smelled sweet, a mixture of sandalwood and perfume. Their thin, hairless arms brushed against her. They lit her cigarette, poured more champagne, and laughed. Mitsuko's finger was still on her knee.

Sarah laid the necklace on the table. Then she took off the bracelet. The girls bent over the jewels, whispered, and giggled. Sarah encouraged them, pointing out emeralds, diamonds, and rubies. She pushed the jewels toward them. Mitsuko held up the necklace, admiring the gold filigree, while Hatsuko snapped on the bracelet. The necklace shone against Mitsuko's long neck. Mitsuko stroked Sarah's wrist, and Hatsuko's foot brushed her thigh. They touched the jewels lightly as they flattered.

Her head pounded.
The gold glittered.
Saburo told a joke.
The beefy man laughed.

She rose. Her cheeks were wet, and her knees shook. Mitsuko pointed to the restrooms. Sarah nodded. She moved past the table where Saburo sat, then the long bar, and finally to the man in the tuxedo suit. She hesitated. The man nodded. The door opened. She walked into the emptiness of the misty Tokyo night.

But Saburo was all she had. One ring of the bell, and she would reverse all that happened; the door would open, the *mizu shobai* man would kneel, and she would explain that she had wanted some fresh air. He would nod, and she would walk to the table and collect her jewels. Mitsuko and Hatsuko would laugh as if it had all been a great deal of fun. She would laugh, too. Then Saburo would return, tell a few jokes, and the girls would tease.

Her hand was on the hardwood door. She felt Saburo's fingers against her skin and the excitement of his slow smile. They would go to Sensei's island and live in a house with tatami mats and a moss garden. She would wear Ama-san white and dive for pearls. Between dives she would sit on a high rock and let the sun warm her body. Saburo would fish. At night they would eat rice, seaweed, and broiled fish, and in the spring, marinated baby octopus.

Saburo.

A taxi rolled toward her. Its lights, orange in the mist, moved deliberately down the street as if searching. Closer. Closer. Headlights beamed on the door. She moved forward with her hand raised. The driver braked.

WARNING

It was past one when the taxi dropped her off. The low fog blanketing the ground swirled around her legs and covered the stucco wall. The world bleached white, dreamlike, she moved through a thick cloud toward the house. Saburo. Her mind went to him, racing through the sequence of events, each building on the last and ending with yakuza and Saburo's bargirls.

"Sarah," Scalia's voice barked in the dark. Before she could respond, he pulled her against the wall. "I've been waiting. I was beginning to think I was out of luck."

Sarah twisted, but Scalia held her fast and brought his face close. In the dim glow of the streetlight, she saw his receding hairline and, tonight, a line of perspiration above his upper lip. She tried to dodge past him, but he was too quick. "Not so fast, Sarah-chan." In his grasp she became a little girl again.

Scalia laughed. "Don't even try. You have a great deal to learn. You believe you can trick everybody and that lies don't matter? Well, they do. Your parents think you were at a friend's party. Wouldn't they be surprised to learn you were at a yakuza club? Wouldn't they be shocked to know about Saburo? Where is Saburo? He should escort you home."

"Leave me alone," Sarah said in a low voice.

"Of course I spy," Scalia said, reading her mind. "You should be grateful that I didn't tell Tamara and Alexander that Saburo is your lover. They don't like to talk about Saburo. They feel responsible for his disappearance. But you and I know that nothing terrible happened. Saburo went to Sensei's island and had a fine life with his grandparents and Fumiko-san. I would never let anything terrible happen to Saburo. Never."

Scalia's voice dropped. "Tamara and Alexander worry about you. You are their passport to America. I couldn't bear to be the one to disappoint them. They will stay, Sarah-chan. You cannot understand why the Bermans are so important. Knowing you are in the same city makes me feel alive. Alexander and Tamara remind me of the good times, the secret deals, the Shanghai pearl auction, how close we were, how young—more than a family—living each day in style, scheming to survive.

"The Italian consulate told me about the Japanese submarine full of South Sea pearls, pearls destined for Italy, cash to support the Japanese war effort." It was an old story, one she knew by heart and Scalia needed to repeat, a justification for all his actions, no matter how terrible. "We were so young, and the deal was so sweet."

Scalia's voice whispered high. "Shanghai, the best city. Refugees came from everywhere, intellectuals, merchants, professionals, and adventurers. Everyone was eager to have a conversation, to explore ideas, to make a deal. What a time. What a place. Tamara was the most beautiful and most intriguing of them all. And all of us were the most alive we will ever be."

He paused and loosened his hold on her, but Sarah did not move away. The fog stayed low, drawing them together, swirling, and edging up their legs. She prayed he would let the past take over.

"I got them out of the Shanghai ghetto," Scalia continued in the same trance-like voice. "Nishiguchi convinced the Japanese that because of their long residence in the Orient, they were not Jews but Orientals. With some bribes the officials accepted that. Japanese are paranoid," he whispered. "Your parents owe Sensei, and they owe me." Scalia sighed and wiped his forehead as if the speech had been too much. "You are my family. My family can't leave. Sasha thinks America means freedom. He thinks you will become a great lawyer and will finally belong somewhere. But Sasha is wrong. Sasha and Tamara belong to me, and that means you belong to me as well."

Sarah let her weight fall against him. They touched foreheads, and Scalia held her as if afraid she would disappear. In his arms she floated above the fog. The softness of his voice insisted she understand, and she did, more than he realized and more than she wanted. His love, possessive and demanding, made him barbarous. They were similar, and in that moment she saw herself, obsessed and demented, waiting for Saburo's call.

Scalia's balding head was covered with dots of water, and his cheeks and chin were wet, too. His nose looked longer than she remembered, its tip red and bulbous. She closed her eyes. Scalia reassured her that Sensei would never find out about Saburo's black market money. Saburo would become a rich man, his own person.

Then Scalia's voice hardened. His fingers dug into her flesh. Now Scalia would reveal his purpose. Her heart beat fast. Scalia must have something on her. Something big. The man at the next table at the yakuza club had left the room, returning in minutes with a satisfied smile. Had he called Scalia? Sensei?

Scalia took out a large envelope. He pointed. "Pictures," he said softly. "You and Saburo." He waved them in front of her. The grainy outline of her bottom, Saburo's leg, and her ecstatic expression as Saburo mounted her, hands wide, gripping the zabuton. They were shiny on the surface and slippery to the touch as if made for insult.

"Unless you do exactly what I say," his tone threatening, "you will have no future, not in Japan or America or anywhere. I will show these pictures to Headmaster Williams, quietly, over drinks. It doesn't matter that Saburo is my son. These pictures won't really hurt his future. Saburo will never graduate from that school anyway. He barely speaks English."

Sarah's legs buckled. Scalia pulled her straight. His voice was matterof-fact as he described Williams's old, straight-laced New England family, missionaries in Japan since the turn of the century. Williams's black-cloaked father gave sermons on Christianity in Japanese but supported the family by selling Japanese wood-block prints to New York dealers. "His son is not different. Entrepreneurial puritans are the worst kind of people, and America is full of them."

Sarah pulled back, but he held her.

"Letters will be written to Stanford and all the other colleges," he said in his most gentle, terrifying voice, "and more letters will be written to the State Department. Your file will be stuffed, and every time you make a request, pictures will be dragged out, and men will peer at them—curious, aroused, and disgusted. That's America. You and your parents will live in Japan on Red Cross passports. It won't be a bad life. You will go to Sophia University English program. You will tell your parents that you need one more year in Japan. That year will become a second year, and so on."

Sarah felt dizzy. She wanted to say something that would scare Scalia, something that would make him give her the pictures. Scalia had won by knowing details, Japan's networked obligations, its insistence on preparing, spying, calculating advantage. Sarah had understood only that Saburo was Scalia's plant, a bit of poison, someone she should avoid at all costs. She'd been arrogant, she had known but she hadn't listened.

Scalia held the pictures high and waved them above her head. She reached. He stepped away. She jumped. A dog barked. The fog swirled. They faced each other. Scalia smiled, a soft sad smile. She ran at him. He shook his head. Her hand reached. He turned. "Help me," she muttered. "Help." Scalia stood for a moment as if considering her appeal. His body was rigid and his expression serious. He was considering her appeal. He must see that this was evil. He must smile and hand her the pictures. What possible good could come of this? She would be humble, bow her thanks and gratitude.. But suddenly he pulled away. She reached for him but he stepped back, turned and without a backward glance, he went down the hill. She watched him disappear.

Then she understood. The realization came suddenly, all the pieces coming together, a puzzle assembled, each part fitting perfectly with the next. Sensei. At diner Sensei knew about the pictures. He had insisted that Scalia was his obedient friend, a person he could trust with any assignment. Scalia would obey. Sensei. Sensei's voice had been confident she would do whatever was necessary to bring Ryuzu to him. She would be that desperate. Sensei had discussed his strategy with Scalia, a general outline of blackmail, and in keeping with Japanese tradition, he left all details to his inferior.

Sensei.

THE BARGAIN

The following day Sensei's black car was parked by the school's front gate. She had called that morning asking for a meeting, her voice high, hesitant, understanding the call was an irrevocable step. "Sarah-chan." The car door opened. She slipped in the backseat.

"You must excuse the way I look," Sensei said, patting his loose, blue jacket with its diamond-shaped stitching. "I have just been to *kendo* practice. I hope it is not too casual for you." The loose jacket revealed Sensei's muscular chest, his skin taut except where it gathered by his armpit. A stick of incense glowed in the ashtray.

"I'm glad you called," Sensei said softly. "I knew something must be serious when I heard your voice, the first call in all these years. I know your parents forbid you to phone, but O'ba misses the sound of your voice. Your name is mentioned so often that I feel you are still in the house." Sarah lowered her eyes. Sensei noted her outfit, her schoolgirl white blouse, dark skirt, and thick socks, and folded his arms, waiting for her to make the first move.

A downward push of the handle, and she could

be on the street. Suzie headed toward the car and raised her hand as if expecting to be invited in. Sarah shook her head. Sensei smiled as if he understood Sarah's dilemma. "You always listened to me," Sensei said softly. "I believe that you will do what is right. That's why I paid special attention to you and taught you the old ways. You were daring, alert, and thoughtful. You were always yourself, and that is really why the children loved you so."

Sensei smiled, confident and sure, a look that laid the groundwork for his request. Now Sensei would offer a deal, one that would put her in peril, but one she must accept. "I need your help," Sarah said in a low voice. "I'm in trouble."

Sensei moved close, lit a long-handled pipe, and puffed slowly. Gradually the sweet smell of tobacco mingled with the incense. "I need your help too, Sarah-chan. We are all connected, so it's natural that we need each other. You and I will always need each other." His eyes had a faraway look. Sarah absorbed the silence. The driver tapped his white-gloved forefinger on the steering wheel.

"Will you go to Ryuzu in San'ya today?" Sensei asked softly. "Will you do this for me and for Japan? Ryuzu often spoke of your friendship. He was sad it ended badly. After you left, Ryuzu and the others would include you in their conversations as if you were still with them. Those children will always be your friends, Sarah-chan."

"Ryuzu is a Communist," Sarah said in the same soft tone as Sensei. "He will not listen to me or anyone. He wants to help the poor and work for the union in San'ya. He is doing what he wants. Like his father, Ryuzu is a dreamer and stubborn. Nothing will make Ryuzu return. Nothing. You know."

Sensei smiled. "Perhaps you are correct," he said in the same slow voice as if considering a serious problem. Sensei was playing with her. She tried to look attentive. "I am just a silly, old man," Sensei continued. "Japan is changing, and we all must change with it. I must adjust; that is only right. Japan will imitate America; obligation and honor will disappear. There will be no more *senpai* and *kohai*. Relationships will be practical. All that will remain of old ways will be a suggestion, a faint imprint. Young people like Ryuzu will make their own way. They will do what they want without regard for tradition, the feelings of others, or the good of Japan. It is logical. I understand."

Sarah was quiet. She felt him waiting. They were in a cat and mouse, a game she would lose. Sensei adjusted his kendo robe and puffed his pipe. The car was quiet except for the driver's tap against the steering wheel. Sarah thought of Saburo. Did he know about her call to Sensei? He should protect her. He should, but he couldn't. Her head began to pound. There were too many plots: Sensei's role in Masaru's death, his threat to ruin Ryuzu and expose Sachiko, his knowledge of Scalia's blackmail. She was powerless. Sensei's half-naked body, emanating a faint smell of perspiration, dominated the car.

"But you are the only person Ryuzu might still listen to," Sensei repeated. "You will do whatever is necessary, whatever it takes to bring back Ryuzu-kun." He took loose tobacco from a pouch, twisted it between his fingers, and stuffed it into the bowl of his pipe. His slow movements, like that of an ancient dance, put her in a meditative, trance-like state. Her breathing slowed, and she felt as if she were floating. Sensei's low voice reminded her of the forest and all that she had tried to forget.

"What I'm asking is not logical," he continued, "but we Japanese are not logical. We are emotional, wet, connected to each other and to the past. I know that it is confusing, but you are part of that wet web of connections. You understand the importance of relationships. In the West, people are dry; they change their minds and relationships. At Harvard I was amazed by how easily people moved from one situation to another without regard for how it would affect the group. They planned their lives by switching jobs and relationships according to their advantage. Their attitudes shocked me."

Sensei puffed deeply, talking as if he were trying to understand. "Ryuzu-chan may have changed. He may be doing what he wants, but I know that he keeps us buried in his heart. He thinks of you by day and dreams of you at night. We Japanese never forget our friends, our true nakama. He keeps you close. Ryuzu-kun, like his father Masaru-kun, is real Japanese. If you do this," Sensei said, "I will never forget it."

Sensei's betrayal of Masaru had been great, Sarah thought. He had turned in Masaru quietly with a pointed observation said in the right tone with the right implication to the right people, a remark that would ripple down the ranks until the arrest was made. He betrayed Masaru for the good of Japan. Only when Sensei met Ryuzu—with his high forehead, straight back, deep brown skin, and flashing eyes—did Sensei feel regret. Only then did he appreciate the horror of what he had done.

"You must try," Sensei repeated. "Ryuzu-kun always trusted you. If you do this," Sensei again promised, "I will never forget it."

Whack! Eddie's hand sounded hard against the side window. Sarah bolted upright. His hand knocked again. His eyes teasing, alive with interest, he pointed at the back seat of his bike. She shook her head. Eddie shrugged, waved, and was gone. The sound broke through Sensei's aura. Sensei's dreamy voice was now harsh. Blood flowed into her limbs.

She would meet Sensei on his own terms. Yes, she would guarantee the return of Ryuzu for her freedom. She would stall for time, promise just enough to stop Scalia's blackmail. Her parents had said the family would leave Japan soon. Besides, Sensei's quest was hopeless. Ryuzu would never comply. He was committed to the cause.

Sensei smiled.

She smiled.

"I will go to Ryuzu," Sarah said softly. "I will do my best."

"My car will take you to San'ya," Sensei spoke quietly, reviewing the deal. "The driver will drop you off in front of Ryuzu's union and will wait for you. You will be perfectly safe." Sensei's voice dropped to a whisper. Sarah leaned forward, knowing his words would be the final bargain. "If Ryuzu returns to me, you will have my gratitude for the rest of my life. I will help you and your family in any way I can. I understand that you will leave Japan soon. Your parents want to live in America. That is fine. I agree."

The chauffeur put the car in gear. Sensei smiled. His kimono had loosened further. Sarah could see his entire chest, the chest that she'd first seen as Sensei meditated by the treasure mound. His nipples puckered, and his skin was browner than she remembered but with the same rounded, muscular shape. She wished that he would close the kimono, but he seemed oblivious.

"You must let him know that I am not angry and that I will continue to help his family." Sensei paused for a moment. "Ryuzu's nephew Shimpei-kun asked for him. Sachiko-chan misses him. Ryuzu-kun has obligations to me, to Japan. He must return. He must come back. He must."

SAN'YA

It was just after four.

"We are close," the driver said.

They were in the *shitamachi*, "low city," close to the sea, populated by Koreans, untouchable *Eta*, and other disadvantaged. It all seemed ordinary enough—men watching a baseball game, troops of uniformed school children, people sitting at a noodle shop, and housewives wearing large aprons buying last-minute items for the evening meal.

The car slowed and crossed a large boulevard. "Roll up your window," the driver directed. "Now we are in San'ya."

The landscape changed, altered with the wide street that separated San'ya from the baseball teams, children, housewives, and restaurants. Color and movement were replaced by asphalt and low buildings, a large expanse of gray. The sidewalk splattered with vomit looked like the splashes of color on a painter's palette. Where were the trees and grass? Where were the children, the people returning from work? Where were the shopkeepers? Where were the shops?

Then she saw them, blotches on the pavement with matted hair and open sores, clutching bottles, huddled on newspapers, oblivious to their environment. Wounded, beyond repair, beyond salvation, they filled her with fear. How could Sensei send her on such a dangerous mission? She would say there had been a mistake, and she could not leave the car. The driver would understand. He must be afraid, too. The men might attack. Nothing was sacred in San'ya. But before she could say anything, the driver parked.

Three men, faces bloated, lying in a doorway, pointed. One with a closed, swollen eyelid yelled, "Get lost, gaijin." He repeated this in a slurred voice, then rose and walked unsteadily toward the car. "You don't belong here," he yelled, swaying back and forth, tripping then righting himself, his flushed face twisted in a hideous grin.

"The window," the driver hissed and turned the handle. But he was too late; the man's hand, with its blackened fingernails, grabbed Sarah's shoulder. Her blouse ripped. The stench of alcohol and urine filled the car. She moved back, but the hand, cut and swollen, followed. Sarah pressed against her seat. The man groped for something he could hold on to. The handle turned, and the window squeezed his arm. The man yelled and withdrew.

He stepped back. For a moment it looked like he would join his friends, who hooted, "Do it! Do it!" The man spread his hands wide, grinned as if he understood, and opened his pants. His thick penis, waved like a flag. The men roared. A yellow spray coated the rear window. More spray followed. His friends stood, arms around each other, and shuffled toward the car. They unzipped their pants. Penises flashed. The back window was thick with urine.

The driver cursed, drove several blocks, and examined a map. He pointed to a flat-roofed building. "That's it," he said in a low voice. "That's the Sogidan

Union; that's where you have to go."

Men loitered on the corner, and more gathered across the street. They eyed the car. The men squatting on the sidewalk rolled onto their sides and took a swig from their bottles. Others jeered. A short man, with a swollen eyelid puffed yellow, shook his fist. Sarah remained in her seat, measuring the distance to the building. It was impossible. The lane was crowded with men. She couldn't move. She wouldn't.

"I'll wait right here," the driver said. "I can't drive down the lane. It's too narrow. Go quickly. You'll be OK. Just a couple of blocks." The driver opened Sarah's door and gave her a push.

The putrid odor of garbage, of vomit, rotten eggs, and grease, piled next to doorways and lamp-posts, turned her stomach. Men glared. One mumbled and threw the empty bottle against the wall. The glass shattered. The men laughed. Another man threw a bottle. The glass shards, green, blue, and white, sparkled.

What if the driver didn't wait, the union door was locked, and she couldn't find Ryuzu? What if the driver got the wrong building? What if Ryuzu told her to leave?

The car door slammed.

She ran. A man, surprisingly agile, moved to cut her off. With short hair and bloodshot eyes—demon-like—he blocked the street. He had the thin-skinned look of a drinker. They faced each other. The men jeered. She moved to bypass him, but he stayed with her. It was a dance; she turned, and he followed. His eyes took on the wildness of the hunt. She backed away.

"Go for it," the men cheered.

The man charged, brushed her shoulder, and grabbed her arm. She pulled away and staggered. The sidewalk, dangerously close, gray and uneven, made her move quickly. Her stomach heaved. The man circled and came from behind. Cornered, her back against a building, she imagined the worst. The man grinned; eyes flashing, arms waving, and confident of victory, he turned toward his audience with raised hands. They roared approval. He stayed that way, his arms high and his feet apart, whistling success. The men encouraged him. His whistle grew louder.

Sarah ducked under his raised arm, her legs churning, sprinting past the broken glass, garbage, flies, and semiconscious laborers, toward the Sogidan Union. He was just behind. She smelled his hair oil, his matted clothes, and his filth. His footsteps made her move faster. The high whistle filled her with terror. There were more cheers. Her chest hurt, and her heart pounded. She kept going. The whole street was yelling.

The door to Sogidan Union was open. She ran inside, slammed the door, and leaned against a wall. The space was dark. Tears rolled down her cheeks. Her heart thumped, and her knees shook. She listened for the man. The street was quiet. Her eyes adjusted. A dirt entryway led to a six-mat tatami room and a small alcove. A man slept in the alcove on a rough quilt. His snores filled the air.

She wiped her eyes. The mission was impossible. She was a small girl facing an adult, violent world. What arrogance. Scalia and Sensei must be having a good laugh. She didn't know Ryuzu's last name or where to find him. He had always been just Ryuzu-chan. No one would help. There were no police in San'ya. Nothing.

Sensei wanted results. She must bring back Ryuzu. That was the deal. All her stalling tactics meant nothing. Scalia would do the dirty work. Sensei never made a move without considering all options. He had been trained as a naval intelligence operative. He was

Japanese. He was Sensei.

"Leave the door open," a voice called from the next room. "People need to know that we're open."

A tall, dark-skinned man wearing a white shirt and black pants leaned against the doorway. He had the high forehead of a scholar, long narrow cheeks, and a slender neck. His fingers tapped against the wall as if impatient with life. Then he smiled, and as the grin spread across his face, she recognized his full lips. He moved quickly toward her.

Ryuzu.

"Sarah-chan," Ryuzu said softly. "I recognized you right away."

The years slid away, her rage dissolved, and she remembered only Ryuzu-chan of the forest, his sudden smile, his love of animals, plants, justice, and her. This was the Ryuzu who had befriended her, protected her, and made the others accept her. Memories of their storytelling and easy play came rushing back.

She smiled and then laughed. Ryuzu joined her. Their laughter, bright and high, filled the entryway. Sarah wanted to continue laughing as if the whole journey were an enormous joke, but the sound caught in her throat, unhinged, as if she'd been on a wild ride. Ryuzu put his hand on her shoulder. She moved close. He pointed to the sleeping man.

"Sit," Ryuzu offered and motioned to the table in the main room. He locked the sliding door. "We have a little time before the men return from their jobs. You'll have to go then. They are often in a foul mood by the end of the day. I can't predict their behavior."

The cushion was crusted with dirt, matted down by hundreds of bodies. She tucked her skirt under her. Ryuzu poured green tea from a thermos into thick cups. His slow movements reminded her of Sensei. She felt large and impatient as she watched tea leaves settle to the bottom. Ryuzu turned his cup three times in traditional fashion. Sarah turned hers as well. Their slurps filled the room.

Ryuzu did not seem so brown and strong now. There were bags under his eyes, and in the bright light, his skin looked gray. Tiny wrinkles crisscrossed his neck so that he appeared parched, like old fruit dried in the sun. Broken blood vessels lined his cheeks, delicate scribbles turning dark at the center. His pointed chin, angular face, and thin arms—covered with cuts, gashes turning to purple—made her think of yakuza and Sensei's warning. There were more lacerations on his hands.

"You have made quite an effort to find me," Ryuzu said, more bemused than angry. Sarah was quiet, understanding he must have seen Sensei's car at the end of the street. Moments passed. Ryuzu waited. She wanted dialogue, a conversation where she could explain.

She said forcefully, "Sensei cares about you."

"Sensei cares about Sensei and about preserving his Japan so that he can care about himself even more."

Sarah took a deep breath, at once overwhelmed by Sensei's demand, one that she could never fulfill, and one that Ryuzu should never accept. She had not counted on Ryuzu looking so fragile, as if he could fold entirely. When he spoke, a vein in his forehead throbbed. He was that thin.

"When I was a student in Russia," Ryuzu said in a thoughtful voice, "I learned a great deal about what the Japanese in naval intelligence did during the war. My teachers showed me pictures of Nanjing. Have you seen those pictures? Not pretty: sticks protruding from vaginas, men kneeling patiently waiting to be beheaded, and people buried alive. We Japanese killed six million Chinese civilians. We bashed in the heads of babies to save bullets. We obliterated whole villages to avoid imagined reprisals. We created slave labor and military brothels and performed medical experiments on captured soldiers and civilians. That's what I learned in Russia. We were worse than animals. We should be ashamed. We should bow our heads. We should teach the truth about what happened in China and Asia to Japanese schoolchildren. They need to know. It must never happen again."

Sarah rose and went to the window. Except for Sensei's car, the lane was empty.

The Dickensian atmosphere—small tatami room, greasy pillows, and the man snoring in the next room—removed all doubt. She was simply a ploy in a larger plot. Sensei didn't expect her to seduce Ryuzu and bring him back. That was crazy. She knew it. Sensei knew it. What could Ryuzu's union accomplish against the yakuza, construction companies, and the Nagatacho government? Nothing. Still, Ryuzu's commitment to the union was a symbol, a threat that Sensei and his Nagatacho cronies could not tolerate.

Sensei and Nagatacho had it all worked out. She was a messenger. Ryuzu had been alerted. Ryuzu would realize Sensei had gone to a great deal of trouble to deliver the message. Scalia's blackmail and her risky journey to San'ya meant Sensei was deadly serious. Ryuzu would understand the warning. It was the Japanese way. Nothing went unprepared. With her visit to San'ya, Sensei would have fulfilled his obligation. Had his friend Masaru been adequately informed? Certainly. If Ryuzu persisted with union activities, there would eventually be a fatal or crippling accident.

"It's the workers of San'ya who are building modern Japan," Ryuzu continued, "but modern Japan spurns them. It's about payoffs." His voice hardened as

he described the system: construction companies working hand in hand with yakuza and politicians to make
San'ya profitable. Death awaited those who protested.
They fell from buildings or were run down by trucks.
All was accepted. There could be no real dialogue in
a place like San'ya. No real dialogue in Japan. Ryuzu
finished by holding up a newspaper. He pointed to a
picture. "What country has news pictures of politicians
sitting next to gangsters?" he asked. "This one is a major
yakuza character," he continued, indicating a large man
on the right. "This picture celebrates a known killer."

Sarah fell quiet.

"Look at me." Ryuzu's voice became impatient.
"I'm twenty years old, and most people think I'm forty.
San'ya is a jail without walls, and it kills even without
yakuza. Yama men have nowhere else to go. Shame has
chased them to this place. Alcohol. Gambling. Debt. If
they are Korean or Burakunin, they can't get work. Initially they think San'ya will save them. They can make
money to send home, money that will buy their way
back into society. It never happens. I came here to help,
and now I can't leave either."

Ryuzu looked as if she could shake him into pieces if she wanted. Perspiration dripped off his forehead.
Fine moisture covered his neck and arms. Delicate veins
lined his eyelids, and more veins throbbed on his neck.
His Adam's apple protruded in lumpy detail beneath his
thin skin. His hands trembled. Did he have TB? Heart
problems? She wanted to feed him, make him rest, relax, and smile. She couldn't imagine him working at the
bank, being introduced to Sensei's friends at Nagatacho, and attending the University of Tokyo. Sensei was
dreaming. Ryuzu was made of another cloth.

His grave eyes, full of resolve, were eyes Sarah
remembered. She wanted to take his hand. She felt

privileged to sit next to him. He had integrity and all that she admired. She imagined that his father, Masaru, had looked like this, an overheated wire, taut and ready to die for justice, for the rights of others. Would Sensei repeat his betrayal of Masaru with Ryuzu? Did he need to repeat all of it?

Footsteps sounded in front of the building. The man in the next room stirred. Soon the Yama men, exhausted from a day's work, furious with their lives, would descend on the union in an alcoholic rage. Ryuzu could not protect her. No one could protect her.

She would let Sensei know that she had tried. A man of substance had replaced Ryuzu, the boy with the open smile and soft, curious eyes. Her troubles were nothing compared to his. He was fighting a grand battle, one that would change people's lives, while she plotted her own survival. She imagined him high on scaffolding above the city, noting conditions, talking to workers, developing bargaining points to use against construction companies and yakuza. She was not a friend but a terrible messenger, a courier with a warning, one he should despise with all his heart.

Sarah stood and turned toward the door. She felt softer now, filled with understanding and less determined to win. Meeting Ryuzu had erased the future. It didn't exist. America was too far, too foreign to think about. Nothing mattered but doing right. Sensei, Scalia— they lived an illusion. This was real. Ryuzu was a person she could never be. He had drawn her into his orbit as a child, and as a child she believed that they were one. But it wasn't so. Ryuzu understood the wide arch of things. He brushed details aside and looked at the large picture, a vision that he worked to fulfill and one that he believed in. Her fear vanished. She would walk, head high, to the car. There was nothing to fear.

Yama men would understand and leave her alone.

"Tell me what Sensei has on you," Ryuzu said, his warm voice interrupting her thoughts. "Tell me, Sarah-chan. It must be big to bring you all the way to San'ya."

The room was silent, pregnant with knowledge, loaded with an understanding, an acknowledgment of legacies enacted through them. Ryuzu's lecture on China and the union was his way of postponing this moment. He took her hand and turned her palm up, gently tracing his finger over her lifeline, like Saburo and the bargirls, hesitating at the break, then following the line to the base of her thumb. If she remained with him, he would listen. She knew it from his soft touch, the yearning in his voice, and his tender smile. Sensei was right. Ryuzu loved her.

There were more footsteps outside the building. Ryuzu closed the door and turned the key in the lock. "Tell me, Sarah-chan," he said gently. His breath caressed her cheek. "Tell me."

The clock ticked. The men drifted into the next room, their voices demanding a place at the table, beer, and a cushion to rest. Bangs on the door increased, but Ryuzu did not rush her, folding his arms across his chest and nodding encouragement. Sarah sat close. Tears of pain and regret poured down her cheeks.

She told him everything.

CHOICE

S arah met Ryuzu every day. Ryuzu pulled her across Tokyo to Minami Senju Station and his San'ya world. She checked into homeroom, walked to Naka Meguro Station, and took the Hibya line through the up-and-coming districts of Hiro and Ropponji to elegant Ginza, where the train turned west to the sea. The long journey prepared her for San'ya. By the time the train reached Minami Senju Station, she was ready, disguised with a hooded jacket and baggy pants.

Ryuzu was at the station with a broad smile. They walked through San'ya, stopping at food stalls hawking pig entrails and drinking joints that reeked of cheap alcohol. Ryuzu knew each Yama man's history. He understood the reason he was in San'ya, his drinking habits, his health problems, and his current debt. "Come to the Sogodan Union," he said at the end of each conversation. "We will help." The men laughed.

She felt safe with Ryuzu, content to trail behind him hearing the stories of the Yama men, defensively told and laced with humor. The men on the sidewalks, ill, drunk, or semiconscious, left them alone. Others questioned Ryuzu on the union and then asked about her in a rough tone. Ryuzu answered questions carefully, explaining that she was his childhood friend, that he had known her always. The men looked bewildered.

Between conversations they sat on park benches and spoke of the past: Ryuzu's father, Masaru, Ryuzu's hatred of Nagatacho politicians, Sensei, yakuza, and his terror of dying in San'ya. In turn she described her fear of leaving Japan and her dread of being trapped. The talk absorbed her. Gradually the conversation widened and moved away from Sensei, Scalia, the past, and their fears.

They argued about writers, Sarah preferring Tolstoy's ability to reveal, while Ryuzu admired Dostoevsky's fatalistic passion. They also argued about politics, about the viability of the Russian Constituent Assembly, and about the brutal class politics of Socialist Revolutionaries, Mensheviks, and Bolsheviks. They debated whether Trotsky should have been Lenin's successor, whether Lenin's New Economic Policy might have succeeded, and whether Russia could have defeated Hitler without Stalin's collectivization.

They never touched, but the dialogue made her yearn for a larger world of ideas, values that she believed in, thoughts she could never express to her friends at school, Buttericks, or Saburo. Despite Ryuzu's Soviet education, he questioned and read widely. Idealistic but pragmatic, he wanted to know, to think, to have an effect. He defined the world through books, using novelists and philosophers as a reference point. In quiet moments he quoted poems of Basho, Pushkin, Rilke, Frost, and Shakespeare in Russian, Japanese, or English.

And San'ya, Ryuzu's laboratory of desperation, provided a role for Ryuzu. There was no shortage of Yama men's need for advice. They wanted a strong shoulder, an impartial voice, and a kind word. Ryuzu was respected in San'ya, depended on, and trusted.

Yama men asked what to say on the phone call to their wives or how to respond to a parent's letter. They listened to his answers with a solemn expression.

Talk with Ryuzu reminded her of her parents. The subjects, philosophical, replete with unanswerable questions, were familiar. She felt a release of energy, a great wind moving through her, freeing her from the mundane and allowing her to think. Her mind soared with opportunities, explorations of subjects and ideas remote from her friends and her life at school.

Her hours in San'ya were spent thinking of others. The Yama men's stories absorbed her. She advised Ryuzu in each case. Ito should get a TB test, Moto should call his wife and apologize, and Sato should have his cuts treated in a proper clinic. Ryuzu listened. She brought Ryuzu sandwiches and fruit, insisting that he eat properly. He shared the food with his Yama men, and she brought more—leftovers from dinner, roast beef, chicken, beet salad, and pickled fish. They picnicked on wood benches and on the low table in the Sogodan Union. He laughed and obliged her, talking through each mouthful. It was stolen time.

Saburo had disappeared without warning. Since the yakuza nightclub—jewels on the table, thin-wristed girls, and hoods with hacked digits—Saburo had stopped coming to school. When her friends asked after Saburo, Sarah shrugged as if he were of no consequence. Yet late at night, after her homework and her sister Vera's bedtime story, she thought of his swift movement, his slicked-back hair, and his desire. In her dreams Saburo's voice, tender, coming from a great distance, made her long for his touch. His soft eyes revealed his vulnerability. Yet her heart hardened at the thought of the Yakuza club. And she had questions. Had Saburo given the jewels to the girls? Did he sleep with the girls? Was he enraged? Did he know about the blackmail? Those were painful moments, feelings, and questions she could not speak of to anyone.

Eddie sat close in class, laughed at her jokes, and quoted her to friends in a loud voice. Sarah continued to help him on tests. He did not ask about her life but made side comments like, "Hey, missed you," when she appeared for homeroom checkout. Eddie had been accepted to Hope College in Utah. His gangster father was pleased and invested in a nearby ski resort. Eddie raced his cycle. He hooked up with Suzie, playing with her fingers in class, stroking her bottom as she mounted his cycle. Ah, Eddie. It seemed only moments ago that she was that free.

In ten days Scalia and Sensei expected her at the Flamingo Club with her answer and Ryuzu in tow. She marked off days in her calendar with small dots, desperate at the thought of what was ahead. Yet despite her worries, San'ya was becoming comprehensible. Now she noted "watchers," young men standing at street corners sent by their yakuza bosses. Now she recognized Yama men, the ones who could work and those who couldn't. Now she saw yakuza following them, marking their activities, recording whom they spoke to, where they ate. When she mentioned it to Ryuzu, he laughed as if all her observations were obvious. When she tried to disappear, her hood pulled over her face, Ryuzu chided, "You are an outsider; of course you are noticed."

Sarah skirted topics that might bring up Sensei's demands or Scalia and the blackmail. It was enough to be with Ryuzu, to wander and give voice to ideas and thoughts. Their history, the golden days, Sensei, and all of it created an understanding, a platform of trust. Occasionally, Ryuzu would ask after her mother, but that was all. The more time they spent together, the greater the ease between them. Ryuzu noticed when she was silent and when she needed to talk. He called her "little sister." She laughed. At the end of each day, Ryuzu escorted her to the train platform and waited until she boarded.

On a Wednesday morning, Sarah arrived at San'ya's Minami Senju Station. Ryuzu ran toward her. "Come," he said. "Yama men are gathering. It is finally happening."

He pulled her across the street, explaining that a Yama man arrested and beaten for complaining about pay and work hours was being held at the local police box. Yakuza were there in force backing the police. Ryuzu spoke quickly, perspiration dripping from his forehead, and his lips pressed thin. "We will do battle. We will win. Yes, this time we will win. Everyone wants change."

Sarah pulled her wool cap over her forehead. They crossed the boulevard and took a sharp right. Surrounded by Yama men, they walked in step toward the police station. More men poured from buildings and alleys. They clogged the narrow street. All eyes focused on the police box surrounded by yakuza hoods. Sarah recognized Hiro, a gambler and drinker who, hearing there was good money in San'ya, had left a wife and two children in Hokkaido. "I'm ashamed," he'd confessed. "I drink, I gamble, I don't call home anymore." But now Hiro, head high, moved deliberately, his arm linked with the others.

The crowd thickened, and the stench of the Yama men, alcohol engrained in their skin and hair, made her cover her face. They smelled of moving rot. Dirt caked their necks and the creases around their ears. More dirt-edged pant cuffs, necklines, and shirts. Sneakers, torn and filthy, exposed their swollen, bruised feet. Nylon jackets, rubber shoes, and dirty clothes covered their wounded bodies. Red, swollen faces balanced on thin necks made them old. Young and aged, diseased and healthy, clogged the street.

Ryuzu pulled her close, gathering her to him, and murmured her name. Ryuzu's need bolted through her. It was the first time they had touched. Her face was against his shoulder. His ribs felt sharp through the thin jacket. Hiro called, but Ryuzu ignored him. Others yelled. His attention was on her. The crowd's energy wrapped around them. His arm brushed her breast, his lips pressed against her cheek. He whispered that he would protect her, that he needed her, and that she mustn't worry.

White-helmeted police with raised clubs took demonstrators one by one. The Yama men knew it. This was their fight. No union had organized this march; the demonstration had erupted spontaneously, a protest rising from a Yama man who dared complain. Word of the injustice spread, his story told in cheap bars, in food stalls, in dormitory hotels, and in parks where the homeless slept. The police, elbow to elbow with yakuza and intent on destruction, dominated the street. The May Day demonstration was nothing compared to this. "Come on," they challenged. "Come on, we're ready if you are. We will crack your heads and break your backs. Come on."

Ryuzu's grip tightened. He pressed her head against his shoulder and shielded her face with his hand. The pulse in his throat quickened. The crowd's energy encouraged her. The police and death meant nothing. She was with the Yama men. Their smell did not bother her. They were a unified force against corporations, police, and the government. She owned this fight—it was in her blood—in her history.

Nothing could stop this. They had right on their side. Justice must prevail. A great cry went up from the crowd. She yelled with them. The Yama men were determined to be seen—"Look at our ragged clothes, bloodshot eyes, and bloated faces. Breathe the alcohol stench on our hair and skin. Peel the maggots off our bodies and wipe the dirt from our ears. We want our Yama man back. He is one of us. We will right this wrong for all wrongs."

The police and yakuza raised their shields and advanced with swinging sticks, moving from right to left and back again. Bodies collapsed. Yama men replaced them. Screams filled the air. A man with a bloodied face fell, and another held his eye. Bones cracked, and blood dripped. They went down like rag dolls, crumpled blotches on cement. More helmeted police streamed in.

Sarah's lungs hurt. Gas. Her eyes stung. Gas. Her throat swelled and ached. Gas. Tears rolled down her cheeks. Her membranes poured liquid, steams of saliva clogging her throat, running from her nose, coursing down her face. Her skin burned. More gas. Men coughed, doubled over, and wretched. Unlike the May Day demonstration, the narrow lane held the gas. They were suffocating, groping, delirious with pain. She felt strangled. Her larynx swelled. She clutched her throat and stretched her neck. There was no air. The pain intensified. Men screamed in agony and held bits of cloth against their faces.

A deep fear took hold: Yama men could turn on her, police could hit her, and gas could paralyze her. Whack, whack, more bones broke; more men went down. Sarah shook. The trembling wouldn't stop. Ryuzu continued to march, his expression set, his hand pressed on her neck. She wanted to break free, but loyalty held her. This time she would be with Ryuzu to the

end. Nothing could make her leave. Canisters rolled on
the street. Flames leapt from the police box. The Yama
men yelled. Yakuza's hachimaki headbands, a moving
ribbon of black and white, filled the lane.

Then, "Run," Ryuzu said. "Run." His voice was
sure. He pointed down the street in the opposite direction from the police box. Ryuzu should be with his
union, but he went against the crowd, away from the
violence, police, and knot of Yama men to a side street.
Buildings on either side blocked the noise. The lane was
empty. It seemed impossible after the crowd, gas and
police. They absorbed the silence in disbelief, and headed west toward the main boulevard. Ryuzu's hand went
around her waist. He lowered his head, so his cheek
brushed her neck. She felt his breath. Both arms were
around her. They bundled together and moved in slow
motion. He whispered her name. She could not speak,
her voice gone, her body ached. Blood ran into her shoe.
Ryuzu wasn't in any better shape. They smelled of soot,
alcohol, and grime.

Ryuzu stopped. He turned toward her, stroking
her neck, his fingers soft, and murmured endearments.
His light touch stirred her. She leaned into him. He
pulled her close. They swayed, moving back and forth,
the motion calming. He ran his fingers to the base of her
spine. His hands were everywhere. She closed her eyes.
He covered their faces with his jacket. Tented, they held
each other.

Then Ryuzu stood straight. "Sarah-chan," he
whispered and steered them right. "Sarah-chan." The
red blink of a hotel light was just ahead. She put her
hand on his long cheek, and he closed his eyes. He
stroked her face and her back. His fragility touched
her. She whispered his name and felt his desire, a hunger that drew her close. His lips were on hers, and she

pressed against him.

"Sarah-chan," he whispered. "Let me. Let me."

Then they went inside.

* * *

By three o'clock, Sarah was back at school. No one noticed the rip in her blouse, the grime on her pants, her matted hair, or the gash on her leg. She stood in the main hall waiting for questions. None came. The school felt strange. Who were these people talking and laughing? They looked young, oblivious. Were they friends? Impossible. She was a stranger in a foreign place. Details she hadn't noticed loomed large. The classrooms looked shabby. The floors needed a good wash. The map in Mr. Buttericks's office was ripped. His bookshelf was untidy.

Eddie had a motorcycle race that night, the Wu twins twisted their jade bangles and whispered of acceptance to the University of Nebraska, and Tom talked football. Sarah moved from one group to another as if in a dream. She laughed at jokes and nodded. What was Ryuzu doing now? Had he returned to the union? Had the wounded been treated? Were yakuza still on the rampage? Had the Yama man been set free? She sat in the library with her head in her hands, waves of hysteria washing over her, her agitation growing. Her head pounded. Her stomach ached, and her skin was wet with perspiration. She washed her face in the girls' room, sponged her skin, and rinsed her hair.

At four she heard the news. The demonstration had ended with no deaths, and there were ten thousand police in San'ya. She walked slowly toward the door.

"Sarah-chan."

She looked up.

Saburo smiled a knowing smile as if they'd been

apart too long. He stood before her with his thumbs hooked in his belt. At once her rage about the Yakuza club, bargirls, all of it, dissolved. She missed him. His absence, initially a relief, had been replaced by a dull ache. She never mentioned his name, not to Ryuzu, her parents, or her friends. Saburo was her private sorrow. Now he stood next to her, his arm on her waist. She felt his rounded muscles and heard his low voice saying she was his princess, his love, and his soul. She wanted all of it.

Did Saburo know where she had been for the past weeks? Did he understand what Scalia and Sensei wanted? Did he know about the blackmail, the pictures, and Ryuzu? His expression was open. Wide-eyed, his cheeks puffed with pride. He owned the moment. Saburo did not hold grudges or regrets. A hero in his own story, he was protected. Nothing could change that. Past and future did not exist for Saburo. He took what he wanted and enjoyed life with boundless passion. No wonder her classmates and teachers liked Saburo. He was fun. He was earnest. He was innocent. Saburo knew nothing.

Sarah smiled into his eyes. Her skin tingled as he pulled her to him. He touched her matted hair and her torn blouse tentatively, as if she might break, before folding her close. "My darling," he said softly, "my darling. What happened to you? You're a mess. Where have you been, my little bird?" She laughed and held him, inhaling his pomade hair oil and tea breath, relieved at his presence, gentle voice, and concern. His body molded to her, breathing her in, slowly, carefully, as if afraid to lose her.

Her friends watched.

The last bell rang.

She followed Saburo out the door.

❋❋❋

The next day Ryuzu waited by the Minami Sanju station gate. They sat on a low bench. San'ya was quiet except for police cars idling at corners. He told her she was beautiful, that she had brought him back to life, to a reality he had forgotten, one that allowed him to feel. The grass and the wood bench looked different. Everything had texture, movement. The world had come alive. The leaves were green, the earth a rich brown, the sky, a fathomless blue. She was his awakening. He gave himself to her. They were outsiders who spoke the same language.

Ryuzu was wrong, she protested. She was the outsider. Everyone else belonged. But Ryuzu ignored her murmurings. He toyed with her fingers and spoke softly. She was magic. The Yama men knew it. They asked about her. She had an effect on them. She had joined the protest against the Yakuza and police. She yelled their slogans. She risked her life. She was fearless, a fighter who knew right from wrong. Ryuzu's hand moved slowly down her back. She closed her eyes.

He spoke of San'ya in a voice that asked for reassurance. This time Yama men had lost and won. In the end the union must represent all Yama men. It would make a difference. He would study law. He would challenge the system. There were others like him. He would find them. It would be a long struggle. Eventually they would force politicians to listen. They must win.

She turned to him, moved close, and touched his thin cheek. Perhaps Ryuzu was right. They were both outsiders. She wished it were true. She wanted a friend that she could understand, share a point of view with, and depend on. Ryuzu closed his eyes. Her fingers moved to his mouth, and his soft lips pressed against her hand. He kissed her palm, letting his tongue linger. They hovered, uneasy with the present and terrified of the future.

The man behind the hotel desk pointed to a room in back overlooking a parking lot. They held each other. Sarah played Ryuzu's thin body like an instrument, plucking strings until she felt his desire. The heat rose between them. They fell on the narrow futon, licking, touching, and sucking. He flattened himself against her.

Ryuzu talked, his speech in rapid fire, afraid she would disappear unless San'ya, Sensei, and the blackmail were discussed. Her blackmail and San'ya were the same. Sensei pulled all the strings. The old ways must be destroyed. Justice must prevail. Sarah covered his mouth, but he spoke through her fingers, the sound muffled, his words hardly intelligible. She answered his questions with more questions, and soon the room was full of words, nothing left untouched. The dark gave permission for a necessary dialogue,, a conversation they needed to interrupt their topsy-turvy world. When Ryuzu entered her, they were still talking.

❊ ❊ ❊

By three she was back at school. At three thirty, Saburo was at the back gate. Sarah made love to Saburo and Ryuzu in a barren, tatami room with nothing but the smell of grass and dank clay walls, and in the back room of a hotel on a moldy quilt. When she was with one, she could not imagine life with the other, adjusting her behavior and thoughts to each. With Saburo she expressed herself by buying small presents and listening while he planned a future on the island, in the black market, or at the Flamingo Club. She poured his tea, brushed the lint from his jacket, and told him amusing stories. She did not ask about the gasoline business or

Scalia. She did not question his comings and goings, whom he met with, and where he spent time. All was taboo. With Saburo she was in the moment. Nothing outside his small room was of consequence. He whispered his plans in a dreamlike voice. He never asked about her life. Her acceptance by Stanford University and her family's plans to leave Japan was taboo. "You are my island," Saburo said. "Yes," she answered softly.

Sarah described her feelings, thoughts, and dilemmas with Ryuzu—her fear of America and her greater fear of leaving Japan. She talked about Japanese values she cherished. American beliefs terrified her. Americans were out for themselves. They were barbaric. In America she would disappear. She would be nothing. Ryuzu listened, put his arm around her, and in a tone that suggested that she would survive spoke of his adjustment to Russia, its crude humor, physicality, and the Russian acceptance of secrecy and deceit.

She avoided talking to Ryuzu about the blackmail and meeting with Sensei. She would protect Ryuzu at all costs. When he mentioned it, she changed the subject; if he referred to Scalia or Sensei, she went silent. In each case he squeezed her hand as if he understood her dilemma. It was easier to discuss large issues like the union, Yakuza roaming the streets, Nagatacho politics, and favors given and taken between politicians, bureaucrats, and big business.

Did Saburo notice the smell of San'ya, the bite marks on her neck? Wasn't he curious about her wet hair and swollen lip? Didn't he wonder where she had been during the day? Didn't he think of Sensei's request? Sometimes she caught him looking at her with a quizzical expression, the gaze long, penetrating, a troubled look full of remorse. She turned away then, waiting for the moment to pass, unsure how to answer his questions. But he never asked.

Did Ryuzu see the chafe mark on her stomach or the tiny bruise on her left thigh, or smell Saburo's cheap cologne? Didn't he wonder why she knew so much about the Shimbashi black market and gasoline prices? Didn't he notice her lipstick before returning to school? Didn't he wonder about the new gold chain around her neck? Wasn't he aware of Saburo's relationship to Sensei? He knew that Saburo had taken her to the Flamingo Club and that Saburo worked with Sensei in the black market.

Nothing was ever said.

After dinner, watching her parents hold hands and talk softly of the future, Sarah banished thoughts of Saburo and Ryuzu. Her parents would not understand her life, one that was against their values, morals, and assumptions. She would go from being their hero to their great disappointment. They were right. It shouldn't be. She was on a `slippery slope, traveling without a compass, a descent that was certain to end in disaster. Her days, divided between Saburo and Ryuzu, between opposing values, created havoc. There was no Sarah.

Her dreams, filled with violent movement, images of sturdy, Mongolian ponies, restless, racing across a vast plain, obsessed her. Steam from the ponies' nostrils and the sound of pounding hoofs filled the air. Their wild eyes moved frantically left to right in search of space. Shoulder to shoulder, keeping pace with each other, they advanced, coming from nowhere and going nowhere. The madness created a torrent of dirt, sand, and grass that sprayed across her mind, making her dizzy, confused, and short of breath. She awoke on the floor, her throat clogged and limbs bruised.

Fragile but fixated, she ignored her school friends'

quizzical looks and Eddie's quiet question, "Are you OK?" They were right to be worried. She was sensitive to touch, to cold, and to heat. She wrapped herself in sweaters, jackets, and socks and tucked her hair under a worker's wool cap. She shivered in warm rooms and folded her arms around her torso to keep warm. Her body felt awkward and disjointed as if it could not settle comfortably into a space. At night she slept with a pillow under her knee and one on each side of her head. During the day, she walked with her head down, eyes on the space in front of her. Her face peeled, in tiny bits, then in large flakes. When she brushed her hair, white dusted her shoulders and floated to the floor. She rubbed her scalp with moisturizing cream, but the flaking persisted. Then her skin loosened, like translucent fish scales, the dead layers covered the pillows and sheets. She examined the leavings, noting large cell like patterns, and wrapped everything in rice paper and placed in at the bottom of her underwear drawer. She covered raw patches on her face with makeup, hiding the red, the chafed forehead, the bruised chin, and the pink elbow.

One way or another, this life must stop.

The clock ticked. The calendar closed in a day at a time, a march toward the dreaded meeting.

Two days to report to Scalia.

Then one day left.

RESOLUTION

Politicians, US military, Japanese and American executives, and elegant women streamed up the Flamingo Club's red-carpeted steps. Sarah slipped past the doorman and was inside. A black pianist played on a low stage, waiters scurried between tables, and elegant people laughed, reached for their drinks, and studied one another.

She mounted the stairs. What if Sensei did not believe her? What if he knew about her days with Ryuzu? What if he knew about Saburo? Sensei's spies left nothing to chance. It was in his interest to know. The Yama man Hiro had asked about her relationship to Ryuzu, about her background and her school, questions she didn't answer. Were they paid to report? Had Sensei already questioned Saburo?

A jazz trumpet accompanied by laugher echoed in the small hall. She pressed her forehead against the door and knocked. The door opened. Sensei nodded and waved her inside. The office was stark, with a desk, a painted screen, and several prints. She flinched at the memory of the table set with blue and white dishes, her made-up face, and her Chinese dress with the high slit. It was another life, another Sarah.

"You have come alone," Sensei observed in a dry voice, indicating a chair opposite the desk. He stood with his hands folded.

"I tried," she said, her voice sounding as if it came from a great distance. "Ryuzu is involved with the union and the workers in San'ya."

"Yes?" Sensei answered.

"He is not well," Sarah said.

"San'ya is a very bad environment," Sensei said, changing the subject. "There have been riots in San'ya. That kind of trouble is not good for Nagatacho. Government ministers don't like trouble. There is much work to be done."

Sarah bent at the waist, lowered her eyes, and folded her hands, as if she accepted all Sensei had to say, all that he stood for. Her head bowed, her chin on her chest, she kept that posture.

Sensei cleared his throat. "I understand you were with Ryuzu-kun at the San'ya riot."

Sarah's head remained lowered; a line of perspiration pricked her upper lip. This was more difficult than she imagined. Who had squealed—Hiro, the gambler, Ishi, who slept at the union office, or the hotel clerk? Sensei knew everything. He had reports from the Yama men, his watchers, and the Yakuza. They called or sent messages through reliable people. Mortified by her own behavior, actions all contrary to Sensei's teaching, she saw the events through Sensei's eyes: San'ya, a necessary rubbish heap; Ryuzu's self-destructive behavior; herself, a bad woman; and Saburo, a useful half-caste. She could not raise her head.

A knock.

Scalia entered, hair slicked back, cheeks powdered, and jacket pressed, with a smile and a mock bow. "We are gathered for a purpose," Scalia said in Japanese. "Sarah, you are the key. For very different reasons, Nishiguchi-sama-Sensei and I want you to stay in

Japan. Tonight you were to come to my office with your answer. Sensei expected Ryuzu to be here. But that's all beside the point. What's important is that we reach an understanding."

Scalia flipped an envelope open and spread the pictures like a deck of cards across the desk. The grainy images revealed a breast, a buttock, and an arm—a glow of flesh, limbs askew, mouth open, and a head turned. Scalia pointed to the pictures, but Sensei frowned and with a violent shake of his head indicated that Scalia had made a serious miscalculation. Scalia retreated. But the pictures remained images of disgrace for all to see.

The door swung open. Saburo entered and with a swift glance at Scalia walked to the desk and gathered the pictures, his approach practical, as if all had been discussed. This was another Saburo—aloof, a man of action who knew his world. This was business. He had come to put things right. Sensei nodded. Scalia stepped back. Saburo held the pictures close to his chest.

Saburo walked to the door, but before he could leave, Ryuzu, dark from the sun and smelling of San'ya, brushed Saburo aside and strode to Sarah's side. His lean body and the strong lines around his mouth made him powerful. He was in command, and the others looked pale beside him. Ryuzu, with moral certainty, understood the legacy of betrayal and yet persisted. He was undefeatable. His thin frame filled the room. Right was on his side. He was impressive. His large hand gripped her shoulder. Scalia grimaced. Saburo looked away. Only Sensei, his face at once youthful, eagerly stepped forward.

A hush took over.

They had assembled so suddenly, each with his own determination, that no one could respond. It was the Japanese way. All knew the details. Sensei had used every bit of ammunition to get to Ryuzu. It was his business to use, to grasp all details, and to warn. She tried to protect Ryuzu, never telling him the time or place of the meeting. But Ryuzu had that information. Had Saburo spoken to Ryuzu? Had Scalia? A go-between? She tried to untangle the networks, the probabilities. Her mind stopped.

But till now Ryuzu had escaped. Leave, her mind screamed, leave this place while you have a chance. Get out before Sensei blackmails you into servitude. You are better than this. Don't be jailed by the past. Stand up to tyranny. Despots always back down. He can't put you in jail. He won't have you killed. Let Sachiko take her chances. She will survive. Sensei is bluffing. If you are really an outsider, go back to the streets. Death is better than Sensei.

But Ryuzu, his expression determined, lips drawn, and eyes fierce, faced Sensei. He looked more alive than she had ever seen him, all his energy stored for this moment. He had planned this confrontation, rehearsed each move, and anticipated the outcome. His face was calm, his body taut, and his focus absolute. There was nothing that Ryuzu didn't know about Sensei, nothing that needed to be explained.

By contrast, Saburo's face was blank as if suddenly his soul had died quietly without his knowledge, destroyed by an alliance not of his making. His skin looked gray in the bright light as if all his blood had drained. He held the pictures loosely. His body hunched as if the drama had exhausted him. He didn't look at Sensei, Ryuzu, or Scalia. His gasoline business did not matter here. Money did not count either. He backed against the wall.

Scalia crossed the room and took the envelope from Saburo. He held the pictures close, head low-

ered in thought. The room waited. Sensei coughed.
Saburo looked away. Ryuzu stepped forward. A trumpet sounded. Laughter. More music. Scalia handed the
envelope to Sarah. It happened quickly. She held the
pictures against her chest. Scalia put his hand on Saburo's shoulder. They stood close, their expressions solemn, part of a great ceremony. Saburo bowed to Sensei.
Ryuzu bowed, quick and direct. He kept his head lowered. It was an ancient act of homage, regret, and understanding. His stiff torso bent, warrior-like, a gesture
of acknowledgement. Sensei's face softened as he put
his hand on Ryuzu's shoulder. Scalia's arm was around
Saburo. Everyone had ownership of another except her.
She stood tall, white, and separate.

Sensei moved to her side. He glanced at the door
with a look that said, "Go, go and be quick about it.
Take this moment and run. You have what you want,
what you came for. The blackmail is over. Scalia has
Saburo, and Ryuzu is here. I could change my mind,
Scalia might renege, Saburo could grab you, or Ryuzu
could say something that would enrage everyone. In
seconds it might all be different. There is only this moment. Run. You will make a new life. You have brought
Ryuzu back. I will clear my debt. Go."

Ryuzu and Saburo raised their heads and turned
toward her, understanding she would leave, disappearing as if she had never been. She saw it in their eyes and
in their posture, straight and distant, of waiting. They
wanted her to walk, head high, out of their lives. It was
time. This is what she'd dreamed of. She had plotted,
planned, made mistakes, and corrected the ones she
could, all to this end. Yet with their dismissal, her desire to leave disappeared; against this rejection winning
didn't matter. She belonged to this world, a universe
where she felt most natural and a place she understood.

Ryuzu and Saburo were part of her and she of them. They'd come from a time between times, a moment in history, the end of an era and the beginning of a future. They had roamed with freedom, spoken a special language, known the smell of a city in cinders, and witnessed the scavengers, the beggars, the clogged train stations, the tents, and the starvation.

"Sarah-chan," Sensei said, his eyes kind, the small wrinkles disappearing into a smile, leaving his lips soft. Kabuki-like, his head waggled from side to side as if he understood her dilemma, the weight of history, and her childish need of him. He moved close. His long cheeks and the dark shadowed eyes made him powerful. He expected to be obeyed, that his presence would be a command. He bowed, stiff, and unyielding, waiting for her to accept. The large clock ticked.

Her body ached with unshed tears.

Saburo watched. Ryuzu watched. Scalia nodded. Sensei moved to the door. The others followed. All her planning had led to this. She took one step and another, her fear replaced by numbness. She was nothing, a person born of a large illusion, a fantasy gone awry. She had demanded to be part of Japan, cherished as a beloved oddity, and she was. There was nothing to keep her in this room.

Sarah swiftly walked out the door and descending the steps, moved past tables of Japanese and Americans and into the night. Outside a fine mist covered the sidewalk. She would not have noticed the rain but for the bubbles that popped on dark puddles. Then the rain began in earnest, slowly and steadily, its volume increasing. Drops landed on her forehead, and she let them stream down her throat. Water pelted her eyelids and plastered her blouse against her skin. Thunder followed lightning, and rain bounced off the cement, large drops hitting her legs and back. She stood, eyes closed, welcoming the wash, a cleansing just for her.

People bumped against her. "Gaijin baka," a man said in a rough voice and pushed her from behind, his elbow at her back. "Move." Sarah tripped. The envelope fell slowly, carried by the wind, circling, landing on a large drain. She reached for it, but the world spun, and her knee hit the pavement.

A hand caught her elbow from behind. Saburo. He had followed her. He remembered their ancient oath. He had understood that they must never part. Her mind churned with possibilities. Ryuzu would never be mentioned. They would bury that history as if it hadn't happened. Her parents would leave. She would stay. Sensei would find a role for her, a suitable occupation, and work that only she could do—a liaison in the Shimbashi black market, an officer in the Flamingo Club. She would attend Sophia night school. In the summer they would go to the island. Saburo would fish. She would dive for oysters. They would be happy. Her mind soared.

But instead of Saburo, a Japanese couple—tiny, wrinkled, with short-cropped hair—stood before her. The woman explained that they had an extra umbrella and that the rain would continue all night. Did she live far away? It was late. The woman kept talking and placed the umbrella in Sarah's hand. It dangled at her side, and the woman righted it. The envelope, ragged from the rain, was some feet away, but the woman blocked her, speaking earnestly of the rains before the summer heat, the danger of chest colds and other ailments. The pictures' shiny surfaces spread over a grating. She reached to retrieve them, but a passerby was there first, kicking them one by one, going down in clumps, crumpled, batches of paper and the brown envelope, tattered and gone.

"Go home now," the woman said in an urgent tone. "This is a bad place." She repeated. "Whatever happened is over. You will be all right. You will see." She righted Sarah's umbrella. The woman continued talking about the rain and the cold in a soothing voice. She leaned close. The woman patted her wet hair and wiped water off her blouse. The man stood by. Then the woman shook her gently. "Go home," she repeated. "Go home." The woman stood for a moment, watching Sarah absorb her words. Then nodding abruptly she and her companion melted into the crowd.

Only then did Sarah hear her own cry, loud and desperate, coming from a place sick with grief. The sounds burst forth, animal-like, a force that she could not control. She continued, building to a wail, horrifying even herself. Lights from the club, blurred by rain, shone in the distance.

She straightened, and the sobs subsided. She went toward the club. In minutes she would be inside. She didn't need Saburo to lead her back. It was her will. She belonged in that room. Sensei would accept her decision. Scalia would be glad. Ryuzu would understand. She crossed the street. Yes. She started down the lane. Yes. She moved between parked cars. Yes. The large door loomed. The doorman bowed. Yes. Yes.

Her foot hit the carpeted step. The umbrella fell. Stinging rain pelted her face. Water clogged her eyelids. She shivered against the cold. Men and women pushed by. Eager waiters took their umbrellas, coats, and packages. Piano and trumpet filled the doorway. She took another step. The round look of astonishment on the doorman's face jolted her. One woman covered her mouth, and another waved her back.

Sarah turned slowly, picked up the umbrella, and headed home.

TRUTH

At five o'clock on Friday, Sarah met her mother, recently returned from Europe, for tea in the lobby of the St. Francis Hotel. Her mother claimed St. Francis's high ceiling and attentive service reminded her of Frank Wright's Imperial Hotel in Tokyo. Sarah nodded, knowing the Imperial had been torn down and the lobby relocated to a mock Meiji historical village.

"I have a letter from O'ba," her mother said, picking up a cucumber sandwich. It had been twelve years since they left Japan. Sarah only recently learned that her mother corresponded with O'ba and Scalia. "O'ba wrote in *hiragana*. I can read most of it."

Sarah had blocked out the past. When her mind drifted to any of it, a wall descended, forcing her to stay in the moment. She focused on her law practice, taking care of her young family, and helping her husband's quest for tenure. She had made American friends, spoke American English, and lived as if her Japanese life had never happened.

"You never really knew Nishiguchi-san," her mother said. "Sensei. Just as well," she added when Sarah remained silent. "But do you remember our first house, the one by the forest, the house you loved?" Her mother spoke slowly. "Scalia arranged for us to live there through his connections with Nishiguchi-san in Shanghai. They were in business together, then and after the war. I didn't like Nishiguchi much, but in many ways he helped us, the family."

Sarah nodded, uncertain of how to proceed. Discussion of the past was taboo. When she mentioned Japan, her mother would say, "Sarah, there is only the present. You are a success. An American." Was her mother really unaware of her history with Sensei? She had always assumed the opposite. Scalia knew. O'ba knew. Had they not told her parents about her frequent meetings with Sensei in the forest? Did they not know about Sensei's obsession with Ryuzu and Ryuzu's father, Masaru? Did they not realize that Saburo and Fumiko worked for Sensei?

Her parents' dream had been realized. They held American passports. Sarah had gone to Stanford and Bolt Law School. She had a thriving law practice, a young family, and a good marriage. It was enough. Her mother, elegant in a silk suit, dark hair pulled into a bun, sipped her tea. She continued to work in the antique business as a buyer for Gumps, her father did real estate, and Vera had become an American teenager.

"Nishiguchi-san was powerful. A right-wing politician," her mother continued. "O'ba wrote that the house was sold and then demolished. Nishiguchi now runs a private boys' school in the old neighborhood. He lives in a small apartment behind the school and teaches the boys tales of samurai and old Japan." Sarah's mother paused. "I hope you aren't too sad about the house. It was bound to happen. The forest and the lake are gone too, everything transformed into cement and concrete." Her voice dropped, and her eyes looked restless. There was more.

"O'ba?"

"Oh, I thought I told you," her mother said. "When Nishiguchi-san sold the house, O'ba returned to Niigata. She runs a small sake shop with her uncle."

Her mother gave Sarah a sharp look. Sarah stirred her tea and nibbled her sandwich. She knew from her mother's hesitant voice that something big was brewing—information that her mother could not bury, events that must be discussed. Sarah put down the sandwich.

"Remember Ryuzu-chan?" her mother asked. "The little boy who yelled for you at the back gate and studied beetles, the one who reminded me of my brother Osyka? O'ba writes that he went to University of Tokyo and is a lawyer in private practice with other radical lawyers. It seems they take cases that no one else will touch—foreign workers and day laborers, that sort of thing. You told me he had a scholarship to study in Russia of all places. I wonder if he ever went."

"He went."

"Why now, Mama?" Sarah wondered, watching her mother, who hardly ate, down three sandwiches and the second pot of tea. A crease ran from her mother's mouth to her chin. The line saddened her. Yes, it had to be big, Sarah decided. They were going through the list, the forbidden names, taboo people, places never mentioned.

"Ryuzu's choice makes sense then," her mother said.

"Yes," Sarah agreed softly. "That choice makes sense."

Her mother's lips twitched with untold information. Sarah tried to keep her voice even. "Beppe?"

Her mother gave her a quick glance. "Beppe died two weeks ago while we were in Europe," she said in a low, anguished voice. "I suppose I am still upset about that. He died in Monte Carlo in an apartment overlooking the sea. The landlord gave us a picture of him and a Japanese girl. Look." She placed a picture in Sarah's hand. "You see, Beppe was not alone."

Sarah took a deep breath. Beppe sat next to a girl looking into the camera. The girl—a young Fumiko, with the same bangs, wide forehead, protruding teeth, and wearing a flowered dress with puffed sleeves, her head cocked to one side—laughed.

"Heart," her mother said. "When your father heard, he tried to find out more from Beppe's family. An uncle who owned a coral shop on the Ponte Vecchio cabled the office, and that's how we heard more details. Since we were in Europe, we immediately went to Monte Carlo."

Sarah crossed her legs and folded her arms. Sunset tinted the couch and chairs to golden-brown. Her mother, silhouetted against the darkening room, hunched over her teacup.

"When we arrived in Monte Carlo, only the landlord had heard of Beppe," her mother said. "He disappeared without a trace. Relatives from Beppe's village claimed the body, and the Japanese girl left in the middle of the night. There was no funeral, and the contents of his apartment were simply given away."

"How is that possible?"

"Taxes," her mother said. "Beppe never paid any taxes to any country and was proud of it. He vanished as if he'd never been born. Once a month he would go to Zurich and bring back a bag of money from a numbered account that Mr. Widdig handled. There is no record of Beppe. He never used a credit card or signed a check. Everything was in cash. Your father had a numbered account, but we closed it—too risky, tax evasion and that sort of thing. Beppe kept his account right up to the end. That was how he lived."

Sarah sipped more tea. For many years she had wished Scalia dead. His cruel laugh and flaccid face filled her dreams, but now, caught in the warmth of her mother's voice, she remembered his gentle tone as he explained the Japanese idea of shizen, "naturalness," and his love of bamboo and all that was green. "It's the most wondrous land, Sarah-chan," he would whisper. "Someday I'll take you to Seto Nan Kai Inland Sea, and you will feel the Japanese kami spirits, in the water, in the air, and on the beaches. Your spirit will join them and be at peace."

"Ah, well," her mother continued. "We all have to die. You knew Beppe when he was terrible, but I knew him when he was grand," she added, as if reading Sarah's thoughts. "He was a tremendous friend and a terrible foe. That was his nature. I've never seen such generosity and malice in the same human being—really two people, one wise and thoughtful, the other, well, the other sadistic, a person who knows vulnerability, when and where to strike. The worst."

Her tone flattened as she continued talking about Shanghai: evenings with Beppe starting at the Grand Hotel, moving on to dinner, then to nightclubs, and ending at sunrise dancing with gypsies on the outskirts of the city. Her voice slowed. "Your father would not have survived the Japanese jail, and we would not have made it to Japan without Beppe. But you know all this."

Sarah waited.

They sat quietly while Sarah absorbed the new information: Sensei's school, Ryuzu's law practice, and Scalia's death. She sensed there was more, information tightly held in her mother's hunched posture, the lines on her face, and her thin lips.

"Yes, a lifetime ago."

Her mother had unlocked the door to the past. But where was Saburo? How was he? Her heart still quickened when she saw a man with a certain stride dressed in black, and she'd hurry to check. Saburo knew enough English to manage the Flamingo Club and to work in the black market. Had he married? Did he have children? Did he still think of her? Did his heart stop when he saw a tall, dark-haired, blue-eyed foreigner? Did he run ahead just to make sure?

"I knew that Saburo was Beppe's son," Sarah ventured.

"Yes, I supposed you did."

"I knew that Fumiko, Beppe, and Saburo were in the black market with Nishiguchi-sensei."

Her mother nodded as if this information was important.

Sarah waited. Her mother grimaced and ordered more tea. "I didn't want to tell you, Sarah," her mother said softly. "I didn't think it was important. You have gone on with your life. Your father and I are so proud of you. You are a successful lawyer married to a successful political scientist. Max loves you and is a good father to your beautiful children. Soon he will have tenure, and your future will be secure."

Tell me, Sarah thought. I have to know. Tell me. I have a right to know. I buried the past. You started this, and you can't stop now.

"You helped Vera adjust to America," her mother continued, "and you helped us, too. I don't know what we would have done without you. When I missed the Orient, you arranged a Sunday dim sum brunch in Chinatown. When your father was worried about his business, you listened and advised. You gave and gave. You simply took care of us all. I know it wasn't easy. I felt terrible about the pressure to perform at the American school. You were our key to America. I never told you how truly grateful I am. Really grateful."

Her mother was on a roll. She had too much information stored carefully in every cell and nerve ending. Her eyes were glazed, as if with Beppe's death the past had surfaced with its own demands, and she was at a loss for how to handle it.

Stop. Tell me. What happened to Saburo-chan? Did he try to contact me? Did he? Does he want to see me? Is that what this is about? Tell me. Do I just have to walk down the street to meet him? Tell me then. I am ready, she thought, the past and present merging, barriers melted, borders dissolved, and boundaries disappeared. She closed her eyes. Just tell me. Say it.

"The past is the past," her mother said as a mantra. She gazed into the distance and kept talking. At once Sarah understood that her mother's pain had nothing to do with her. This was her mother's story, and she finally had to tell it. "There are many things that I regret—letting Saburo and Fumiko live in the hut behind the house. I know Saburo affected you, playing the flute outside the house day after day, calling you, wanting your soul. Eventually I gave in, but I knew it was wrong." Her mother dabbed her eye with a napkin. "In time you and Saburo became one, finishing each other's sentences, making up stories that only you understood a fantasy world full of adventure, and samurai. It was crazy. We should have moved."

Diffused light from the high windows made the room glow. For the first time since leaving Japan, Sarah felt clear. Her mother was still talking about how they should have moved, but Sarah barely heard. She would find Saburo. They were the same person, untamed in the same way. They would recognize each other immediately, and it would be as always. They would make love in a small, bare room. He would undress her slowly and stroke her arms, breasts, and face, and as the heat rose between them, he would draw her close, suck her nipples, bury his head between her legs, and pound into her. Wildness spread. She wanted Saburo at any cost.

Sarah's mind raced. Yes, she would run from her brilliant husband, her demanding children, and her growing law practice. She would soak in the dankness of Japan's ditches, the grass smell of tatami rooms, and the rich odor of tea. Once more she would share its obsession with order, politeness, and obligation, and its chaotic nights. She understood. She would be home and free.

Then she stopped. It was not true. She loved Saburo, yes, but she could never leave herself again. She had done that once for too long, and it nearly destroyed her. That was over. There was no more merging, expecting others to pick up the pieces and make her whole. Her anguished howl, the rain, the small woman holding the umbrella, and the pictures over the grating — it all came back in a rush. She had walked into herself that night, illusion replaced by understanding. Still, she could know him in the present, aging, with responsibilities.

In time Saburo would take his proper place. They would exchange New Year's greetings, short notes that revealed little but said a great deal. After some years she would include a picture of herself and the children. He would reciprocate. Their children would meet in San Francisco or Tokyo. They would wonder at each other. She would explain that Saburo was an old childhood friend and with a certain unease they would accept that explanation. Yes, everything in time. She'd seen it happen with her parents and Scalia. No one wanted trauma. It was too fraught, unsafe in every dimension, stirring feelings about decisions that had long become fact. She nodded for her mother to continue.

"Then there was play in the forest with Ryuzu and the other children," her mother continued. "It was not wise. Too much freedom. But I was so ill for so long. When I got home from the hospital, there were patterns that I didn't have the strength to break. Forgive me."

"I loved the forest, my friends, and Ryuzu-chan," Sarah said in an equally somber tone. "Those were my golden days."

"Yes."

"But I really loved Saburo." At once she knew that was truer than she realized, that Ryuzu was her great friend and true companion, but Saburo was her love. It had been that way from the beginning. When she saw him, her heart raced, and when he spoke her eyes followed his lips. She breathed him in. Even now she looked for him. She wished Ryuzu the best but didn't care if he'd married, had children, or how he earned his living. Saburo. She could taste the salt on his lips and smell his wheat tea breath. She needed to know everything.

"Yes, Beppe said that he sent Saburo to the American school. He said you became close. I didn't realize," her mother acknowledged in a more hesitant tone.

"I never loved anyone the way I loved Saburo," Sarah insisted. "More than Ryuzu-chan or any of my friends, I loved Saburo. It was always Saburo." Her mother flushed and adjusted the collar of her suit. Sarah knew that her last statement, a command, left her mother no choice.

"Saburo died eight years ago, Sarah," her mother said softly. "Beppe wrote us. Terrible. After that Beppe left Japan and settled in Monte Carlo. I wanted to tell you, but you were just married and finally established. I just couldn't bear to bring up all that."

Sarah could not breathe, she could not think. Saburo, dead. Saburo—living and breathing and doing his deals at the Yakuza Club with his swagger, brilliant smile, and assumptions about life—gone? Saburo, his leg on her thigh, his lips on her neck, was no longer? Saburo, his dark, leather jacket, massive Honda, and gold chain, energized and ready to go, buried? No. Never. There must be a mistake. It was not possible. Yet Sarah knew it was true.

"How?"

"After we left, Saburo refused to work with Beppe and would not attend school. An ainoko, 'mixed-love child,'" her mother said with a sigh. "Japan is nothing but networks and connections. Saburo didn't fit into any. Perhaps the black market might have worked for Saburo. Beppe didn't understand why he left the Flamingo Club." Her mother sighed again. "Beppe was beside himself. He even asked me to intervene. But what could I do? I never had a real relationship with Saburo or Fumiko. And involving you was out of the question." This last sentence was uttered as an impassioned declaration. "Out of the question!" her mother repeated.

Sarah sat still. The pain returned, this time with a terrible force. It settled in her stomach. Her arms hurt. She could not breathe. The worst was coming. Her mother could not stop. Her eyes glittered with the energy that came from too much knowledge. The glazed look intensified. Sarah knew she had to tell the story. Sarah had clients like that. For days they would be tight lipped and reveal nothing. Logic, bribes, and commands would not work. Then something would happen—a phone call, a letter—and the switch would be tripped, and they would begin to speak, a dam of words released.

"Saburo was a test driver for Honda," her mother said in a low voice. "Beppe felt responsible, having given Saburo his first bike, a bribe to attend the American school."

Sarah nodded. Her mother gave her a sharp look.

"Saburo raced every day. He earned good money. Beppe was impressed. He sent us a picture of Saburo on a Honda in a black leather jacket."

Sarah held her breath. Her mother appeared to be measuring the wisdom of continuing the story. She ordered vodka. The two women sat in silence — Sarah with her hand on her stomach and her mother cradling her chin — until the waiter returned with a flask and two glasses. Her mother poured each of them a shot and immediately downed hers.

"One day Saburo was told not to test drive in muddy conditions. The course was full of puddles and ruts, but Saburo insisted. He had been drinking heavily, bar hopping every night. Beppe knew he was in trouble." Her mother's voice dropped. "Beppe wasn't to blame. He loved Saburo in his own way and brought him back from the Inland Sea so that he would have a better life than a fisherman. Only later did Beppe realize that that was a mistake; Saburo had found a place in his grandparents' village. He loved the ocean, mending nets, and the smell of seaweed in his tea. Parents are often stupid, but Beppe did care. He showed us a picture of Saburo with a wide smile standing in front of fishing nets, brown and wrinkled from the sun and sea, at every opportunity."

Her mother took another drink. Words that had been buried deep now rushed to the surface. "Beppe regretted so much: his obsession with me and his impact on the family. He made peace with us. In his last years, he took up meditation, spending hours with his hands folded, staring at the sea. I believe he found some peace. I hope so."

Her mother waited while Sarah took this in. "That day Beppe had gone to the driving course to meet Saburo and have a serious talk. But Beppe arrived too late," her mother said. "The manager told him that Saburo went around and around." Her mother paused and reached in her purse. "I have Beppe's letter to you."

Sarah shook her head, knowing what her mother knew: Beppe's letter, documenting his fear of loss, his need to control, was intended for her. Her mother had kept the letter for eight years, buried in a drawer waiting for this moment. Now her mother nodded, ripped the letter in half, and placing it in the ashtray lit a match. The paper burned for several seconds.

A hush settled between them. Her mother swallowed her third vodka. The ashes from the letter curled and went dead. Sarah's body felt cold, her stomach hurt, and her mouth was dry. Saburo. Gone. Her past. Just like that.

"The manager said Saburo was crazy," her mother continued in a softer tone. "They ordered him to stop. They held up flags. Saburo wouldn't listen, around and around twenty-eight times. They clocked him at 120 when his bike sped out of control." Her mother's face turned ashen, taking on the bewildered look of a small child whose energies had been exhausted over a tantrum. "My God, what have I done? I didn't mean to. My God."

Sarah tried to speak, wanting to console her — she had to know; it was better this way — but the words wouldn't come. Until this moment she hadn't realized that hope, creating possibilities by day and fueling dreams at night, had energized her. In between wake and sleep, when morning light blurred past and present and when her husband reached for her, she imagined Saburo.

Her mother reached across the table. Her hand felt cold, and the skin wrinkled under pressure. Sarah drew back, but her mother's grip tightened. "You mustn't," she said. "You mustn't. It's over. I'm sorry." The words sputtered, but her grasp, determined and insistent, remained. Her mother's vodka glass toppled, but no one moved. Her grip, vice-like, locked on. "It's OK," her mother said softly. "In time. In time."

Sarah swayed. The waiter hovered, the light dimmed, and the people at the next table paid their bill. Her mother held her. Her fingers tightened. She came close, her arm on Sarah's shoulder and around her waist. Their foreheads touched. She felt her mother's tears. She pulled back but her mother remained, whispering that she loved her, that she was her precious girl, that she was sorry. The words poured out in a steady stream, words that had been stored for too long, words she had to speak. Then silence. The waiter lit a candle. A young boy yelled for ice cream. The next table asked for sherry. Gradually her mother loosed her grip. Their breaths matched. Sarah lifted her head.

"Oh, Mama."

"Sarah-chan," her mother said softly.

A Note About the Author

Patricia Gercik was born in Vancouver, BC, Canada in 1944 and grew up in Tokyo, Japan. She graduated from the University of California with a BA and received an MA from Tufts University. She worked at Massachusetts Institute of Technology for over two decades as Managing Director of the MIT Japan Program and as Associate Director of MIT International Science and Technology Initiatives. Her dedication to international education was recognized by the Japan Society of Boston, which presented her with the John E. Thayer, III Award for her significant contribution to the advancement of understanding between Japan and the United States. She was awarded the 2010 Excellence Award by MIT in the category of "Bringing Out the Best: everyday leadership throughout MIT." She published *On Track With the Japanese: A Case-By-Case Approach to Building Successful Relationships* with Kodansha International as well as several CD-ROMS on negotiating with the Japanese. She also co-authored *The Opium Trail*, published by Concerned Asian Scholars, and was a contributor to *Our Bodies, Ourselves*, by the Boston Women's Health Book Collective.

Made in the USA
Middletown, DE
20 December 2014